LIVE WIRE

HARLAN

LIVE WIRE

COBEN

DUTTON

DUTTON
Published by Penguin Group (USA) Inc.
375 Hudson Street, New York, New York 10014, U.S.A.
Penguin Group (Canada), 90 Eglinton Avenue East, Suite 700, Toronto, Ontario M4P 2Y3, Canada (a
division of Pearson Penguin Canada Inc.); Penguin Books Ltd, 80 Strand, London WC2R 0RL, England;
Penguin Ireland, 25 St Stephen's Green, Dublin 2, Ireland (a division of Penguin Books Ltd); Penguin
Group (Australia), 250 Camberwell Road, Camberwell, Victoria 3124, Australia (a division of Pear-
son Australia Group Pty Ltd); Penguin Books India Pvt Ltd, 11 Community Centre, Panchsheel Park,
New Delhi–110 017, India; Penguin Group (NZ), 67 Apollo Drive, Rosedale, North Shore 0632, New
Zealand (a division of Pearson New Zealand Ltd); Penguin Books (South Africa) (Pty) Ltd, 24 Sturdee
Avenue, Rosebank, Johannesburg 2196, South Africa

Penguin Books Ltd, Registered Offices: 80 Strand, London WC2R 0RL, England

Published by Dutton, a member of Penguin Group (USA) Inc.

First printing, March 2011
1 3 5 7 9 10 8 6 4 2

Copyright © 2011 by Harlan Coben
All rights reserved

 REGISTERED TRADEMARK—MARCA REGISTRADA

LIBRARY OF CONGRESS CATALOGING-IN-PUBLICATION DATA
has been applied for

ISBN 978-0-525-95206-0

Printed in the United States of America
Set in Sabon
Designed by Leonard Telesca

PUBLISHER'S NOTE
This book is a work of fiction. Names, characters, places, and incidents either are the product of the
author's imagination or are used fictitiously, and any resemblance to actual persons, living or dead, business establishments, events, or locales is entirely coincidental.

For Anne,
because the best is yet to come

LIVE WIRE

1

The ugliest truth, a friend once told Myron, is still better than the prettiest of lies.

Myron thought about that now as he looked down at his father in the hospital bed. He flashed back sixteen years, to the last time he had lied to his father, the lie that caused so much heartbreak and devastation, a lie that started a tragic ripple that, finally, disastrously, would end here.

His father's eyes remained closed, his breathing raspy and uneven. Tubes seemed to snake out from everywhere. Myron stared down at his father's forearm. He remembered as a child visiting his dad in that Newark warehouse, the way his father sat at his oversized desk, his sleeves rolled up. The forearm had been powerful enough back then to strain the fabric, making the cuff work tourniquet-like against the muscle. Now the muscle looked spongy, deflated by age. The barrel chest that had made Myron feel so safe was still there, but it had grown brittle, as though a hand pressing down could snap the rib cage like dried twigs. His father's unshaven face had gray splotches instead of his customary five o'clock shadow, the skin around his chin loose, sagging down like a cloak one size too big.

Myron's mother—Al Bolitar's wife for the past forty-three years—sat next to the bed. Her hand, shaking with Parkinson's, held his. She too looked shockingly frail. In her youth, his mother had been an early feminist, burning her bra with Gloria Steinem, wearing T-shirts that read stuff like "A Woman's Place Is in the House . . . and Senate." Now, here they both were, Ellen and Al Bolitar ("We're El-Al," Mom always joked, "like the Israeli airline") ravaged by age, hanging on, luckier by far than the vast majority of aging lovers—and yet this was what luck looked like in the end.

God has some sense of humor.

"So," Mom said to Myron in a low voice. "We agree?"

Myron did not reply. The prettiest of lies versus the ugliest truth. Myron should have learned his lesson back then, sixteen years ago, with that last lie to this great man he loved like no other. But, no, it wasn't so simple. The ugliest truth could be devastating. It could rock a world.

Or even kill.

So as his father's eyes fluttered open, as this man Myron treasured like no other looked up at his oldest son with pleading, almost childlike confusion, Myron looked at his mother and slowly nodded. Then he bit back the tears and prepared to tell his father one final lie.

2

SIX DAYS EARLIER

Please, Myron, I need your help."

This was, for Myron, a bit of a fantasy: a shapely, gorgeous damsel in distress sauntering into his office like something out of an old Bogey film—except, well, the saunter was more of a waddle and the shapeliness was coming from the fact that the gorgeous damsel was eight months pregnant, and really, sorry, that kind of killed the whole fantasy effect.

Her name was Suzze T, short for Trevantino, a retired tennis star. She had been the sexy bad girl of the tour, better known for her provocative outfits, piercings, and tattoos than for her actual game. Still Suzze won a major and made a ton in endorsements, most notably as the spokeswoman (Myron loved that euphemism) for La-La-Latte, a chain of topless coffee bars, where college boys loved to snicker for "extra milk." Good times.

Myron spread his arms. "I'm here for you, Suzze, twenty-four/seven—you know that."

They were in his Park Avenue office, home of MB Reps, the *M* standing for Myron, the *B* for Bolitar, and the Reps because they represented athletes, actors, and writers. Literal-Monikers-R-Us.

"Just tell me what I can do."

Suzze began to pace. "I'm not sure where to begin." Myron was about to speak when she held up her hand. "And if you dare say, 'Start at the beginning,' I will rip off one of your testicles."

"Just one?"

"You're engaged now. I'm thinking of your poor fiancée."

The pace turned more into a stomp, picking up speed and intensity so that a small part of Myron feared that she might go into labor right here in his recently refurbished office.

"Uh, the carpet," Myron said. "It's new."

She frowned, paced some more, started biting her exuberantly polished fingernails.

"Suzze?"

She stopped. Their eyes met.

"Tell me," he said.

"You remember when we first met?"

Myron nodded. He was just a few months out of law school and starting up his fledgling firm. Back then, at the inception, MB Reps had been known as MB SportsReps. That was because initially Myron represented only athletes. When he started representing actors and writers and others in the field of the arts and celebrity, he dropped the Sports from the name, ergo, MB Reps.

Again with the literal.

"Of course," he said.

"I was a mess, wasn't I?"

"You were a great tennis talent."

"And a mess. Don't sugarcoat it."

Myron put his palms toward the ceiling. "You were eighteen."

"Seventeen."

"Seventeen, whatever." Quick memory flash of Suzze in the sun: blond hair in a ponytail, a wicked grin on her face, her forehand whipping the ball as though it had offended her. "You'd just turned pro. Adolescent boys hung your poster in their bedrooms. You were supposed to beat legends right away. Your parents redefined pushy. It's a miracle you stayed upright."

"Good point."

"So what's wrong?"

Suzze glanced down at her belly as though it had just appeared. "I'm pregnant."

"Uh, yeah, I can see that."

"Life is good, you know?" Her voice was soft now, wistful. "After all the years, when I was a mess . . . I found Lex. His music has never been better. The tennis academy is doing great. And, well, it's just all so good now."

Myron waited. Her eyes stayed on her belly, cradling it as though it were its contents, which, Myron surmised, it kind of was. To keep the conversation going, Myron asked, "Do you like being pregnant?"

"The actual physical act of carrying a child?"

"Yes."

She shrugged. "It's not like I'm glowing or any of that. I mean,

I'm so ready to deliver. It's interesting though. Some women love being pregnant."

"And you don't?"

"It feels like someone parked a bulldozer on my bladder. I think the reason women like being pregnant is because it makes them feel special. Like they're minor celebrities. Most women go through life without the attention, but when they're pregnant, people make a fuss. This may sound uncharitable, but pregnant women like the applause. Do you know what I mean?"

"I think so."

"I've already had my share of applause, I guess." She moved toward the window and looked out for a moment. Then she turned back toward him. "By the way, did you notice how huge my boobs are?"

Myron said, "Um," and decided to say no more.

"Come to think of it, I wonder whether you should contact La-La-Latte for a new photo shoot."

"Strategically angled shots?"

"Exactly. Might be a great new campaign in these puppies." She cupped them in case Myron wasn't sure what puppies she was referencing. "What do you think?"

"I think," Myron said, "that you're stalling."

Her eyes were wet now. "I'm so damned happy."

"Yeah, well, I can see where that would be a problem."

She smiled at that. "I put the demons to rest. I've even reconciled with my mother. Lex and I couldn't be more ready to have the baby. I want those demons to stay away."

Myron sat up. "You're not using again?"

"God, no. Not that kind of demon. Lex and I are done with that."

Lex Ryder, Suzze's husband, was one half of the legendary band/ duo known as HorsePower—the much lesser half, to be frank, to the supernaturally charismatic front man, Gabriel Wire. Lex was a fine if troubled musician, but he would always be John Oates to Gabriel's Daryl Hall, Andrew Ridgeley to Gabriel's George Michael, the rest of the Pussycat Dolls next to Nicole Scherz-i-something.

"What kind of demons then?"

Suzze reached into her purse. She plucked out something that from across the desk looked as though it might be a photograph. She stared at it for a moment and then passed it to Myron. He took a quick glance and again tried to wait her out.

Finally, just to say something, he went with the obvious: "This is your baby's sonogram."

"Yep. Twenty-eight weeks old."

More silence. Again Myron broke it. "Is there something wrong with the baby?"

"Nothing. He's perfect."

"He?"

Suzze T smiled now. "Going to have my own little man."

"That's pretty cool."

"Yeah. Oh, one of the reasons I'm here: Lex and I have been talking about it. We both want you to be the godfather."

"Me?"

"Yep."

Myron said nothing.

"Well?"

Now it was Myron who had wet eyes. "I'd be honored."

"Are you crying?"

Myron said nothing.

"You're such a girl," she said.

"What's wrong, Suzze?"

"Maybe nothing." Then: "I think someone is out to destroy me."

Myron kept his eyes on the sonogram. "How?"

And then she showed him. She showed him two words that would echo dully in his heart for a very long time.

3

An hour later, Windsor Horne Lockwood III—known to those who fear him (and that was pretty much everyone) as Win—swaggered into Myron's office. Win had a great swagger, like he should be wearing a black top hat and tails and twirling a walking stick. Instead he sported a pink-and-green Lilly Pulitzer tie, a blue blazer with some kind of crest on it, and khakis with a crease sharp enough to draw blood. He had loafers, no socks, and basically looked as though he'd just gone yachting on the SS *Old Money*.

"Suzze T just stopped by," Myron said.

Win nodded, jaw jutted. "I saw her on the way out."

"Did she look upset?"

"Didn't notice," Win said, taking a seat. Then: "Her breasts were engorged."

Win.

"She has a problem," Myron said.

Win leaned back, crossed his legs with his customary coiled ease. "Explain."

Myron spun his computer monitor so Win could see. An hour ago, Suzze T had done something similar. He thought about those two small words. Harmless enough on their own, but life is about context. And in this context, those two words chilled the room.

Win squinted at the screen and reached into his inside breast pocket. He plucked out a pair of reading glasses. He'd gotten them about a month ago, and though Myron would have said it was impossible, they made Win look even more haughty and stuck-up. They also depressed the hell out of him. Win and he weren't old— not by a long shot—but to use Win's golf analogy when he had first unveiled the glasses: "We are officially on the back nine of life."

"Is this a Facebook page?" Win asked.

"Yes. Suzze said she uses it to promote her tennis academy."

Win leaned a little closer. "Is that her sonogram?"

"Yes."

"And how does a sonogram promote her tennis academy?"

"That's what I asked. She said you need the personal touch. People don't just want to read self-promotion."

Win frowned. "So she posts a sonogram of a fetus?" He glanced up. "Does that make sense to you?"

In truth, it did not. And once again—with Win wearing reading glasses and the two of them whining about the new world of social networks—Myron felt old.

"Check out the picture comments," Myron said.

Win gave him the flat eyes. "People comment on a sonogram?"

"Just read them."

Win did. Myron waited. He had pretty much memorized the page. There were, he knew, twenty-six comments in all, mostly various good wishes. Suzze's mother, the aging poster child for Evil Stage (Tennis) Mom, for example, had written: "I'm going to be a grandma, everyone! Yay!" Someone named Amy said, "Aww cute!!!" A jocular "Takes after his old man! ;)" came from a session drummer who used to work with HorsePower. A guy named Kelvin wrote, "Congrats!!" Tami asked, "When's the baby due, sweetie?"

Win stopped three from the bottom. "Funny guy."

"Which one?"

"Some turdlike humanoid named Erik typed"—Win cleared his throat, leaned closer to the screen—"'Your baby looks like a sea horse!'" and then Erik the Riot put the letters "LOL."

"He's not her problem."

Win was not placated. "Old Erik still might be worth a visit."

"Just keep going."

"Fine." Win's facial expressions rarely changed. He had trained himself in both business and combat to show nothing. But a few seconds later, Myron saw something darken in his old friend's eyes. Win looked up. Myron nodded. Because now Myron knew that Win had found the two words.

They were there, at the bottom of the page. The two words were in a comment made by "Abeona S," a name that meant nothing to him. The profile picture was some sort of symbol, maybe Chinese lettering. And there, all in caps, no punctuation, were the two simple yet wrenching words:

"NOT HIS"

Silence.

Then Win said, "Yowza."

11

"Indeed."

Win took off his glasses. "Need I ask the obvious question?"

"That being?"

"Is it true?"

"Suzze swears that it's Lex's."

"Do we believe her?"

"We do," Myron said. "Does it matter?"

"Not on a moral basis, no. My theory? This is the work of some neutered crank."

Myron nodded. "The great thing about the Internet: It gives everyone a voice. The bad thing about the Internet: It gives everyone a voice."

"The great bastion for the cowardly and anonymous," Win agreed. "Suzze should probably delete it before Lex sees it."

"Too late. That's part of the problem. Lex has sort of run off."

"I see," Win said. "So she wants us to find him?"

"And bring him home, yes."

"Shouldn't be too difficult to find a famous rock star," Win said. "And the other part of the problem?"

"She wants to know who wrote this."

"The true identity of Mr. Neutered Crank?"

"Suzze thinks it's something bigger. That someone is truly out to get her."

Win shook his head. "It's a neutered crank."

"Come on. Typing 'Not his'? That's pretty sick."

"A *sick* neutered crank. Do you ever read the nonsense on this Internet? Go to any news story anywhere and look at the racist, homophobic, paranoid 'comments.' " He made quote marks with his fingers. "It will make you howl at the moon."

"I know, but I promised I'd look into it."

Win sighed, put the glasses back on, leaned toward the screen. "The person who posted it is one Abeona S. Is it safe to assume that's a pseudonym?"

"Yep. Abeona is the name of a Roman goddess. No idea what the S stands for."

"And what about the profile photograph? What's this symbol?"

"I don't know."

"You asked Suzze?"

"Yep. She said she had no idea. It looks almost like Chinese lettering."

"Perhaps we can find someone to translate it." Win sat back and re-steepled the fingers. "Did you notice the time the comment was posted?"

Myron nodded. "Three seventeen A.M."

"Awfully late."

"That's what I was thinking," Myron said. "This could just be the social-networking equivalent of drunk texting."

"An ex with issues," Win said.

"Is there any other kind?"

"And if I recall Suzze's rambunctious youth, there could be—conservatively speaking—several candidates."

"But none that she imagines doing something like this."

Win continued to stare at the screen. "So what's our first step?"

"Really?"

"Pardon?"

Myron moved around his renovated office. Gone were the posters of Broadway plays and Batman memorabilia. They'd been taken down during the paint job, and Myron wasn't really sure if he wanted to put them back up. Gone too were all his old trophies and awards from his playing days—his NCAA championship rings, his *Parade* All-American certificates, his College Player of the Year award—with one exception. Right before his first professional game as a Boston Celtic, as his dream was finally coming true, Myron had seriously injured his knee. *Sports Illustrated* put him on the cover with the tagline, IS HE DONE? and while they don't answer the question, it ended up being a big fat YUP! Why he kept the framed cover up he wasn't quite sure. If asked, he said that it was a warning to any "superstar" entering his office how quickly it can all go away, but Myron somehow suspected it went deeper than that.

"That's not your usual modus operandi," Myron said.

"Oh, do tell."

"This is usually the part where you tell me that I'm an agent, not a private eye, and that you don't see any purpose in doing this because there is no financial benefit to the firm."

Win said nothing.

"Then you usually complain that I have a hero complex and always need to rescue someone in order to feel complete. And lastly—or I should say, most recently—you tell me how my interfering has actually done more harm than good, that I've ended up hurting and even killing maybe more than I've saved."

Win yawned. "Is there a point?"

"I thought it was pretty obvious but here it is: Why suddenly are you willing—enthusiastic even—about taking on this particular rescue mission when in the past—"

"In the past," Win interrupted, "I always helped out, didn't I?"

"For the most part, yes."

Win looked up, tapped his chin with his index finger. "How to explain this?" He stopped, thought, nodded. "We have a tendency to believe good things will last forever. It is in our nature. The Beatles, for example. Oh, they'll be around forever. *The Sopranos*—that show will always be on the air. Philip Roth's Zuckerman series. Springsteen concerts. Good things are rare. They are to be cherished because they always leave us too soon."

Win rose, started for the door. Before he left the room, he looked back.

"Doing this stuff with you," Win said, "is one of those good things."

4

It did not take much to track down Lex Ryder.

Esperanza Diaz, Myron's business partner at MB Reps, called him at eleven P.M. and said, "Lex just used his credit card at Three Downing."

Myron was staying, as he often did, at Win's co-op in the legendary Dakota building, overlooking Central Park West on the corner of Seventy-second Street. Win had a spare bedroom or three. The Dakota dates back to 1884 and it looks it. The fortresslike structure was beautiful and dark and somehow wonderfully depressing. It's a hodgepodge of gables, balconies, finials, pediments, balustrades, half domes, cast iron, archways, ornate railing, stepped dormers—a bizarre blend that was somehow seamless, hauntingly perfect rather than overwhelming.

"What's that?" Myron asked.

"You don't know Three Downing?" Esperanza asked.

"Should I?"

"It's probably the hippest bar in the city right now. Diddy, super-models, the fashionista, that crowd. It's in Chelsea."

"Oh."

"It's a little disappointing," Esperanza said.

"What?"

"That a playah of your magnitude doesn't know all the trendy spots."

"When Diddy and I go clubbing, we take the white Hummer stretch and use underground entrances. The names blur."

"Or being engaged is cramping your style," Esperanza said. "So do you want to head over there and pick him up?"

"I'm in my pajamas."

"Yep, a playah. Do the pajamas have feetsies?"

Myron checked his watch again. He could be downtown before midnight. "I'm on my way."

"Is Win there?" Esperanza asked.

"No, he's still out."

"So you're going down alone?"

"You're worried about a tasty morsel like me in a nightclub on my own?"

"I'm worried you won't get in. I'll meet you there. Half hour. Seventeenth Street entrance. Dress to impress."

Esperanza hung up. This surprised Myron. Since becoming a mother, Esperanza, former all-night, bisexual party girl, never went out late anymore. She had always taken her job seriously—she now owned 49 percent of MB Reps and with Myron's strange travels of late had really carried the load. But after a decade-plus of leading a

17

night lifestyle so hedonistic it would have made Caligula envious, Esperanza had stopped cold, gotten married to the uber-straight Tom, and had a son named Hector. She went from Lindsay Lohan to Carol Brady in four-point-five seconds.

Myron looked in his closet and wondered what to wear to a trendy nightspot. Esperanza had said dress to impress, so he went with his tried and true—jeans-blue-blazer-expensive-loafer look—Mr. Casual Chic—mostly because that was all he owned that fit the bill. There was really little in his closet between jeans-blazer and all-out suit, unless you wanted to look like the sales guy at an electronics store.

He grabbed a cab on Central Park West. The cliché of Manhattan taxi drivers is that they are all foreign and barely speak English. The cliché may be true, but it had been at least five years since Myron had actually spoken to one. Despite recent laws, every single cabdriver in New York City wore a mobile-phone Bluetooth in his ear, twenty-four/seven, quietly talking in his native tongue to whoever was on the other end. Manners aside, Myron always wondered whom they had in their lives that wanted to talk to them all day. In this sense, one could argue that these were very lucky men.

Myron figured that he'd see a long line, a velvet rope, something, but as they approached the Seventeenth Street address, there was no sign of any nightclub. Finally he realized that the "Three" stood for the third floor and that "Downing" was the name of the quasi-high-rise in front of him. Someone went to the MB Reps School of Literal Business Naming.

The elevator arrived on the third floor. As soon as the doors slid open, Myron could feel the music's deep bass in his chest. The long queue of desperate wanna-enters started immediately. Purportedly, people went to clubs like this to have a good time, but the truth was, most stood on a line and ended up with a sharp reminder that they still weren't cool enough to sit at the popular kids' lunch table. VIPs walked right past them with nary a glance and somehow that made them want to go in more. There was a velvet rope, of course, signaling their lower status, and it was guarded by three steroid-stuffed bouncers with shaved heads and practiced scowls.

Myron approached with his best Win-like swagger. "Hey, fellas."

The bouncers ignored him. The biggest of the three wore a black suit with no shirt. None. Suit jacket, no shirt. His chest was nicely waxed, displaying impressive metrosexual cleavage. He was currently dealing with a group of four maybe-twenty-one-year-old girls. They all wore ridiculously high heels—heels were definitely in this year—so that they teetered more than strutted. Their dresses were skimpy enough for a citation, but really, that was nothing new.

The bouncer was examining them cattle-call style. The girls posed and smiled. Myron half expected them to open their mouths so he could examine their teeth.

"You three are okay," Cleavage told them. "But your friend here is too chunky."

The chunky girl, who was maybe a size eight, started to cry. Her three waiflike friends gathered in a circle and debated if they should go in without her. The chunky girl ran off in sobs. The friends shrugged and entered. The three bouncers smirked.

Myron said, "Classy."

The smirks turned his way. Cleavage met Myron's eyes, offering up a challenge. Myron met his gaze and did not look away. Cleavage looked Myron up and down and clearly found him wanting.

"Nice outfit," Cleavage said. "You on your way to fight a parking ticket in traffic court?"

His two compadres, both sporting tourniquet-tight Ed Hardy T-shirts, liked that one.

"Right," Myron said, pointing at the cleavage. "I should have left my shirt at home."

The bouncer on Cleavage's left made a surprised O with his mouth.

Cleavage stuck out his thumb, umpire-style. "End of the line, pal. Or better yet, just head out."

"I'm here to see Lex Ryder."

"Who says he's here?"

"I say."

"And you are?"

"Myron Bolitar."

Silence. One of them blinked. Myron almost shouted, "Ta-da," but refrained.

"I'm his agent."

"Your name isn't on the list," Cleavage said.

"And we don't know who you are," Surprised O added.

"So"—the third bouncer waved with five beefy fingers—"buh-bye."

"Irony," Myron said.

"What?"

"Don't you guys see the irony?" Myron asked. "You are gatekeepers at a place you yourselves would never be allowed in—and yet, rather than seeing that and thus adding a human touch, you act like even bigger overcompensating ass-clowns."

More blinking. Then all three stepped toward him, a giant wall of pecs. Myron felt his blood thrum. His fingers tightened into fists. He relaxed them, kept his breathing even. They moved closer. Myron did not step back. Cleavage, the leader, leaned toward him.

"You better go now, bub."

"Why? Am I too chunky? By the way, seriously, do these jeans make my ass look big? You can tell me."

The long line of wanna-enters quieted at the sight of this challenge. The bouncers glanced at one another. Myron scolded himself. Talk about counterproductive. He had come here to fetch Lex, not get into it with raging 'roid heads.

Cleavage smiled and said, "Well, well, looks like we have a comedian here."

"Yeah," Surprised-O Bouncer said, "a comedian. Ha-ha."

"Yeah," his partner said. "You're a real comedian, aren't you, funny man?"

"Well," Myron said, "at the risk of appearing immodest, I'm also a gifted vocalist. I usually open with 'The Tears of a Clown,' move into a stripped-down version of 'Lady'—more Kenny Rogers than Lionel Richie. Not a dry eye in the house."

Cleavage leaned in close to Myron's ear, his buddies nearby. "You do realize, of course, that we're going to have to kick your ass."

"And you do realize, of course," Myron said, "that steroids make your testicles shrink."

Then from behind him, Esperanza said, "He's with me, Kyle."

Myron turned, saw Esperanza, and managed not to say, "Wow," out loud, though it wasn't easy. He had known Esperanza for two decades now, had worked side by side with her, and sometimes, when you see someone every day and become best friends, you just forget what a total knee-knocking sizzler she is. When they met, Esperanza had been a scantily clad professional wrestler known as Little Pocahontas. Lovely, lithe, and teeth-meltingly hot, she left being the glamour girl of FLOW (Fabulous Ladies of Wrestling) to become his personal assistant while getting her law degree at night. She had moved up the ranks, so to speak, and was now Myron's partner at MB Reps.

Kleavage Kyle's face broke into a smile. "Poca? Girl, is that really you? You look good enough to lick like an ice cream cone."

Myron nodded. "Smooth line, Kyle."

Esperanza offered her cheek for a buss. "Nice to see you too," she said.

"Been too long, Poca."

Esperanza's dark beauty brought on images of moonlit skies, night walks on the beach, olive trees in a gentle breeze. She wore hoop earrings. Her long black hair always had the perfect muss to it. Her sheer white blouse had been fitted by a benevolent deity; it may have been open a button too low but it was all working.

The three goons stepped back now. One released the velvet rope. Esperanza rewarded him with a dazzling smile. As Myron followed, Kleavage Kyle positioned himself to bump into Myron. Myron braced himself and made sure that Kyle got the worst of it. Esperanza muttered, "Men."

Kleavage Kyle whispered to Myron: "We ain't through, bub."

"We'll do lunch," Myron said. "Maybe catch a matinee of *South Pacific*."

As they headed inside, Esperanza shot Myron a look and shook her head.

"What?"

"I said dress to impress. You look like you're heading to a parent-teacher conference for a fifth grader."

Myron pointed at his feet. "In Ferragamo loafers?"

"And what were you starting up with those Neanderthals for?"

"He called a girl chunky."

"And you came to her rescue?"

"Well, no. But he said it right to her face. 'Your friends can come in but you can't because you're chunky.' Who does that?"

The main room in the club was dark with neon accents. There were large-screen TVs in one section because if you're out at a nightclub, what you really want to do, Myron guessed, was watch TV. The sound system, approximately the size and dimension of a Who stadium concert's, assaulted the senses. The DJ played "house music," a practice whereby the "talented" DJ takes what might ordinarily be a decent song and absolutely destroys it by adding some kind of synthesized bass or electronic beat. There was a laser show, something Myron thought went out of style after a Blue Öyster Cult tour in 1979, and a bevy of young thin-sticks oohed and ahhed over a special effect on the dance floor whereby said floor belched steam, as though you couldn't see that on the street near any Con Ed truck.

Myron tried to shout over the music, but it was pointless. Esperanza led him to a quiet area with, of all things, Web-access terminals. All stations were taken. Again Myron shook his head. You come to a nightclub to surf the Net? He turned back to the dance floor. The women were, in this smoky light, largely on the attractive side, albeit young, and dressed more like they were playing adults than actually being ones. The majority of the women had their cell phones out, skinny fingers tapping off texts; they danced with a languorousness that bordered on comatose.

Esperanza had a small smile on her face.

"What?" Myron said.

She gestured to the right side of the dance floor. "Check out the ass on that chick in the red."

Myron looked at the crimson-clad dancing buttocks and re-membered an Alejandro Escovedo lyric: "I like her better when she walks away." It had been a long time since Myron had heard Espe-ranza talk like this.

"Nice," Myron said.

"Nice?"

"Awesome?"

Esperanza nodded, still smiling. "There are things I could do with an ass like that."

Looking at the rather erotic dancer and then at Esperanza, an image popped into Myron's head. He immediately forced it out. There were places your mind best not go when you're trying to concentrate on other matters. "I'm sure your husband would love that."

"I'm married, not dead. I can look."

Myron watched her face, watched the excitement there, the strange feeling that she was back in her element. When her son, Hector, was born two years ago, Esperanza had immediately gone into Mommy-mode. Her desk was suddenly filled with a corny potpourri of classic images: Hector with the Easter Bunny, Hector with Santa Claus, Hector with Disney characters and on kiddie rides at Hershey Park. Her best business clothes were often stained with baby spit-up and rather than hide it, she loved to tell how said spit-up made its way onto her person. She made friends with Mommy types who would have made her gag in the past, and discussed Maclaren strollers and Montessori preschools and bowel movements and what ages their various offspring first crawled/walked/talked. Her entire world, like many mothers before her—and yes, this was something of a sexist statement—had shrunk down into a small mass of baby flesh.

"So where would Lex be?" Myron asked.

"Probably one of the VIP rooms."

"How do we get in?"

"I undo one more button," Esperanza said. "Seriously, let me work it alone for a minute. Check out the bathroom. I bet you twenty bucks you can't take a pee in the urinal."

"What?"

"Just bet me and go," she said, pointing to the right.

Myron shrugged and headed into the restroom. It was black and dark and marble. He stepped over to the urinal and saw immediately what Esperanza meant. The urinals sat on a giant wall of one-way glass like something in a police interrogation room. In short, you saw everything on the dance floor. The languorous women were literally feet away from him, some using the mirror side of the glass to check themselves out, not realizing (or maybe definitely realizing) that they were staring at a man trying to relieve himself.

He headed out. Esperanza had her hand extended, palm up. Myron crossed it with a twenty-dollar bill.

"Still got the shy bladder, I see."

"Is the women's room the same?"

"You don't want to know."

"So what next?"

Esperanza gestured with her chin at a man with slicked-back

hair oiling his way toward them. When he filled out his job application, Myron had little doubt that it read, *Last Name: Trash. First Name: Euro*. Myron checked the man's wake for slime tracks.

Euro smiled with ferret teeth. "Poca, mi amor."

"Anton," she said, letting him kiss her hand with a tad too much enthusiasm. Myron feared that he might use those ferret teeth to gnaw the skin to bone.

"You are still such a magnificent creature, Poca."

He spoke with a funny maybe-Hungarian, maybe-Arabic accent, like something he made up for a comedy sketch. Anton was unshaven, the stubble on his face glistening in a not-pleasant way. He wore sunglasses even though it was cave-dark in here.

"This is Anton," Esperanza said. "He says Lex is in bottle service."

"Oh," Myron said, having no idea what bottle service was.

"This way," Anton said.

They traveled into a sea of bodies. Esperanza was in front of him. Myron got a kick out of watching every neck turn for a second glance. As they continued to wind through the crowd, a few women met Myron's gaze and held it, though not as many as one, two, five years ago. He felt like an aging pitcher who needed this particular radar gun to tell him that his fastball was losing velocity. Or maybe there was something else at work here. Maybe women just sensed that Myron was engaged now, had been taken off the market by the lovely Terese Collins and thus was no longer to be treated as mere eye candy.

Yeah, Myron thought. Yeah, that *had* to be it.

Anton used his key to open a door into another room—and seemingly another era. Where the actual club was techno and sleek with hard angles and smooth surfaces, this VIP lounge was done up in Early American Bordello. Plush sofas of burgundy, crystal chandeliers, leather moldings on the ceiling, lit candles on the wall. The room also had another one-way glass wall, so the VIPs could watch the girls dance and maybe choose a few to join them. Several robustly implanted soft-porn model types wore period corsets and merry widows and walked around with champagne bottles, ergo, Myron figured, the term "bottle service."

"Are you looking at all the bottles?" Esperanza asked.

"Um, close."

Esperanza nodded, smiled at a particularly well-endowed hostess in a black corset. "Hmm . . . Could do with a little bottle service myself, if you know what I'm saying."

Myron thought about it. Then: "Actually, I don't. You're both women, right? So I'm not sure I get the bottle reference."

"God, you're literal."

"You asked if I was looking at all the bottles. Why?"

"Because they're serving Cristal champagne," Esperanza said.

"So?"

"How many bottles do you see?"

Myron glanced around. "I don't know, nine, maybe ten."

"They go for eight grand a pop here, plus tip."

Myron put his hand to his chest, feigning heart palpitations. He spotted Lex Ryder sprawled on a couch with a colorful assortment of lovelies. The other men in the room all shouted aging musician/ roadie—long hair weaves, bandanas, facial hair, wiry arms, soft guts. Myron made his way through them.

"Hello, Lex."

Lex's head lolled to the side. He looked up and shouted with too much gusto, "Myron!"

27

Lex tried to get up, couldn't, so Myron offered him a hand. Lex used it, managed to get to his feet, and hugged Myron with the slobbering enthusiasm men save for too much drink. "Oh man, it's so good to see you."

HorsePower had started off as a house band in Lex and Gabriel's hometown of Melbourne, Australia. The name had come from Lex's last name Ryder (Horse-Ryder) and Gabriel's last name Wire (Power-Wire), but from the moment they started together, it was all about Gabriel. Gabriel Wire had a wonderful voice, sure, and he was ridiculously handsome with nearly supernatural charisma—but he also had that elusive, intangible, the "you know it when you see it" quality that raises the greats to the status of legendary.

Must be hard, Myron often thought, for Lex—or anyone—to live in that shadow. Sure, Lex was famous and rich and technically speaking, all songs were Wire-Ryder productions, though Myron, being the one who handled his finances, knew Lex's cut was 25 percent to Gabriel's 75. And sure, women still hit on him, men still wanted to be his friend, but Lex was also the ultimate late-night punch line, the butt of all jokes involving second-to-the-point-of-irrelevancy bananas.

HorsePower was still huge, maybe bigger than ever, even though Gabriel Wire had gone completely underground after a tragic scandal more than fifteen years ago. With the exception of a few paparazzi shots and a lot of rumors, there had been pretty much no sign of Gabriel Wire in all that time—no touring, no interviews, no press, no public appearances. All that secrecy just made the public hunger for Wire all the more.

"I think it's time to go home, Lex."

"Nah, Myron," he said, voice thick with what Myron hoped

was just drink. "Come on now. We're having fun. Aren't we having fun, gang?"

Various vocalizations of agreement. Myron looked around. He may have met one or two of the guys before, but the only one he knew for certain was Buzz, Lex's longtime bodyguard/personal assistant. Buzz met Myron's eye and shrugged as if to say, what can you do?

Lex threw his arm around Myron, draping it over his neck like a camera strap. "Sit, old friend. Let's have a drink, relax, unwind."

"Suzze is worried about you."

"Is she now?" Lex arched an eyebrow. "And so she sent her old errand boy to come fetch me?"

"Technically speaking, I'm your errand boy too, Lex."

"Ah, agents. That most mercenary of occupations."

Lex wore black pants and a black leather vest, and it looked like he'd just gone clothes shopping at Rockers R Us. His hair was gray now, cut very short. Collapsing back on the couch, he said, "Sit, Myron."

"Why don't we take a walk, Lex?"

"You're my errand boy too, right? I said, sit."

He had a point. Myron found a spot and sank deep and slow into the cushions. Lex turned a knob to his right and the music lowered. Someone handed Myron a glass of champagne, spilling a bit as they did. Most of the tight-corset ladies—and let's face it, in any era, that's a look that works—were gone now, without much notice, as though they'd faded into the walls. Esperanza was chatting up the one she'd been checking out when they entered the room. The other men in the room watched the two women flirt with the fascination of cavemen first seeing fire.

Buzz was smoking a cigarette that smelled, uh, funny. He looked to pass it off to Myron. Myron shook his head and turned toward Lex. Lex lounged back as though someone had given him a muscle relaxant.

"Suzze showed you the post?" Lex asked.

"Yes."

"So what's your take, Myron?"

"A random lunatic playing head games."

Lex took a deep sip of champagne. "You really think so?"

"I do," Myron said, "but either way it's the twenty-first century."

"Meaning?"

"Meaning it's not that big a deal. You can get a DNA test, if you're so concerned about it—establish paternity for certain."

Lex nodded slowly, took another deep sip. Myron tried to stay out of agent mode, but the bottle held 750 ml, which is approximately 25 ounces, divided by $8,000 dollars, equaled $320 per ounce.

"I hear you're engaged," Lex said.

"Yup."

"Let's drink to that."

"Or sip. Sipping is cheaper."

"Relax, Myron. I'm filthy rich."

True enough. They drank.

"So what's bothering you, Lex?"

Lex ignored the question. "So how come I haven't met your new bride-to-be?"

"It's a long story."

"Where is she now?"

Myron kept it vague. "Overseas."

"May I give you some advice on marriage?"

"How about, 'Don't believe stupid Internet rumors about paternity'?"

Lex grinned. "Good one."

Myron said, "Meh."

"But here's the advice: Be open with each other. Totally open."

Myron waited. When Lex didn't follow up, Myron said, "That's it?"

"You expected something deeper?"

Myron shrugged. "Kinda."

"There's this song I love," Lex said. "The lyric says, 'Your heart is like a parachute.' Do you know why?"

"I think the line is about a mind being like a parachute—it only functions when it's open."

"No, I know that line. This one is a better, 'Your heart is like a parachute—it only opens when you fall.'" He smiled. "Good, right?"

"I guess."

"We all have friends in our lives, like, well, take my mates in here. I love them, I party with them, we talk about weather and sports and hot pieces of ass, but if I didn't see them for a year—or really, ever again—it wouldn't make much difference in my life. That's how it is with most people we know."

He took another sip. The door behind them opened. A bunch of giggling women entered. Lex shook his head, and they vanished back out the door. "And then," he went on, "every once in a while, you have a real friend. Like Buzz over there. We talk about everything. We know the truth about each other—every sick, depraved flaw. Do you have friends like that?"

"Esperanza knows I have a shy bladder," Myron said.

"What?"

"Never mind. Go on. I know what you're saying."

"Right, so anyway, real friends. You let them see the sick crap that goes on in your brain. The ugly." He sat up, getting into it now. "And you know what's odd about that kind of thing? You know what happens when you're totally open and let the other person see that you're a total degenerate?"

Myron shook his head.

"Your friend loves you even more. With everyone else, you put up this façade so you can hide the crud and make them like you. But with real friends, you show them the crud—and that makes them care. When we get rid of the façade, we connect more. So why don't we do that with everyone, Myron? I ask you."

"I guess you're going to tell me."

"Damned if I know." Lex sat back, took a deep sip, tilted his head in thought. "But here's the thing: The façade is, by nature, a lie. That's okay for the most part. But if you don't open up to the one you love most—if you don't show the flaws—you can't connect. You are, in fact, keeping secrets. And those secrets fester and destroy."

The door opened again. Four women and two men stumbled in, giggling and smiling and holding obscenely overpriced champagne in their hands.

"So what secrets are you keeping from Suzze?" Myron asked.

He just shook his head. "It's a two-way street, mate."

"So what secrets is Suzze keeping from you?"

Lex did not reply. He was looking across the room. Myron turned to follow his gaze.

And then he saw her.

Or at least he thought that he did. A blink of an eye across the VIP lounge, candlelit and smoky. Myron hadn't seen her since that snowy night sixteen years ago, her belly swollen, the tears running down her cheeks, the blood flowing through her fingers. He hadn't even kept tabs on them, but the last he had heard they were living somewhere in South America.

Their eyes met across the room for a second, no more. And as impossible as it seemed, Myron knew.

"Kitty?"

His voice was drowned out by the music, but Kitty did not hesitate. Her eyes widened a bit—fear maybe?—and then she spun. She ran for the door. Myron tried to get up fast, but the cushion-sucking sofa slowed him down. By the time he got to his feet, Kitty Bolitar—Myron's sister-in-law, the woman who had taken away so much from him—was out the door.

5

Myron ran after her.

As he reached the VIP lounge exit, here was the image that flashed across his brain: Myron age eleven, his brother, Brad, age six with the crazy curly hair, in the bedroom they shared, playing Nerf basketball. The backboard was flimsy cardboard, the ball basically a round sponge. The rim was attached to the top of the closet door by two orange suction cups you had to lick to make stick. The two brothers played for hours, inventing teams and giving themselves nicknames and personas. There was Shooting Sam and Jumping Jim and Leaping Lenny, and Myron, being the older brother, would control the action, making up a fake universe with good-guy players and bad-guy players and high drama and close games with buzzer beaters. But most of the time, in the end, he let Brad win. At night, when they got into their bunk beds—Myron on

34

top, Brad beneath him—they would recap the games in the dark like TV sportscasters doing postgame analysis.

The memory cleaved his heart anew.

Esperanza spotted him sprinting. "What?"

"Kitty."

"What?"

No time to explain. He hit the door and pushed through it. He was back in the club now with the deafening music. The old man in him wondered who enjoyed socializing when you could not hear anyone speak. But really, now, his thoughts were totally focused on reaching Kitty.

Myron was tall, six-four, and standing on his toes, he could look over most of the crowd. No sign of the Maybe-Kitty. What had she been wearing? Turquoise top. He looked for flashes of turquoise.

There. Her back to him. Heading toward the club exit.

Myron had to move. He shouted excuse-me's as he tried to swim through the bodies, but there were too many of them. The strobe lights and quasi-laser show weren't helping either. Kitty. What the hell was Kitty doing here? Years ago, Kitty had been a tennis wunderkind too, training with Suzze. That was how they first met. It could be that the two old friends were back in touch, of course, but did that really answer why Kitty was here, in this club, without his brother, tonight?

Or was Brad here too?

He started moving faster. He tried not to knock into anyone, but of course that was impossible. There were dirty looks and cries of "Hey!" or "Where's the fire?" but Myron ignored them, pressed on, the whole exercise beginning to take on a dream quality, one of those where you're running and not going anywhere,

where your feet are suddenly heavy or you're trudging through deep snow.

"Ouch!" a girl shrieked. "Dumbass, you stepped on my toe!"

"Sorry," Myron said, still trying to get through.

A big hand landed on Myron's shoulder and spun him around. Someone pushed him hard from behind, nearly knocking him off his feet. Myron got his balance and faced what might have been an open audition for *Jersey Shore: The Ten-Year Reunion* show. There was a blend of hair mousse and faux tans and plucked eyebrows and waxed chests and poser muscles. They had the tough-guy sneers, a strange look on those who primp and manscape to within an inch of their lives. Punching them in the face would hurt; messing up their hair would hurt even more.

There were four or five or maybe six of them—they tended to blur together into a mass of slippery unpleasantness and overbearing Axe cologne—and they were excited about the possibility of proving what men they were in defending the honor of some girl's toe.

Still Myron was nothing if not diplomatic. "I'm sorry, guys," he said. "But this is an emergency."

One douchebag said, "Whoa, where's the fire? You see a fire here, Vinny?"

Vinny: "Yeah, where's the fire? Because I don't see one. You see one, Slap?"

Before Slap could speak, Myron said, "Yeah, I get it. No fire. Look, again, I'm really sorry, but I'm in big hurry."

Still Slap had to get involved: "Nope, I don't see no fire either."

No time for this. Myron started to move—damn, no sign of Kitty—but the men closed ranks. Douchebag, with his hand still on Myron's shoulder, went for the vise grip. "Say you're sorry to Sandra."

"Uh, what part of 'I'm really sorry' confused you?"

"To Sandra," he said again.

Myron turned to the girl who, judging by her dress and the company she kept, never got enough attention from her daddy. He shook his shoulder to dislodge the annoying hand. "I'm really sorry, Sandra."

He said this because it was the best course of action. Try to make peace and move on. But Myron knew. He could see it in the red in their faces, the wet in their eyes. The hormones were engaged now. So as he turned back toward the guy who'd first pushed him, Myron was not surprised to see a fist heading toward his face.

Fights normally last mere seconds—and those seconds are chockfull of three things: confusion, chaos, and panic. So when people see a fist heading toward them, they naturally overreact. They try to duck all the way down or fall all the way back. That was a mistake. If you lose your balance or lose sight of your adversary, you end up, of course, in more danger. Good fighters will often throw blows for just this reason—not necessarily to connect but to make the opponent put himself in a more vulnerable position.

So Myron's move to avoid the blow was a slight one—only a few inches. His right hand was already up. You don't have to knock the fist away hard with some big karate move. You just need to divert its course a little. That was what Myron did.

Myron's goal here was simple: Put this guy down with a minimum of fuss or injury. Myron redirected the traveling fist and then, with the same hand already up, he put his index and middle finger together and snapped a dart blow right at the soft hollow of his attacker's throat. The blow landed flush. Jerzie Boy made a gurgling sound. Both his hands instinctively flew to his throat, leaving him totally exposed. In a normal fight, if there was such a thing, this was where Myron would put him down for good. But that wasn't what he wanted here. He wanted to get away.

So even before Myron could gauge his next shot, he started past the guy, trying to move swiftly away from the scene. But all avenues of escape were blocked now. The patrons at the crowded club had moved in closer, drawn by the smell of a fight and the base desire to see a fellow human being hurt or maimed.

Another hand reached out and grabbed his shoulder. Myron brushed it off. Someone dived for his legs, wrapping Myron up by the ankles, attempting a tackle. Myron bent his knees. He used one hand for balance on the floor. With the other, he tucked his fingers down and delivered a palm strike to the man's nose. The man let go of Myron's legs. The music stopped now. Someone screamed. Bodies began to topple.

This was not good.

Confusion, chaos, and panic. In a crowded nightclub, those things are both enhanced and ridiculously contagious. Someone nearby gets jostled and panics. He throws a punch. People back up. Spectators who'd been enjoying the relative safety of that passive act realize that they are now in harm's way. They begin to flee, crashing into others. Pandemonium.

Someone hit Myron in the back of the head. He spun. Someone hit him in the midsection. Myron's hand instinctively whipped out and grabbed the man's wrist. You can learn the best fighting techniques and be trained by the best, but there is no substitute for being born with amazing hand-eye coordination. As they used to say in his basketball days, "You can't teach height." You also can't really teach coordination or athleticism or competitive instinct either, try as parents might.

So Myron Bolitar, the superior athlete, was able to snatch a wrist mid-blow. He pulled the man toward him and using that momentum, threw a forearm into the man's face.

The man went down.

More screams now. More panic. Myron turned, and in the rush of people, he saw the Maybe-Kitty by the door. He started toward her, but she vanished behind an onslaught of bouncers, including two of the guys who'd given Myron a hard time on the way in. The bouncers—and there were a lot of them now—headed straight toward Myron.

Uh-oh.

"Whoa, fellas, slow down here." Myron lifted his hands, showing that he had no intention of fighting them. As they drew closer, Myron kept his hands up. "Someone else started it."

One tried to get him in a full nelson, an amateur move if ever there was one. Myron calmly slipped out of it and said, "It's over, okay? It's—"

Three more bouncers tackled him hard. Myron hit the floor with a thud. One of the guys from out front climbed on top of him. Someone else kicked Myron's legs. The guy on top of him tried to put his bloated forearm on Myron's throat. Myron ducked his chin, blocking it. The guy tried harder, moving his face close enough for Myron to smell the guy's stale hot-dog breath. Another kick. The face came closer. Myron rolled hard, catching the guy's face with his elbow. The man cursed and backed off.

As Myron started to rise, he felt something hard and metallic push against the bottom of his rib cage. He had a tenth of a second, maybe two, to wonder what it was. Then Myron's heart exploded.

At least, that was what it felt like. It felt like something in his chest had just gone boom, like someone had placed live wires on every nerve ending, sending his parasympathetic system into total spasm. His legs turned to water. His arms dropped away, unable to offer up the least bit of resistance.

A stun gun.

Myron dropped like a fish on a dock. He looked up and saw Kleavage Kyle grinning down at him. Kyle released the trigger. The pain stopped, but only for a second. With his fellow bouncers surrounding him so no one in the club could see, Kyle dug the stun gun back into Myron's lower rib cage and zapped him again. Myron's scream was muffled by a hand closing over his mouth.

"Two million volts," Kyle whispered.

Myron knew something about stun guns and Tasers. You are only supposed to hold the trigger for a few seconds, no more, so as to incapacitate but not seriously injure. But Kyle, maniacal smile on high, did not let up. He kept the trigger pressed down. The pain increased, became overwhelming. Myron's whole body started to quake and buck. Kyle kept his finger on the trigger. Even one of the bouncers said, "Uh, Kyle?" But Kyle held on until Myron's eyes rolled back and there was blackness.

6

What must have been seconds later, Myron felt someone pick him up and carry him fireman-style over a shoulder. His eyes remained closed, his body limp. He was on the cusp of unconsciousness, but he was still aware of where he was, what was happening to him. His nerve endings were shot. He felt exhausted and shaky. The man carrying him was big and muscular. He heard the club music start up again and a voice over the sound system shouted, "Okay, folks, the freak show is ovah! Let's get back to the par-tay!"

Myron remained still, letting the man carry him. He didn't resist. He used the time to regroup, recover, start to plan. A door opened and closed, smothering the music. Myron could feel the brighter light through his closed eyes.

The big man carrying him said, "We should just toss him outside now, right, Kyle? I think he's had enough, don't you?"

It was the same voice that said, "Uh, Kyle," when Myron had been getting zapped. The voice had just a lilt of fear in it. Myron did not like that.

Kyle said, "Put him down, Brian."

Brian did so with surprising gentleness. Lying on the cold floor, his eyes not yet opened, Myron did some quick calculating and knew what his next steps were: Keep your eyes closed, pretend you've totally blacked out—and then slowly start snaking your hand toward the BlackBerry device in your pocket.

Back in the nineties, when cell phones were just starting to become the norm, Myron and Win had developed a techno-savvy and occasionally life-saving mode of communication: When one or the other of them was in trouble (read: Myron), he would hit his speed-dial #1 button on his cell phone and the other (read: Win) would pick up, put the phone on mute, and listen in or rush to or at least help the other. At the time, fifteen years ago, this trick had been cutting edge; today it was about as cutting edge as a Betamax.

That meant, of course, taking it to the next level. Now, with modern breakthroughs, Myron and Win could have each other's back in a much more efficient way. One of Win's tech experts had enhanced their BlackBerrys so that they had a special two-way satellite radio that worked even in spots where there was no cell service, as well as both audio and visual recording devices, and a GPS tracker so that one knew exactly where the other was, within four feet, at any given moment—all of which could be activated anytime with the push of a button.

Ergo the snaking hand heading toward the BlackBerry in his pocket. With his eyes closed, he faked a groan so he could roll just enough to get his hand closer to the pocket. . . .

"Looking for this?"

It was Kleavage Kyle. Myron blinked open his eyes. The floor of the room was Formica and maroon. The walls too were maroon. There was one table with what looked liked a box of Kleenex on it. No other furniture. Myron turned his gaze toward Kyle. Kyle was grinning.

He was also holding up Myron's BlackBerry.

"Thanks," Myron said. "I was looking for that. You can just toss it over here."

"Oh, I don't think so."

There were three other bouncers in the room, all with shaved heads, all steroid-and-too-much-gym huge. Myron spotted one who looked a little frightened and figured that had been his carrier, so to speak. The frightened guy said, "I better head back out to the front, make sure everything is okay."

Kyle said, "You do that, Brian."

"Seriously, his friend, that hot chick wrestler, knows he's here."

"Don't worry about her," Kyle said.

"I would," Myron said.

"Excuse me?"

Myron tried to sit up. "You don't watch much TV, do you, Kyle? You know that part of the show where they triangulate the cell phone signal and find the guy? Well, that's what's happening here. I don't know how much longer it will take but—"

Holding the BlackBerry up, his expression two steps past smug, Kyle hit the off button and watched the device power down. "You were saying?"

Myron did not reply. Frightened Big Guy left.

"First," Kyle said, tossing Myron back his wallet, "please escort Mr. Bolitar from the premises. We request that you never return."

"Even if I promise not to wear a shirt?"

"My two men will escort you out the back entrance."

This was a curious development—letting him go. Myron decided to play it out, see if it was going to be this easy. He was, to put it kindly, skeptical. The two men helped lift Myron to his feet. "What about my BlackBerry?"

"You can have it back when you exit the premises," Kyle said.

One man held Myron's right arm, the other the left. They led him into the corridor. Kyle followed, closing the door behind them. When they were all out of the room, Kyle said, "Okay, good, that should do it. Bring him back in."

Myron frowned. Kyle opened the same door again. The two men gripped Myron harder and started dragging him back into the room. When Myron resisted, Kyle showed him the stun gun. "You want another two million volts?"

Myron did not. He moved back to the maroon room. "What was that all about?"

"That part was for show," Kyle said. "Please move to the far corner." When Myron didn't obey immediately, he flashed the stun gun. Myron inched backward, not turning his back on Kyle. There was a small table by the door. Kyle and the two bouncers moved toward it. They reached into what looked like a box of tissues and pulled out surgical gloves. Myron watched them slip the gloves onto their hands.

"Let me just state for the record," Myron said, "that I'm getting a little turned on by the rubber gloves. Will this involve my bending over?"

"Defense mechanism," Kyle said, snapping the gloves on with a little too much zeal.

"What?"

"You use humor as a defense mechanism. The more frightened you are, the more your mouth flaps."

Bouncer-cum-therapist, Myron thought, perhaps proving the man's point.

"So let me explain the situation so even you'll understand," Kyle said in a singsong tone. "We call this the beating room. Hence the maroon color. The blood blends in, as you will soon see."

Kyle stopped and smiled. Myron kept still.

"We just videotaped you leaving this room under your own volition. As you may have guessed, the camera is now off. So that's the official record—you leaving of your own accord, relatively unharmed. We also have witnesses who will state that you assaulted them, that our response was proportional to the threat you posed, that you initiated the ruckus. We have longtime club patrons and employees who will pretty much sign any statement we put in front of them. No one will back up any claim you have. Any questions?"

"Just one," Myron said. "Did you really use the word 'ruckus'?"

Kyle stayed with the grin. "Defense mechanism," he said again.

The three men spread out, fists tightened, muscles at the ready. Myron moved a little farther into the corner.

"So what's your plan here, Kyle?" Myron asked.

"It's pretty simple, Myron. We are going to hurt you. How badly depends on how much you resist. At best, you're going to end up hospitalized. You will be pissing blood for a while. We may break a bone or two. But you will live and probably recover. If you resist, I will use the stun gun to paralyze you. It will be very painful. And then your beating will be longer and more savage. Am I making myself clear?"

They started to inch closer. Their hands flexed. One cracked his neck. Kleavage Kyle actually took off his jacket. "I don't want to get it dirty," he explained. "What with the blood stains and all."

Myron pointed lower. "What about your pants?"

Kyle was topless now. He did that flex thing where you make your pecs dance. "Don't worry about them."

"Oh, but I do," Myron said.

Then, as the men inched closer, Myron smiled and crossed his arms. The move made the men pause. Then Myron said, "Did I tell you about my new BlackBerry? The GPS feature? The two-way satellite radio? It all works when you press one button."

"Your BlackBerry," Kyle said, "is off."

Myron shook his head and made a buzzing noise as though he had heard the wrong answer on a game show. Win's voice came from the BlackBerry's tinny speaker: "No, Kyle, I'm afraid it's not."

The three men stopped.

"So let me explain the situation," Myron said, doing his best Kyle singsong, "so even you'll understand. The button you have to press to activate all the newfangled features? You guessed it: It's the off button. In short, everything that's been said has been recorded. Plus the GPS is on. How far away are you, Win?"

"Heading through the club entrance now. I also activated the three-way caller. Esperanza's on the line on mute. Esperanza?"

The mute button was clicked off. The club music came through the phone speaker. Esperanza said, "I'm by the side door where they dragged Myron out. Oh, and guess what? I found an old friend here, a police officer named Roland Dimonte. Say hi to my friend Kyle, Rolly."

The male voice said, "I better see Bolitar's ugly, untouched mug out here in thirty seconds, asswipe."

It took more like twenty.

"It might not have been her," Myron said.

It was two A.M. by the time Myron and Win got back to the Dakota. They sat in a room rich people called "a study," with Louis the Something wood furniture and marble busts and a large antique globe and bookshelves with leather-bound first editions. Myron sat in a burgundy chair with gold buttons on the arm. By the time things had calmed down at the club, Kitty had vanished, if she'd ever been there in the first place. Lex and Buzz had cleared out too.

Win opened a leather-bound first-edition false front bookcase to reveal a refrigerator. He grabbed a Yoo-hoo chocolate drink and tossed it to Myron. Myron caught it, and reading the directions—"Shake It!"—did just that. Win opened the decanter and poured himself an exclusive cognac called, interestingly enough, The Last Drop.

"I could have been wrong," Myron said.

Win lifted his snifter and checked it against the light.

"I mean, it's been sixteen years, right? Her hair was a different color. The room was dark and I saw her for only a second. So really, when I add it up, it might not have been her."

"It might not have been *she*," Win said. "Subject pronoun."

Win.

"And it was Kitty," Win said.

"How do you know?"

"I know you. You don't make those kinds of mistakes. Other mistakes, yes. But not those kind."

Win took a sip of cognac. Myron splashed down some of the Yoo-hoo. Cold, chocolaty, sweet nectar. Three years ago Myron had all but given up this, his favorite beverage, in favor of boutique coffees that eat away the stomach lining. When he returned home from the stress of being overseas, he started up again with Yoo-hoo, more for the comfort than the actual taste. Now he loved it again.

"On the one hand, it doesn't matter," Myron said. "Kitty hasn't been part of my life for a long time."

Win nodded. "And on the other hand?"

Brad. That was what the other hand, the first hand, both hands, every hand—the chance, after all these years, to see and maybe reconcile with his baby brother. Myron took a moment, shifted his seat. Win watched and said nothing. Eventually Myron said, "It can't be a coincidence. Kitty in the same nightclub—same VIP room even—as Lex."

"It would seem unlikely," Win said. "So what's our next step?"

"Find Lex. Find Kitty."

Myron stared at the Yoo-hoo label and wondered, not for the first time, what the heck "dairy whey" was. The mind stalls. It dodges, weaves, finds irrelevancies on soda cans, all in the hopes of avoiding the unavoidable. He thought about when he first tried this drink, in that house in Livingston, New Jersey, he now owned, how Brad always had to have one too because Brad always wanted to do what big brother, Myron, did. He thought about the hours he shot baskets in the backyard, letting Brad have the honor of fetching him rebounds so Myron could concentrate on shooting. Myron spent so many hours out there, shooting, moving, getting the pass from Brad, shooting again, moving, hours and hours alone, and while Myron did not regret one moment of it, he had to wonder about his priorities—the priorities of most top athletes. What we so admire and call "single-minded dedication" was really "obsessive self-involvement." What in that exactly is admirable?

An alarm clock beeping—a truly grating ringtone the Black-Berry people had for some reason labeled "Antelope"—interrupted them. Myron glanced down at his BlackBerry and flicked off the offending noise.

"You might as well take that," Win said, standing. "I have somewhere to go anyway."

"At two thirty A.M.? You want to tell me her name?"

Win smiled. "Maybe later."

Given the demand for the one computer in the area, two thirty A.M., Eastern Daylight Time—seven thirty A.M. in Angola—was pretty much the only time that Myron could get his fiancée, Terese Collins, alone, if only technologically.

Myron signed on to Skype, the Internet equivalent of a video-phone, and waited. A moment later, a video box came up and Terese appeared. He felt the heady rush and the lightness in his chest.

"God, you're beautiful," he said to her.

"Good opening line."

"I always open with that line."

"It doesn't get old."

Terese looked great, sitting at the desk in a white blouse, hands folded so that he could see the engagement ring, her bottle-brunette hair—she was normally a blonde—pulled back into a ponytail.

After a few minutes, Myron said, "I was with a client tonight."

"Who?"

"Lex Ryder."

"The lesser half of HorsePower?"

"I like him. He's a good guy. Anyway, he said the secret of a good marriage is being open."

"I love you," she said.

"I love you too."

"I didn't mean to interrupt, but I love that I can just blurt that out. I never had that before. I'm too old to feel this way."

"We are always eighteen, waiting for our lives to begin," Myron said.

"That's corny."

"You're a sucker for corny."

"True enough. So Lex Ryder said we should be open. Aren't we?"

"I don't know. He had this theory on flaws. That we should reveal them to each other—the worst things about us—because somehow that makes us more human and thus closer."

Myron gave her a few more details from the conversation. When he was done, Terese said, "Makes sense."

"Do I know yours?" he asked.

"Myron, remember when we first got to that hotel room in Paris?"

Silence. He remembered.

"So yeah," she said softly, "you know my flaws."

"I guess I do." He shifted in his seat, trying to meet her eyes by gazing straight into the camera. "I'm not sure you know all mine."

"Flaws?" she said, feigning shock. "What flaws?"

"I'm pee shy, for one."

"And you think I don't know that?"

He laughed a little too hard.

"Myron?"

"Yes."

"I love you. I can't wait to be your wife. You're a good man, maybe the best man I've ever known. The truth won't change that. Whatever you're not telling me? It may fester or whatever Lex said. Or it may not. Honesty can be overrated too. So don't torment yourself. I will love you either way."

Myron sat back. "Do you know how great you are?"

"I don't care. Tell me how beautiful I am again. I'm a sucker for that."

7

Three Downing was closing up for the night.

Win watched the patrons stumble outside, blinking in the unnatural light of Manhattan at four A.M. He waited. After a few minutes he spotted the large man who had used the stun gun on Myron. The large man—Kyle—was tossing someone out as though he were a bag of laundry. Win stayed calm. He thought back to a time not that long ago when Myron had vanished for weeks, was tortured probably, a time when he, Win, couldn't help his best friend or even avenge him after the fact. Win remembered the horrible feeling of powerlessness. He hadn't felt that way since his youth in the wealthy suburbs on Philadelphia's Main Line, since those who hated him on sight tormented and beat him. Win had sworn back then that he would never feel that way again. Then he did something about it. Now, as an adult, the same rule held.

If you are hurt, you strike back. Massive retaliation. But with a purpose. Myron didn't always agree with this doctrine. That was okay. They were friends, best friends. They would kill for each other. But they weren't the same person.

"Hello, Kyle," Win called out.

Kyle looked up and scowled.

"Do you have a moment for a private conversation?" Win asked.

"You kidding me?"

"Normally, I'm a great kidder, a regular Dom DeLuise, but no, Kyle, tonight I kid you not. I want us to chat in private."

Kyle actually licked his lips. "No cell phones this time?"

"None. No stun guns either."

Kyle looked around, making sure that the proverbial coast was clear. "And that cop is gone?"

"Long gone."

"So it's just you and me?"

"Just you and me," Win repeated. "In fact, my nipples are getting hard at the thought."

Kyle moved closer. "I don't care who you know, pretty boy," Kyle said. "I'll bust your ass up but good."

Win smiled and gestured for him to lead the way. "Oh, I can't wait."

Sleep used to be an escape for Myron.

No more. He would lie in bed for hours, stare at the ceiling, afraid to close his eyes. It brought him back often to a place he was supposed to forget. He knew that he should deal with this—visit a shrink or something—but he also knew that he probably wouldn't. Trite to say, but Terese was something of a cure. When he slept with her, the night terrors kept their distance.

His first thought when the alarm clock jarred him back to the present was the same as when he'd tried to close his eyes: Brad. It was odd. Days, sometimes weeks, maybe even months passed without thinking about his brother. Their estrangement worked a bit like grief. We are often told during times of bereavement that time heals all wounds. That's crap. In truth, you are devastated, you mourn, you cry to the point where you think you'll never stop— and then you reach a stage where the survival instinct takes over. You stop. You simply won't or can't let yourself "go there" anymore because the pain was too great. You block. You deny. But you don't really heal.

Seeing Kitty last night had knocked away the denial and sent Myron reeling. So now what? Simple: Talk to the two people who could tell him something about Kitty and Brad. He reached for his phone and called his house in Livingston, New Jersey. His parents were visiting from Boca Raton for the week.

His mom answered. "Hello?"

"Hey, Mom," Myron said, "how are you?"

"I'm great, honey. How are you?"

Her voice was almost too tender, as if the wrong answer could shatter her heart.

"I'm great too." He'd thought about asking her about Brad, but no, this would take some tact. "I thought maybe I'd take you and Dad out to dinner tonight."

"Not Nero's," she said. "I don't want to go to Nero's."

"That's fine."

"I'm not in the mood for Italian. Nero's is Italian."

"Right. No Nero's."

"You ever have that?"

"Have what?"

"Where you're just not in the mood for a kind of food? Take me right now, for example. I simply don't want Italian."

"Yep, I got that. So what kind of food would you like?"

"Can we do Chinese? I don't like the Chinese in Florida. It's too greasy."

"Sure. How about Baumgart's?"

"Oh, I love their kung pao chicken. But, Myron, what kind of name is Baumgart's for a Chinese restaurant? It sounds like a Jewish deli."

"It used to be," Myron said.

"Really?"

He had explained the origin of the name to her at least ten times. "I really have to hurry here, Mom. I'll be by the house at six. Tell Dad."

"Okay. Take care of yourself, honey."

Again with the tender. He told her to do the same. After he hung up, he decided to text his father to confirm tonight. He felt bad about that, as if he were somehow betraying his mother, but her memory . . . well, enough with the denial, right?

Myron quickly showered and got dressed. Since returning from Angola, Myron had, at Esperanza's rather strong suggestion, made walking to work a morning ritual. He entered Central Park at West Seventy-second and took it south. Esperanza loved to walk, but Myron had never really gotten it. His temperament was not suited for head clearing or settling his nerves or solace or whatever putting one foot in front of the other was supposed to accomplish. But Esperanza had convinced him that it would be good for his head, making him promise to give it three weeks. Alas, Esperanza was wrong, though maybe he hadn't given it a fair shake. Myron spent most of the time with the Bluetooth in his ear, chatting up clients, gesturing wildly like, well, like most of the other park dwellers. Still it felt better, more "him," to be multitasking. So with that in mind, he jammed the Bluetooth into his ear and called Suzze T. She picked up on the first ring.

"Did you find him?" Suzze asked.

"We did. Then we lost him. Have you heard of a nightclub called Three Downing?"

"Of course."

Of course. "Well, Lex was there last night." Myron explained about finding him in the VIP room. "He started talking about festering secrets and not being open."

"Did you tell him the post wasn't true?"

"Yes."

"What did he say?"

"We kind of got interrupted." Myron walked past the children frolicking in the fountain in Heckscher Playground. There might be happier kids somewhere else on this sunny day, but he doubted it. "I have to ask you something."

"I already told you. It's his baby."

"Not that. Last night, at that club, I could have sworn I saw Kitty."

Silence.

Myron stopped walking. "Suzze?"

"I'm here."

"When was the last time you saw Kitty?" Myron asked.

"How long ago did she run away with your brother?"

"Sixteen years ago."

"Then the answer is sixteen years."

"So I was just imagining seeing her?"

"I didn't say that. In fact, I bet it was her."

"Do you want to explain?"

"Are you near a computer?" Suzze asked.

"No. I'm walking to the office like a dumb animal. I should be there in about five minutes."

"Forget that. Can you grab a cab and swing by the academy? I want to show you something anyway."

"When?"

"I'm just about to start a lesson. An hour?"

"Okay."

"Myron?"

"What?"

"How did Lex look?"

"He looked fine."

"I just got a bad feeling. I think I'm going to mess up."

"You won't."

"It's what I do, Myron."

"Not this time. Your agent won't let you."

"Won't let you," she repeated, and he could almost see her shaking her head. "If anyone other than you said that, I would think it was the lamest thing I ever heard. But coming from you . . . no, sorry, it's still really lame."

"I'll see you in an hour."

Myron picked up his pace and headed into the Lock-Horne

Building—yes, Win's full name was Windsor Horne Lockwood, and as they used to say in school, you do the math—and took the elevator to the twelfth floor. The doors opened right into the MB Reps reception area and sometimes, when children on the elevator pressed the wrong button and the door opened, they screamed at what they saw.

Big Cyndi. Receptionist extraordinaire at MB Reps.

"Good morning, Mr. Bolitar!" she cried out in the high-pitched squeal of a little girl seeing her *Teen Beat* idol.

Big Cyndi was six-five and had recently completed a four-day juice-cleansing "evacuation" diet so that she now tipped the scales at three-ten. Her hands were the size of throw pillows. Her head resembled a cinder block.

"Hey, Big Cyndi."

She insisted that he call her that, never just Cyndi or, uh, Big, and even though she had known him for years, she liked the formality of calling him Mister Bolitar. Big Cyndi was, he guessed, feeling better today. The diet had darkened Big Cyndi's usually sunny demeanor. She had growled more than talked. Her makeup, usually a Joseph-and-the-Technicolor-Dreamcoat display, had been a harsh black 'n' white, landing somewhere between nineties' goth and seventies' Kiss. Now, as usual, her makeup looked as though it'd been applied by laying a sixty-four box of Crayolas on her face and turning up the heat lamp.

Big Cyndi leapt to her feet and while Myron was beyond being shocked by what she wore anymore—tube tops, spandex bodysuits—this outfit almost made him step back. Her dress was chiffon, maybe, but it was more like she'd tried to wrap her entire body in party streamers. What appeared to be bands of flimsy purplish pink crepe paper started at the top of her breasts and wound and wound and wound down past her hips and stopped too short on the upper thigh. There were rips in the fabric, pieces dangling off like something Bruce Banner sported after turning into the Hulk. She smiled at him and spun hard on one leg, the earth teetering on its axis as she did. There was a diamond-shaped opening on her lower back near the coccyx bone.

"Do you like it?" she asked.

"I guess."

Big Cyndi turned back toward him, put her hands on her crepe-paper-clad hips, and pouted. " You 'guess'?"

"It's great."

"I designed it myself."

"You're very talented."

"Do you think Terese will like it?"

Myron opened his mouth, stopped, closed it. Uh-oh.

"Surprise!" Big Cyndi shouted. "I designed these bridesmaid dresses myself. It's my gift to you both."

"We don't even have a date yet."

"True fashion stands the test of time, Mr. Bolitar. I'm just so glad you like them. I was going to go with a sea-foam color, but I think the fuchsia is warmer. I'm more a warm-tone person. I think Terese is too, don't you?"

"I do," Myron said. "She's all about fuchsia."

Big Cyndi gave him the slow smile—tiny teeth in a giant mouth—that sent children shrieking. He smiled back. God, he loved this big, crazy woman.

Myron pointed at the door on the left. "Is Esperanza in?"

"Yes, Mr. Bolitar. Should I let her know that you're here?"

"I got it, thanks."

"Would you please tell her that I'll be in for her fitting in five minutes?"

"Will do."

Myron knocked lightly on the door and entered. Esperanza sat at her desk. She was wearing the fuchsia dress, though on her, with the strategic rips, it looked a bit more like Raquel Welch in *One Million Years B.C.* Myron stifled a chuckle.

"Make one comment," Esperanza said, "and die."

"*Moi?*" Myron sat. "I do think, however, that sea foam would work better on you. You're not a warm-tone person."

"We have a meeting at noon," she said.

"I'll be back by then, and hopefully you'll be changed. Any hits on Lex's credit cards?"

"Nothing."

She didn't look up at him, her eyes down examining some paper on her desk with a tad too much concentration.

"So," Myron said, aiming for nonchalant. "What time did you get home last night?"

"Don't worry, Daddy. I didn't break curfew."

"That's not what I meant."

"Sure it is."

Myron looked at the swirl of trite-but-true family photographs on her desk. "Do you want to talk about it?"

"No, Dr. Phil, I don't."

"Okay."

"And don't give me that sanctimonious face. I didn't do anything beyond flirting last night."

"I'm not here to judge."

"Yeah, but you do it anyway. Where are you off to?"

"Suzze's tennis academy. Have you seen Win?"

"I don't think he's in yet."

Myron grabbed a taxi west toward the Hudson River. The Suzze T Tennis Academy was located near Chelsea Piers in what looked like, and maybe was, a giant white bubble. When you entered the courts, the air pressure used to inflate the bubble made your ears pop. There were four courts, all filled with young women/teens/girls playing tennis with instructors. Suzze was on court one, all eight months pregnant of her, giving instructions on how to approach the net to two sun-soaked blond teens with ponytails. Forehands were being drilled on court two, backhands court three, serves on court four. Someone had put down hula hoops in the corners of the service line as targets. Suzze spotted Myron and signaled for him to give her a minute.

Myron moved back into the waiting room overlooking the courts. The moms were there, all in tennis whites. Tennis was the only sport where spectators liked to dress like the participants, as if they might suddenly be called out of the stands to play. Still—and Myron knew that this was politically incorrect—there was something hot about a mom in tennis whites. So he looked. He did not ogle. He was too sophisticated for that. But he looked.

The lust, if that was what this was, quickly dissipated. The mothers scrutinized their daughters with too much intensity, their lives seemingly riding on every shot. Looking out the picture window at Suzze, watching her sharing a laugh with one of her pupils, he remembered Suzze's own mom, who used terms like "driven" or "focused" to cover up what should have been labeled "innate cruelty." Some believe that these parents go overboard because they are living their lives through their children, but that wasn't the case because they wouldn't ever treat themselves so callously. Suzze's mother wanted to create a tennis player, period, and felt the best way to do that was to tear asunder anything else that might give her child either joy or self-esteem, making her wholly dependent on how she swung a racket. Beat your opponent, you're good. Lose, you're meaningless. She did more than withhold love. She withheld any inkling of self-worth.

Myron had grown up in an era in which people blamed their parents for all their problems. Many were whiners, pure and simple, not willing to look in the mirror and get a grip. The Blame Generation, finding fault with everyone and everything but ourselves. But Suzze T's situation was different. He had seen the torment, seen the years of struggle, trying to rebel against everything tennis, wanting to quit but also loving the actual game. The court became both her torture chamber and her one place of escape, and it was hard to reconcile that. Eventually, almost inevitably, it led to drugs and self-destructive behavior until finally even Suzze, who could have played the blame game with a fair amount of legitimacy, looked in the mirror and found her answer.

Myron sat and paged through a tennis magazine. Five minutes later, the kids started filing off the court. The smiles fled as they left the pressure-air confines of the bubble, their heads held down by their mothers' forceful gazes. Suzze came out after them. A mother stopped her, but Suzze kept it short. Without breaking stride, she walked past Myron and gestured for him to follow. Moving target, Myron thought. Harder for a parent to nab.

She headed into her office and closed the door after Myron.

"This isn't working," Suzze said.

"What's not?"

"The academy."

"Looks like a pretty good crowd to me," Myron said.

Suzze collapsed into her desk chair. "I came in with what I thought would be a great concept—a tennis academy for top players that would also let them breathe and live and become more well-rounded. I argued the obvious—that such a setting would make them better-adjusted, happier people—but I also argued that in the long run, it would make them better tennis players."

"And?"

"Well, who knows what the long run means? But the truth is, my concept isn't working. They aren't better players. The kids who are single-minded and have no interest in art or theater or music or friends—those kids become the best players. The kids who just want to beat your brains in, destroy you, show no mercy—those are the ones who win."

"Do you really believe that?"

"You don't?"

Myron said nothing.

"And the parents see it too. Their kids are happier here. They won't burn out as fast, but the better players are leaving for the intense boot camps."

"That's short-term thinking," Myron said.

"Maybe. But if they burn out when they're twenty-five, well, that's late in a career anyway. They need to win now. We get that, don't we, Myron? We were both blessed athletically, but if you don't have that killer instinct—the part of you that makes you a great competitor if not a great human being—it is hard to be an elite."

"So are you saying we were like that?" Myron asked.

"No, I had my mom."

"And me?"

Suzze smiled. "I remember seeing you play at Duke in the NCAA finals. The expression on your face . . . you'd rather die than lose."

For a moment neither of them spoke. Myron stared at tennis trophies, the shiny trinkets that represented Suzze's success. Finally Suzze said, "Did you really see Kitty last night?"

"Yes."

"How about your brother?"

Myron shook his head. "Brad may have been there, but I didn't see him."

"Are you thinking what I'm thinking?"

Myron shifted in his seat. "You think Kitty posted that 'Not His'?"

"I'm raising the possibility."

"Let's not jump to conclusions yet. You said you had something you wanted to show me. About Kitty."

"Right." She started gnawing on her lip, something Myron hadn't seen her do in years. He waited, gave her a little time and space. "So yesterday after we talked, I started checking around."

"Checking around for what?"

"I don't know, Myron," she said, a little impatience sneaking in. "Something, a clue, whatever."

"Okay."

Suzze started typing on her computer. "So I started looking at my own Facebook page, where that lie was posted. You know anything about how people fan you?"

"I assume they just sign up."

"Right. So I decided to sort of do what you suggested. I started looking for old boyfriends or tennis rivals or fired musicians—someone who might want to harm us."

"And?"

Suzze was still typing. "And I started going through the people who'd signed up recently for the fan page. I mean, I now have forty-five thousand followers. So it took some time. But eventually . . ."

She clicked the mouse and waited. "Okay, here. I stumbled across this profile from someone who signed up three weeks ago. I thought it was pretty odd, especially in light of what you told me about last night."

She gestured toward Myron, who stood and circled around to see what was on the screen. When he saw the name in bold on the top of the profile page, he wasn't really all that surprised.

Kitty Hammer Bolitar.

8

Kitty Hammer Bolitar.

Back in the privacy of his office, Myron took a closer look at the Facebook page. No question about it when he saw the profile photo: It was his sister-in-law. Older, sure. A little more weathered. The cuteness from her tennis days had hardened a bit, but her face still had that perky-pretty thing going on. He stared at her for a moment and tried to quell the hatred that naturally rose to the surface whenever he thought of her.

Kitty Hammer Bolitar.

Esperanza came in and sat next to him without a word. Some would assume that Myron would want to be alone. Esperanza knew better. She looked at the screen.

"Our first client," she said.

"Yep," Myron said. "Did you see her at the club last night?"

"Nope. I heard you call her name, but by the time I turned, she was gone."

Myron checked the wall posts. Sparse. Some people playing Mafia Wars or Farmville or quizzes. Myron saw that Kitty had forty-three friends. "First thing," he said. "Let's print out a list of her friends, see if there is anybody we know."

"Okay."

Myron hit a photo album icon called "Brad and Kitty—A Love Story." Then he started looking through the photographs, Esperanza at his side. For a long time, neither spoke. Myron just clicked, looked, clicked. A life. That was what he was seeing. He had made fun of these social networks and didn't get them and thought of all the strange, even quasi-perverse stuff about the whole thing, but what he was seeing here, what he was watching go by, click by click, was nothing less than a life, or in this case, two.

His brother's and Kitty's.

Myron watched Brad and Kitty age. There were photographs on a sand dune in Namibia, canyoning in Catalonia, sightseeing on Easter Island, helping the natives in Cusco, cliff-diving in Italy, backpacking in Tasmania, doing an archeological dig in Tibet. In some photographs, like the ones with the hilltop villagers in Myanmar, Kitty and Brad sported native garb. In others they wore cargo shorts and tees. Backpacks were almost always present. Brad and Kitty often posed cheek to cheek, one smile almost touching the other. Brad's hair remained a constant curly dark mess, at times getting long and unruly enough to mistake for a Rastafarian's. He hadn't changed much, his brother. Myron studied his brother's nose and saw that it was a little more crooked now—or maybe that was projecting.

Kitty had lost weight. There was something both wiry and brittle about her physique now. Myron kept clicking. The truth was—a truth he should be happy about—Brad and Kitty glowed in every shot.

As if reading his mind Esperanza said, "They look damn happy."

"Yep."

"But they're vacation pictures. You can't tell anything from them."

"Not vacation," Myron said. "This is their life."

Christmas was in Sierra Leone. There was a Thanksgiving in Sitka, Alaska. Another festival of some kind in Laos. Kitty listed her current address as "Planet Earth's Obscure Corners," and her occupation as "Former Miserable Tennis Wunderkind Now Happy Nomad Looking to Better the World." Esperanza pointed at her "occupation" and made a gagging gesture with her finger and mouth.

When they finished looking through that first album, he went back to the photo page. Two more albums were there—one called "My Family," the other labeled "The Best Thing in Our Lives—Our Son, Mickey."

Esperanza said, "You okay?"

"Fine."

"Then let's get to it."

Myron clicked on the Mickey folder and the thumbs—small iconlike photos—loaded up. For a moment he just stared, his hand on the mouse. Esperanza kept still. Then, almost mechanically, Myron started clicking through the photographs of the boy, starting when Mickey was a newborn infant and ending sometime recently, when the boy was probably about fifteen. Esperanza bent for a closer look, watching the images whir by, when under her breath she whispered, "My God."

Myron said nothing.

"Go back," she said.

"Which one?"

"You know which one."

He did. He went back to the photograph of Mickey playing basketball. There were a lot of him playing hoops—in Kenya, Serbia, Israel—but in this particular picture, Mickey was taking a fadeaway jumper. His wrist was cocked, the ball near his forehead. His taller opponent was reaching to block it, but he never would. Mickey had hops, yes, but he also had the fadeaway, drifting back to safety from that outstretched hand. Myron could almost see the gentle release, the way the ball would rise with perfect backspin.

"May I state the obvious?" Esperanza asked.

"Go for it."

"That's your move. This could be a picture of you."

Myron did not reply.

"Except, well, you had that ridiculous perm back then."

"It wasn't a perm."

"Sure, right, the natural curls that left when you were twenty-two."

Silence.

"How old would he be now?" Esperanza asked.

"Fifteen."

"He looks taller than you."

"Could be."

"No question he's a Bolitar. He's got your build, but he's got your dad's eyes. I like your dad's eyes. They're soulful."

Myron said nothing. He just stared at the photographs of the nephew he'd never met. He tried to sort through the emotions ricocheting through him and then decided to just let them be.

"So," Esperanza said, "what's our next step?"

"We find them."

"Why?"

Myron figured the question was rhetorical or maybe he didn't have a good answer. Either way he let it be. After Esperanza left, Myron went through the photographs of Mickey again, slower this time. When he finished, he clicked the message button. Kitty's profile picture appeared. He typed a message to her, deleted it, typed it again. The wording was wrong. Always. The message was also too long, too much explanation, too much rationalization and couching, and too many "on the other hands." So finally he gave it one last try with three words:

Please forgive me.

He looked at it, shook his head, and then, before he could change his mind, he hit the send button.

Win never showed. He used to keep his office upstairs, corner of the trading floor of Lock-Horne Securities, but when Myron was indisposed for a significant period of time, he moved down to MB Reps (literally and figuratively) so as to shore up Esperanza and assure the clients that they were still in good hands.

It was not unusual for Win not to come in or be in contact. Win disappeared a fair amount—not much recently, but whenever he did, it was usually not good. Myron was tempted to call him, but as Esperanza had pointed out earlier, he was not either of their mothers.

The rest of the day was about the clients. One was upset because he had recently been traded. One was upset because he wanted to be traded. One was upset because she had been forced to attend a movie premiere in a town car when she was promised a stretch limousine. One was upset (notice the trend here) because he was staying in a hotel in Phoenix and couldn't find his hotel key. "Why do they use these stupid cards as keys, Myron? Remember the days when you had the big ones with the tassels? I never lost those. Make sure they put me in hotels with those from now on, okay?"

"Sure thing," Myron said.

An agent wore many hats—negotiator, handler, friend, financial consultant (Win did most of that), real estate agent, personal shopper, travel agent, damage controller, branding merchandiser, chauffeur, babysitter, parental figure—but what clients liked most was that an agent got more worked up over your interests than you did. Ten years ago, during a tense negotiation with a team owner, the client calmly told Myron, "I don't take what he's saying personally" and Myron replied, "Well, your agent does." The client smiled. "That's why I'll never leave you."

And that pretty much sums up the best agent-talent relationships.

At six o'clock, Myron made the very familiar turn onto his hometown street in the suburban paradise known as Livingston, New Jersey. Like much of the suburbs surrounding Manhattan, Livingston had been farmland, considered the boondocks, until the early 1960s when someone realized that it was less than an hour from the big city. Then the split-levels invaded and conquered. In the past few years, the McMansions—definition: how much interior square footage could we fit on how tiny a plot of land—had made serious inroads, but not yet on his street. When Myron pulled up to the familiar abode, second from the corner, the same one he'd lived in pretty much his whole life, the front door opened. His mother appeared.

Not that long ago—a few years ago even—his mother would sprint out down the concrete walk upon his arrival, as though it were a tarmac and he was a returning POW. Today she stayed by the door. He kissed her cheek and gave her a big hug. He could feel the gentle quake from her Parkinson's. Dad was behind her, waiting and watching, as was his way, until it was his turn. Myron kissed his cheek too, always, because that was what they did.

They were so glad to see him, and yes, at his age, he should be over that, but he wasn't and so what? Six years ago, when his father had finally retired from the warehouse in Newark and his parents decided to migrate south to Boca Raton, Myron had bought his childhood home. Yes, those in the psychiatric profession would scratch their chins and mutter something about arrested development or uncut umbilical cords, but Myron found the move to be a practical one. His parents came up a lot. They'd need a place to stay. It was a good investment—Myron owned no real estate. He could come here when he wanted to escape the city, and he could stay at the Dakota when he didn't.

Myron Bolitar, Master of Self-Rationalization.

Whatever. He had recently done some renovations, updating the bathrooms, painting the walls something neutral, remodeling the kitchen—and mostly, so Mom and Dad wouldn't have to navigate the stairs, Myron had turned what had been the downstairs den into a bedroom suite for them. Mom's first reaction: "Will this hurt resale value?" After he assured her that it would not—he really had no idea one way or the other—she had settled into it just fine.

The TV was on. "What are you watching?" Myron asked.

"Your father and I never watch anything live anymore. We used that DMV machine to record the shows."

"DVR," Dad corrected.

"Thank you, Mr. Television, Mr. Ed Sullivan, ladies and gentlemen. The DMV, the DVR, whatever. We record a show, Myron, then we watch it and skip the commercials. Saves time." She tapped her temple, indicating that doing this displayed intelligence.

"So what were you watching?"

"I," Dad said, stressing that one word, "wasn't watching anything."

"Yes, Mr. Sophistication over there would never ever watch any television. This from a man who wants to buy the box set of *The Carol Burnett Show* and still longs for those Dean Martin roasts."

Dad just shrugged.

"Your mother," his mother went on, loving that third person, "is much more hip, much more today and watches reality shows. Sue me, but that's how I roll or rock or whatever. Anyway, I'm thinking of writing a letter to that Kourtney Kardashian. Do you know who she is?"

"Pretend I do."

"Pretend nothing. You do. No shame in it. What is a shame is that she's still with that drunken idiot with the pastel suit like he's a giant Easter duck. She's a pretty girl. She could do so much better, don't you think?"

Myron rubbed his hands together. "So who's hungry?"

They drove to Baumgart's and ordered the kung pao chicken

plus a bunch of appetizers. His parents used to eat with the gusto of rugby players at a barbecue, but now their appetites were small, their chewing slow, their whole manner suddenly dainty.

"When are we going to meet your fiancée?" Mom asked.

"Soon."

"I think you should have a huge wedding. Like Khloe and Lamar's."

Myron looked a question at his father. Dad said by way of explanation: "Khloe Kardashian."

"And," Mom added, "Kris and Bruce got to meet Lamar before the wedding and he and Khloe barely knew each other! You've known Terese for, what, ten years."

"Something like that."

"So where are you going to live?" Mom asked.

Dad said, "Ellen," in that voice.

"Shush, you. Where?"

"I don't know," Myron said.

"I'm not butting in," she began, which was nothing if not a prequel to butting in, "but I wouldn't keep our old house anymore. I mean, don't live there. It'd just be bizarre, the whole attachment thing. You'll need a place of your own, someplace new."

Dad: "El . . ."

"We'll see, Mom."

"I'm just saying."

When they'd finished, Myron drove them back home. Mom excused herself, claiming that she was fatigued and wanted to lie down for a bit. "You boys talk." Myron looked at his father, concerned. Dad gave him a look that said not to worry. Dad held up a finger as the door closed. A few moments later, Myron heard the tinny sound belonging, he assumed, to one of the Kardashians saying, "Oh my God, if that dress was, like, any sluttier, it would be taking the walk of shame."

His father shrugged. "She's obsessed right now. It's harmless."

They moved to the wooden deck out back. The deck had taken almost a year to build and was strong enough to withstand a tsunami. They grabbed the outdoor chairs with the faded cushions and looked out over the backyard Myron still saw as the Wiffle-ball stadium. He and Brad had played that game for hours. The double tree was first base, a permanently browned-out grass spot was second, third was a rock buried in the ground. If they hit the ball really hard, it would land in Mrs. Diamond's vegetable garden and she would come out in what they used to call a housedress and scream at them to stay off her property.

Myron heard laughter from a party three doors up. "The Lubetkins are having a barbecue?"

"The Lubetkins moved out four years ago," Dad said.

"So who's there now?"

Dad shrugged. "I don't live here anymore."

"Still. We used to be invited to all the barbecues."

"When it was our time," his father said. "When our children were young and we knew all the neighbors and had kids going to the same school and playing on the same sports teams. Now it's someone else's turn. That's how it should be. You need to let things go."

Myron frowned. "And you're usually the subtle one."

Dad chuckled. "Yeah, sorry about that. So while I'm playing this new role, what's wrong?"

Myron skipped the "how do you know" because what would be

the point? Dad wore a white golf shirt, even though he never played the game. His gray chest hair jutted through the V. He looked off, knowing that Myron was not a huge fan of intense eye contact.

Myron decided to dive right in. "Have you heard from Brad recently?"

If his father was surprised to hear Myron say that name—the first time Myron had done so in front of his father in fifteen-plus years—he did not show it. He took a sip of his iced tea and pretended to think about it. "We got an e-mail, oh, maybe a month ago."

"Where was he?"

"In Peru."

"And what about Kitty?"

"What about her?"

"Was she with him?"

"I assume so." Now his father turned and faced him. "Why?"

"I think I saw Kitty last night in New York City."

His father sat back. "I guess it's possible."

"Wouldn't they have contacted you if they were in the area?"

"Maybe. I could e-mail him and ask."

"Could you?"

"Sure. Do you want to tell me what this is about?"

He kept it vague. He'd been looking for Lex Ryder when he saw Kitty. His father nodded as Myron spoke. When he finished, Dad said, "I don't hear from them much. Sometimes months go by. But he's okay. Your brother, I mean. I think he has been happy."

"Has been?"

"Excuse me?"

"You said 'has been happy.' Why didn't you just say he's happy?"

"His last few e-mails," Dad said. "They've been, I don't know, different. Stiffer maybe. More newsy. But then again, I'm not very close to him. Don't get me wrong. I love him. I love him as much as I do you. But we aren't particularly close."

His dad took another sip of iced tea.

"You were," Myron said.

"No, not really. Of course, when he was young, we were all a bigger part of his life."

"So what changed that?"

Dad smiled. "You blame Kitty."

Myron said nothing.

"Do you think you and Terese will have children?" Dad asked.

The subject change threw him. Myron wasn't sure exactly how to reply. "It's a delicate question," he said slowly. Terese couldn't have any more children. He had not told his parents about this yet because, until he got her to the right doctors, he still couldn't accept it himself. Either way, this was not the time to raise the issue. "We're on the old side, but who knows."

"Well, either way, let me tell you something about parenting, something none of those self-help books or parenting magazines will tell you." Dad turned and leaned in closer. "We parents grossly overestimate our importance."

"You're being modest."

"No, I'm not. I know you think that your mother and I are the most amazing parents. I'm glad. I really am. Maybe for you, we were, though you've blocked out a lot of the bad."

"Like what?"

"I'm not going to rehash my mistakes right now. That's not the point anyway. We were good parents, I guess. Most are. Most are trying their best and if they make mistakes, it's from trying too hard. But the truth is, we parents are at the most, say, auto mechanics. We can tune up the car and make sure it has the proper fluids. We can keep it running, check the oil, make sure it is road ready. But the car is still the car. When the car comes in, it's already a Jaguar or Toyota or Prius. You can't turn a Toyota into a Jaguar."

Myron made a face. "A Toyota into a Jaguar?"

"You know what I mean. I know the analogy isn't the best and now that I think about it, it doesn't really hold because it sounds like a judgment, like the Jaguar is better than the Toyota or something. It is not. It's just different with different needs. Some kids come out shy, some are outgoing, some are bookish, some are jocks, whatever. The way we raise you doesn't really have much to do with it. Sure we can instill values and all that, but we usually mess up when we try to change what is already there."

"When you try," Myron added, "to turn the Toyota into the Jaguar?"

"Don't be a wise guy."

Not long ago, before running off to Angola and under very different circumstances, Terese had made this exact same argument to him. Nature over nurture, she insisted. Her argument was both a comfort and a chill, but in this case, with his father sitting on the deck with him, Myron wasn't really buying it.

"Brad wasn't meant to stay at home or settle down," his father said. "He was always itching to escape. He was meant to wander. A nomad, like his ancestors, I guess. So your mother and I let him go. When you were kids, you were both amazing athletes. You thrived on competition. Brad didn't. He hated it. That doesn't make him less or more, just different. God, I'm tired. Enough. I assume you have a very good reason for trying to find your brother after all these years?"

"I do."

"Good. Because despite what I said, you two falling out has been one of the biggest heartaches of my life. So it would be nice to see you reconcile."

Silence. It was broken when Myron's cell phone buzzed. He checked the caller ID and was surprised to see that the call was coming from Roland Dimonte, the NYPD cop who'd helped out in Three Downing last night. Dimonte was a friend/adversary from way back. "I need to take this," Myron said.

His father signaled for him to go ahead.

"Hello?"

"Bolitar?" Dimonte barked. "I thought he stopped pulling this crap."

"Who?"

"You know who. Where the hell is the psycho Win?"

"I don't know."

"Well, you better find him."

"Why, what's up?"

"We got a big freaking problem, that's what. Find him now."

9

Myron looked through the metal-meshed window in the emergency room. Roland Dimonte stood to his left. Dimonte reeked of both chewing tobacco and what might have been a rancid bottle of Hai Karate. Despite being born and raised in Manhattan's Hell's Kitchen, Dimonte liked to go with the urban cowboy look, sporting right now a tight shiny shirt with snap buttons and boots so garish that he might have stolen them off a San Diego Charger cheerleader. His hair was a reformed mullet by way of a retired hockey player who now did color commentary on a local television station. Myron could feel Dimonte's eyes on him.

Lying on his back in the bed, eyes wide open and staring at the ceiling, tubes coming out of at least three locations, was Kleavage Kyle, head bouncer from Three Downing.

"What's wrong with him?" Myron asked.

"Lots of stuff," Dimonte said. "But the main thing is a ruptured kidney. The doctor says it was caused by—and I quote—'precise and severe abdominal trauma.' Ironic, don't you think?"

"Ironic how?"

"Well, our friend here will be pissing blood for quite some time. Maybe you remember earlier last evening. That's exactly what our victim told you would happen to you." Dimonte crossed his arms for effect.

"So, what, you think I did this?"

Dimonte frowned. "Let's pretend for a brief moment that I'm not a mentally dehydrated numb nut, okay?" He had an empty can of Coke in his hands. He spit tobacco juice into it. "No, I don't think you did this. We both know who did it."

Myron gestured with his chin toward the bed. "What did Kyle say?"

"He said he was mugged. A bunch of guys broke into the club and jumped him. He never saw their faces, can't identify them, doesn't want to press charges anyway."

"Maybe that's true."

"And maybe one of my ex-wives will tell me that she no longer wants her alimony check."

"What do you want me to say here, Rolly?"

"I thought you had him under control."

"You don't know it was Win."

"We both know it was Win."

Myron took a step away from the window. "Let me put it another way. You don't have any evidence it was Win."

"Sure I do. There was a surveillance video for a bank outside the club. Gets the whole area. It shows Win approaching our pectorally gifted friend here. They talk for a few moments and then they both go back into the club." Dimonte stopped, looked off. "Odd."

"What?"

"Win is usually much more careful. Guess he's slipping as he gets older."

Not likely, Myron thought. "What about the surveillance tapes inside the club?"

"What about them?"

"You said Win and Kyle here walked back into the club. So what do the interior tapes show?"

Dimonte spit into the can again, trying hard to cover up his obvious body language. "We're still working on it."

"Uh, let's pretend for a brief moment that I'm not a mentally dehydrated numb nut."

"They're gone, okay? Kyle says the guys who jumped him must have taken them."

"Sounds logical."

"Take a look at him, Bolitar."

Myron did. Kyle's eyes were still on the ceiling. His eyes were wet.

"When we found him last night, that Taser he nailed you with was lying on the floor next to him. The battery was empty from overuse. He was shaking, nearly catatonic. He'd crapped his pants. For twelve hours he couldn't form words. I showed him a picture of Win, and he started sobbing to the point where the doctor had to sedate him."

Myron looked back at Kyle. He thought about the Taser, thought about the gleam in Kyle's eyes as he held down the trigger, thought about how close he, Myron, had come to ending up in a bed like that. Then Myron turned and looked at Dimonte. His voice was pure monotone. "Wow. I. Feel. Just. Terrible. For. Him."

Dimonte just shook his head.

Myron said, "Can I go now?"

"You heading back to your place at the Dakota?"

"Yes."

"We got a man waiting there for Win. When he arrives, I want to have a little chat with him."

"Good evening, Mr. Bolitar."

"Good evening, Vladimir," Myron said as he breezed by the Dakota doorman and passed through the famed wrought-iron gate. There was a cop car sitting out front, sent by Dimonte. When Myron arrived at Win's apartment, the lights were low.

Win sat in his leather club chair with a snifter of cognac. Myron was not surprised to see him. Like most old buildings with a storied past, the Dakota held secret underground passageways. There was one Win had shown him that started in the basement of a highrise near Columbus Avenue, another from a spot a block uptown bordering Central Park. Vladimir, Myron was sure, knew Win was here, but he wouldn't say anything. The cops didn't give Vladimir his Christmas bonus.

Myron said, "And here I thought you went out last night in search of casual sex. Now I found out it was to beat up Kyle."

Win smiled. "Who said I couldn't do both?"

"It wasn't necessary."

"The sex? Well, it never is, but that never stops a man, does it?"

"Funny."

Win steepled his hands. "Do you think you're the first guy Kyle dragged to that maroon room—or just the first to escape without a hospital visit?"

"He's a bad guy, so what?"

"He's a very bad guy. Three assault beefs in the past year—in all cases, witnesses from the club helped clear him."

"So you took care of it?"

"It's what I do."

"Not your job."

"But I so enjoy it."

No point in getting into this now. "Dimonte wants to talk to you."

"As I'm aware. But I don't want to talk to him. So my attorney will contact him in about half an hour and tell him that unless he has an arrest warrant, we will not be chatting. End of story."

"Would it help if I told you that you shouldn't have done it?"

"Wait," Win said, starting his mime act. "Before you start, let me tune up my air violin."

"What exactly did you do to him anyway?"

"Did they find the Taser?" Win asked.

"Yes."

"Where?"

"What do you mean, where? Next to his body."

"*Next* to it?" Win said. "Oh. Well. He must have been able to help himself a little bit at least."

Silence. Myron reached into the fridge and grabbed a Yoo-hoo. The television screen had the Blu-ray Disc logo bouncing across it.

"How did Kyle put it?" Win said, twirling the cognac in its snifter, his cheeks flushed red. "He will be pissing blood for a while. Maybe he broke a bone or two. But in the end he'll recover."

"But he won't talk."

"Oh no. He won't ever talk."

Myron sat. "You're a scary dude."

"Well, I don't like to brag," Win said.

"Still this was not a wise move."

"Wrong. It was a very wise move."

"How so?"

"There are three things you must remember. One"—Win lifted a finger—"I never hurt innocents, only those most deserving. Kyle fit that category. Two"—another finger—"I do this to protect us. The more fear I instill in people, the safer we are."

Myron almost smiled. "That's why you let yourself get caught on that street video," he said. "You wanted everyone to know it was you."

"Again I don't like to brag, but, well, yes. Three," Win said, holding up the third finger, "I always do it for reasons other than vengeance."

"Like justice?"

"Like getting information." Win picked up the remote and pointed it at the television. "Kyle was kind enough to provide me with all the surveillance tapes from last night. I've spent most of the day looking through them for both Kitty and Brad Bolitar."

Whoa. Myron turned toward the screen. "And?"

"I'm still going through them," Win said, "but so far, it isn't good."

"Explain."

"Why explain when I can show?" Win poured a second snifter of cognac and showed it to Myron. Myron shook it off. Win shrugged, put the snifter down next to him, and pressed the play button on the remote. The screen's bouncing logo vanished. A woman appeared. Win hit pause. "This is the best view of her face."

Myron leaned forward. One of the fascinating things about surveillance videos was that they were shot from cameras set up high, so that you rarely got a great look at the face. This seemed counterintuitive, but perhaps there was no better alternative. This particular shot was a touch blurry, a close-up, and Myron imagined that someone had cropped and zoomed in on her face. Either way it ended any doubt about identity.

"Okay, so we know it's Kitty," Myron said. "What about Brad?"

"No sign of him."

"So what—to use your vernacular—isn't good?"

Win thought about that. "Well, perhaps 'isn't good' was an ineffective way for me to have put it," he said.

"How should you have put it?"

Win tapped his chin with his index finger. "Really, really bad."

Myron felt the chill and turned back toward the screen. Win pressed another button on the remote. The camera zoomed out. "Kitty entered the club at ten thirty-three P.M. with approximately ten other people. Lex's entourage, if you will."

There she was, turquoise blouse, her face pale. The video was one of those that took pictures every two or three seconds so that the effect was jerky, like one of those flip books or old footage of Babe Ruth running the bases.

"This was taken in a small chamber off the VIP room at ten forty-seven P.M."

Not long before he and Esperanza arrived, Myron thought. Win

hit a skip button and reached a frozen image. Again the camera angle was from above. It was hard to see Kitty's face. She was with another woman and a guy with long hair tied into a ponytail. Myron did not recognize them. The guy with the ponytail had something in his hand. A rope maybe. Win hit the play button and the actors in this little drama came to life. Kitty put out her arm. Ponytail leaned closer to her and wrapped the . . . nope, not rope . . . around her bicep and tied it off. Then he tapped her arm with two fingers and took out a hypodermic needle. Myron felt his heart sink as Ponytail put the needle in Kitty's arm with a seemingly practiced hand, pushed the plunger, and untied the cord around her bicep.

"Wow," Myron said. "That's new, even for her."

"Yes," Win said. "She's stepped up from cokehead to heroin addict. Impressive."

Myron shook his head. He should have been shocked, but pitifully he wasn't. He thought about the Facebook photographs, the big smiles, the family trips. He'd been wrong before. It wasn't a life. It was a lie. Take "life" and remove the *f*. One big fat ol' lie. Classic Kitty.

"Myron?"

"Yep."

"This isn't the worst part," Win said.

Myron just looked at his old friend.

"This won't be easy to watch."

Win was not one for hyperbole. Myron turned back to the TV and waited for Win to hit the play button. Without looking away from the screen, Myron put the Yoo-hoo on a coaster and put out his hand. Win had the previously poured snifter of the cognac at the ready. Myron accepted it now, took a sip, closed his eyes, let it sting his throat.

"I'm skipping ahead fourteen minutes," Win said. "In short, this picks up a few minutes before you spotted her entering the VIP room."

Win finally pressed the play button. The view was the same—that small chamber room from above. But this time there were only two people in the room: Kitty—and the man with the long ponytail. They were talking. Myron risked a quick glance at Win. Win's face, as always, showed nothing. On the screen, Ponytail started twisting his fingers in Kitty's hair. Myron just stared. Kitty began to kiss the man's neck, moving down to his chest, unbuttoning his shirt as she went, until her head disappeared from the frame. The man let his head fall back. There was a smile on his face.

"Turn it off," Myron said.

Win pressed the remote. The screen went dark. Myron closed his eyes. Utter sadness and deep rage coursed through him in equal measure. His temples started pounding. He dropped his head into his hands. Win was there now, standing over him, his hand on his shoulder. Win did not say anything. He just waited. A few moments later, Myron opened his eyes and sat upright.

"We find her," Myron said. "Whatever it takes, we find her now."

"Still no sign of Lex," Esperanza said.

After another night of limited sleep, Myron sat behind his desk. His body ached. His head pounded. Esperanza sat across from him. Big Cyndi leaned against the door frame, smiling in a way someone with vision trouble might call demure. She was packed in a shimmering purple Batgirl costume, a somewhat bigger-sized replica of the one Yvonne Craig made famous on the old TV show. The fabric looked strained at the seams. Big Cyndi had a pen stuck behind one cat ear, a Bluetooth in the other.

"No hits on his credit card," Esperanza said. "No cell phone use. In fact, I even got our old friend PT to run a GPS on his smartphone. It's turned off."

"Okay."

"We also got a pretty good close-up of the ponytailed guy who was, uh, friendly with Kitty at Three Downing. Big Cyndi is going to head down to the club in a few hours with the still frame and question the staff."

Myron looked over at Big Cyndi. Big Cyndi batted her eyes at him. Picture two tarantulas on their backs baking in the desert sun.

"We also checked on your brother and Kitty," Esperanza continued. "Nothing in the United States. No credit cards, no driver's license, no property, no liens, no tax returns, no parking tickets, no marriage or divorces listed, nothing."

"I have another idea," Myron said. "Let's check out Buzz."

"Lex's roadie?"

"He's more than a roadie. Anyway, Buzz's real name is Alex I. Khowaylo. Let's try his credit cards and cell phone—he might have left his on."

"Pardon me," Big Cyndi said. "I have a call coming in." Big Cyndi tapped her Bluetooth and put on her receptionist voice. "Yes, Charlie? Okay, yes, thank you." Charlie, Myron knew, was the security guard downstairs. Big Cyndi tapped the Bluetooth off and said, "Michael Davis from Shears is coming up the elevator."

"You got this?" Esperanza asked him.

Myron nodded. "Show him in."

Shears, along with Gillette and Schick, dominate the razor blade market. Michael Davis was the VP in charge of marketing. Big Cyndi waited at the elevator for the new arrival. New arrivals often gasped when the elevator first opened and Big Cyndi was standing there. Not so with Michael. He barely broke stride, rushing ahead of Big Cyndi and directly into Myron's office.

"We got a problem," Michael said.

Myron spread his arms. "I'm all ears."

"We're taking Shear Delight Seven off the market in a month."

Shear Delight Seven was a razor or, if you believe the Shear marketing department, the latest in "shaving innovation technology" featuring a "more ergonomic grip" (who has trouble holding a razor?), a "professional blade stabilizer" (Myron had no idea what that meant), "seven thinner, precision blades" (because other blades are fat and imprecise) and "micro-pulse power operation" (it vibrates).

Myron's NFL All-Pro defensive back, Ricky "Smooth" Sules, was featured in the ad campaign. The tagline: "Get Twice as Smooth." Myron didn't really get it. In the TV commercial, Ricky shaves, smiling as though it is a sex act, says the Shear Delight Seven gives him the "closest, most comfortable shave possible," and then a hot girl coos, "Oh, Smooth . . . ," and runs her hands along his cheeks. In short, it is the same shaving commercial all three companies have been running since 1968.

"Ricky and I were under the impression it was doing great."

"Oh, it is," Davis said. "Or it was. I mean, the response is through the roof."

"So?"

"It works too well."

Myron looked at him, waited for him to say more. When he didn't, Myron said, "And that's a problem how?"

"We sell razor blades."

"I know."

"So that's how we make money. We don't make it selling the actual razors. Heck, we practically give away the razors. We make it by selling you the refills—the razor blades."

"Right."

"So we need people to change blades at least, say, once a week. But the Shear Delights are working better than expected. We have reports of people going six to eight weeks on a single razor. We can't have that."

"You can't have blades that work too well."

"Exactly."

"And because of that, you're going to cancel the whole campaign?"

"What? No, of course not. We've built tremendous goodwill off the product. The consumer loves it. What we will do is start offering a new, improved product. The Shear Delight Seven Plus with a new comfort lubricant strip—for the best shave of your life. We feed it slowly into the market. Over time, we phase out the Shear Sevens in favor of the improved Plus."

Myron tried not to sigh. "And—let me make sure I follow—the Plus blades won't last as long as the regular blades."

"But"—Davis held up a finger and smiled widely—"it gives the consumer a comfort strip. The comfort strip will make it the most comfortable shave possible. It is like a spa for your face."

"A spa where the refills will have to be changed once a week rather than once a month."

"It's a wonderful product. Ricky will love it."

Myron would make a moral stand here, but, well, nah. His job was to represent his client's best interest, and in the case of endorsements, that meant getting said client the most money possible. Yes, there were always ethical questions to consider. Yes, he would tell Ricky exactly what was up with the Plus versus the regular model. But it was Ricky's decision and there was little doubt if it meant more money, he would and should go for it. One could spend a lot of time bemoaning how this was clearly an attempt to con the public via advertising, but one would be hard-pressed to find any product or marketing campaign that did not do exactly that.

"So," Myron said, "you want to hire Ricky to endorse the new product."

"What do you mean, hire?" Davis looked deeply offended. "He's already under contract."

"But now you want him to redo the commercials. For the new Plus blades."

"Well, yes, of course."

"So I'm thinking," Myron said, "that Ricky should get twenty percent more money for the new commercial."

"Twenty percent more how?"

"Twenty percent over what you paid him to endorse the Shear Delight Seven."

"What?" Davis shouted, hand to heart as though warding off a heart attack. "Are you kidding? It's practically a reshoot of the first. Our lawyers say that under the contract, we can ask him to do the reshoot and not pay one cent more."

"Your lawyers are wrong."

"Come on. Let's be reasonable. We are generous people, aren't we? Because of that—even though, really, we shouldn't—we can give him a ten percent bonus over what he's already getting."

"Not enough," Myron said.

"You're joking, right? I know you. You're a funny guy, Myron. You're being funny right now, right?"

"Ricky is happy with the razor as it is," Myron said. "If you wish to have him endorse a whole new product with a whole new marketing campaign, he will certainly need to make more money."

"More? Are you out of your mind?"

"He won Shear's Stubble Destroyer's Man of the Year. That upped his worth."

"What?" Total outrage now. "We gave him that award!"

And so it goes.

Half an hour later, when Michael Davis left cursing under his breath, Esperanza came into Myron's office.

"I found Lex's friend Buzz."

10

Adiona Island is exactly five miles wide, exactly two miles long, and, as Win once put it, the "epicenter of the WASP." It is located a scant four miles off the coast of Massachusetts. According to the Census Bureau, 211 people inhabited the island year-round. That number grew—it was hard to say by how much but it was at least several fold—during the summer months as the blue bloods from Connecticut, Philadelphia, and New York flocked in by jet or ferry. Recently, the Adiona Golf Course was named one of the top twenty-five courses by *Golf Magazine*. This upset rather than pleased the club members because Adiona Island was their private world. They don't want you to visit or even know about the island. Yes, there was a "public" ferry, but the ferry was small, the departure schedule hard to figure out, and if you somehow managed to get there, the beaches and pretty much all land on the island were private and guarded. There was only one restaurant on Adiona Island, the Teapot Lodge, and it was more of a drinking pub than an eatery. There was one food market, one general store, one church. There were no hotels or inns or anyplace to stay. The mansions, most with cute names like Tippy's Cottage or The Waterbury or Triangle House, were both spectacular and understated. If you wanted to buy one, you could—this was a free country—but you wouldn't be welcomed, wouldn't be allowed to join the "club," wouldn't be allowed on the tennis courts or the beaches and you would be discouraged from patronizing the Teapot Lodge. You had to be invited onto this private enclave or agree to go it alone as a social outcast—and pretty much no one chose to go it alone. The island was kept secure less by real guards and more with Old-World scowls of disapproval.

With no true restaurant, how did the well-heeled dine? They ate meals prepared by help. Dinner parties were the norm, almost in rotation, Bab's turn and then a night at Fletcher's place and maybe Conrad's yacht on Friday and, well, Windsor's estate on Saturday. If you summer here—and one clue might be that you use the word "summer" as a verb—chances are your father and grandfather summered here too. The air was heavy with ocean spray and eau du blue blood.

On either side of the island, there were two mysterious, fenced-off areas. One was near the grass tennis courts and owned by the military. No one knew exactly what went on there, but the rumors of covert operations and Roswell-type secrecy were endless.

The other secluded enclave was on the southern tip of the island. The land was owned by Gabriel Wire, the eccentric, ultra-reclusive lead singer of HorsePower. Wire's compound was bathed in secrecy—a full twenty-one acres protected by security guards and the latest in surveillance technology. Wire was the exception on this island. He seemed fine alone, secluded, an outcast. In fact, Myron thought, Gabriel Wire insisted upon it.

Over the years, if rumors were to be believed, the island's blue bloods had pretty much accepted the reclusive rocker. Some claim that they see Gabriel Wire shopping at the market. Others say that he often swam, either alone or with only a stunning beauty, on a quiet strip of beach in the later afternoons. Like much with Gabriel Wire, nothing could be confirmed.

The only real approach to Wire's compound was a dirt road with about five thousand Keep Out signs and a guard booth with a drop arm. Myron ignored the signs because he was a crazy rule-breaker like that. Upon arrival via private boat, he had borrowed the car, a totally rad Wiesmann Roadster MF5 with retail price over a quarter of a million dollars, from Baxter Lockwood, Win's cousin, who had a place on Adiona Island. Myron debated driving straight through the drop arm, but ol' Bax might not appreciate the scratches.

The guard looked up from his paperback. He sported a severe crew cut and aviator sunglasses and had a hard military bearing. Myron gave him a five-finger toodle-oo wave and Smile Seventeen—charmingly shy via early Matt Damon. Pretty dazzling.

The guard said, "Turn around and leave."

Mistake. Smile Seventeen only worked on da ladies. "If you were a lady, you'd be dazzled right now."

"By the smile? Oh, I am. On the inside. Turn around and leave."

"Aren't you supposed to call the house and make sure I'm not expected?"

"Oh." The guard made a phone with his fingers and mimed a conversation. Then he hung up his fingers and said, "Turn around and leave."

"I'm here to see Lex Ryder."

"I don't think so."

"My name is Myron Bolitar."

"Should I genuflect?"

"I'd prefer it if you just lift the drop arm."

The guard put down his book and slowly made his way to his feet. "I don't think so, Myron."

Myron had expected something like this. Over the past sixteen years, since the death of a young woman named Alista Snow, only a handful of people had even seen Gabriel Wire. Back then, when the tragedy first occurred, the media had gorged on images of the charismatic front man. Some claimed that he got preferential treatment, that at the very least, Gabriel Wire should have been charged with involuntary manslaughter, but the witnesses backed away and even Alista Snow's father eventually stopped demanding justice. Whatever the reason—cleared or swept under the rug—the incident changed Gabriel Wire forever. He ran off and, if rumors were to be believed, spent the next two years in Tibet and India before returning to the United States under a cloud of secrecy that would have made Howard Hughes envious.

Gabriel Wire had not been seen in public since.

Oh, there were plenty of rumors. Wire joined the conspiracy legends of the moon landing, JFK assassination, and Elvis sightings. Some say that he wore disguises and moved freely, going to movies and clubs and restaurants. Some say that he got plastic surgery or that he shaved off his famed curly hair and grew a goatee. Some say that he simply loves the seclusion of Adiona Island and that he sneaks in supermodels and assorted lovelies. This last rumor was given extra credence when one tabloid interrupted a phone call between a famous young starlet and her mother discussing her weekend with "Gabriel at Adiona," but many, Myron included, smelled a planted story timed, by eerie coincidence, the week before said starlet's big movie opening. Sometimes a paparazzo would be tipped off that Gabriel would be somewhere, but the picture would never be conclusive, always appearing in whatever rag with the headline IS THIS GABRIEL WIRE? Other rumors had it that Wire spent considerable time institutionalized while others insisted that the reason he kept out of sight was simple vanity: His beautiful face had been sliced up during a bar fight in Mumbai.

Gabriel Wire's vanishing act did not spell the end of HorsePower. Just the opposite, in fact. Not surprisingly, the legend of Gabriel Wire grew. Would people remember Howard Hughes if he was just another rich guy? Were the Beatles hurt by the rumors of Paul McCartney's death? Eccentricity sells. Gabriel, with Lex's help, managed to keep their music production level steady, and while there was some lost revenue because they couldn't tour anymore, the record sales more than offset that.

"I'm not here to see Gabriel Wire," Myron said.

"Good," the guard said, "because I never heard of him."

"I need to see Lex Ryder."

"Don't know him either."

"Mind if I make a call?"

"After you turn around and leave," the guard said, "you can have sex with Rhesus monkeys for all I care."

Myron looked at him. There was something familiar about the

man, but he couldn't put his finger on it. "You're not your average rent-a-cop."

"Hmm." The guard arched an eyebrow. "Dazzling now with flattery on top of the smile?"

"Double dazzle."

"If I were a hot chick, I'd probably be disrobing by now."

Yep, definitely not your average rent-a-cop. He had the eyes, the mannerisms, the relaxed coil of a pro. Something here was not adding up.

"What's your name?" Myron asked.

"Guess my answer. Go ahead. Take a wild guess."

"Turn around and leave?"

"Bingo."

Myron decided not to argue. He backed up, surreptitiously taking out his modified Win-spy BlackBerry. There was a zoom camera on it. He headed to the end of the drive, got the camera up, snapped a quick pic of the guard. He sent it off to Esperanza by e-mail. She'd know what to do. Then he called Buzz, who must have seen on his caller ID that it was Myron: "I'm not going to tell you where Lex is."

"First of all, I'm fine," Myron said. "Thanks for having my back at the club last night."

"My job is to take care of Lex, not you."

"Second, you don't have to tell me where Lex is. You're both at Wire's place on Adiona Island."

"How did you figure that out?"

"GPS on your phone. In fact, I'm right outside the gate now."

"Wait, you're already on the island?"

"Yep."

"Doesn't matter. You can't get in here."

"Really? I could call Win. If we put our minds to it, we'll figure a way."

"Man, you're a pest. Look, Lex doesn't want to go home. That's his right."

"Good point."

"And you're his agent, for crying out loud. You're supposed to be looking out for his interests too."

"Another good point."

"Exactly. You're not a marriage counselor."

Maybe, maybe not. "I need to talk to him for five minutes."

"Gabriel won't let anyone in. Hell, I'm not allowed out of the guest cottage."

"There's a guest cottage?"

"Two. I think he keeps girls in the other one and shuffles them in one at a time."

"Girls?"

"What, you want the more politically correct 'women'? Hey, it's still Wire. I don't know their ages. Anyway, no one is allowed in the recording studio or main house except through some tunnel. It's spooky here, Myron."

"Do you know my sister-in-law?"

"Who's your sister-in-law?"

"Kitty Bolitar. You might know her better as Kitty Hammer. She was at Three Downing with you guys last night."

"Kitty's your sister-in-law?"

"Yes."

Silence.

"Buzz?"

"Hold on a second." After a full minute had passed, Buzz came back on the phone. "You know the Teapot?"

"The town pub?"

"Lex will meet you there in half an hour."

Myron expected the only pub on an island of the stuffy old-moneys to be like Win's office—dark woods, burgundy leather, antique wooden globe, decanters, heavy crystal, oriental carpets, maybe paintings of a fox hunt. That wasn't the case. The Teapot Lodge looked like a neighborhood drinking hole in a seedier section of Irvington, New Jersey. Everything looked worn. The windows were loaded up with neon beer signs. There was sawdust on the floor and a popcorn stand in the corner. There was also a small dance floor with a mirrored disco ball. "Mack the Knife" by Bobby Darin played over the sound system. The dance floor was packed. Age range: wide—from "barely legal" to "foot in grave." The men wore either blue oxfords with sweaters tied around their shoulders or green blazers Myron had only seen on Masters golf champions. The well-kept, though not surgically or Botox enhanced, women wore pink Lilly Pulitzer tunics and blazing white trousers. The faces were ruddy from inbreeding, exertion, and drink.

Man, this island was weird.

Bobby Darin's "Mack the Knife" neatly segued into an Eminem and Rihanna duet about watching a lover burn and loving the way said lover lies. It is a cliché that white people can't dance, but the cliché here was concrete and unshakable. The song may have changed, but the limited dance steps did not alter in any discernible way. Not even the rhythm or lack thereof. Too many of the men snapped when they danced, as if they were Dino and Frank performing at the Sands.

The bartender sported a receding-hairline pompadour and a suspicious smile. "Help you?" he said.

"Beer," Myron said.

Pompadour just stared at him, waited.

"Beer," Myron said again.

"Yes, I heard you. I just never heard someone order that before."

"A beer?"

"Just the word 'beer.' It is customary to say a kind. Like Bud or Michelob or something."

"Oh, what have you got?"

The bartender started ripping off about a million titles. Myron stopped him on the Flying Fish Pale Ale, mostly because he liked the name. The beer ended up being awesome, but Myron wasn't much of a connoisseur. He grabbed a wooden booth near a group of lovely young, uh, girls-cum-women. It was indeed hard to tell ages anymore. The women were speaking something Scandinavian— Myron wasn't good enough with foreign languages to know more than that. Several of the ruddy-faced men dragged them out on the dance floor. Nannies, Myron realized, or more specifically, au pairs.

A few minutes later, the pub door flew open. Two large men stomped in as though putting out small brush fires. Both wore aviator sunglasses, jeans, and a leather jacket, even though it was maybe a hundred degrees out. Aviator sunglasses inside a dark pub—talk about trying too hard. One of the men took a step left, the other a step right. The one on the right nodded.

Lex entered, looking understandably embarrassed by the bodyguard spectacle. Myron raised his hand and gave a little wave. The two bodyguards started toward him, but Lex stopped them. They didn't look happy about it, but they stayed by the door. Lex bounced over and slid into the booth.

"Gabriel's guys," Lex said by way of explanation. "He insisted they come too."

"Why?"

"Because he's a schizo who grows more paranoid by the day, that's why."

"By the way, who was the guy at the gate?"

"Which guy?"

Myron described him. The color ebbed from Lex's face.

"He was at the gate? You must have set off a sensor when you drove in. He's normally inside."

"Who is he?"

"I don't know. He's not exactly chummy."

"You've seen him before?"

"I don't know," Lex said a little too quickly. "Look, Gabriel doesn't like me talking about his security. Like I said, he's paranoid. Forget it; it's not important."

Fine with Myron. He wasn't here to learn about the lifestyle of a rock star. "You want a drink?"

"Nah, we're working late tonight."

"So why are you hiding?"

"I'm not hiding. We're working. This is how we always do it.

Gabriel and I holed up alone in his studio. Making music." He glanced back at the two big bodyguards. "So what are you doing here, Myron? I already told you: I'm fine. This doesn't concern you."

"This isn't about just you and Suzze anymore."

Lex sighed, sat back. He, like lots of aging rockers, had the emaciated thing going on, with skin like weathered tree bark. "What, it's about you all of a sudden?"

"I want to know about Kitty."

"Dude, I'm not her keeper either."

"Just tell me where she is, Lex."

"I don't have a clue."

"You don't have an address or a phone number?"

Lex shook his head.

"So how did she end up with you at Three Downing?"

"Not just her," Lex said. "There were, what, a dozen of us."

"I don't care about the others. I'm asking how Kitty ended up with you guys."

"Kitty is an old friend," Lex said with an exaggerated shrug. "She called out of the blue and said she could use a night out. I told her where we were."

Myron looked at him. "You're kidding, right?"

"What?"

"Just called you out of the blue for a night out? Please."

"Look, Myron, why are you asking me these questions? Why don't you ask your brother where she is?"

Silence.

"Ah," Lex said, "I see. So you're doing this for your bro?"

"No."

"You know I love to wax philosophical, right?"

"I do."

"Here is a simple one: Relationships are complicated. Especially matters of the heart. You have to let people work their own stuff out."

"Where is she, Lex?"

"I told you. I don't know."

"Did you ask her about Brad?"

"Her husband?" Lex frowned. "Now it's my turn to say, 'You're kidding, right?'"

Myron handed him a copy of the still frame he'd gotten off the security camera of the ponytailed guy. "Kitty was with this guy at the club. Do you know him?"

Lex took a look at it and shook his head. "Nope."

"He was part of your entourage."

"No," Lex said, "he wasn't." He sighed, picked up a cocktail napkin, started tearing it into strips.

"Tell me what happened, Lex."

"Nothing happened. I mean, not really." Lex looked toward the bar. A pudgy man in a fitted golf shirt was chatting up one of the au pairs. Tears for Fears's "Shout" was on and literally everyone else in the bar yelled "Shout" at the appropriate time. The guys who'd been snapping on the dance floor still snapped.

Myron waited, gave Lex space.

"Look, Kitty called me," Lex said. "She said she needed to talk. She sounded pretty desperate. You know we go way back. You remember those days, right?"

There had been a time when the rock gods partied with the tennis starlets. Myron had been there for part of it, fresh out of law school and seeking clients for his start-up agency. So had his younger brother, Brad, enjoying the summer before his freshman year of college by "interning" for his big bro. That summer had started off with such promise. It ended with the love of his life breaking his heart—and Brad gone from his life for good.

"I remember," Myron said.

"So anyway I figured that Kitty just wanted to say hi. For old times' sake. I always felt bad for her, you know, the whole career gone up in flames like that. I guess I was curious too. It's been, what, fifteen years since she quit."

"Something like that."

"So Kitty meets up with us at the nightclub, and right away I know something isn't right."

"In what way?"

"She has a bad case of the shakes. Her eyes are glazed, and man, I know strung out when I see it. I stopped using a long time ago. Suzze and me, we went through that war already. Kitty, no offense, but she was still using. She hadn't come to me to say hello. She came to me to score. When I told her I wasn't into that scene, she asked for money. I told her no on that too. So she moved on."

"Moved on?"

"Yep."

"What do you mean, moved on?"

"What part is hard to understand, man? It's a simple equation. Kitty is a junkie—and we wouldn't give her a fix. Ergo, she hooked up with someone who could, uh, help her out."

Myron held up the photo of Ponytail. "This guy?"

"I guess."

"And then what?"

"Then nothing."

"You said Kitty was an old friend."

"Yeah, so?"

"So you didn't think to try to help her?"

"Help her how?" Lex said, turning his palms to the sky. "Like, organize an intervention right there in the nightclub? Like, drag her by force to rehab?"

Myron said nothing.

"You don't know junkies."

"I remember when you were one," Myron said. "I remember when you and Gabriel were throwing all your cash at blow and blackjack."

"Blow and blackjack. I like that." Lex smiled. "So how come you never helped us out?"

"Maybe I should have."

"Nah, you couldn't have helped. A man has to find his own way."

Myron wondered about that. He wondered about Alista Snow, whether earlier intervention with Gabriel Wire could have helped her out. He almost said that, but what would be the point?

"You keep wanting to fix things," Lex said, "but the world has a certain ebb and flow. You screw with it, you just make it worse. It isn't always your fight, Myron. Do you mind if I give you a quick example from, well, from your past?"

"I guess not," Myron said, regretting the words the moment they passed his lips.

"When I first met you all those years ago, you had a serious girlfriend, right? Jessica something. The writer."

The regret started taking shape and expanding.

"And something bad happened between you. I don't know what. Here you were, what, twenty-four, twenty-five years old?"

"What's your point, Lex?"

"I was a huge basketball fan, so I knew your whole story. First-round draft pick of the Boston Celtics. Supposed to be the next big superstar, all the planets aligned, and then, bam, you wreck your knee in a preseason game. Career over, just like that."

Myron made a face. "Uh, your point?"

"Just listen a second, okay? So you go to Harvard Law and then you come down to Nick's tennis camp to recruit these tennis players. You had no chance against the big guys like IMG and TruPro. I mean, who are you? You're barely out of school. But you land Kitty, the top prospect, and then when she quits the game, you get Suzze. You know how you did that?"

"I really don't see the relevance."

"Just stay with me a moment. Do you know how?"

"I made a good pitch, I guess."

"No. You landed them the same way you landed me when I heard you were branching out of sports. There's a decency to you, Myron. A person senses it right away. Yeah, you give good meeting and let's face it, having Win as your financial guy gives you a big head start. But what separates you is that we know you care. We know you'd rescue us if we were in trouble. We know you'd rather lose a limb than steal a nickel from us."

"With all due respect," Myron said, "I still don't see your point."

"So when Suzze calls you because we've had a tiff, you come

running. That's your job. You're hired to do that. But unless a person is hired, well, I have a different philosophy: Things ripple."

"Wow, can I jot that down?" Myron faked taking out a pen and scribbling. "Things . . . ripple. Great, got it."

"Stop being a wiseass. What I'm saying is, people shouldn't butt in, even with the best of intentions. It's dangerous and an invasion. When you and Jessica had your big problem, would you have wanted all of us to try to butt in and help?"

Myron gave him the flat eyes. "Did you just compare my problems with a girlfriend to you going missing when your wife is pregnant?"

"Just in this way: It is foolhardy and frankly egomaniacal to think you have that kind of power. What's going on with me and Suzze—that isn't your business anymore. You have to respect that."

"Now that I found you and know you're safe, I do respect that."

"Good. And unless your brother or sister-in-law asked for your help, well, you're meddling in a matter of the heart. And the heart is like a war zone. Like us going overseas to Iraq or Afghanistan. You think you're being heroic and saving stuff, but really you're just making it worse."

Myron gave him the flat eyes again. "Did you just compare my concern for my sister-in-law to overseas wars?"

"Like the US of A, you're meddling. Life is like a river and when you change its course, you're responsible for where it goes."

A river. Sigh. "Please stop."

He smiled and rose. "I better go."

"So you have no idea where Kitty is?"

He sighed. "You didn't listen to a word I said."

"No, I listened," Myron said. "But sometimes people are in trouble. Sometimes they need saving. And sometimes people who need help don't have the courage to ask for it."

Lex nodded. "Must be godlike," he said, "to know when that is."

"I don't always make the right call."

"No one does. Why it's best to leave it alone. But I will tell you this much if it helps. Kitty said she was leaving in the morning. Going back to Chile or Peru or somewhere like that. So my guess is, if you want to help, you may be a little late to the party."

11

"Lex is fine," Myron said.

Suzze and Lex owned a penthouse in a high-rise along the Hudson River in Jersey City, New Jersey. The penthouse took up the entire top floor and had more square feet than your average Home Depot. Despite the hour—it was midnight by the time he got back from Adiona Island—Suzze was dressed and waiting for him on the enormous terrace. The terrace was waaay over the top, what with those Cleopatra sofas and plush chairs and Greek statues and French gargoyles and Roman arches, especially when all you needed—indeed all you saw anyway—was the killer view of the Manhattan skyline.

Myron had wanted to go straight home. There was really nothing more to discuss now that they knew Lex was safe, but on the phone Suzze had seemed oddly needy. With some clients, coddling came with the territory. With Suzze, that had never been the case.

"Tell me what Lex said."

"He's with Gabriel recording some songs for their next album."

Suzze stared at the Manhattan skyline through the summer mist. In her hand, she held a glass of what looked like wine. Myron was not sure what to say about that—pregnancy and wine—so he just kind of cleared his throat.

"What?" Suzze said.

Myron pointed at the wineglass. Mr. Subtle.

"The doctor says it's fine to have one," she said.

"Oh."

"Don't look at me like that."

"I'm not."

She looked out at the skyline from the arch, her hands on her belly. "We're going to need better guard rails up here. What with a baby on the way. I don't even let drunk friends up here."

"Good idea," Myron said. She was stalling. That was okay. "Look, I don't really know what's up with Lex. I admit he's acting a little weird, but he also made a convincing case that it's not my business. You wanted me to find out if he was okay. I have. I can't force him to come home."

"I know."

"So what else is there? I could keep looking into who posted the 'Not His' comment—"

"I know who posted that," Suzze said.

That surprised him. He studied her face and when she didn't say anything else, he asked, "Who?"

"Kitty."

She took a sip of wine.

"You're sure?"

"Yes."

"How?"

"Who else would want that kind of payback?" she asked.

The humidity weighed on Myron like a heavy blanket. He looked at Suzze's belly and wondered what it must be like to lug that around in this weather.

"Why would she want revenge on you?"

Suzze ignored the question. "Kitty was a great player, wasn't she?"

"So were you."

"Not like her. She was the best player I'd ever seen. I became a pro, won a few tournaments, had four year-end top ten finishes. But Kitty? She could have been one of the greats."

Myron shook his head. "It would have never happened."

"What makes you say that?"

"Kitty was a screwup. The drugs, the partying, the lies, the manipulation, the narcissism, the self-destructive streak."

"She was young. We were all young. We all made mistakes."

Silence.

"Suzze?"

"Yes?"

"Why did you want to see me tonight?"

"To explain."

"Explain what?"

She came over to him, spread her arms, and hugged him. Myron held her tight, feeling the warm belly against him. He didn't know if that was weird. But as the hug lasted, it started to feel good, therapeutic. Suzze lowered her head into Myron's chest and stayed there for a while. Myron just held her.

Finally Suzze said, "Lex is wrong."

"About?"

"Sometimes people do need help. I remember nights you saved me. You held me like this. You listened. You never judged me. Maybe you don't know it, but you saved my life a hundred times."

"I'm still here for you," Myron said softly. "Tell me what's wrong."

She held on, keeping her ear against his chest. "Kitty and I were both about to turn seventeen. I wanted to win the juniors so badly that year. Get into the Open. Kitty was my top competition. When she beat me in Boston, my mother went crazy."

Myron said, "I remember."

"My parents explained to me that everything is fair in competition. You do whatever you have to to win. To get an edge. Do you know about the Shot Heard 'Round the World? The home run by Bobby Thomson in the 1950s?"

The change of subjects threw him. "Yeah, sure. What about it?"

"He cheated, my dad said. Thomson. I mean, they all did. People think it just happens now with steroids. But those old New York Giants were stealing signs. Other pitchers scuffed up the baseball. That guy who ran the Celtics, the one who drafted you, he intentionally made it extra hot in the visiting team's locker rooms. Maybe it's not cheating. Maybe it's just looking for the edge."

"And you looked for the edge?"

"Yes."

"How?"

"I spread rumors about my competitor. I made her out to be

more of a slut than she was. I tried to ruin her focus by adding stress to her life. I told you that her baby was probably not Brad's."

"You weren't the only one who told me that. And I knew Kitty on my own. I didn't base my opinion on what you told me anyway. She was a mess, right?"

"So was I."

"But you weren't manipulating my brother. You weren't leading him on and then sleeping around with a bunch of other guys."

"But I was all too ready to tell you about that, wasn't I?" Suzze nestled her head in closer to his chest. "You know what I didn't tell you?"

"What?"

"Kitty also loved your brother. Truly and deeply. When they were broken up, her play suffered. Her heart wasn't in it. I pushed her into partying more. I keep telling her that Brad wasn't for her, that she should play the field."

Myron thought back to the happy photographs of Kitty, Brad, and Mickey on her Facebook and wondered what could have been. He tried to let his mind settle on those blissful images, but the mind goes where it wants. Right now the mind was veering back to the video of Kitty and Ponytail in that private room at Three Downing. "Kitty made her own mistakes," he said, hearing the bitterness in his tone. "What you said or didn't say made no difference. She lied to Brad about everything. She lied about her drug use. She lied to him about my role in their little drama. She even lied about being on the pill."

But as he said that last part, something in his own words didn't mesh. Here Kitty was, on the verge of being the next Martina, Chrissie, Steffi, Serena, Venus—and she ends up getting pregnant. Maybe it was, as she claimed, an accident. Anyone who took middle school health class knows that the pill doesn't work 100 percent of the time. But Myron had never given that excuse an iota of plausibility.

"Does Lex know all this?" he asked.

"All?" She smiled. "No."

"He told me that was the big issue. People have secrets and those secrets fester and then destroy trust. You can't have a good relationship without total transparency. You need to know all your spouse's secrets."

"Lex said that?"

"Yes."

"That's sweet," she said. "But he's wrong again."

"How's that?"

"No relationship survives total transparency." Suzze lifted her face off his chest. Myron saw the tears on her cheeks, felt the wetness on his shirt. "We all keep secrets, Myron. You know that as well as anyone."

By the time Myron made it back to the Dakota, it was three in the morning. He checked to see whether Kitty had replied to his "Please forgive me" message. She hadn't. On the off chance that Lex had told him the truth—and that Kitty had told Lex the truth—he sent Esperanza an e-mail to see if they could check passenger manifests for Kitty's name on flights out of Newark or JFK heading to South America. He signed on to the computer to see if Terese was around. She wasn't.

He thought about Terese. He thought about Jessica Culver, the ex-love Lex had mentioned. After claiming for years that marriage was not for her—the years she was with Myron—Jessica had recently wed a man named Stone Norman. Stone, for crying out loud. What kind of name was that? His friends probably called him "The Stoner" or "Stone Man." Thinking about old lovers, especially ones you wanted to marry, was never a productive endeavor, so Myron made himself stop.

Half an hour later, Win came home. He was accompanied by his latest girlfriend, a tall modelesque Asian named Mee. There was a third person too, another attractive Asian woman Myron had never seen before.

Myron looked over at Win. Win wiggled his eyebrows.

Mee said, "Hi, Myron."

"Hi, Mee."

"This is my friend, Yu."

Myron held back the sigh and said hello. Yu nodded. When the two women left the room, Win grinned at Myron. Myron just shook his head. "Yu?"

"Yep."

When Win had first started up with Mee, he loved to share jokes using her name. *"Mee so horny . . . It's Mee time . . . Sometimes I just want to make love to Mee."*

"Yu and Mee?" Myron said.

Win nodded. "Wonderful, don't you think?"

"No. Where have you been all night?"

Win leaned in conspiratorially. "Between Yu and Mee . . ."

"Yes?"

Win just smiled.

"Oh." Myron sighed. "I get it. Good one."

"Be happy. It used to be all about Mee. But then I realized something. It's about Yu too."

"Or, uh, in this case, Yu and Mee together."

"Now you're in the spirit," Win said. "How was your sojourn to Adiona Island?"

"You want to hear this now?"

"Yu and Mee can wait."

"By that, you mean the girls, not us, right?"

"It does get confusing, doesn't it?"

"Not to mention perverse."

"Don't worry. When I'm not around, Yu can keep Mee occupied." Win sat, steepled his fingers. "Tell me what you learned."

Myron did. When he finished, Win said, "Methinks Lex doth protest too much."

"You got that too?"

"When a man does that much philosophizing, he's covering."

"Plus that last line about her going back to Chile or Peru in the morning?"

"Throwing you off the track. He wants you to stay away from Kitty."

"Do you think he knows where she is?"

"It wouldn't surprise me."

Myron thought about what Suzze said, about transparency and everyone having secrets. "Oh, one more thing." Myron fumbled for his BlackBerry. "Gabriel Wire had a guard working the gate. He looked familiar to me, but I can't place him."

He handed Win the BlackBerry, the photograph on the home screen. Win studied it for a moment.

"This," Win said, "is also not good."

"You recognize him?"

"I haven't heard his name in years." Win handed the BlackBerry back. "But it looks like Evan Crisp. Big-time pro. One of the best."

"Who'd he work for?"

"Crisp was always freelance. The Ache brothers used to bring him in when there was serious trouble."

The Ache brothers, Herman and Frank, had been two leading Old-World mobsters. RICO had finally moved in and closed them down. Like many of his elder brethren, Frank Ache was serving time in a maximum security federal penitentiary, mostly forgotten. Herman, who had to be seventy by now, had managed to slither out of his indictment and used his ill-gotten booty to feign legitimacy.

"A hit man?"

"To some degree," Win said. "Crisp was brought in when your muscle needed a little finesse. If you wanted someone to make a lot of noise or shoot up a place, Crisp wasn't your man. If you wanted someone to die or vanish without raising suspicion, you called Crisp."

"And now Crisp works as a rent-a-cop for Gabriel Wire?"

"That would be a no," Win said. "It's a small island. Crisp got tipped off the moment you arrived and then awaited your imminent arrival. My theory is, he knew you'd take the photograph and that we would figure out his identity."

"To scare us away," Myron said.

"Yes."

"Except we don't scare easily."

"Yes," Win said with only a small eye roll. "We are so very macho."

"Okay, so first we have this weird post on Suzze's board, probably put there by Kitty. Then we have Lex meeting up with Kitty. We have Crisp working for Wire. Plus Lex hiding out at Gabriel Wire's place and probably lying to us."

"And when you add those together, what do you come up with?"

"Bubkes," Myron said.

"No wonder you're our leader." Win rose, poured himself a cognac, tossed Myron a Yoo-hoo. Myron did not shake or open it. He just held the cold can in his hand. "Of course, just because Lex may be lying, that doesn't mean his basic message to you is wrong."

"What message is that?"

"You interfere with the best intentions. But you interfere nonetheless. Whatever your brother and Kitty are going through, perhaps it isn't your place. You haven't been part of their lives for a very long time."

Myron thought about that. "That may be my fault."

"Oh, please," Win said.

"What?"

"Your fault. So when Kitty, for example, told Brad that you hit on her, was she telling the truth?"

"No."

Win spread his hands. "So?"

"So maybe she was just striking back. I said some horrible things about her. I accused her of trapping Brad, manipulating him. I didn't believe the baby was his. Maybe she was using the lie to defend herself."

"Boo"—Win started playing air violin—"hoo."

"I'm not defending what she did. But maybe I messed up too."

"And, pray tell, how would you have messed up?"

Myron said nothing.

"Go ahead," Win said. "I'm waiting."

"You want me to say, 'by interfering.'"

"Bingo."

"So perhaps this is my chance to make amends."

Win shook his head.

"What?"

"How did you mess up in the first place? By interfering. How do you intend to make up for it? By interfering."

"So I should just forget what I saw on that surveillance camera?"

"I would." Win took a deep long sip. "But, alas, I know you can't."

"So what do we do?"

"What we always do. At least in the morning. Tonight I have plans."

"And those would again be between Yu and Mee?"

"I would say bingo again, but I so hate repeating myself."

"You know," Myron said, choosing his words carefully, "and I don't mean to moralize here or judge."

Win crossed his legs. When he did it, the crease remained perfect. "Oh, this is going to be rich."

"And I recognize that Mee has been a part of your life for longer than any woman I remember, and I'm glad that you seem to have at least curtailed your appetite for hookers."

"I prefer the term 'upscale escorts.'"

"Super. In the past, your womanizing, your being a cad . . ."

"A *rakish* cad," Win said with a rakish smile. "I always liked the word 'rakish,' don't you?"

"It fits," Myron said.

"But?"

"When we were in our twenties and even thirties, it was all somewhat, I don't know, endearing."

Win waited.

Myron stared at the can of Yoo-hoo. "Forget it."

"And now," Win said, "you think my behavior, for a man of my years, is somewhat closer to pathetic."

"I didn't mean it that way."

"You think I should settle down a bit."

"I just want you to be happy, Win."

Win spread his hands. "So do I."

Myron gave him the flat eyes. "You're referring to the Yu in the other room again, aren't you?"

The rakish grin. "Love me for all my faults."

"Again, by me, do you mean, uh, Mee?"

Win stood. "Don't worry, old friend. I am happy." Win started moving toward the bedroom door. He stopped suddenly, closed his eyes, looked troubled. "But you may have a point."

"That being?"

"Maybe I'm not happy," he said, a wistful distant look on his face. "Maybe you're not either."

Myron waited, almost sighed. "Go ahead. Say it."

"So perhaps it's time to make Yu and Mee happy."

He vanished into the other room. Myron stared at the Yoo-hoo can for a little while. There was no noise. Win had mercifully soundproofed his room years ago.

At seventy thirty A.M., a mussed Mee came out in a robe and started making breakfast. She asked Myron if he wanted something. Myron politely declined.

At eight A.M., his phone rang. He checked the number and saw it was from Big Cyndi.

"Good morning, Mr. Bolitar."

"Good morning, Big Cyndi."

"Your ponytailed drug dealer was at the club last night. And I tailed him."

Myron frowned. "In the Batgirl costume?"

"It's dark. I blend."

That image came and thankfully fled.

"Did I tell you that Yvonne Craig herself helped me make it?"

"You know Yvonne Craig?"

"Oh, we're old friends. You see, she told me that the material was one-way stretch. It's sort of like a girdle fabric, not as thin as Lycra, but not as thick as neoprene. It was very hard to find."

"I'm sure."

"Did you know Yvonne starred as the superhot green chick on *Star Trek*?"

"Marta, the Orion slave girl," Myron said, because he couldn't help himself. He tried to get them back on track. "So where is our drug dealer now?"

"Teaching French at Thomas Jefferson Middle School in Ridgewood, New Jersey."

12

The cemetery overlooked the schoolyard.

Who came up with that—placing a school full of kids, just budding into adolescence, directly across the street from a resting place for the dead? These children walk by this cemetery or look out on it literally every day. Did it bother them? Did it remind them of their own mortality, that in what would amount to infinity's breath, they'd grow old and end up there too? Or, more likely, was the cemetery an abstract, something that had nothing to do with them, something so commonplace to them that they barely saw it anymore?

School, cemetery. Talk about life's bookends.

Big Cyndi, still in the Batgirl costume, knelt by a gravestone, head lowered, shoulders hunched, so that from a distance, one might mistake her for a Volkswagen Beetle. When Myron approached, she looked out of the corner of her eye and whispered, "I'm blending," and then started sobbing again.

"So where exactly is Ponytail?"

"Inside the school, room two-oh-seven."

Myron looked toward the school. "A drug-dealing middle school French teacher?"

"It seems that way, Mr. Bolitar. Shame, don't you think?"

"I do."

"His real name is Joel Fishman. He lives in Prospect Park, not far from here. He's married and has two kids, a boy and a girl. He has taught French for more than twenty years. No real record. One DUI eight years ago. Ran for town council six years ago."

"A citizen."

"A citizen, yes, Mr. Bolitar."

"How did you get all that information?"

"At first, I considered seducing him so that he'd take me back to his place. You know. Pillow talk. But I knew you'd be against my defiling myself like that."

"I would never let you use your body for evil, Big Cyndi."

"Only sin?"

Myron smiled. "Exactly."

"So I followed him from the club. He took public transportation, the last train out at two seventeen A.M. He walked home to Seventy-four Beechmore Drive. I called the address in to Esperanza."

From there, it would only take a few keystrokes to learn all. Welcome to the computer age, boys and girls. "Anything else?" he asked.

"Joel Fishman goes by the name Crush at the club."

Myron shook his head.

"And the ponytail is a clip-on. Like a hair extension."

"You're kidding."

"No, Mr. Bolitar, I'm not. I guess he wears it as a disguise."

"So now what?"

"There's no school today, only teacher conferences. Normally the security here is pretty tight, but I bet you could go in pretending you're a parent." She put her hand up, stifling a grin. "As Esperanza might note, in those jeans and blue blazer, you'd fit right in."

Myron pointed to his feet. "In Ferragamo loafers?"

He headed across the street and waited until he saw a few parents heading for the door. Then he caught up to them and said hello like he knew them. They said hello back, pretending the same. Myron held the door, the wife walked through, the husband insisted Myron follow, Myron did with a hearty parental laugh.

And Big Cyndi thought she knew how to blend.

There was a signup sheet and a security guard behind the desk. Myron walked over, signed in as David Pepe, making the last name somewhat unreadable. He took a sticker name tag, wrote "David" on it, "Madison's Dad" in smaller print beneath. Myron Bolitar, Man of a Thousand Faces, Master of Disguise.

The old saw is that public schools never change except that they seem smaller. The old saw held serve in here—linoleum floor, metal lockers, wooden classroom doors with metal-mesh glass windows. He arrived at room 207. There was a sign on the window so you couldn't see in. The sign read, RÉUNION EN COURS. NE PAS DÉRANGER. Myron didn't speak much French, but he knew that the second part was asking him to please wait.

He looked for a schedule sheet, something listing times and parents and whatever. Nothing. He wondered what to do here. There were two laminated class chairs in front of most of the doors. The chairs looked sturdy and practical and about as comfortable as a tweed thong. Myron debated waiting in one of them, but suppose the parents for the next meeting showed up?

He chose instead to wander the corridor and keep a close eye on the door. It was 10:20 A.M. Myron assumed that most meetings ended on the half hour or maybe quarter hour. This was a guess, but probably a good one. Fifteen minutes per meeting, maybe thirty minutes. At a minimum, it would be every ten minutes. Either way, the next meeting would be at ten thirty. If no one showed by, say, 10:28, Myron would meander back to the door and try to get in at ten thirty A.M.

Myron Bolitar, Master Planner.

But parents did show up by 10:25 A.M. and pretty much in a steady stream until noon. So that no one would notice him hanging around, Myron wandered downstairs when meetings would start, hid in the bathrooms, stayed in the stairwell. Serious boredom set in. Myron noticed that most of the fathers wore blue blazers and jeans. He had to update his wardrobe.

Finally at noon, there appeared to be an opening. Myron waited by the door and smiled as the parents exited. So far, Joel Fishman had not made an appearance. He waited in the room while one set of parents replaced another. The parents would knock on the door, and Fishman would call out, "*Entrez.*"

Now Myron knocked, but this time there was no reply. He knocked again. Still nothing. Myron turned the knob and opened the door. Fishman sat at his desk, eating a sandwich. There was a can of Coke and package of Fritos on the desk. Ponytail looked so different without the, well, ponytail. His faded yellow dress shirt was short sleeved with material thin enough to see the wife-beater tee below. He wore one of those UNICEF kid ties that were all the rage in 1991. His hair was short, close-cropped, parted on the side. He looked exactly like a middle school French teacher and nothing like a nightclub drug dealer.

"May I help you?" Fishman said, clearly annoyed. "Parent meetings start up again at one."

Another one fooled by the clever disguise. Myron pointed at the Fritos. "Got the munchies?"

"Excuse me?"

"Like when you're high. You got the munchies?"

"Excuse me?"

"It's a clever reference to . . . never mind. My name is Myron Bolitar. I'd like to ask you a few questions."

"Who?"

"Myron Bolitar."

Silence. Myron again almost added, "Ta-da," but refrained. Maturity.

"Do I know you?" Fishman asked.

"You don't."

"I don't have your child in any of my classes. Mrs. Parsons also teaches French. Perhaps you're supposed to be there. Room two-eleven."

Myron closed the door behind him. "I'm not looking for Mrs. Parsons. I'm looking for Crush."

Fishman froze mid-chew. Myron moved across the room, grabbed the parent chair, twirled it around, straddled it macholike. Mr. Intimidation. "On most men, a ponytail reeks of midlife crisis. But I kind of liked it on you, Joel."

Fishman swallowed whatever was in his mouth. Tuna fish from the smell. On whole wheat, Myron saw. Lettuce, tomato. Myron wondered who'd made it for him or whether he'd made it himself and then he wondered why he wondered stuff like that.

Fishman slowly reached for the Coke, looking to stall, and took a sip. Then he said, "I don't know what you're talking about."

"Can you do me a favor?" Myron asked. "It's a small one, really. Can we skip the silly denials? It will really save time and I don't want to hold up the parents coming in at one."

Myron tossed him one of the stills from the nightclub.

Fishman glanced at the photograph. "That's not me."

"Yes, Crush, it is."

"That man has a ponytail."

Myron sighed. "I just asked for one small favor."

"Are you a police officer?"

"No."

"When I ask like that, you have to tell the truth," he said. Not true, but Myron didn't bother to correct him. "And I'm sorry, but you have me mistaken for someone else."

Myron wanted to reach across the desk and bop the guy on the forehead. "Last night at Three Downing, did you notice a large woman in a Batgirl costume?"

Fishman said nothing, but the guy would not have made a great poker player.

"She followed you home. We know all about your club visits, your drug dealings, your—"

That was when Fishman pulled a gun out of his desk drawer.

The suddenness caught Myron off guard. A cemetery goes with a school about as much as a teacher pulling a gun on you inside of his classroom. Myron had made a mistake, gotten overconfident in this setting, let down his guard. A big mistake.

Fishman quickly leaned across the desk, the gun inches from Myron's face. "Don't move or I'll blow your goddamn head off."

When someone points a gun at you, the whole world has a tendency to shrink down to the approximate size of the opening at the end of the barrel. For a moment, especially if it is your first time having a firearm thrust in your face at eye level, that opening is all you see. It is your world. It paralyzes you. Space, time, dimensions, senses are no longer factors in your life. Only that dark opening matters.

Still, Myron thought, slow time down.

The rest happened in less than a second.

First: The mental-state "would he pull the trigger" calculation. Myron looked past the gun and into Fishman's eyes. They were wide and wet, his face shiny. Plus Fishman had pulled a gun on him in a classroom while people were still in the school. His hand shook. The finger was on the trigger. You put those pieces together and you realize a simple truth: The man was crazy and thus may indeed shoot you.

Second: Size up your opponent. Fishman was a married school-teacher with two kids. Playing drug dealer at night in a tony night-club did not really change that. The chances that he had real combat training seemed remote. He had also made a truly amateur move, putting the gun this close to Myron's face, leaning over the desk like that, slightly off balance.

Third: Decide your move. Picture it. If your assailant is not at close range, if he is across the room or even more than a few feet away, well, there would be no choice. You can't disarm him, no matter what kind of martial art kicks you've seen in the movies. You have to wait it out. That was still option A. Myron could indeed stay still. That would be expected. He could talk him down. They were in a school, after all, and you'd have to be not just "crazy" but "Crazy with a capital C" to fire a gun in here.

But if you were a man like Myron, a man who had the reflexes of a professional athlete along with years of training, you might take a serious look at option B: Disarming your opponent. If you choose B, you cannot hesitate. If you choose B, you're best off getting him right away, before he realized that it was a possibility and backed away or grew more cautious. Right now, in the split second he had pulled the gun and shouted for Myron not to move, Joel Fishman was still high off that adrenaline, which leads to . . .

Fourth: Execute.

Surprisingly—or maybe not—it is easier to disarm a man with a gun than one with a knife. If you dart out your hand toward a blade, you could slice open your palm. Knives are hard to grab. You need to go for the wrist or forearm rather than the weapon itself. There is very little room for error.

For Myron, the best way to disarm a person with a firearm involved two steps. One, before Fishman could react in any way, Myron quickly jerked himself out of the discharge line. You don't have to move far, which isn't really an option anyway. It just involves a lightning-quick tilt to the right—the side of Myron's dominant hand. There are many complicated techniques you could use here, depending upon what kind of handgun your assailant was carrying. Some say, for example, to grasp the hammer with your thumb so you can prevent certain weapons from firing. Myron never bought that. There was too little time and too much precision involved, not to mention in the rush to calculate your reaction, trying to figure out whether you're dealing with a semiautomatic or revolver or whatever.

Myron went for something simpler and again, kiddies, if you're not professionally trained and physically gifted, don't try this at home. With his dominant hand, Myron snatched the gun away. Just like that. Like he was taking a toy from a bratty kid. Using his superior strength, athletic skill, knowledge, leverage, and element of surprise, he snapped out his hand and took away the weapon. As he pulled the weapon free, he lifted his elbow and struck Fishman flush on the face, sending him sprawling back in the chair.

Myron leapt across the desk, knocking the chair back. Fishman landed hard on his back. He tried to snake-crawl off the chair. Myron leapt on him, straddling his chest. He even pinned Fishman's arms to the floor with his knees, like a big brother picking on a little one. Old-school.

"Are you out of your goddamn mind?" Myron asked.

No reply. Myron boxed Fishman's ears hard. Fishman squealed in terror and tried to cover up, cowering, helpless. Myron flashed to the video with Kitty, the satisfied smirk, and he punched Fishman hard in the face.

"The gun's not loaded!" Fishman yelled. "Check! Please."

Still pinning down the man's wiggling arms, Myron checked. Fishman was telling the truth. There were no bullets. Myron tossed the gun across the room. Myron cocked his fist to deliver another blow. But Fishman was sobbing now. Not just crying or cringing or scared. He was sobbing in a way you rarely saw in an adult. Myron rolled off him, still at the ready—two could play at the sudden, surprise attack.

Fishman curled himself into a little ball. He made fists, jammed them into his eyes, and kept sobbing. Myron just waited.

"I'm so sorry, man," Fishman managed between sobs. "I'm such a mess. I'm really, really sorry."

"You pulled a gun on me."

"I'm a mess," he said again. "You don't understand. I'm so screwed."

"Joel?"

He kept sniffling.

"Joel?" Myron slid another photograph across the floor to him. "See the woman in that picture?"

He still had his eyes covered.

Myron made his voice firm. "Look, Joel."

Fishman slowly put his hands down. His face was slick from tears and probably phlegm. Crush, the tough Manhattan drug dealer, wiped his face with his sleeve. Myron tried to wait him out, but he just stared.

"A few nights ago, you were at Three Downing with that woman," Myron said. "If you start telling me you don't know what I'm talking about, I will take off my shoe and beat you with it. Do you understand me?"

Fishman nodded.

"You remember her, right?"

He closed his eyes. "It's not what you think."

"I don't care about any of that. Do you know her name?"

"I'm not sure I should tell you."

"My shoe, Joel. I could just beat it out of you."

Fishman wiped his face, shook his head. "That doesn't seem your style."

"What do you mean by that?"

"Nothing. I just don't think you'll hit me anymore."

In the past, Myron thought, I would have in a Big Apple second. But right now, yeah, Fishman was right. He wouldn't.

Seeing Myron hesitate, Fishman said, "Do you know anything about addiction?"

Oh boy. Where was this headed? "Yes, Joel, I do."

"From personal experience?"

"No. Are you going to tell me you're a drug addict, Joel?"

"No. I mean, well, sure, I use. But that's not really what this is about." He tilted his head, suddenly the inquisitive teacher. "Do you know when addicts finally go for help?"

"When they have to."

He grinned as though pleased. Myron Bolitar, prize pupil. "Precisely. When they hit rock bottom. That's what just happened here. I get it now. I get that I have a problem, and I'm going to get help."

Myron was about to crack wise, but he stopped himself. When a guy you wanted info from was talking, it was best to keep him that way. "That sounds like a productive move," Myron said, trying not to gag.

"I have two kids. I have a wonderful wife. Here, take a look."

As Fishman started reaching into his pocket, Myron jumped closer. Fishman nodded, moved slower, took out a set of keys. He handed Myron one of those photo key chains. It was a family shot taken, according to the background, at Six Flags Great Adventure. A costumed Bugs Bunny and Tweety Bird stood left and right of the Fishman family. Mrs. Fishman was heartbreakingly lovely. Joel was kneeling. On his right was a girl, maybe five or six with blond hair and the kind of wide smile that's so damn contagious Myron realized that the corner of his own lips were curling upward. On the other side of Joel was a boy, maybe two years younger than the girl. The boy was shy, half hiding his face in his father's shoulder.

He handed the key chain back. "Beautiful kids."

"Thank you."

Myron remembered something his father once told him: People have an amazing capacity to mess up their own lives.

Out loud, Myron said, "You're a dumb-ass, Joel."

"I'm sick," he corrected. "There's a difference. I want to get better though."

"Prove it."

"How?"

"Start showing that you're ready to change by telling me about the woman you were with three nights ago."

"How do I know you don't mean her harm?"

"The same way you know I won't take off my shoe and beat you."

Joel Fishman looked at the key chain and started to cry again.

"Joel?"

"I honestly want to move past this."

"I know you do."

"And I will. I swear to God. I'll get help. I will be the best father and husband in the world. I just need a chance. You get that, right?"

Myron wanted to vomit. "I do."

"It's just . . . Don't get me wrong. I love my life. I love my family and my kids. But for eighteen years I've woken up and come to this school and taught middle schoolers French. They hate it. They never pay attention. When I started, I had this vision of what it was going to be like—me teaching them this beautiful language that I love so much. But it's nothing like that. They just want to get As and move on. That's it. Every class, year after year. We go through this dance. Amy and I are always struggling to make ends meet. It's just the same, you know. Every day. Year after year. The same drudgery. And what will tomorrow be like? The same. Every day the same, until, well, until I die."

He stopped, looked off.

"Joel?"

"Promise me," Fishman said. "Promise me that if I help you, you won't tell on me." Tell on me. Like he was one of his students who cheated on a test. "Give me that chance, please. For the sake of my kids."

"If you tell me all you know about this woman," Myron said, "I won't tell."

"Give me your word."

"You have my word."

"I met her at the club three nights ago. She wanted to score. I set it up."

"By set it up, you mean you gave her drugs."

"Yes."

"Anything else?"

"No, not really."

"Did she tell you her name?"

"No."

"How about a phone number? In case she wanted to score again?"

"She didn't give me one. That's all I know. I'm sorry."

Myron was not buying it. "How much did she pay you?"

"Excuse me?"

"For the drugs, Joel. How much money did she give you?"

Something crossed his face. Myron saw it. Here came the lie. "Eight hundred dollars," Fishman said.

"In cash?"

"Yes."

"She was carrying eight hundred dollars?"

"I don't take Visa or MasterCard," he said with the chuckle of a liar. "Yes, of course."

"And where did she give you the money?"

"At the club."

"When you gave her the drugs?"

His eyes narrowed a little. "Of course."

"Joel?"

"What?"

"Remember I showed you those still photographs?"

"What about them?"

"They came off surveillance videos," Myron said. "Do you get my drift?"

Fishman's face blanched.

"To put it grossly," Myron said, "I saw fluids exchanged, not cash."

Joel Fishman began to sob again. He put his hands in prayer position, the key chain between his fingers like rosary beads.

"If you're going to lie to me," Myron said, "I see no reason to keep my word."

"You don't understand."

Again with the understand.

"What I did was terrible. I'm ashamed. I didn't see the point in telling you that part. It doesn't change anything. I don't know her. I don't know how to reach her."

Fishman started wailing again, holding up the photo key chain now like wolfsbane to ward off a vampire. Myron waited, considered his options. He stood, crossed the room, and pocketed the gun. "I'm going to turn you in, Joel."

The crying stopped. "What?"

"I don't believe you."

"But I'm telling you the truth."

Myron shrugged and reached for the doorknob. "You also aren't helping me. That was part of the deal."

"But what can I do? I don't know anything. Why would you punish me for that?"

Myron shrugged. "I'm bitter." He turned the knob.

"Wait."

Myron didn't.

"Listen to me, okay? Just for a second."

"No time."

"Do you promise not to say anything?"

"What have you got, Joel?"

"Her cell number," he said. "Just keep your word, okay?"

13

I t's a prepaid mobile phone," Esperanza said. "No way to trace it."

Damn. Myron pulled his Ford Taurus out of the cemetery lot. Big Cyndi was jammed into the seat so that it looked as though her air bag had gone off. Yep, a Ford Taurus. Exterior color: Atlantis Green Metallic. When Myron cruised by, supermodels swooned.

"Point of purchase was a T-Mobile store in Edison, New Jersey," Esperanza said. "Paid with cash."

Myron started to turn the car back around. Time to visit Joel Fishman for one more favor. Ol' Crush would be delighted to see him.

"Something else," Esperanza said.

"I'm listening."

"Remember that weird symbol next to the 'Not His' post?"

"Yep."

"Like you suggested, I put it on a fan page for HorsePower to see if anyone knew about it. A woman named Evelyn Stackman replied, but she won't talk over the phone."

"Why not?"

"She wouldn't say. She wants to meet in person."

Myron made a face. "Over some symbol?"

"That's correct."

"Do you want to handle it?" Myron asked.

"Maybe you didn't hear me," Esperanza said. "I said, she. She, as in a reluctant-to-talk female."

"Ah," Myron said. "So you figure, what, I could use my wiles and manly charm to seduce the information out of her?"

"Yeah," Esperanza said, "let's run with that."

"Suppose she's gay?"

"I thought you had the kind of wiles and manly charm that work on all preferences."

"Yes, of course. My bad."

"Evelyn Stackman lives in Fort Lee. I'll set up the meet for this afternoon."

She hung up. Myron turned the engine off. "Come on," he said to Big Cyndi. "We'll pretend to be parents of a middle schooler."

"Oh, fun." Then Big Cyndi seemed to consider that. "Wait, do we have a boy or girl?"

"Which would you prefer?"

"I really don't care as long as he or she is healthy."

They made their way back into the school. Two parents waited outside the classroom. Big Cyndi cued her tears for them, claiming that their "little Sasha" had a "French emergency" that would only take a second. Myron used the distraction to enter the classroom alone. No reason for Joel to see Big Cyndi and freeze up.

Not surprisingly, Joel Fishman was very unhappy to see him. "What the hell do you want?"

"I need you to call her and set up a meet."

"Why would we meet?"

"How about—oh, I don't know—pretending you're a drug dealer seeing if she needs to score?"

Joel frowned. He was about to protest, but Myron just shook his head. Joel did a quick calculation and realized that the best way to get through this was to cooperate. He took out his cell phone. He had her in his contacts as "Kitty"—no last name. Myron kept his ear near the phone. When he heard the tentative, skittish "hello" on the other end of the line, his face fell. No doubt about it: The voice belonged to his sister-in-law.

Fishman played his part with the perfection of a sociopath. He asked her if she wanted to meet up again. She said yes. Myron nodded at Fishman. Fishman said, "Okay, cool, I'll come to your place. Where do you live?"

"That won't work," Kitty said.

"Why not?"

And then Kitty whispered something that made Myron's heart freeze: "My son is around."

Fishman was good. He said that he could take a rain check, just drop off the "package," whatever she wanted, but Kitty was equally cagey. They ended up agreeing to meet near the merry-go-round at the Garden State Plaza Mall in Paramus. Myron checked his watch. He'd have enough time to talk to Evelyn Stackman about the symbol on the "Not His" post and then be back to see Kitty.

Myron wondered what he would do when that happened— when he met up with Kitty. Should he jump out and confront her? Ask her gentle questions? Or maybe not show up at all. Maybe the best move was to have Fishman cancel after she showed up so that he could follow her home.

Half an hour later, Myron parked the car in front of a modest brick cape off Lemoine Avenue in Fort Lee. Big Cyndi stayed in the car and fiddled with her iPod. Myron headed up the walk. Evelyn Stackman had the door opened before Myron could even ring the bell. She looked to be fiftyish with curled frizz that reminded him of Barbra Streisand in *A Star Is Born*.

"Ms. Stackman? I'm Myron Bolitar. Thank you for seeing me."

She invited him inside. The living room had a worn green sofa, an upright piano of light cherry wood, and posters of HorsePower concerts. One was from their first show at the Hollywood Bowl more than two decades ago. The poster was signed by both Lex Ryder and Gabriel Wire. The inscription—in Gabriel's handwriting— read, "To Horace and Evelyn, You Both Rock."

"Wow," Myron said.

"I've been offered ten thousand dollars for it. I could use the money but . . ." She stopped. "I Googled you. I don't follow basket-ball, so I didn't know your name."

"That was a long time ago anyway."

"But you now manage Lex Ryder?"

"I'm an agent. It's slightly different. But, yes, I work with him."

She mulled that over. "Follow me." She led him to the steps heading down to the basement. "My husband, Horace. He was the real fan."

The small finished basement had a ceiling so low Myron could not stand upright. There was a gray futon and an old television on a fiberglass black stand. The rest of the basement was, well, HorsePower. A fold-out table, the kind you might put out when your dining room table couldn't handle all your family, was covered with all things HorsePower—photographs, album covers, files of sheet music, concert advertisements, guitar picks, drumsticks, shirts, dolls. Myron recognized a black shirt with snap buttons.

"Gabriel actually wore that during a concert in Houston," she said.

There were two fold-out chairs. Myron saw several photographs of "Wire sightings" from the tabloids.

"I'm sorry it's such a mess. After the whole Alista Snow tragedy, well, Horace was heartbroken. He used to study the paparazzi sightings of Gabriel. See, Horace was an engineer. He was so good with math and puzzles." She gestured toward the tabloids. "They're all fake."

"What do you mean?"

"Horace always found a way to prove the images weren't really Gabriel. Like this one. Gabriel Wire had a scar on the back of his right hand. Horace got the original negative and blew it up. There was no scar. On this one he ran a mathematical equation—don't ask me to explain how—and figured that this man was wearing a size ten shoe. Gabriel Wire has a size twelve."

Myron nodded, said nothing.

"It must seem weird. This obsession."

"No, not really."

"Other men follow a sports team or go to the racetrack or collect stamps. Horace loved HorsePower."

"How about you?"

Evelyn smiled. "I was a fan, I guess. But not like Horace. It was something we did together. We camped out for concerts. We would turn the lights low and listen and try to come up with the real meaning behind the lyrics. It might not sound like much, but I'd give anything for one more night like that."

A shadow crossed her face. Myron wondered whether he should go there and then decided, yes, maybe he should.

"What happened to Horace?" he asked.

"He died this past January," she said, a small choke in her voice. "Heart attack. He had it crossing the street. People thought a car hit him. But Horace just fell in the crosswalk and died. Just like that. Gone. He was only fifty-three. We were high school sweethearts. Raised two kids in this house. We made plans for our old age. I'd just retired from my job at the post office, so we could travel more."

She flashed a quick "what can you do" smile and looked away. We all have our scars and torment and ghosts. We all walk around and smile and pretend everything is okay. We are polite to strangers and share the road with them and stand in line at the supermarket and we manage to disguise the hurt and desperation. We work hard and make plans and more often than not, that all goes to hell.

"I'm really sorry for your loss," Myron said.

"I shouldn't have said anything."

"It's okay."

"I know I should get rid of this stuff. Sell it. But I just can't yet."

Not knowing what to say, Myron went with a classic: "I understand."

She managed a smile. "But, really, you want to know about the symbol."

"If you don't mind."

Evelyn Stackman crossed the room and opened up the filing cabinet. "Horace tried to figure out what it meant. He looked up Sanskrit and Chinese and hieroglyphics, things like that. But he could never place it."

"Where did you first see it?"

"The symbol?" Evelyn reached into the cabinet and pulled out what appeared to be the cover for a CD. "Did you know about this album?"

Myron looked at it. It was the artwork, if that was what you called it, for an album cover. He had never seen it. On the top it read, "LIVE WIRE." Then under that in smaller print, HORSE-POWER LIVE AT MADISON SQUARE GARDEN. But that wasn't what drew your eye. Under the letters was a strange photograph of Gabriel Wire and Lex Ryder. The shot was from the waist up, both shirtless, back-to-back with their arms folded. Lex was on the left, Gabriel on the right, both turning to look at their prospective music buyer with serious glares.

"Right before the Alista Snow tragedy, they were going to do a live album," Evelyn said. "Were you with them then?"

Myron shook his head. "I came on later."

Myron couldn't stop staring. Gabriel and Lex had thrown some "guyliner" on their eyes. Both men were given equal space in the photograph—if anything, Lex had a better spot, being on the left where your eye naturally goes first—but what you noticed here, what you couldn't help but feel, was that your eyes were drawn to Gabriel Wire, almost exclusively, as though there were a bright beacon shining down on that half of the photograph. Wire was—and Myron believed this with all due hetero respect—so damn handsome. His gaze did more than smolder; it called out to you, demanded attention, insisted you look back.

Successful musicians have a variety of strengths, but rock superstars, like their athletic or thespian counterparts, also have the intangibles. That was what transformed Gabriel from musician into rock legend. Gabriel had almost supernatural charisma. Onstage or even in person, it blew you away, but even here, in a photograph from an album cover never released, you could feel it all again. It was more than just good looks. You sensed in those smoldering eyes sensitivity, tragedy, anger, intelligence. You wanted to listen to him. You wanted to know more.

Evelyn said, "Gorgeous, isn't he?"

"Yes."

"Is it true about his face being destroyed?"

"I don't know."

Next to Gabriel, working the pose too hard, was Lex. His folded arms were tensed up, as if he were doing the quiet bicep flex. He was strictly average-looking with somewhat nondescript features, and perhaps, if you paid him any attention at all, you realized that Lex was the sensible one, the consistent one, the stable one—in short, the boring one. Lex was the grounded yin next to Gabriel's hypnotically volatile yang. But then again, every long-running group needs that balance, don't they?

"I don't see the symbol here," Myron said.

"It never made it to the cover." Evelyn was back in the file cabinet. She pulled out a manila envelope with the wraparound string. She took the string between her thumb and index finger, stopped, and looked up. "I keep wondering if I should show you this."

"Mrs. Stackman?"

"Evelyn."

"Evelyn. You know Lex is married to Suzze T, right?"

"Of course."

"Someone is trying to hurt her. And Lex too, I guess. I'm trying to figure out who."

"And you think this symbol is a clue?"

"It could be, yes."

"You seem like a good man."

Myron waited.

"I told you Horace was a big-time collector. His favorite items were the one of a kinds. A few years ago, the photographer Curk Burgess contacted him. A week before Alista Snow died, Burgess took the photograph you're looking at now."

"Okay."

"But he took a bunch that day, of course. It was a long photo shoot. I guess Gabriel wanted to go with something more risqué, so they took some of these pictures naked. Do you remember a few years ago when a private collector bought a Marilyn Monroe porn film so that no one else would see it?"

"Yes."

"Well, that's more or less what Horace did. He bought the negatives. We really couldn't afford it, but that was the level of his commitment." She pointed to the album cover in his hand. "This was originally a full body shot, but they cropped it."

She unwrapped the manila folder, slid out a photograph, showed it to him. Myron looked. The two men were shot from the side and, yes, they were naked but the shadows were, uh, tasteful and worked like fig leaves.

"I still don't see it."

"See that mark on Gabriel's, er, upper thigh, I guess?"

Evelyn handed him another photograph, an extreme blowup. And there it was, on the right thigh, very close to Gabriel Wire's somewhat legendary groin—a tattoo.

A tattoo that looked exactly like the symbol in the "Not His" post on Suzze's Facebook page.

14

There were still two hours until his meet with Kitty at the Garden State Plaza Mall. On the way to the bus stop by the George Washington Bridge, Myron filled in Big Cyndi on what he'd learned from Evelyn Stackman.

"Curious," Big Cyndi said.

"What?"

Big Cyndi tried to shift in her seat to face him. "As you know, Mr. Bolitar, I spent many years as a rock groupie."

He hadn't known. In the glory heyday of the Fabulous Ladies of Wrestling on WPIX Channel 11 in the New York area, Big Cyndi had been known as Big Chief Mama. As a tag team, Big Cyndi's Big Chief Mama and Esperanza's Little Pocahontas were Intercontinental Champions, whatever "Intercontinental" means. They were the good guys. Little Pocahontas would usually be winning on skill before her evil adversary would do something illegal—throw sand in her eye, use the dreaded "foreign object," distract the referee so she could be double-teamed—and then, when the crowd was in a total frenzy, crying out seemingly in vain at the horrible injustice being done to a smoking-hot babe, Big Chief Mama would roar and leap from the top rope and free her lithe, babe-a-licious partner from bondage and together, with the throngs on their feet cheering, Little Pocahontas and Big Chief Mama would restore world order and, of course, defend their Intercontinental Tag Team title.

Massively entertaining.

"You were a groupie?"

"Oh yes, Mr. Bolitar. A big one."

She batted her eyes at him again. Myron nodded. "I didn't know."

"I've had sex with many rock stars."

"Okay."

She arched her right eyebrow. "*Many*, Mr. Bolitar."

"Got it."

"Some of your favorites even."

"Okay."

"But I would never kiss and tell. I'm the model of discretion."

"That's nice."

"But you know your favorite axe man in the Doobie Brothers?"

"Discretion, Big Cyndi."

"Right. Sorry. But I was making a point. I followed in the footsteps of Pamela des Barres, Sweet Connie—you remember, from the Grand Funk song?—Bebe Buell—and my mentor, Ma Gellan. You know who she is?"

"No."

"Ma Gellan considered herself a rock star cartographer. Do you know what that is?"

He tried not to roll his eyes. "I know a cartographer is a mapmaker."

"That's right, Mr. Bolitar. Ma Gellan made up topographical and topological nude body maps of rock stars."

"Ma Gellan," Myron said, seeing it now. He nearly groaned. "Like Magellan?"

"You're very quick, Mr. Bolitar."

Everyone's a wiseass.

"Her maps are wonderful—very detailed and precise. They show scars, piercings, abnormalities, body hair, even areas where they were colossally or inadequately equipped."

"For real?"

"Of course. You know about Cynthia Plaster Caster? She used to make plaster casts of penises. By the way, it's true about front men. They are always gifted. Oh, except for one from a very famous British band, I won't say who, but he's hung like a small kitten."

"Is there a point here?"

"An important one, Mr. Bolitar. Ma Gellan made a topographical map of Gabriel Wire. The man was gorgeous—face and body. But he had no tattoos. Not a mark on him."

Myron thought about that. "Evelyn Stackman's picture was taken within weeks of his becoming a total recluse. Maybe he got it after she did her, uh, study of him."

They arrived at the bus stop.

"That could be," Big Cyndi said. As she rolled out, the car creaked and rolled like the opening credits of *The Flintstones* when Fred gets those ribs. "Would you like me to check with Ma?"

"I would. Are you sure I can't just get you a taxi back?"

"I prefer taking the bus, Mr. Bolitar."

And there she stalked away like a middle linebacker, still in the Batgirl costume. No one gave her a second glance. Welcome to the New York–New Jersey–Connecticut tristate area. Visitors often think that the locals are uncaring or cold or rude. The truth is, they are frighteningly polite. When you live in a congested area, you learn to give people their space, allow them their privacy. Here you can be surrounded by people and still enjoy being alone.

The Garden State Plaza Mall was two million–plus square feet of retail space located in the epicenter of retail malls, Paramus, New Jersey. The word "Paramus" comes from the Lenape Native Americans and means either "place of fertile soil" or "make room for another megastore." Paramus boasts more retail shopping than any other zip code in the USA, and Myron's guess was, it wasn't even close.

He pulled into the lot and checked the time. Another hour until Kitty was supposed to arrive. His stomach grumbled. He checked out the eating options and felt his arteries harden: Chili's, Johnny Rockets, Joe's American Bar & Grill, Nathan's Famous hot dogs, KFC, McDonald's, Sbarro, and both Blimpie and Subway, which Myron actually thought were the same restaurant. He settled on California Pizza Kitchen. He ignored the cheery waiter's attempt at selling him an appetizer and after looking over all the international pizza topping choices—Jamaican Jerk, Thai Chicken, Japanese eggplant—he went with plain ol' pepperoni. The waiter looked disappointed.

Malls are malls. This was one was gi-normous, but really, what makes most malls stand out is the depressing sameness within. Gap, Old Navy, Banana Republic, JCPenney, Nordstrom, Macy's,

Brookstone, AMC Theatres, you get the idea. There were strange super-specific specialty stores, like the one that only sold candles or, winner of most moronically highbrow name of all, The Art of Shaving—how did that place stay in business? What Myron noticed now were the crappy kiosk-type stores in the middle of the corridor. There were the Perfume Palace and Piercing Pagoda. There were at least four that sold flying remote-controlled toys with some bozo intentionally flying the helicopter in your way. Yes, four. And yet have you ever seen a child using one of those in real life?

As Myron made his way to the merry-go-round, he spotted the most odious, dishonest, snake oil–like mall booth of all—the bogus "talent/model scouts," who basically stopped everyone they could with wide-eyed come-ons like, "Wow, you have the look we're searching for! Have you ever thought of modeling?" Myron stood and watched the commission-seeking con artists—mostly attractive women in their early twenties—work the crowd, trying not so much to find a certain look as, Myron assumed, a lobotomy scar so as to locate a person naïve enough to be "accepted" into their "scouting program" and buy a four-hundred-dollar "photography portfolio" so they could start posing for major catalogues and making TV commercials immediately.

Right. Does that TV commercial come with a Nigerian bank account?

Myron was not sure what was more depressing—the fact that these young dream scammers didn't mind exploiting people's desire for fame, or that their victims were so needy that they fell for it?

Enough. Myron knew that this was his way of stalling. Kitty would be here in fifteen minutes. He debated spending the time in Spencer's Gifts, his and Brad's favorite store growing up in Livingston, New Jersey, what with the beer jokes, explicit shot glasses, safe sexual innuendo, and weird blue-light posters in the back. He thought again about the last time he saw Brad and Kitty. He thought about what he had done. He thought about the confused, wounded look in Brad's eyes. He thought about the way the blood trickled between Kitty's fingers.

He shook it off and moved to one side, out of view so that she wouldn't see him. Myron debated getting a newspaper to hide his face, but nothing would stick out in a mall more than someone actually reading.

Fifteen minutes later, as Myron watched the merry-go-round from behind a mannequin at Foot Locker, Kitty arrived.

15

Win's private jet landed on the only runway at Fox Hollow Airport. A black limousine waited on the tarmac. Win chastely kissed his stewardess Mee and headed down the plane steps.

The limo dropped him off at the United States Penitentiary in Lewisburg, Pennsylvania, home of the "worst of the worst" among federal prisoners. A guard greeted Win and led him through the maximum-security prison to G Block or, as it is more commonly known, "Mafia Row." John Gotti had served time here. So had Al Capone.

Win moved into the facility's visiting room.

"Please have a seat," the guard said.

Win obliged.

"Here are the rules," the guard said. "No shaking hands. No touching. No physical contact of any kind."

"How about French-kissing?" Win asked.

The guard frowned, but that was about it. Win had managed to get this appointment fast. That meant, the guard had obviously concluded, that this was a man with serious juice. What Lewisburg calls Phase 1 and 2 prisoners were allowed only video visitations. Phase 3 prisoners were permitted noncontact visitors. Only Phase 4—and it was unclear how you became Phase 4—were permitted what were called "contact visits" with family. Frank Ache, the former mafioso leader from Manhattan, was granted Phase 3 for the purpose of Win's visit. That was fine with Win. He had no interest in making physical contact with the man.

The heavy door swung open. When Frank Ache shackle-shuffled into the visiting area wearing the prison-issue, neon orange jumpsuit, even Win was surprised. In his prime—one that probably lasted better than two decades—Frank had been a gritty, deadly Old-World mafia boss. He cut an impressive figure. He'd been a big man, barrel-chested, sporting polyester-cum-velour sweat suits too tacky for a monster truck rally. There were rumors that Scorsese wanted to do a film about his life and that Tony Soprano was in some ways based on Frank, except Frank didn't have the loving family or any of the semi-humanity of Soprano. Frank Ache's name struck fear. He'd been a dangerous killer, a man who had murdered many and made no apologies for it.

But prison has a way of shrinking a man. Ache must have lost fifty, sixty pounds inside these walls. He looked sapped, dry as an old twig, frail. Frank Ache squinted at his visitor and tried to smile.

"Windsor Horne Lockwood the third," he said. "What the hell are you doing here?"

"How are you, Frank?"

"Like you care."

"No, no, I've always been very concerned with your well-being."

Frank Ache laughed a little too long and hard at that one. "You're lucky I never whacked you. My brother always stopped me, you know."

Win did know. He looked into the dark eyes and saw blankness.

"I'm on Zoloft now," Frank said as if reading his mind. "You believe that? They have me on suicide watch. Don't much see the point, do you?"

Win didn't know if he meant the point of taking the drug or committing suicide or even trying to prevent the suicide. He also didn't care. "I have a favor to ask," Win said.

"Were we ever buddies?"

"No."

"So?"

"Favor," Win said again. "As in, you do one for me, I do one for you."

Frank Ache stopped. He sniffled, used a once-giant hand to wipe his face. His receding hairline was gone now, though big tufts stayed on the side. His dark olive skin was now the gray of a city street after a rainstorm.

"What makes you think I could use a favor?"

Win did not answer that. There was no reason to elaborate. "How did your brother slither out of an indictment?"

"That's what you want to know?"

Win said nothing.

"What difference does that make?"

"Humor me, Frank."

"You know Herman. He looked classy. Me, I looked like a dago."

"Gotti looked classy."

"No, he didn't. He looked like a goomba dressed up in expensive suits."

Frank Ache looked off now, his eyes wet. He put his hand up to his face again. It started with another sniffle and then the big, scary man's face crumbled. He started to cry. Win waited for him to regain his composure. Ache cried some more.

Finally: "You got a tissue or something?"

"Use your neon orange sleeve," Win said.

"You know what it's like in here?"

Win said nothing.

"I sit alone in a six-by-eight cell. I sit in it twenty-three hours a day. Alone. I eat my meals in there. I crap in there. When I go out in the yard for one hour, no one else is outside. I go days without hearing a voice. I try sometimes to talk to the guards. They won't say a word back to me. Day after day. I sit alone. I talk to no one. That's how it's gonna be till the day I die." He started sobbing again.

Win was tempted to take out his air violin, but he refrained. The man was talking—needed to talk, it seemed. This was a good thing. Still: "How many people did you kill, Frank?"

He stopped crying for a moment. "Me myself or that I ordered?"

"Your pick."

"Got me. I personally whacked, what, twenty, thirty guys."

Like he was talking about parking tickets he beat. "I'm feeling sorrier for you by the moment," Win said.

If Frank took offense, he didn't show it. "Hey, Win, you want to hear something funny?"

He kept leaning forward as he talked, desperate for any kind of conversation or contact. Amazing what humans, even ones as wanton as Frank Ache, crave when left alone—other humans. "The floor is yours, Frank."

"You remember one of my men named Bobby Fern?"

"Hmm, perhaps."

"Big fat guy? Used to run underage girls out of the Meatpacking District?"

Win remembered. "What about him?"

"You see me crying in here, right? I don't try to hide it anymore. I mean, what's the point? You know what I mean. I cry. So what? Truth is, I always did. I used to kinda go off and cry alone. Even back in the day. I don't know why either. Hurting people actually made me feel good, so that wasn't it, but then, like one time, I was watching *Family Ties*. You remember that show? With the kid who's got that shaking disease now?"

"Michael J. Fox."

"Right. Loved that show. That sister Mallory was a hot number. So I'm watching it and it must be the last season and the father on the show has a heart attack. It's kinda sad and see, that's how my old man died. It's no big deal, I mean, it's a dumb sitcom, and next thing I know I'm bawling like a baby. Used to happen to me like that all the time. So I'd make an excuse and go off. I'd never let anyone see me. You know my world, right?"

"Right."

"So one day when I go off like that, Bobby walks in on me and sees me crying." Frank smiled now. "Now me and Bobby, we go back. His sister was the first girl who let me go to third base. Eighth grade. It was awesome." He looked off, lost in this happy moment. "So anyway, Bobby walks in and I'm crying, and man, you should have seen his face. He didn't know what to do. Bobby, he kept swearing he'd never tell anyone, not to worry, hell, he cried all the time. I loved Bobby. He was a good man. Nice family. So I thought I'd let it slide, you know."

"You were always such a prince," Win said.

"Right, sure, I tried. But see, now, whenever I was with Bobby, I felt, I don't know, ashamed or something. He didn't do or say nothing, but now suddenly he was jumpy around me. Wouldn't meet my eye, that kinda thing. And Bobby smiled a lot, you know, he had this big smile and loud laugh. But now, when he smiled and laughed, I'm thinking maybe he was making fun of me, you get what I'm saying?"

"So you killed him," Win said.

Frank nodded. "Used a fish-line garrote. I don't use that too often. Nearly sliced Bobby's head off. But I mean, can you blame me?"

Win spread his hands. "How could anyone?"

Frank laughed too hard again. "Nice having you visit."

"Oh yes, good times."

Frank laughed some more.

He just wanted to talk, Win thought again. It was pathetic, really. This former mountain of a man was that broken, desperate, and thus Win could use it. "You said before that Herman looked classy. That he appeared to be more legitimate than you."

"Right, so?"

"Could you elaborate?"

"You were there, you know how it was with me and Herman. Herman wanted to be legit. He wanted to go to fancy parties and play old golf clubs like yours and he got the midtown office in the nice high-rise. He put dirty money into real businesses, like that suddenly made the money clean or something. So toward the end, Herman only wanted to handle gambling and loan sharking. Guess why?"

Win said, "Because there was less violence?"

"No, if anything, they're more violent, what with collecting and stuff." Frank Ache leaned forward, and Win could smell the decay on his breath. "Gambling and loan sharking felt legit to him. Casinos do gambling and they're legit. Banks do loans and they're legit. So why can't Herman do the same?"

"And you?"

"I handled the other stuff. Whores, drugs, like that, though let me tell you, if Zoloft ain't a drug that don't work better than blow, I'll suck off a hyena. And don't get me started on whores being illegal. Oldest profession. And when you think about it, what man doesn't pay for sex in the end?"

Win did not argue.

"So why you here?" Frank smiled and the sight was still eerie. Win wondered how many people had died, their last sight being that smile. "Or maybe I should ask, whose ass has Myron stuck his finger up now?"

Time to show his hand. "Evan Crisp's."

That widened Frank's eyes. "Whoa."

"Yes."

"Myron met up with Crisp?"

"That he did."

"Crisp is nearly as deadly as you," Frank said.

"I'm flattered."

"Man, you going up against Crisp. Should be fun watching that."

"I'll send you the DVD."

Something dark ran across Frank's face. "Evan Crisp," he said slowly, "is one of the main reasons I'm here."

"How's that?"

"See, one of us—me or Herman—had to go down. You know how RICO is. They needed a scapegoat."

Scapegoat, Win thought. The man has no idea how many people he personally murdered, including one for seeing him cry. But he's a scapegoat.

"So it was either me or Herman. Crisp worked for Herman. Suddenly Herman's witnesses vanish or recant. Mine didn't. The end."

"So you went down for the crimes?"

Frank leaned forward again. "I got thrown under the bus."

"Meanwhile, Herman lives on, happy and legit," Win said.

"Yep," Frank said.

Their eyes met for a moment. Frank gave Win the smallest nod.

"Evan Crisp," Win said, "is now working for Gabriel Wire. Do you know who that is?"

"Wire? Sure. His music is pure, one hundred percent, grade-A crap. Does Myron rep him?"

"No, his partner."

"Lex something, right? Another no-talent."

"Any clue why Crisp might be working for Gabriel Wire?"

Frank smiled with small teeth that looked like Tic Tacs. "In the old days, Gabriel Wire did it all. Blow, whores—but mostly gambling."

Win arched an eyebrow. "Do tell."

"The favor?"

"Done."

Nothing else said on that. Nothing else needed.

"Wire owed Herman big," Frank said. "At one point—now I'm going back before he started the Howard Hughes act, what, fifteen, twenty years—his tab was more than half a million."

Win considered that for a moment. "There are rumors that someone messed up Wire's face."

"Not Herman," Frank said with a headshake. "He ain't that stupid. Wire can't sing a lick, but his smile could unsnap a bra from thirty paces. So no, Herman wouldn't mess with the breadwinner."

Outside the room and down the hall, a man screamed. The guard by the door did not move. Neither did Frank. The screaming continued, grew louder, and then it was cut off as though with a switch.

Win asked, "Do you have any thoughts on why Crisp would be working for Wire?"

"Oh, I doubt he's working for Wire," Frank said. "My bet? Crisp is there for Herman. He's probably on the scene making sure Mr. Rock 'n' Roll pays up."

Win sat back, crossed his legs. "So you believe that your brother is still involved with Gabriel Wire then?"

"Why else would Crisp be watching him?"

"We thought that perhaps Evan Crisp had gone legit. Perhaps he took a cushy security job for a recluse."

Frank smiled again. "Yeah, I can see how you might think that."

"But I'm wrong?"

"We never go legit, Win. We just become bigger hypocrites. The world is dog-eat-dog. Some get eaten, some don't. All of us, even your buddy Myron, would kill a million strangers to protect the few he cares about—and anyone who tells you different is a liar. We do it every day in one way or another. You can either buy that nice pair of shoes or you can use that money to save some starving kids in Africa—and yet you always buy the shoes. That's life. We all kill if we feel justified. A man has a starving family. If he kills another man, he can steal his loaf of bread and save his kids. If he doesn't kill the man, he doesn't get the bread and his family dies. So he kills the man. Every single time. But see, the rich man doesn't need to kill to get a loaf of bread. So he says, 'Oh, it's wrong to kill' and makes up rules so no one hurts him or takes the million loaves he's saving for him and his fat family. You hear what I'm saying?"

"Morality is subjective," Win said, making a production of stifling a yawn. "What a philosophical insight, Frank."

Frank chuckled at that. "I don't get many visitors. I'm enjoying this."

"Wonderful. So, pray tell, what are Crisp and your brother up to?"

"Truth? I don't know. But it might explain where a lot of Herman's money came from. When the RICO guys came crashing down, they froze all our assets. Herman had a cash cow somewhere paying for the lawyer and, hell, for Crisp. It could have been Gabriel Wire, why not?"

"Could you ask?"

"Ask Herman?" Frank shook his head. "He don't visit much."

"Ah, how sad. You two used to be so close."

That was when Win felt his cell phone double-vibrate. The double-vibrate was a specific setting for emergencies only. He took out the cell phone, read the text, and closed his eyes.

Frank Ache looked at him. "Bad news."

"Yes."

"Do you have to go?"

Win rose. "Yes."

"Hey, Win? Come back, okay? It's good to talk like this."

But they both know that he wouldn't. Pathetic. Twenty-three hours in a cell alone. You shouldn't do that to a man, Win thought, even the worst. You should take him out in the back, put a gun behind his head, and fire two bullets into his skull. Before you pulled the trigger, the man, even one as broken as Frank, would beg for his life. That was how it worked. The survival instinct always kicked in—men, all men, begged for their lives when faced with death. Still, putting down the animal was cost-effective, wiser, and in the end, more humane.

Win nodded to the guard and hurried back toward his plane.

16

Myron watched Kitty walk tentatively through the mall, afraid the ground might give way. Her face was pale. Her once-defining freckles had faded away, but not in a healthy way. She kept cringing and blinking, as though someone had raised a hand and she was bracing for the strike.

For a moment, Myron just stood there, the tinny mall acoustics roaring in his ears, flashing back to those early tennis days, when Kitty was so confident, so sure of herself, you just knew that she was destined for greatness. Myron remembered taking Suzze and Kitty to a mall like this one when they had downtime before a tournament in Albany. The two budding tennis greats strolled the mall like, well, two teenage girls, dropping the adult pretenses for a while, using "like" and "you know" in every sentence, talking too loudly, laughing about the dumbest things, just as two teenage girls should.

Would it be too hackneyed to wonder where it all went so wrong?

Kitty's eyes darted left and right. Her right leg started to shake. Myron needed to make a decision. Should he make a gradual approach? Should he just wait and follow her back to her car? Should he try direct confrontation or something subtler?

When her back was turned, Myron started walking toward her. He hurried his step, afraid she'd turn, see him, and bolt. He angled himself to block any such quick getaway, heading toward a corner between Macy's and Wetzel's Pretzels. He was two steps from Kitty when he felt his BlackBerry vibrate. As though sensing his approach, Kitty began to turn toward him.

"Good to see you again, Kitty."

"Myron?" She recoiled as though slapped. "What are you doing here?"

"We need to talk."

Her mouth dropped open. "What . . . how did you find me?"

"Where's Brad?"

"Wait, how did you know I'd be here? I don't understand."

He spoke quickly, wanting to get past this. "I found Crush. I told him to call you and set this up. Where's Brad?"

"I have to go." Kitty started past him. Myron stepped in her way. She moved to her right. Myron grabbed her arm.

"Let go of me."

"Where is my brother?"

"Why do you want to know?"

The question made him pull up. He was unsure how to answer. "I just want to talk to him."

"Why?"

167

"What do you mean, why? He's my brother."

"And he's my husband," she said, suddenly standing her ground. "What do you want with him?"

"I told you. I just want to talk to him."

"What, so you can make up more stuff about me?"

"Me make stuff up? You're the one who said I—" Unproductive. He made himself stop. "Look, I'm sorry about everything. Whatever I said or did. I want to put it in the past. I want to make amends."

Kitty shook her head. Behind her, the merry-go-round started up again. There were maybe twenty children on board. Some parents joined them. They stood by the horse, making sure that the offspring were secure. Most watched from the sidelines, their heads moving in small circles so they could watch their child and only theirs. Each time the child circled around, the parent's face would light up anew.

"Please," Myron said.

"Brad doesn't want to see you."

Her tone was that of a petulant teenager, but the words still stung. "He said that?"

She nodded. He tried to meet her eye, but her gaze was everywhere but on him. Myron had to take a step back and put his emotions on hold. Forget the past. Forget the history. Try to connect.

"I wish I could take it back," Myron said. "You have no idea how much I regret what happened."

"Doesn't matter anymore. I have to go."

Connect, he thought. You have to connect. "Do you ever think about regrets, Kitty? I mean, do you ever wish you could go back and do one little thing differently and then everything, your whole world, would be something else? Like if I made a right turn instead of a left at a stoplight. If you hadn't picked up that tennis racket when you were, what, three years old? If I didn't hurt my knee and then I wouldn't have been an agent and then you would have never met Brad? You ever wonder about stuff like that?"

It may have been a ploy or line on his part, but that didn't mean it wasn't true. He felt drained now. For a moment they both just stood there, their world gone quiet while the mall rush raged about them.

When Kitty finally spoke, her voice was soft. "It doesn't work that way."

"What doesn't?"

"Everyone has regrets," she said, looking off. "But you don't want to go back. If I made a right instead of a left or if I never picked up a racket, well, I wouldn't have met Brad. And we would have never had Mickey." At the mention of her son, her eyes welled up. "Whatever else happened, I could never go back and risk that. If I changed one thing—even if I got an A in sixth-grade math instead of a B—maybe that chain reaction would have changed one sperm or one egg and then there would be no Mickey. Do you see?"

Hearing about the nephew he never met worked like a lasso around Myron's heart. He tried to keep his voice even. "What's Mickey like?"

For a moment the drug addict was gone, the tennis player was gone—and color came to her face. "He's the greatest kid in the world." She smiled, but Myron could see the devastation behind it. "He's so smart and strong and kind. He awes me every day. He loves playing basketball." A small chuckle escaped her lips. "Brad says he may be better than you."

"I'd love to see him play."

Her back stiffened, and her face shut like a slammed gate. "That's not going to happen."

He was losing her—time to change tacks again, keep her off balance. "Why did you post 'Not His' on Suzze's wall?"

"What are you talking about?" she countered, but there was no conviction in her voice. She opened her purse and started reaching inside. Myron peered over her and saw two crushed packets of cigarettes. She withdrew one and put it in her mouth, looking up at him as though daring him to say something. He didn't.

She started toward the exit. Myron stayed with her.

"Come on, Kitty. I already know it was you."

"I need a smoke."

They walked between two restaurants, Ruby Tuesday and Mc-Donald's. The McDonald's had the most garish Ronald McDonald statue sitting in a booth. Ronald had a big smile and was too brightly painted and looked as though it might wink as they passed. Myron wondered whether it gave kids nightmares because, when Myron was unsure of his next move, he wondered about things like that.

Kitty already had her lighter at the ready. She inhaled hard, closing her eyes, and let loose a long ream of smoke. Cars slowly cruised around in search of open spaces. Kitty took another hit. Myron waited.

"Kitty?"

"I shouldn't have posted that," she said.

So there it was. Confirmation. "Why did you?"

"Good old-fashioned revenge, I guess. When I was pregnant, she told my husband it wasn't his."

"So you decided to do likewise?"

Puff. "It seemed like a good idea at the time."

At 3:17 in the morning. Little wonder. "How high were you?"

"What?"

Mistake. "Never mind."

"No, I heard you." Kitty shook her head, tossed the rest of the cigarette onto the walk, and stomped on it with her foot. "This isn't your business. I don't want you to be part of our lives. Neither does Brad." Something again flicked in her eyes. "I gotta go."

She turned to head back inside, but Myron put his hands on her shoulders.

"What else is going on here, Kitty?"

"Get your hands off me."

He didn't. He looked at her and saw that whatever connection he had made, it was gone now. She looked like a cornered animal now. A cornered, spiteful animal.

"Let. Go. Of. Me."

"There's no way Brad would put up with this."

"With what? We don't want you in our lives. You may want to forget what you did to us—"

"Just listen to me, okay?"

"Get your hands off me! Now!"

There was no talking to her. Her irrationality enraged him. Myron could feel his blood boil. He thought about all the terrible things she had done—how she had lied, how she had made his brother run away. He thought about her shooting up at the club and then he thought about her with Joel Fishman.

His voice had an edge now. "Have you really burned through that many brain cells, Kitty?"

"What are you talking about?"

He leaned in so that his face was inches from her. Through clenched teeth he said, "I found you via your drug dealer. You hit up Lex hoping to score drugs."

"Is that what Lex told you?"

"For crying out loud, look at yourself," Myron said, no longer disguising his disgust. "Are you really going to try to tell me you're not using?"

Tears flooded her eyes. "What are you, my drug counselor?"

"Think about how I found you."

Kitty's eyes narrowed in confusion. Myron waited. And then she saw it. He nodded.

"I know what you did at the club," Myron said, trying not to lose it. "I even have it on videotape."

She shook her head. "You don't know a thing."

"I know what I saw."

"You son of a bitch. Now I get it." She wiped the tears from her eyes. "You want to show it to Brad, right?"

"What? No."

"I can't believe this. You videotaped me?"

"Not me. The club. It's a surveillance video."

"And you tracked it down? You goddamn bastard."

"Hey," Myron snapped, "I'm not the one going down on a guy in a nightclub so I can shoot up."

She stepped back as though he'd slapped her. Dumb. He had forgotten his own warning. With strangers he knew how to talk, knew how to interrogate. With family, it always goes down the wrong road, doesn't it?

"I didn't mean . . . Look, Kitty, I really do want to help."

"Liar. Tell the truth for once."

"I am telling the truth. I do want to help."

"Not about that."

"What are you talking about?"

Kitty had the eerie, cagey smile of, well, a drug addict looking for a fix. "What would you say if you saw Brad again? Tell the truth."

That made him pull up. What, after all, did he want here? Win always cautioned him to keep his eyes on the prize. Accomplish the goals. One: Suzze had asked him to find Lex. Done. Two: Suzze had wanted to know who posted the "Not His" to her profile. Done.

Didn't Kitty, drug-addled and all, have a point? What would he say if he saw Brad? Sure, he would apologize and try to reconcile. But what then?

Would he just keep what he'd seen on the videotape a secret?

"Just as I thought." Kitty's expression was so smug and triumphant that more than anything in the world, he wanted to wallop her right in the face. "You'd tell him I'm some kind of whore."

"I don't think I'd have to tell him anything, Kitty. The tape kind of speaks for itself, doesn't it?"

She slapped him across the face. The drugs hadn't dulled the former great athlete's reflexes. The smack stung, the sound echoing. Kitty started to push past him again. With his cheek reddening, Myron reached out and grabbed her elbow, maybe a little too roughly. She tried to pull away. He tightened the grip, hitting the pressure point. She winced and said, "Ow, that hurts."

"You all right, ma'am?"

Myron turned. Two men from mall security were there. Myron let go of Kitty's elbow. Kitty dashed back into the mall. Myron started to follow, but the security guards stood their ground.

"It's not what it looks like," Myron told them.

They were too young to truly roll their eyes in the world-weary way such a line deserved, but they tried. "I'm sorry, sir, but we—"

No time to explain. Like a halfback, Myron juked right and then ran past them. "Hey! Stop!"

He didn't. He sprinted down the corridor. The security guards gave chase. He stopped by the merry-go-round's cross section, looked left toward Spencer's Gifts, straight ahead toward Macy's, right toward Starbucks.

Nothing.

Kitty was gone. Again. But maybe that was better. Maybe it was time to reevaluate, figure out what he should really do here. The security guards caught up to him. One looked ready to make a flying tackle, but Myron raised his hands in surrender.

"It's over, guys. I'm leaving."

By now, eight other mall security guards had appeared, but none wanted to create a scene. They escorted him outside of the mall. He slipped into his car. Way to go, Myron, he thought. You really handled that so well. But again, when he took a step back, what was left to do here anyway? He wanted to see his brother, but was it right to force the issue? He had waited sixteen years. He could wait a little more. Forget Kitty. He would try to reach out to Brad via that e-mail address maybe or through their father or something.

Myron's phone buzzed. He gave the nice security guards a little wave and reached into his pocket. The caller ID read: LEX RYDER.

"Hello?"

"Oh God . . ."

"Lex?"

"Please . . . hurry." He started sobbing. "Wheeling her out."

"Lex, calm down."

"My fault. Oh my God. Suzze . . ."

"What about Suzze?"

"You should have left it alone."

"Is Suzze okay?"

"Why didn't you just leave it alone?"

More sobbing. Myron felt icy fear in his chest. "Please, Lex, listen to me. I need you to calm down, so you can tell me what's going on."

"Hurry."

"Where are you?"

He started sobbing some more.

"Lex? I need to know where you are."

There was a choking noise, more sobs, and then three words: "In the ambulance."

It was hard to get more out of Lex.

Myron managed to learn that Suzze was being rushed to St. Anne's Medical Center. That was it. Myron texted Win and called Esperanza. "I'm on it," Esperanza said. Myron tried to plug in the hospital on his GPS, but his hand kept shaking and then the GPS kept taking too long, and when he started driving the car, that damn safety feature wouldn't let him plug the information in.

He got caught up in traffic on the New Jersey Turnpike, started laying on the horn and waving people over like a madman. Most drivers just ignored him. Some, he could see, picked up cell phones, probably calling the cops to warn them about the crazy person losing his mind in traffic.

Myron called Esperanza. "Any word?"

"The hospital won't say anything over the phone."

"Okay, call me if you learn anything. I should be there in another ten, fifteen."

It was fifteen. He pulled into the hospital's full and rather complicated lot. He circled a few times and then just figured the hell with it. He double-parked, blocking someone in, and left his keys. He ran toward the entrance, past the huddled smokers in the hospital scrubs, and into the ER. He stopped at the front desk, three people back, bouncing from one foot to the other like a six-year-old needing to go potty.

Finally, it was his turn. He told her why he was here. The woman behind the desk gave him the implacable "seen it all" face.

"Are you family?" she asked in a tone that would need technological help to be any flatter.

"I'm her agent and a close friend."

A practiced sigh. This, Myron could see, was going to be a waste of time. His eyes started darting around the room, looking for Lex or Suzze's mother or something. In the far corner, he was surprised to see Loren Muse, head county investigator. Myron had met Muse when a teenager named Aimee Biel vanished a few years back. Muse had her little cop pad out. She was talking to someone hidden behind the corner and taking notes.

"Muse?"

She spun toward him. Myron moved to his right. Whoa. He could see now that she'd been interviewing Lex. Lex looked beyond awful, all color drained from his face, his eyes staring up at nothing, his body leaning limply against the wall. Muse snapped the pad closed and started toward Myron. She was a short woman, barely five feet tall, and Myron was six-four. She stopped in front of him, looked up, and met his eye. Myron did not like what he saw.

"How is Suzze?" Myron asked.

"She's dead," Muse said.

17

It was a heroin overdose.

Muse explained it to Myron as he stood next to her, vision blurred, shaking his head no over and over again. When he was finally able to speak, he asked, "What about the baby?"

"Alive," Muse said. "Delivered via caesarean. A boy. He seems fine, but he's in the neonatal intensive care unit."

Myron tried to feel some kind of relief at this news, but the stunned and numb still won out. "Suzze wouldn't have killed herself, Muse."

"Might have been accidental."

"She wasn't using."

Muse nodded in that way cops do when they don't want to argue. "We'll investigate."

"She was clean."

Another patronizing nod.

"Muse, I'm telling you."

"What do you want me to say here, Myron? We'll investigate, but right now all signs point to a drug overdose. There was no forced entry. No signs of a struggle. She also had a pretty rich history of drug use."

"History. As in her past. She was having a baby."

"Hormones," Muse said. "They make us do stupid things."

"Come on, Muse. How many women eight months pregnant commit suicide?"

"And how many drug addicts really go clean forever and ever?"

He thought about his darling sister-in-law, Kitty, another addict who couldn't stay clean. Exhaustion started to weigh down his bones. Oddly—or maybe not—he started to think about his fiancée. Beautiful Terese. He suddenly wanted to walk away from this, right now, just give it up. He wanted to chuck it all. Screw the truth. Screw justice. Screw Kitty and Brad and Lex and whoever else and just grab the first flight back to Angola and be with the one person who could make all the madness disappear.

"Myron?"

He focused in on Muse.

"Can I see her?" he asked.

"You mean Suzze?"

"Yes."

"Why?"

He wasn't sure himself. Maybe it was a classic case of needing it to be real, of needing—and God, he hated that word—some sort of closure. He thought about Suzze's bouncing ponytail when she played tennis. He thought about her posing for those hilarious La-

La-Latte ads and her easy laugh and the way she chewed gum on the court and the look on her face when she asked him to be the godfather.

"I owe her," he said.

"Are you going to investigate this?"

He shook his head. "The case is all yours."

"There's no case right now. She's a drug overdose."

They headed back down the corridor and stopped in front of a door in the delivery wing. Muse said, "Wait here."

She slipped inside. When she came back out, she said, "The hospital's pathologist is with her. He, uh, cleaned her up, you know, after the caesarean."

"Okay."

"I'm doing this," Muse said, "because I still owe you a favor."

He nodded. "Consider it paid in full."

"I don't want it paid in full. I want you to be honest with me."

"Okay."

She opened the door and led him into the room. The man standing next to the gurney—Myron assumed that he was the pathologist—wore scrubs and stood perfectly still. Suzze was laid out on her back. Death does not make you look younger or older or peaceful or agitated. Death makes you look empty, hollow, like everything has fled, like a house suddenly abandoned. Death turns a body into a thing—a chair, a filing cabinet, a rock. Dust to dust, right? Myron wanted to buy all the rationales, all the stuff about life going on, that an echo of Suzze would live on in her child in the nursery down the hall, but right now it wasn't happening.

"So do you know anyone who'd want her dead?" Muse asked.

He offered up the easy answer: "No."

"The husband seems pretty shook up, but I've seen husbands who could channel Olivier after killing their wives. Anyway, Lex claims he flew in on a private jet from Adiona Island. When he got there, they were wheeling her out. We can check his time frame."

Myron said nothing.

"They own the building—Lex and Suzze," Muse went on. "There are no reports yet of anyone going in or out, but the security is pretty lax in that place. We might look into it more if we feel the need."

Myron approached the body. He put his hand on Suzze's cheek. Nothing. Like putting your hand on a chair, a file cabinet. "Who called it in?"

"That part seems a bit unusual," Muse said.

"How so?"

"A man with a Spanish accent made the call from the phone in her penthouse. When the paramedics got there, he was gone. We figured it was probably an illegal working in the building and didn't want to get in trouble." That made no sense, but Myron didn't want to get into that. Muse added, "Could be someone who was shooting up with her and didn't want trouble. Or even her dealer. Again, we'll look into it."

Myron turned to the pathologist. "Can I look at her arms?"

The pathologist glanced over at Muse. Muse nodded. The pathologist pulled back the sheet. Myron checked the veins. "Where did she shoot up?" he asked.

The pathologist pointed at a bruise in the crook of her elbow.

"You see some old tracks here?" Myron asked.

"Yes," the pathologist said. "Very old."

"Anything else fresh?"

"Not on the arms, no."

Myron looked at Muse. "That's because she hasn't used drugs in years."

"People shoot up in all different spots," Muse said. "Even in her heyday, what with wearing tennis outfits, rumor has it Suzze shot up in, er, less conspicuous places."

"So let's check that."

Muse shook her head. "What's the point?"

"I want you to see that she hadn't been using."

The pathologist cleared his throat. "There's no need," he said. "I already did a cursory examination of the body. I did indeed find some old scarring there, near the tattoo on her upper thigh, but there's nothing fresh."

"Nothing fresh," Myron repeated.

"That still doesn't prove it wasn't self-inflicted," Muse said. "Maybe she decided to do it in one big swoop, Myron. Maybe she was indeed clean and overdid it or overdosed intentionally."

Myron spread his hands, giving her incredulous. "When she was eight months pregnant?"

"Okay, fine, then you tell me: Who would want to kill her? And more than that, how? Like I said, no signs of struggle. No signs of forced entry. Show me one thing that says it wasn't a suicide or accidental OD."

Myron wasn't sure how much to say here. "She got a post on Facebook," he began. And then he stopped. A cold finger traced down his spine. Muse saw it.

"What?" she asked.

Myron turned to the pathologist. "You said she shot up near her tattoo?"

Again the pathologist looked toward Muse.

"Hold up a second," Loren Muse said. "What were you saying about a post on Facebook?"

Myron didn't wait. He reminded himself again that this wasn't Suzze, but this time he felt the tears push into his eyes. Suzze had survived so much, had finally come out on the right end, and now, just when she seemed to have everything within her grasp, well, it was time for Myron to step up. Screw the excuses. Suzze had been his friend. She had come to him for help. He owed her.

He pulled back the sheet before Muse could object. His eyes fell to her upper thigh, and yes, there it was. The tattoo. The same tattoo that was in the 'Not His' post. The same tattoo that Myron had just seen in the photo of Gabriel Wire.

"What's wrong?" Muse asked.

Myron stared down at the upper thigh. Gabriel Wire and Suzze had the same tattoo. The implication was obvious.

Muse: "What's that a tattoo of?"

Myron tried to slow down the swirl in his head. The tattoo had been in the online post—so how did Kitty know about it? Why did she put it in her post? And, of course, wouldn't Lex know about the same tattoo being on both his wife and his music partner?

Add it up. The words 'Not His.' A symbol that adorned the upper thighs of both Suzze and Gabriel Wire. No wonder that post had rocked Lex.

"Where's Lex?" Myron asked.

Muse folded her arms across her chest. "Are you really going to hold out on me?"

"It's probably nothing. Is he with the baby?"

She frowned, waited.

"Plus I can't say anything," Myron said. "At least not right now."

"What are you talking about?"

"I'm an attorney, Muse. I work for both Lex and Suzze."

"You're an agent."

"I'm also an attorney."

"Oh no. You're not going to pull out your Harvard JD on me. Not now. Not after I let you come in here and see the body."

"My hands are tied, Muse. I need to speak with my client."

"Your client?" Muse got up in his face and pointed at Suzze's corpse. "Go right ahead, but I'm not sure she'll hear you."

"Don't be cute. Where's Lex?"

"You're serious?"

"I am."

"You were the one who suggested I may be looking at a homicide here," Muse said. "So answer this for me: If indeed Suzze was murdered, who's my prime suspect?"

Myron didn't say anything. Muse cupped her hand around her ear. "I can't hear you, big boy. Come on, you know the answer because in these cases it's always the same: the husband. The husband is always the prime suspect. So what then, Myron? What if one of your clients killed another?"

Myron took one more glance down at Suzze. Dead. He felt so numb, as though his blood had stopped flowing. Suzze, dead. It was beyond his comprehension. He wanted to collapse now and pound on the floor and cry. He left the room and followed the signs for the nursery. Muse followed him.

"What were you saying about a Facebook post?" she asked.

"Not now, Muse."

He followed the arrow left. The nursery was on the left. He turned and looked through the window. There was a line of six newborns in those rolling acrylic cribs, all wearing a baby beanie and swaddled in a white blanket with pink and aqua stripes. The newborns were lined up as if for inspection. They'd all been immediately catalogued with an index card, either blue or pink, with name and time of birth.

Divided off from the nursery by more Plexiglas was the neonatal intensive care unit. There was only one parent with one child in there now. Lex sat in a rocking chair, but the chair didn't move. He wore a yellow smock. He cupped his son's head with his left hand, cradling the child on his right forearm. Tears lined his face. For a long moment, Myron just stood and watched him. Muse joined him.

"What the hell is going on here, Myron?"

"I don't know yet."

"Do you have any idea what the media is going to be like on this?"

Like he cared. He started for the door. A nurse stopped him and made him wash his hands. Then she put a yellow surgical smock and matching mask on him. Myron pushed open the door with his back. Lex did not look up.

"Lex?"

"Not now."

"I think we should talk."

Lex finally looked up. His eyes were bloodshot. When he spoke now, his voice was soft. "I asked you to leave it alone, didn't I?"

Silence. Later, Myron was sure, the words would sting. Later, when he settled down and tried to sleep, the guilt would reach into his chest and crush his heart like a Styrofoam cup. "I saw her tattoo," Myron said. "It was in that post."

He closed his eyes. "Suzze was the only woman I ever loved. And now she's gone. I mean, forever. I will never see Suzze again. I will never hold her. This boy—your godson—will never know his mother."

Myron said nothing. He felt a tremor start in his chest.

"We have to talk, Lex."

"Not tonight." His voice was surprisingly gentle now. "Tonight I just want to sit here and protect my son."

"Protect him from what?"

He didn't respond. Myron felt his phone buzz. He took a surreptitious glance and saw that the call was coming from his father. He stepped out of the room and put the phone to his ear. "Dad?"

"I heard about Suzze on the radio. Is it true?"

"Yes. I'm at the hospital now."

"I'm so sorry."

"Thanks. I'm kind of busy here. . . ."

"When you're done, do you think you could swing by the house?"

"Tonight?"

"If possible."

"Is something wrong?"

"I just need to talk to you about something," Dad said. "Don't worry how late. I'll be awake."

18

Before leaving the hospital, Myron played lawyer and warned Loren Muse not to speak to his client Lex Ryder without legal counsel. She responded that he should be fruitful and multiply, but not in those exact words. Win and Esperanza arrived. Win filled him in on his prison encounter with Frank Ache. Myron wasn't sure what to make of it.

"Perhaps," Win said, "we should meet with Herman Ache."

"Perhaps," Myron said, "we should meet with Gabriel Wire." He turned to Esperanza. "Let's also check on our favorite French teacher, see where Crush was at the time of Suzze's death."

"Okay," Esperanza said.

"I can drive you home," Win said.

But Myron shook him off. He needed the downtime. He needed to take a step back. Maybe Muse was right. Maybe it was a drug overdose. Last night, on that balcony overlooking Manhattan, all that talk about secrets, all that guilt about Kitty and the past— maybe it summoned up old demons. Maybe the answer would be as simple as that.

Myron got into his car and headed back to his home in Livingston. He called Dad to let him know that he was on his way. "Drive safely," his father said. Myron hoped that maybe his father would offer up a clue about what they needed to discuss, but he didn't. AM radio was already reporting the death of "former troubled tennis sensation Suzze T," and Myron again wondered about the inept shortcutting of the media.

It was dark by the time Myron pulled up to his familiar abode. The light in the upstairs bedroom—the one he had shared with Brad when they were both very young—was on, and Myron looked up at it. He could see the outline of the long-faded Tot Finder sticker, something the Livingston Fire Department had handed out during the early Carter administration. The image on the sticker was dramatic, a brave fireman, his chin up, carrying a limp, long-haired child to safety. Now the room was a home office.

His car lights caught a For Sale sign on the Nussbaums' front lawn. Myron had gone to high school with their son Steve, though everyone called him either "Nuss" or "Baum," a friendly kid Myron really liked but for some reason never hung out with. The Nussbaums had been one of the original families, buying in when this farmland was originally turned into housing forty years ago. The Nussbaums loved it here. They loved to garden and putter and work on the gazebo in the backyard. They brought the Bolitars the extra tomatoes from their garden, and if you've never tried a Jersey tomato in August, you just don't get it. Now even the Nussbaums were moving out.

Myron parked in the driveway. He saw movement in the window. Dad had probably been watching, the ever-present silent sentinel. When Myron was a teen, he had no curfew because, his father explained, he'd shown enough responsibility not to need one. Al Bolitar was a terrible sleeper, and Myron could not remember a time, no matter what hour he returned home, when his father was not up waiting for him. His father needed everything in place before he could close his eyes. Myron wondered whether it was still that way for him, and how his sleep had changed when his younger son ran off with Kitty and never returned.

He parked the car. Suzze was dead. He had never been big on denial, but he was still having trouble wrapping his brain around that one. She was about to start the next big chapter of her life—motherhood. He often imagined the day his own parents first came by this dwelling, his father struggling at the plant in Newark, his mom pregnant. He pictured El-Al, young, holding hands the way they always do, walking up the concrete path, gazing at this split-level and deciding, yes, this would be the place that would shelter their new family and hold their hopes and dreams. He wondered now, as they looked back, whether those dreams came true or whether there were regrets.

Soon Myron would be married too. Terese couldn't have children. He knew that. He had spent his whole life wanting the American Dream family—the house, the picket fence, the two-car garage, the two-point-four kids, the barbecue in the back, the basketball hoop on the garage—in short, the life of the people here like the Nussbaums and the Browns and the Lyons and the Fonteras and the El-Al Bolitars. Apparently it was not meant to be.

Mom, blunt as she was, had made a good point about selling

the house. You can't hold on too tightly. He wanted Terese home, with him, where she belonged, because in the end, only your lover can make the world disappear, and yes, he knew how corny that sounded.

Myron trudged up the concrete walk, lost in this thought, and maybe that was why he didn't sense the danger before it struck. Or maybe his attacker was good, patient, crouching in the dark, waiting until Myron was close enough or distracted enough to pounce.

First came the flash of light. Twenty years ago, Dad had installed motion-detector lights in the front of the house. This had been a big marvel to his parents, on par with the discovery of electricity or cable television. For weeks, El-Al had tested this new technology, trying to walk or even crawl deliberately, seeing whether they could fool the motion detector. Mom and Dad would approach from various angles, at various speeds, laughing heartily whenever the light would snap on, catching them every time. The simple pleasures.

Whoever had jumped out of the bush had been picked up by the motion detector. Myron saw a flash of light, heard a noise, a rush of wind, the sound of exertion, maybe words. He turned toward it, and saw the fist heading straight for his face.

There was no time to duck, no time to get up a forearm block. The blow was going to land. Myron turned from it. It was simple science. Move with the punch, not against it. Turning lessened the impact, but the powerful blow, delivered clearly by a strong man, still packed a wallop. For a moment Myron saw stars. He shook his head, tried to clear it.

An angry snarl of a voice: "Leave us alone."

Another punch came at Myron's head. The only way to get away from it, Myron saw, was to fall on his back. He did, the knuckles grazing the top of his skull. It still hurt. Myron was about to start rolling away, rolling to safety so he could regroup, when he heard another noise. Someone had opened the front door. And then a panicked voice: "Myron!"

Damn. It was Dad.

Myron was about to call out for his father to stay where he was, that he'd be fine, that he should go inside and call the police, that whatever he did, he should not come out.

Not a chance.

Before Myron could open his mouth, Dad was already in mid-sprint.

"You son of a bitch!" his father shouted.

Myron found his voice. "Dad, no!"

Useless. His son was in trouble, and as he always had, his father hurled himself toward it. Still flat on his back, Myron looked up at the silhouette of his attacker. He was a tall man, his hands balled into fists, but he made the mistake of turning at the sound of Al Bolitar's approach. His body language altered in a surprising way. The hands suddenly went loose. Myron moved fast. Using his feet, he wrapped up his attacker's right ankle. He was about to turn hard, trapping the ankle, snapping it or tearing the tendons ten ways to Sunday when he saw his father leap—actually leap at the age of seventy-four—toward the attacker. The attacker was big. Dad had no chance, and he probably knew it. But that didn't matter to him.

Myron's father reached out his arms like a linebacker blitzing the quarterback. Myron tightened the ankle trap, but the big man didn't even lift a hand to protect himself, just letting Al Bolitar knock him off balance.

"Get away from my son!" Dad yelled, wrapping his arms around the assailant, both crumpling to the ground.

Myron moved fast now. He rolled up to his knees, getting his hand ready for a palm strike to the nose or throat. Dad was involved now—no time to waste. He had to put this guy out of commission in a hurry. He grabbed the man's hair, pulled him out of the shadows, and straddled his chest. Myron cocked his fist. He was just about to snap a right into the nose when the light hit the attacker's face. What Myron saw made him pause for a split second. The attacker's head was turned toward the left, looking with concern at Myron's father. His face, his features . . . they were so damned familiar.

Then Myron heard the man—no, he was a kid, really—beneath him say one word: "Grandpa?"

The voice was young; the snarl gone.

Dad sat up. "Mickey?"

Myron looked down as his nephew turned back toward him. Their eyes met, a color so much like his own, and Myron would swear later that he felt a physical jolt. Mickey Bolitar, Myron's nephew, pushed the hand off his hair and rolled hard to the side.

"Get the hell off me."

Dad was out of breath.

Myron and Mickey both snapped out of the stun and helped him to his feet. His face was flushed. "I'm fine," Dad said with a grimace. "Let go of me."

Mickey turned back to Myron. Myron was six-four, and Mickey

looked to be about the same. The kid was broad and powerfully built—every kid today lifts weights—but he was still a kid. He jabbed Myron's chest with his finger.

"Stay away from my family."

"Where's your father, Mickey?"

"I said—"

"I heard you," Myron said. "Where's your father?"

Mickey took a step back and looked toward Al Bolitar. When he said, "I'm sorry, Grandpa," he sounded so damn young.

Dad had his hands on his knees. Myron went to help him, but he shook him off. He stood straight and there was something akin to pride on his face. "It's okay, Mickey. I understand."

"What do you mean, you understand?" Myron turned back to Mickey. "What the hell was that all about?"

"Just stay away from us."

Seeing his nephew for the very first time—like this—it was surreal and overwhelming. "Look, why don't we go inside and talk this out?"

"Why don't you go to hell?"

Mickey took one last concerned look at his grandfather. Al Bolitar nodded, as if to say all was fine. Then Mickey shot Myron a hard glare and ran into the darkness. Myron was about to go after him, but Dad put a hand on his forearm. "Let him go." Al Bolitar was red-faced and breathing hard, but he was also smiling. "Are you okay, Myron?"

Myron touched his mouth. His lip was bleeding. "I'll live. Why are you smiling?"

Dad kept his eyes on the road where Mickey had vanished into the darkness. "Kid's got balls."

"You're kidding, right?"

"Come on," Dad said. "Let's go inside and talk."

They headed into the downstairs TV room. For most of Myron's childhood, Dad had a Barcalounger, reserved specifically for him, the kind of dinosaur of a recliner that was eventually held together with duct tape. Nowadays there was a five-piece sectional called the "Multiplex II" with built-in recliners and storage areas for beverages. Myron had bought it from a place called Bob's Discount Furniture, though originally he had been resistant because Bob's radio commercials were four steps beyond grating.

"I'm really sorry about Suzze," Dad said.

"Thank you."

"Do you know what happened?"

"Not yet, no. I'm working on it." Dad's face was still red from the exertion. "Are you sure you're okay?"

"I'm fine."

"Where's Mom?"

"She's out with Aunt Carol and Sadie."

"I could use a glass of water," Myron said. "How about you?"

"Okay. And put some ice on your lip so it doesn't swell."

Myron headed up the three steps to the kitchen, grabbed two glasses, filled them up from the overpriced water dispenser. There were ice packs in the freezer. He grabbed one and headed back to the TV room. He handed a glass to Dad and sat in the recliner on the right.

"I can't believe that just happened," Myron said. "The first time I see my nephew and he attacks me."

"Do you blame him?" Dad asked.

Myron sat up. "Excuse me?"

"Kitty called me," Dad said. "She told me about your run-in at the mall."

Myron should have known. "Did she now?"

"Yes."

"And that's the reason Mickey jumped me?"

"Didn't you suggest his mother was something"—Dad stopped, searched for the word, couldn't find it—"something bad?"

"She is something bad."

"And if someone suggested that about your mother? How would you have reacted?"

Dad was smiling again. He was riding some kind of high from the adrenaline rush of combat or maybe pride in his grandson. Al Bolitar had been born poor in Newark and grew up on the city's tougher streets. He started working for a butcher on Mulberry Street when he was just eleven. The majority of his adult life was spent running an undergarment factory in Newark's North Ward near the Passaic River. His office, as it were, loomed above the assembly line floor, all glass so he could see out and his employees could see in. He tried to save the plant during the riots in 1967, but the looters burned it down, and while Dad eventually rebuilt it and went back to work, he never quite looked at his employees or the city the same again.

"Think about it," Dad said. "Think about what you said to Kitty. Suppose someone had said that to your mother."

"My mother isn't Kitty."

"You think that matters to Mickey?"

Myron shook his head. "Why would Kitty tell him what I said?"

"What, a mother should lie?"

When Myron was eight years old, he got into a pushing fight

195

with Kevin Werner outside Burnet Hill Elementary School. His parents sat in the school office and heard a stern lecture from the principal, Mr. Celebre, on the evils of fighting. When they got home, Mom headed upstairs without saying a word. Dad sat him down in this very room. Myron expected a fairly severe punishment. Instead his father leaned forward and looked him dead in the eye. "You'll never get in trouble with me for getting in a fight," he said. "If you find yourself in a situation where you need to step outside and settle it, I'm not going to question your judgment. You fight if you have to. You never run away from it. You never back down." And as crazy and surprising as this advice may have seemed, Myron had indeed backed down from fights in the years to come, doing the "prudent" thing, and the truth—a truth that probably explained what his friends described as his hero complex—was that no beating hurts as much as backing down.

"This is what you wanted to talk to me about?" Myron said.

Dad nodded. "You need to promise me you'll leave them alone. And you already know this, but you shouldn't have said what you did to your brother's wife."

"I just wanted to talk to Brad."

"He's not around," Dad said.

"Where is he?"

"He's on some kind of charity mission in Bolivia. Kitty didn't want to give me the details."

"Maybe there's trouble."

"Between Brad and Kitty?" Dad took a sip of water. "Maybe there is. But that's not our business."

"So if Brad is off in Bolivia, what are Kitty and Mickey doing here?"

"They're looking to settle back in the States. They're debating between this area and California."

Another lie, Myron was sure. Way to manipulate the old man, Kitty. Get Myron off my back and maybe we will want to live near you. Keep him bugging us and we move across the country. "Why now? Why did they come back home after all these years?"

"I don't know. I didn't ask."

"Dad, I know you like to give your kids privacy, but I think you're taking this not-interfering thing a little too far."

He chuckled at that. "You have to give them room, Myron. I never told you how I felt about Jessica, for example."

Again with his old girlfriend. "Wait, I thought you liked Jessica."

"She was bad news," Dad said.

"But you never said anything."

"It wasn't my place."

"Maybe you should have," Myron said. "Maybe it would have saved me a lot of heartache."

Dad shook his head. "I would do anything to protect you"—he almost glanced outside, having proved the point mere minutes ago—"but the best way to do that is to let you make your own mistakes. A mistake-proof life is not worth living."

"So I just let it go?"

"For now, yes. Brad knows you reached out—Kitty will tell him. I e-mailed him too. If he wants to reach back, he will."

Myron flashed to another memory: Brad, age seven, getting bullied at sleepaway camp. Myron remembered Brad just sitting out by the old softball field by himself. Brad had made the last out and the bullies had taunted en masse. Myron tried to sit with him but Brad just kept crying and telling Myron to go away. It was one of those times you feel so helpless you'd kill to make the pain go away. He remembered another time, when the entire Bolitar family went to Miami during the February school break. He and Brad shared a hotel room, and one night, after a fun-filled day at the Parrot Jungle, Myron asked him about school and Brad broke down and cried and said that he hated it and had no friends and it broke Myron's heart in about a thousand places. The next day, sitting out by the pool, Myron asked Dad what he should do about it. His father's advice had been simple: "Don't raise it. Don't make him sad now. Just let him enjoy his vacation."

Brad had been gawky, awkward, a later bloomer. Or maybe it had just been growing up behind Myron.

"I thought you wanted us to reconcile," Myron said.

"I do. But you can't force it. Give them room."

His father was still breathing hard from the earlier altercation. There was no reason to get him all upset now. It could wait until the morning. But then: "Kitty is using drugs," Myron said.

Dad raised an eyebrow. "You know this?"

"Yes."

Dad rubbed his chin and considered this new development. Then: "You still need to leave them alone."

"Are you serious?"

"Did you know that at one point your mother was addicted to painkillers?"

Myron said nothing, stunned.

"It's getting late," Dad said. He started to get up from the couch. "You okay?"

"Wait, you're just going to drop this bomb on me and walk away?"

"It wasn't a big deal. That's my point. We worked it out."

Myron didn't know what to say. He also wondered what Dad would make of it if he told him about Kitty's sex act in the night-club, and man, he hoped that Dad wouldn't use another Mom-did-same analogy on that one.

Give it a rest for the night, Myron thought. No reason to do anything hasty. There will be nothing new until daylight. They heard a car pull into the driveway and then the sound of a car door slamming shut.

"That will be your mother." Al Bolitar rose gingerly. Myron stood too. "Don't tell her about tonight. I don't want her worrying."

"Okay. Hey, Dad?"

"Yes?"

"Nice tackle out there."

Dad tried not to smile. Myron looked at the aging face. He had that overwhelming feeling, the melancholy one he got when he realized that his parents were getting older. He wanted to say more, wanted to thank him, but he knew that his father knew all that and that any additional discussion on the subject would be unseemly or superfluous. Let the moment alone. Let it breathe.

19

At two thirty A.M., Myron headed upstairs to that same childhood bedroom he'd shared with Brad, the one that still had the Tot Finder sticker on the window, and flipped on the computer.

He logged on to Skype. The screen opened on Terese's face, and as always, he felt the heady rush and, yep, the lightness in his chest.

"God, you're beautiful," he said.

Terese smiled. "May I speak frankly?"

"Please."

"You are the sexiest man I've ever known, and right now, just looking at you is driving me up a wall."

Myron sat up a little taller. Talk about the perfect medicine. "I'm trying very hard not to preen," he said. "And I'm not even sure what preening is."

"May I continue to be frank?" she asked.

"Please."

"I would be willing to try, uh, something via video, but I don't quite get it, do you?"

"I confess I don't."

"Does that make us old-fashioned? I don't get computer sex or phone sex or any of that."

"I tried phone sex once," Myron said.

"And?"

"And I never felt so self-conscious in my life. I started laughing at a particularly inopportune stage."

"Okay, so we're in agreement."

"Yep."

"You're not just saying that? Because, you know, I mean, I know we're far apart—"

"I'm not just saying that."

"Good," Terese said. "So what's going on over there?"

"How much time do you have?" Myron asked.

"Maybe another twenty minutes."

"How about we spend ten of it just talking like this and then I'll tell you?"

Even through a computer monitor, Terese looked at him as though he were the only man in the world. Everything vanished. There was just the two of them. "That bad?" she said.

"Yes."

"Okay, handsome. You lead, I will follow."

But that didn't work. He told her right away about Suzze. When he finished, Terese said, "So what are you going to do?"

"I want to chuck it all. I'm just so tired."

She nodded.

"I want to come back to Angola. I want to marry you and just stay there."

"I want that too," she said.

"There's a 'but' coming."

"Not really, no," Terese said. "Nothing would make me happier. I want to be with you more than you could ever know."

"But?"

"But you can't leave. You're not built that way. For one, you can't just abandon Esperanza and the business."

"I could sell her my share."

"No, you can't. And even if you could, you need to learn the truth about Suzze. You need to figure out what's going on with your brother. You need to look after your parents. You can't just dump that all and come here."

"And you can't come home," Myron said.

"Not yet, no."

"So what does that mean?"

Terese shrugged. "We're screwed. But just for a little while. You will find out what happened to Suzze and settle things."

"You sound confident."

"I know you. You'll do all that. And then, well, when things are settled, you can come for a long visit, right?"

She arched an eyebrow and smiled at him. He smiled back. He could actually feel the muscles in his shoulders relax.

"Definitely right," he said.

"Myron?"

"Yes."

"Do it quickly."

Myron called Lex in the morning. No reply. He called Buzz. Same. Chief County Investigator Loren Muse, however, answered her cell phone—Myron still had the number from their previous encounter. He persuaded her to meet him at Suzze and Lex's high-rise, the scene of the drug overdose.

"If it will help wrap this up," Muse said, "you're on."

"Thank you."

An hour later, Muse met up with him in the front lobby. They got into the elevator and started up to the top floor.

"According to the preliminary autopsy," Muse said, "Suzze T died of respiratory arrest caused by an overdose of heroin. I don't know if you know much about opiate overdoses, but classically the drug just decreases the victim's ability to breathe until it just stops. Often the victim still has a pulse and survives for several minutes without breathing. I think that's what helped save the baby, but I'm not a doctor. There were no other drugs in her system. No one conked her on the head or anything like that—no signs of any physical altercation whatsoever."

"In short," Myron said, "nothing new."

"Well, there's one thing. I found that post you were talking about last night. On Suzze's Facebook. The one that said, 'Not his.'"

"And you think what?"

"I think," Muse said, "that maybe it's true."

"Suzze swore it wasn't."

Muse rolled her eyes. "And, gee, no woman would ever lie about paternity. Think about it. Suppose the baby isn't Lex Ryder's. Maybe she felt guilty. Maybe she worried about being exposed."

"You could always run a paternity test on the baby," Myron said. "Find out for sure."

"Sure I *could*, if I were investigating a murder. If I were investigating a murder, I might ask for a court order. But like I said, I'm not. I'm giving you a reason why a woman may have taken a drug overdose. Period, the end."

"Maybe Lex will let you do the DNA test anyway."

The elevator arrived as Muse said, "Well, well, well."

"What?"

"You don't know."

"Don't know what?"

"I thought you were Lex's hotshot defense attorney."

"Meaning?"

"Meaning, Lex is already gone with the baby," Muse said.

"What do you mean, 'gone'?"

"This way." They started up the spiral staircase that led to the rooftop terrace.

"Muse?"

"As you, a shining star of a defense lawyer already know, I have no reason to hold Lex Ryder. Early this morning, against doctor's orders, he checked his newborn son out of the hospital—as is his right. He left his pal Buzz behind and hired a pediatric nurse to accompany him."

"Where did they go?"

"Since there's no murder here or even suspicion of one, I had no reason to actively pursue his destination." Muse reached the rooftop. Myron followed. She walked over to the Cleopatra-like chaise near the arch. Muse stopped, looked down, and pointed at the chair.

Her tone turned dead serious. "Here."

Myron looked down at the smooth ivory chaise. No blood, no wrinkles, no sign of death. You would expect a chair would show something about what had taken place. "This is where they found her?"

Muse nodded. "The needle was on the floor. She was passed out, totally unresponsive. The only prints on the needle are hers."

Myron looked out through the arch. In the distance, the Manhattan skyline beckoned. The water was still. The sky was purple and gray. He closed his eyes and traveled back two nights ago. When the wind whipped across the balcony, Myron could almost hear Suzze's words: *"Sometimes people do need help. . . . Maybe you don't know it, but you saved my life a hundred times."*

But not this time. This time, per Lex's request, he had backed off, hadn't he? He had finished up her favor—they knew who posted "Not His," they knew where Lex was—and Myron had chosen to butt out, to leave Suzze on her own.

Myron kept his eyes on the skyline. "You said a guy with a Spanish accent made the nine-one-one call?"

"Yes. He used one of their portable phones. It was on the floor downstairs. Probably dropped it when he was running out. We checked it for prints, but everything is pretty smeared up on it. We have Lex's and Suzze's and that's about it. When the paramedics got here, the door was still open. They came in and found her up here."

Myron jammed his hands into his pockets. The breeze hit his

face. "You realize that your theory about an illegal immigrant or maintenance worker makes no sense."

"Why not?"

"A janitor or whatever walks by, happens to see—what?—the door ajar, comes all the way into the apartment, and then, I guess, goes out on the roof?"

Muse thought about that. "You have a point."

"It is much more likely that the person who called was here with her when she shot up."

"So?"

"What do you mean, so?"

"Like I said before, I'm in this for the crime, not curiosity. If she was shooting up with a friend and if he or she ran, I'm really not up for prosecuting that. If it was her drug dealer, okay, maybe if I can find the person and then prove he sold her the drugs, but really, that's not what I'm trying to find out."

"I was with her the night before, Muse."

"I know."

"I was right here on this very roof. She was troubled, but she wasn't suicidal."

"So you told me," Muse said. "But think about it—troubled but not suicidal. That's a pretty fine distinction. And for the record, I never said she was suicidal. But she was troubled, right? That could have led to her falling off the wagon—and maybe she just fell too hard."

The wind kicked up again. Suzze's voice—was this the last thing she said to him?—came with it: *We all keep secrets, Myron.*

"And here's another thing to think about," Muse said. "If this was a murder, it was pretty much the dumbest one I've ever seen. Let's say you wanted Suzze dead. Let's say you could even somehow get her to take the heroin on her own without physical force. Maybe you put a gun against her head, whatever. You with me?"

"Go on."

"Well, if you want to kill her, why not just kill her? Why call nine-one-one and take the chance that she'd be alive when they got here? For that matter, with the amount of drugs she took, why not lead her under that arch and get her to fall off? Either way, what you do *not* do is call the paramedics or leave with the door open for a janitor or whatever. Do you see what I mean?"

"I do," Myron said.

"Am I making sense?"

"You are."

"Do you have anything that disputes what I said?"

"Not a thing," Myron said, trying to sort it through in his head. "So if you're right, she probably contacted her dealer yesterday. Any clues on who it was?"

"Not yet, no. We know that she took a drive yesterday. There was an E-ZPass hit on the Garden State Parkway near Route Two-eighty. She could have headed to Newark."

Myron considered that. "Did you check her car?"

"Her car? No. Why?"

"Do you mind if I check it?"

"Do you have keys?"

"I do."

She shook her head. "Agents. Go ahead. I have to get back to work."

"One more question, Muse."

Muse just waited.

"Why are you showing me all this after I pulled the attorney-client card last night?"

"Because right now I have no case anyway," she said. "And because if somehow I'm missing something—if somehow this was a murder—it doesn't matter who you're supposed to defend. You cared about Suzze. You wouldn't just let her killer walk."

They headed down the elevator in silence. Muse got off at ground level. Myron went down to the garage. He hit the remote control and listened for the beep. Suzze drove a Mercedes S63 AMG. He opened it and slipped into the driver's seat. He got a whiff of some wildflower perfume and it made him think of Suzze. He opened the glove compartment and found the registration, insurance card, and the car manual. He searched under the seats for—he wasn't sure what, really. Clues. All he found was loose change and two pens. Sherlock Holmes probably could have used them to figure out exactly where Suzze had gone, but Myron couldn't.

He turned the car on, started up the dashboard GPS. He hit "previous destinations" and saw a list of spots Suzze had plugged in for directions. Sherlock Holmes, eat your heart out. The most recent destination was in Kasselton, New Jersey. Hmm. In order to get there, you'd have to take the Garden State Parkway past Exit 146 per the E-ZPass records.

The second-to-last input was an intersection in Edison, New Jersey. Myron pulled out his BlackBerry and started typing in the addresses listed. When he finished he e-mailed them to Esperanza. She could look them up online, figure out whether any of them were important. There were no dates next to inputs, so for all Myron knew, Suzze had visited these places months ago and rarely used the GPS.

Still all signs pointed to the fact that Suzze visited Kasselton recently, maybe even the day of her death. It might be worth a quick visit.

20

The address in Kasselton was a four-store strip mall anchored by a Kings Supermarket. The other three storefronts housed a Renato's Pizzeria, a make-your-own ice cream parlor called SnowCap, and an old-school barbershop dubbed "Sal and Shorty Joe's Hair-Clipping," complete with the classic red-and-white pole out front.

So why had Suzze come out here?

There were, of course, supermarkets and ice cream parlors and pizzerias far closer to her home and somehow Myron doubted that either Sal or Shorty Joe did Suzze's hair. So why drive out this way? Myron stood there and waited for the answer to come to him. Two minutes passed. The answer did not arrive, so Myron decided to give it a nudge.

He started with the Kings Supermarket. Not sure what else to

do, he flashed a picture of Suzze T around and asked whether anyone had seen her. Working old-school. Like Sal and Shorty Joe. A
few people recognized Suzze from her tennis days. A few had seen
her on the news last night and assumed Myron was a cop, an as-
sumption he did little to correct. In the end though, no one had seen
her in the supermarket.

Strike one.

Myron headed back outside. He looked out at the parking lot.
Best odds? Suzze had driven here for a drug buy. Drug dealers,
especially in suburbia, used public lots all the time. You park your
cars side by side, open front windows, someone tosses money from
one car to another, someone tosses drugs back.

He tried to picture it. Suzze, the woman who had told him the
night before about secrets and worried about being too competitive, all eight months pregnant of her, the woman who walked
into his office two days earlier saying, "I'm so damn happy"—that
Suzze had driven out to this strip mall to buy enough heroin to kill
herself?

Sorry, no, Myron wasn't buying it.

Maybe she was meeting someone else, not a drug dealer, in this
lot. Maybe, maybe not. Great detective work so far. Okay, there
was still work to be done. Renato's Pizzeria was closed. The barbershop, however, was doing business. Through the storefront window, Myron could see the older men jabbering away, arguing in
that good-natured ways guys do, looking remarkably content. He
turned to SnowCap ice cream parlor. Someone was hanging up a
sign: HAPPY BIRTHDAY, LAUREN! Girls, probably around the age of
eight, maybe nine, were heading inside toting birthday presents.
Their mothers held their hands, exhausted, harried, happy.

Suzze's voice: *"I'm so damned happy."*

This, he thought, looking at the mothers, should have been Suzze's life. It would have been. It was what Suzze wanted. People do dumb things. They throw away happiness as though it were a soiled napkin. That could have been what happened here—Suzze, so close to true joy, messed it up as was her wont.

He looked through the parlor's front window and watched the little girls pull away from their mothers and greet one another with squeals and hugs. The parlor was a swirl of colors and movement. The mothers moved to the corner with the coffee urn. Myron again tried to picture Suzze here, where she belonged, when he noticed a man standing behind the counter, staring at him. The man was older, midsixties, with the middle-management belly spread and citation-worthy comb-over. He stared at Myron through glasses that were a touch too fashionable, like something a hip urban architect might sport, and he kept pushing them back up his nose.

The manager, Myron figured. Probably always looking out the window like this, guarding the grounds, a busybody. Perfect. Myron approached the door with Suzze T's picture at the ready. By the time he got to the door, the man was already there, holding it open.

"Can I help you?" the man asked.

Myron held up the picture. The man looked at the photograph and his eyes closed.

"Have you seen this woman?" Myron asked.

His voice seemed very far away. "I spoke to her yesterday."

This guy did not look like a drug dealer. "What about?"

The man swallowed, started to turn away. "My daughter," he said. "She wanted to know about my daughter."

*   *   *

"Follow me," the man said.

They walked past the ice cream counter. The woman working behind it was in a wheelchair. She had a great big smile and was telling a customer about the oddly named ice cream flavors and all the possible ingredients you could mix into them. Myron glanced to his left. The party was in full swing. The girls were taking turns mixing and mashing ice cream in order to create their own flavors. Two high school–age girls helped with the heavy scooping while another mixed in Reese's Pieces, cookie dough, Oreos, sprinkles, Gummi Bears, nuts, chocolate chips, even granola.

"Do you like ice cream?" the man asked.

Myron spread his hands. "Who doesn't like ice cream?"

"Not many people, knock wood." The man rapped a Formica tabletop with his knuckles as they passed. "What flavor can I get you?"

"I'm fine, thank you."

But he wouldn't take no for an answer. "Kimberly?"

The woman in the wheelchair looked up.

"Make our guest here the SnowCap Melter."

"Sure thing."

The store was blanketed with the SnowCap ice cream logo. That should have given it to him. SnowCap. Snow. Myron took another look at the man's face. The fifteen years had been neither a friend nor an enemy to the man—normal aging—but now Myron started to put it together.

"You're Karl Snow," Myron said. "Alista's father."

"Are you a cop?" he asked Myron.

Myron hesitated.

"It doesn't matter. I've got nothing to say."

Myron decided to give him a push. "Are you going to help cover up another murder?"

Myron expected shock or outrage, but instead he got a firm headshake. "I read the papers. Suzze T died of an overdose."

Maybe a bigger push: "Right, and your daughter just fell out a window."

Myron regretted the words the moment they escaped his lips. Too much too soon. He waited for the eruption. It didn't come. Karl Snow's face sagged. "Sit down," he said. "Tell me who you are."

Myron sat facing Karl Snow and introduced himself. Behind Snow, Lauren's birthday party was growing happily rowdy. Myron thought about the obvious juxtaposition—a girl's birthday party being hosted by a man who lost his own—but then he let it go.

"The news said she overdosed," Karl Snow said. "Is that true?"

"I'm not sure," Myron said. "That's why I'm looking into it."

"I don't get it. Why you? Why not the police?"

"Could you just tell me why she was here?"

Karl Snow leaned back, pushed his glasses back up his nose. "Let me ask you something before we get into this. Do you have any evidence at all that Suzze T was murdered—yes or no?"

"For one thing," Myron said, "there's the fact that she was eight months pregnant and looking forward to starting a family."

He did not look impressed. "That doesn't sound like much evidence."

"It's not," Myron said. "But here's what I do know for certain.

Suzze drove out here yesterday. She talked to you. A few hours later, she was dead."

He glanced behind him. The young woman in the wheelchair started toward them with an ice cream monstrosity. Myron started to get up to help, but Karl Snow shook his head. Myron stayed where he was.

"One SnowCap Melter," the woman said, putting it in front of Myron. "Enjoy."

The Melter would have trouble fitting in the trunk of a car. Myron half expected the table to tilt over. "This is for one person?" Myron asked.

"Yep," she said.

He looked at her. "Does it come with angioplasty or maybe a shot of insulin?"

She rolled her eyes. "Golly, I've never heard that one before."

Karl Snow said, "Mr. Bolitar, meet my daughter Kimberly."

"Nice to meet you," Kimberly said, awarding him with the kind of smile that makes the cynical think about the celestial. They chatted for a minute or two—she was the store manager, Karl just owned the place—and then she wheeled herself back behind the counter.

Karl was still watching his daughter when he said, "She was twelve when Alista . . ." He stopped, as though not sure what word to use. "Their mother died two years earlier from breast cancer. I didn't handle it well. I started drinking too much. Kimberly was born with CP. She needed constant care. I guess that Alista, well, I guess she slipped through the cracks."

As if on cue, a big laugh exploded from the party behind him. Myron glanced over at Lauren, the birthday girl. She too was smiling, a ring of chocolate around her mouth.

"I have no interest in hurting you or your daughter," Myron said.

"If I talk to you now," he said slowly, "I need you to promise me I won't see you again. I can't have the media back in our lives."

"I promise."

Karl Snow rubbed his face with both hands. "Suzze wanted to know about Alista's death."

Myron waited for him to say more. When he didn't, he asked, "What did she want to know?"

"She wanted to know if Gabriel Wire killed my daughter."

"What did you say?"

"I told her that after meeting privately with Mr. Wire, I no longer believed that he was culpable. I told her that, in the end, it was a tragic accident and that I was satisfied with that result. I also told her that the settlement is confidential, so that was really all I could say."

Myron just stared at him. Karl Snow had said it all in a practiced monotone. Myron waited for Snow to meet his eye. He didn't. Instead Snow shook his head and said softly, "I can't believe she's dead."

Myron didn't know whether he was talking about Suzze or Alista. Karl Snow blinked, looked off toward Kimberly. The sight seemed to give him strength. "Have you ever lost a child, Mr. Bolitar?"

"No."

"I'll spare you the clichés. In fact, I'll spare you altogether. I know how people view me: the unfeeling father who took a big payday in exchange for letting his daughter's killer go free."

"And that wasn't the case?"

216

"Sometimes you have to love a child privately. And sometimes you have to grieve privately."

Myron was not sure what that meant, so he waited.

"Eat some of the ice cream," Karl said, "or Kimberly will notice. That girl has eyes in the back of her head."

Myron reached for the spoon and tried the whipped cream with the first layer of what looked like cookies 'n' cream. Manna.

"Good?"

"Manna," Myron said.

He smiled again, but there was no joy in it. "Kimberly invented the Melter."

"She's a genius."

"She's a good daughter. And she loves this place. I messed up with Alista. I won't make that mistake again."

"Is that what you told Suzze?"

"In part. I tried to make her understand my position at the time."

"Which was?"

"Alista loved HorsePower—and like every teenage girl, she was totally gaga over Gabriel Wire." Something crossed his face. He looked away, lost. "Alista's birthday was coming up. Sweet sixteen. I didn't have the money to throw her a big party, but I knew that HorsePower was going to play a concert at Madison Square Garden. I guess they didn't play many concerts—I never really followed them—but I knew that there was this Ticketmaster on the basement level of this Marshalls Department Store on Route Four. So I woke up at, like, five in the morning and got on line. You should have seen it. No one else there was over thirty, and I'm standing there, waiting for two hours, to buy tickets to the concert. When I got to the window, the woman started typing into the computer and first she tells me that it's sold out and then, well, then she says, 'No, wait, I have only two left,'" and I was never so happy to buy something in my life. Like it was kismet, you know? Like it was supposed to happen."

Myron nodded as noncommittally as he could.

"So I get home and Alista's birthday is still a week away so I figure I'm going to wait. I tell Kimberly about them. And we're both dying. I mean, those tickets are burning a hole in my pocket. You ever have that? Where you buy someone something so special that you just can't wait to give it?"

"Sure," Myron said softly.

"So that's how it is with me and Kimberly. We end up driving to Alista's high school. We park there and I get Kimberly out and into her chair and Alista comes out and we're just smiling like two cats that ate the canary. Alista makes a face at us, the way teenage girls do, and she says, 'What?'" and I just held up the tickets and Alista"—he stopped, his world rolling back all those years—"she just screamed and threw her arms around my neck and squeezed so hard . . ."

His voice faded away. He pulled a napkin from the dispenser, started to go for his eyes, decided against it. He stared down at the table.

"So anyway, Alista took her best friend to the concert. They were supposed to go back to the friend's house afterward. For a sleepover. But they didn't. You know the rest."

"I'm sorry."

Karl Snow shook his head. "A long time ago."

"And you don't blame Gabriel Wire?"

"Blame?" He stopped and thought about that. "The truth is,

I didn't supervise Alista enough after her mother died. So part of it, I mean, when I really look at it closely, the roadie who spotted Alista in the crowd? He was a stranger. The security guy who let her backstage? He was a stranger. Gabriel Wire—he was a stranger too. I was her father—and I didn't look out for her. Why should I have expected them to?"

Karl Snow blinked and flicked a look to the right.

"And that's what you told Suzze?"

"I told her there was no proof that Gabriel Wire did anything wrong that night—at least, nothing the police could prove. They made that very clear to me. Yes, Alista had been in Wire's hotel suite. Yes, she did fall from his balcony—and yes, she did fall thirty-two floors. But to get from A to B, to get from those facts to indicting a powerful celebrity, not to mention securing a conviction . . ." He shrugged. "I had another daughter to worry about. I had no money. Do you know how hard it is to raise a handicapped child? How expensive? And SnowCap is a small chain now. How do you think I got the initial seed money?"

Myron was trying hard to understand, but his voice had more edge than he'd wanted. "From your daughter's killer?"

"You don't get it. Alista was dead. Dead is dead. There was nothing I could do for her anymore."

"But there was something you could still do for Kimberly."

"Yes. But it really isn't as cold as that. Suppose I didn't take the money. Now Wire gets away with it—and Kimberly is still in a bad way. This way, at the very least, Kimberly would be taken care of."

"No offense, but that does sound awfully cold."

"I suppose to an outsider it does, doesn't it? I'm a father. And a father really has only one job. Protect your child. That's it. And once I failed at that, once I let my daughter go off to that concert and I didn't check up on her. . . . Nothing can ever make up for that." He stopped, wiped a tear from his eye. "Anyway, you wanted to know what Suzze wanted. She wanted to know if I thought Gabriel Wire killed Alista."

"Did she say why she wanted to know? I mean, after all these years?"

"No." He blinked, looked away.

"What?"

"Nothing. I should have told her to leave it alone. Alista tangled with Gabriel Wire—and look what happened."

"Are you saying—?"

"I'm not saying anything. The news said she overdosed on heroin. She seemed distraught when she left, so I guess I'm not all that surprised."

Behind him one of Lauren's friends started crying—something about someone getting the wrong goodie bag. Karl Snow heard the commotion. He hurried over to the girls, all someone's daughters, girls who would grow up quickly and have crushes on rock stars. But for now here they were, at a little girl's birthday party, simply wanting ice cream and the right goodie bag.

21

Win knew how to get an immediate meeting with Herman Ache.

Windsor Horne Lockwood III had, like Windsor Horne Lockwood II and Windsor Horne Lockwood, been born with a silver golf tee in his mouth. His family had been original members of Merion Golf Club in Ardmore, outside Philadelphia. Win was also a member of Pine Valley, routinely ranked as the number one course in the world (this despite the fact that the course was located near a cheesy water park in southern New Jersey), and for those times he wanted to play a great course near New York City, Win had joined Ridgewood Golf Club, an A. W. Tillinghast–designed twenty-seven-hole paradise that rivaled the best parkland courses in the world.

Herman Ache—the "former" mobster—loved golf more than he

loved his children. That might be hyperbole, but based on Win's recent visit to a federal penitentiary, Herman Ache certainly loved golf more than he loved his brother Frank. So Win called Herman's office that morning and invited him to play a round at Ridgewood that very day. Without hesitation, Herman Ache said yes.

Herman Ache was too cagey not to realize that Win had an agenda, but he didn't care. This was a chance to play Ridgewood—a rare opportunity for even the wealthiest and most powerful of mob bosses. He would parry and thrust and probably walk headfirst into a fed wiretap sting if it meant that he could tee off on one of Tillinghast's most legendary courses.

"Thanks again for inviting me," Herman said.

"My pleasure."

They were on the first tee, known as One East. No cell phones were allowed on the course, but Win had spoken to Myron right before heading out and was thus filled in on Myron's meeting with Karl Snow. Win was not sure what to make of it. He cleared his mind and stepped up to the ball. He let loose a breath and split the fairway in half with a two-hundred-ninety-yard drive.

Herman Ache, who had a swing uglier than a monkey's armpit, was up next. He hooked it way left over the trees and nearly out to Route 17.

Herman frowned. He stared at the club, ready to blame. "You know something? I saw Tiger hit the same shot on this hole during the Barclay Open."

"Yes," Win said. "You and Tiger are practically interchangeable off a tee."

Herman Ache smiled with aggressively capped teeth. Despite

being in his late seventies, he wore a yellow Nike Dri-Fit golf shirt and, following a recent albeit ill-advised golf fashion trend, form-fitting white pants flared at the cuff and held up by a thick black belt with a silver buckle the size of a hubcap.

Ache called for a Mulligan—basically a do-over and something Win never ever did when he was someone's guest—and placed another ball on the tee. "Let me ask you something, Win."

"Please do."

"As you probably know, I'm an old man."

Ache smiled again. He aimed for kindly grandfather but with the caps it came out more lemurlike. Herman Ache had the kind of tan that was more orange than brown and luxuriously distinguished gray hair, the kind only money could buy—in short, he wore a top-drawer toupee. His face was totally wrinkle-and-movement free. Botox. Lots of it. His skin was too oily, too shiny, so that he looked a bit like something Madame Tussaud created on an off day. The neck gave him away. It was scrawny and baggy, hanging loosely like an old man's scrotum.

"I'm aware," Win said.

"And as you probably know, I operate and own a tremendous and varied portfolio of legal enterprises."

If a man feels the need to tell you that his enterprises are "legal," well, they most definitely are not.

Win made a noise of noncommitment.

"I'm wondering if you'd consider sponsoring me for membership here," Herman Ache said. "With your connections and name, I mean, if you'd be the one doing the sponsoring, I think it might go a long way to acceptance."

Win tried very hard not to blanch. He also managed not to put his hand to his heart and stumble backward, though it was not easy. "We can discuss," Win said.

Herman stood behind the ball, narrowed his eyes, and studied the fairway as though he were searching for the New World. He strolled up to his ball, stood next to it, and took four painfully slow practice swings. The caddies exchanged a glance. Herman looked out at the fairway again. If this were a movie, you'd now start seeing the hands of the clock fly around, days on a calendar blowing in the wind, leaves browning, and snow falling and then the sun coming up and everything turning green.

Win Golf Credo #12: It is perfectly acceptable to stink at golf. It is not perfectly acceptable to stink slowly.

Herman finally took his shot—another duck hook to the left. The ball smacked a tree and came down into play. The caddies looked relieved. Win and Ache made it through the first two holes, talking about utter nonsense. Golf, by nature, is a wonderfully self-involved game. You care about your score and pretty much nothing else. That was a good thing in many ways, but made for anything but stimulating conversation.

On the third-hole tee, the famed par-five mounds hole, they both looked out over the sight, the quiet, the green, the hush. It was breathtaking. For a moment no one moved or spoke. Win breathed evenly, almost closed his eyes. A course is a sanctuary. It was easy to poke fun and yes, golf was the most baffling of endeavors, screwing with the minds of even the most seasoned participants, but when Win was outside on a day like today, when he looked out over the calming spread of green, these were the moments when he, a full-fledged agnostic, felt almost blessed.

"Win?"

"Yes?"

"Thank you," Herman Ache said. There was a tear in his eye. "Thank you for this."

Win looked at the man. The spell broke. This was not the man with whom he wanted to share this moment. Still, Win thought, there was an opening. "About this club sponsorship thing."

Herman Ache looked up at Win with zealotlike hope. "Yes?"

"What would I tell the membership board about your, uh, business interests?"

"I told you. I'm totally legit now."

"Ah, but they will know about your past."

"First of all, that is the past. And that wasn't me anyway. Let me ask you something, Win: What's the difference between Herman Ache now and Herman Ache five years ago?"

"Why don't you tell me?"

"Oh, I will. The difference is that there is no Frank Ache out there anymore."

"I see."

"All the criminal stuff, all the violence—that wasn't me. It was my brother Frank. You know him, Win. Frank is coarse. He is loud and violent. I did my best to rein him in. He's the one who caused all the trouble. You can tell the board that."

Selling his brother out for membership in a golf club. Quite the prince.

"I'm not sure trashing your own brother will sit well with the membership board either," Win said. "They are very big here on family values."

Eye shift, gear shift. "Oh, I'm not trashing him. Look, I love

Frank. He's my baby brother. He'll always be that. I take good care of him. You know he's serving a prison sentence, right?"

"I've heard, yes," Win said. "Do you visit him?"

"Sure, all the time. Funny thing is, Frank loves it there."

"In prison?"

"You know Frank. He practically runs the place. I'll be honest with you. I didn't want him to take the fall alone, but Frank, well, he insisted on it. He wanted to take one for the whole family, so really, the least I can do is make sure he's well taken care of."

Win studied the old man's face and body language. Nothing. Most people assume that somehow you can tell when a man is lying to you—that there are clear-cut signs of deceit and that if you learn those signs, you can discern when someone is telling a lie or the truth. Those who believe such nonsense are just fooled all the more. Herman Ache was a sociopath. He had probably murdered—or more precisely, ordered the murder of—more people than Frank ever could. Frank Ache was obvious—a frontal assault easily spotted and thus taken down. Herman Ache worked more like a snake in the grass, a wolf in sheep's clothing, and thus was far more dangerous.

The tees on the seventh hole were up closer today, so Win passed on the driver in favor of his three-wood. "May I ask you a question about one of your business interests?"

Herman Ache gave Win the eye, and now, yes, the snake was not so hidden.

"Tell me about your relationship with Gabriel Wire."

Even a sociopath can look surprised. "Why the hell would you want to know about that?"

"Myron represents his partner."

"So?"

"I know in the past that you handled his gambling debts."

"And you think that should be illegal? It's fine if the government sells lottery tickets. It's fine if Las Vegas or Atlantic City or a bunch of Indians take bets, but if an honest businessman does it, somehow that's a crime?"

Win tried very hard not to yawn. "So, do you still handle Gabriel Wire's gambling?"

"I can't see how any of this is your business. Wire and I have legitimate business arrangements. That's all you have to know."

"Legitimate business arrangements?"

"That's right."

"But I'm confused," Win said.

"About?"

"What possible legitimate business arrangements involve Evan Crisp guarding Wire's house on Adiona Island?"

Still holding his driver, Ache froze. He handed it back to the caddie and snapped the white glove off his left hand. He moved closer to Win. "Listen to me," he said softly. "This is not a place you and Myron want to interfere. Trust me here. Do you know Crisp?"

"Only by reputation."

Ache nodded. "Then you know it won't be worth it."

Herman gave Win one more hard glare and returned to his caddie. He put his glove back on and asked for his driver. The caddy handed it to him and then headed toward the woods on the left because that was the real estate Herman Ache's golf balls seemed to favor.

"I have no interest in hurting your business," Win said. "I have no interest in Gabriel Wire, for that matter."

"So what do you want here?"

"I want to know about Suzze T. I want to know about Alista Snow. I want to know about Kitty Bolitar."

"I don't know what you're talking about."

"Would you like to hear my theory?"

"About?"

"Let's go back sixteen years," Win said. "Gabriel Wire owes you a substantial sum of money for gambling debts. He's a drug addict, a pleated-skirt chaser—"

"Pleated?"

"He likes them young," Win explained.

"Oh. Now I get it. Pleated."

"So glad. Gabriel Wire is also—more important to you—a compulsive gambler. In short, he's a mess, albeit a profitable one. He has money and tremendous earning potential, ergo the interest owed keeps compounding. Are you with me?"

Herman Ache said nothing.

"Then Wire goes too far. After a concert at Madison Square Garden, he invites Alista Snow, a naïve sixteen-year-old girl, back to his suite. Wire slips her Rohypnol and cocaine and whatever other drugs he has lying around, and the girl ends up leaping off a balcony. He panics. Or perhaps, being that he is such an important asset, you already have a man on the scene. Perhaps Crisp. You clean up the mess. You intimidate the witnesses and even buy off the Snow family—whatever it takes to protect your boy. He owes you even bigger now. I don't know what 'legitimate business arrangement' you made, but I imagine Wire has to pay you, what, half his earnings? That would be several million dollars per year minimum."

Herman Ache just looked at him, trying very hard not to fume. "Win?"

"Yes?"

"I know you and Myron like to think you're tough guys," Ache said, "but neither one of you is bulletproof."

"Tsk-tsk." Win spread his arms. "What happened to Mr. Legal? Mr. Legitimate Businessman?"

"You've been warned."

"By the way, I visited your brother in prison."

Herman's face fell.

"He sends his regards."

22

Back at the office, Big Cyndi was at the ready.

"I have some information on Gabriel Wire's tattoo, Mr. Bolitar."

"Let's hear it."

Big Cyndi wore all pink today with enough blush on her cheeks to coat a minivan. "According to Ma Gellan's extensive research, Gabriel Wire had one tattoo. It was on his left thigh, not his right. This may sound a little strange, so please bear with me."

"I'm listening."

"The tattoo was a heart. That tattoo itself was permanent. But what Gabriel Wire would do is fill in a name temporarily."

"I'm not sure I follow."

"You have seen what Gabriel Wire looks like, correct?"

"Yes."

"He was a rock star and an absolute major yummy, but he had a certain predilection."

"That being?"

"He liked underage girls."

"He was a pedophile?"

"No, I don't believe so. His targets were fully developed. But they were young. Sixteen, seventeen."

Alista Snow, for example. And now that he thought about it, Suzze T, back in those days.

"So even though Gabriel Wire was a tasty rock star, he often needed to convince a girl that she meant something to him."

"I'm not sure how the tattoos fit in."

"It was a red heart."

"So?"

"So it was plain inside. Just red. Gabriel Wire would then take a Sharpie and write in the name of the girl he was pursuing. He would pretend that he had gotten the tattoo especially for that particular girl."

"Wow."

"Yes."

"Talk about diabolical."

Big Cyndi sighed. "You wouldn't believe the things men will do to land some of us hotties."

Myron tried to process this. "How did it work exactly?"

"It would depend. If Gabriel wanted to close the sale immediately, he would actually take the girl to a tattoo parlor that night. He would tell her he was going to the back room and to wait for him. Then he'd draw in the name. Sometimes he would do it before a second date."

"Sort of, say, 'I care about you so much, look, I got a tattoo with your name on it'?"

"Precisely."

Myron shook his head.

"You have to admit," Big Cyndi said, "it is sort of genius."

"More like sick."

"Oh, I believe that was part of it," Big Cyndi said. "Gabriel Wire could have any girl he wants—even young ones. So I ask myself, why would he go to all that trouble? Why not just move on to the next girl?"

"And?"

"And I think, like many men, he needed the girl to truly fall for him. He liked them young. So my guess is he was developmentally stunted, stuck in that stage when a boy gets off breaking a girl's heart. Like in high school."

"Could be."

"It's just a theory," Big Cyndi said.

"Okay, this is all interesting, but what does this have to do with the other tattoo—the one that Suzze had too?"

"The design appears to be original artwork of some kind," Big Cyndi said. "So Ma Gellan theorized that Suzze and Gabriel became lovers. Suzze got the tattoo and—to impress or fool her—Gabriel got one too."

"So it was temporary?"

"There's no way to know for certain," Big Cyndi said, "but it is certainly, based on his past, a strong possibility."

Esperanza was standing in the doorway. Myron looked over at her. "Thoughts?"

"Just the obvious," Esperanza said. "Suzze and Gabriel were

lovers. Someone posts a tattoo that both of them wore with a message about the paternity of her child."

"Kitty admitted that she posted it," Myron said.

"That might add up," Esperanza said.

"Why's that?"

The office phone rang. Big Cyndi moved back to her desk and put on her sugary-sweet voice. "MB Reps." She listened a moment and shook her head at them, pointing to herself: She could handle it.

Esperanza signaled Myron to follow her into her office. "I got Suzze's mobile phone records."

On television, they make getting phone records seem difficult or, for the purposes of the plot, that it takes days or weeks. In truth, it could be done in minutes. In this case, it would take even less. Suzze, like many of MB Rep's clients, had set up all her bill paying via MB Reps. That meant that they had her phone number, her address, her passcodes, her social security number. Esperanza was able to get the calls online as though it were her own phone.

"Her final call was to Lex's cell, but he didn't pick up. I think that he may have been on the plane flying back. But Lex had called her earlier in the day. Right after that—this is the morning before Suzze died—she also called an untraceable disposable mobile. My guess is, the police will believe that she was calling her drug dealer to set up a buy."

"But that wasn't the case?"

Esperanza shook her head. "The number matches the one ol' Crush gave you for Kitty."

"Whoa."

"Yes," Esperanza said. "And maybe that's how Suzze got the drugs."

"From Kitty?"

"Yep."

Myron shook his head. "I still don't believe it."

"What don't you believe?"

"Suzze. You saw her in here. She was pregnant. She was happy."

Esperanza sat back and looked at him for several beats. "Do you remember when Suzze won the US Open?"

"Of course. What does that have to do with anything?"

"She'd cleaned up her act. She focused solely on her tennis, and bam, right away, Suzze wins a major. I never saw someone want something so badly. I can still see that final cross-court forehand to win, the look of pure undiluted joy on her face, the way she threw her racket up in the air and turned and pointed at you."

"At us," Myron said.

"Don't patronize me, please. You've always been her agent and her friend, but you can't be blind here. I want you to think what happened next."

Myron tried to remember. "We had a huge party. Suzze brought the trophy with her. We drank out of it."

"And then?"

Myron nodded, seeing where Esperanza was going. "She crashed."

"Big-time."

Four days after the biggest victory of her career—after appearing on the *Today* show, *Late Show with David Letterman*, and a bunch of other high-profile venues—Myron found Suzze crying, still in bed at two in the afternoon. They say that there is nothing worse than having a dream come true. Suzze had thought the US Open trophy would bring her instant happiness. She thought her breakfast would taste better in the morning, the sun would feel better on her skin, that she'd look in the mirror and see someone more attractive, smarter, more worthy of love.

She thought that winning would change her.

"Just when things were at their best for her," Esperanza said, "she started using again."

"And you think that's what happened here?"

Esperanza raised one weighing hand, then the other. "Happiness, crash. Happiness, crash."

"And her visit to Karl Snow after all the years? Do you think that's a coincidence?"

"Nope. But I think he brought up a lot of emotion. That plays for her using, not against. Meanwhile I checked the addresses you gave me from Suzze's GPS. The first, well, you figured that one out—Karl Snow's ice cream parlor. The rest are all easy to explain, except I don't have a clue about that second one."

"The intersection in Edison, New Jersey?" Then: "Wait. Didn't you say Kitty's disposable phone was purchased at T-Mobile in Edison?"

"Right." Esperanza brought something up on the computer. "Here's the Google Earth satellite picture."

Myron looked. A ShopRite. A Best Buy. A bunch of stores. A gas station.

"No T-Mobile," Esperanza said.

But, Myron thought, worth a drive anyway.

23

Myron's car Bluetooth picked up his cell phone. He spent the first half hour on the phone with clients. Life doesn't stop for death. If you ever need proof of that, head back to work.

A few minutes before arriving, Win called.

"Are you armed?" Win asked.

"I assume you upset Herman Ache."

"I did."

"So he's involved with Gabriel Wire?"

"It would seem so, yes, except for one thing."

"What's that?" Myron asked.

"I presented him with our theory about them controlling Wire via blackmail and gambling debts."

"Right."

"After several minutes," Win said, "Mr. Ache finally admitted that our theory was correct."

"Which means?"

"Herman Ache would lie about what he ate for lunch," Win said.

"So we're missing something."

"Yes. In the meantime, arm yourself."

"I'll pick up a gun when I get back," Myron said.

"No need to wait. There is a thirty-eight under your seat."

Terrific. Myron reached under his seat, felt the bump. "Anything else I need to know?"

"I birdied the last hole. Shot two under par for the round."

"Talk about burying the lead."

"I was trying to be modest."

"I think," Myron said, "that at some point, we will need to talk to Gabriel Wire face-to-face."

"That might mean storming the castle," Win said. "Or at least his estate on Adiona Island."

"Think we can get through his security?"

"I'll pretend you didn't ask that."

When Myron arrived at the intersection in Edison, he parked in the lot of yet another strip mall. He looked to see whether there was an ice cream parlor in this one—he'd start there this time if that was the case—but no, this one was somewhat more generic, Strip Mall USA, featuring a Best Buy, a Staples, and a shoe store called DSW that had the approximate square footage of a small European principality.

So why here?

He worked out yesterday's timeline in his head. First Suzze received a phone call from her husband Lex Ryder. The call lasted forty-seven minutes. Thirty minutes after hanging up, Suzze placed a call to Kitty's disposable cell phone. That call was shorter—four minutes. Okay, fine, what next? There was a time gap now, but four hours later, Suzze confronted Karl Snow at his ice cream parlor about the death of his daughter Alista Snow.

So he needed to try to fill in the four hours.

Following the logic of the GPS, sometime between Suzze's four-minute phone call with Kitty and Suzze's visit to Karl Snow, she had driven down here, to this intersection in Edison, New Jersey. Suzze hadn't put an actual address into the GPS, like she did with Karl Snow's mall. She had just put this intersection. There was a strip mall on one corner. A gas station on another. An Audi dealer on the third. Nothing but woods on the fourth.

So why? Why not put a real address?

Clue One: Suzze had come here right after calling Kitty. Considering their rather long and complicated relationship, a four-minute call seemed awfully brief. Possible conclusion: Suzze and Kitty had talked just long enough to set up a meet. Second possible conclusion: They'd agreed to meet here, at this intersection.

Myron looked for a restaurant or coffee shop, but there were none. It seemed highly unlikely that the two former tennis greats had decided to buy shoes or office supplies or electronics, so that ruled out the rest of one corner. He glanced down the road on the left and then the right. And there, past the Audi dealer, Myron spotted an ornate sign that caught his attention. The lettering was done in an Old English font and read: LENDALE MOBILE ESTATES.

It was, Myron saw after crossing the road, a trailer park. Even trailer parks had gone the way of Madison Avenue and spin doctors, what with the fancy sign and use of the word "estates" as though it were a beloved stop on an elite house tour in Newport, Rhode Island. The trailers were laid out along a grid of roads with names like Garden Mews and Old Oak Drive, though there seemed to be no indication of either a garden or an oak, old or not, and Myron was not sure what a mews was.

Even from his spot on the road, Myron could see several For Rent signs. New conclusion: Kitty and Mickey were staying here. Maybe Suzze didn't know the exact address. Maybe a GPS wouldn't recognize Garden Mews or Old Oaks Drive, so she'd given Suzze the closest intersection.

He didn't have a photograph of Kitty to show around, and even if he did, that would just be too suspicious. He couldn't stop and knock on trailer doors either. In the end, Myron opted for a good old-fashioned stakeout. He got back in his car and parked near the manager's office, giving him a pretty good view of most of the trailers. So how long could he park here and wait? An hour, maybe two. He called his old friend Zorra, a former Mossad agent who was always game for a stakeout. Zorra would head down and take over in two hours.

Myron settled in, used the time to make calls to his clients. Chaz Landreaux, his oldest NBA player and a former All-Star, was hoping to scratch out another year in the pros. Myron kept calling general managers, trying to get the popular veteran a tryout, but there was no interest. Chaz was heartbroken. "I just can't let go yet," he told Myron. "You know what I mean?"

Myron did. "Keep working out," Myron said. "Someone will give you a chance."

"Thanks, man. I know I can help a young team."

"I know it too. Let me ask you something else. Worst-case scenario. If the NBA isn't in the cards, how would you feel about playing a year in China or Europe?"

"I don't think so."

Looking out his front windshield, Myron spotted a trailer door open. This time, however, his nephew, Mickey, came out. Myron sat up. "Chaz, I'll keep working on it. Let's talk tomorrow."

He hung up. Mickey still held the door open. He looked back inside the trailer for a moment before letting the door shut. He was, as Myron had noted last night, a big kid, six-four, and weighing around two-ten. Mickey walked with his shoulders back, his head high. It was, Myron realized, the Bolitar walk. Myron's father walked like that. Brad walked like that. And Myron too.

You can't escape your genes, kid.

Now what?

There was, he guessed, a slight chance that Suzze had spoken or met with Mickey. But really that seemed unlikely. Better to stay here. Better to wait until Mickey was gone and then approach the trailer, hoping Kitty was still inside. If not, if Kitty wasn't there and he needed to track down Mickey, that wouldn't be difficult. Mickey wore a red Staples employee polo. It was safe to assume that Mickey was heading to work.

Did Staples hire employees that young?

Myron wasn't sure. He pulled down the visor. He knew that the sun's reflection would make it impossible for Mickey to spot him. As his nephew came closer, Myron could make out the name tag on his shirt. It read: BOB.

Stranger and stranger.

He waited until Mickey turned toward the intersection before getting out of his car. He walked toward the highway and took a quick look. Yep, Mickey was heading to the Staples. Myron turned back and headed down Garden Mews. The park was clean and well kept. There were lawn chairs in front of some trailers. Others had plastic daisies or those pinwheel decorations stuck into the ground. Chimes blew in the wind. There was also a wide variety of lawn ornaments, the Madonna being far and away the most popular.

Myron reached the door and knocked. No answer. He knocked harder. Still nothing. He tried to peer into a window, but the shades were pulled. He circled the trailer. Every window shade was down in the middle of the day. He moved back to the door and tried the knob. Locked.

The lock was a spring latch, probably not new. Myron wasn't an expert on breaking in, but the truth is, "loiding" an old spring-latch lock was pretty easy. Myron made sure no one was looking. Years ago, Win had taught him how to break in with a thinner-than-credit-card card. The card had sat dormant in his wallet, always there but unused, like an adolescent carrying a condom but without the hope. He took it out now, made sure no one was looking, and slid the card into the door frame, getting between the latch tongue to depress it and thus unlock the door. If the trailer door had a dead bolt or a dead latch or even a dead locking plunger, this would all be for naught. Luckily the lock was cheap and flimsy.

The door swung open.

Myron quickly stepped inside and closed it behind him. The lights were out and with the shades all pulled down, the room held a ghastly glow.

"Hello?"

No reply.

He flipped the light switch. The bulbs sputtered their way to illumination. The room was pretty much what one might expect from a trailer rental. There was one of those ninety-nine-dollar, too-much-assembly-required grid "entertainment centers" with a handful of paperbacks, a small television, and a beat-up laptop computer. There was a coffee table in front of a sleeper couch that had not seen a coaster since the first moon landing. Myron could tell the couch was a sleeper because there was a pillow and folded blankets on it. Mickey probably slept here, his mother taking the bedroom.

Myron spotted a photograph on the end table. He flicked on the lamp and lifted it into view. Mickey was in a basketball uniform, his hair messed, the ringlets in front pasted to his forehead by the sweat. Brad stood next to him, his arm draped around his son's neck as though he was about to put him in a loving headlock. Father and son sported enormous smiles. Brad gazed at his son with such obvious love, the moment so intimate Myron almost felt like turning away. Brad's nose, Myron could see, had a definite bend now. But more than that, Brad looked older, his hair starting to recede from the forehead, and something about that, about the passage of time and all they'd missed, made Myron's heart break anew.

From behind him, Myron heard a noise. He spun quickly. The sound had come from the bedroom. He moved to the door and peered inside. The main room was neat and tidy. The bedroom looked like a tornado had ripped through it, and there, in the eye of the storm, asleep (or worse) on her back, was Kitty.

"Hello?"

She didn't move. Her breath came in short, raspy pants. The

room smelled of old cigarettes and what might have been beer sweat. He moved closer to the bed. Myron decided to do a little poking around before he woke her. The disposable cell was on her bedside table. He checked it. He recognized the calls from Suzze and Joel "Crush" Fishman. There were three or four other calls, some with what looked like an overseas number. He punched them into his BlackBerry and e-mailed them to Esperanza. He searched Kitty's pocketbook and found her and Mickey's passports. There were dozens of stamps for countries on every continent. Myron tore through it, trying to figure out the timeline. A lot of the stamps were smeared. Still it looked as though Kitty had entered the United States eight months ago from Peru.

He put the passports back in the purse and rifled through it. There were no surprises at first, but then he started to feel along the lining and—hello—he felt the hard lump. He reached in, slid the seam open with his fingers, and pulled out a plastic bag with a small amount of brown powder in it.

Heroin.

Anger almost got the better of him. He was about to wake her up with a kick to the bed when he spotted something on the floor. For a moment he just blinked in disbelief. It was there, on the floor near Kitty's head, where you might toss a book or magazine if you were falling asleep. Myron bent down to get a closer look. He didn't want to touch it, didn't want to get fingerprints on it.

It was a gun.

He looked around, found a T-shirt on the floor, and used it to lift the gun into view. A .38. Same as the one sitting in Myron's waistband, courtesy of Win. What the hell was going on here? He was half tempted to report her to family services and leave it at that.

"Kitty?"

His voice was louder now, harsher. No movement. This wasn't sleep. She was passed out. He kicked the bed. Nothing. He debated throwing water on her face. Instead he tried to gently slap her face. He leaned over her and smelled the stale breath. He traveled back again, to when she was that adorable teenager dominating center court, and his favorite Yiddish expression came back to him in a rush: Man plans, God laughs.

This was not a kind laugh.

"Kitty?" he said again, a little harsher now.

Her eyes suddenly opened wide. She rolled quickly, startling Myron back, and then he realized what she was doing.

She was going for the gun.

"Looking for this?"

He held up the gun. She cupped her hands though there was barely any light in there and blinked at him. "Myron?"

24

"Why the hell do you have a loaded gun?"

Kitty hopped out of bed and looked under a closed window shade. "How did you find me?" Her eyes bulged. "My God, were you followed?"

"What? No."

"Are you sure?" Total panic. She ran over and checked another window. "How did you find me?"

"Just calm down."

"I won't calm down. Where's Mickey?"

"I saw him go off to work."

"Already? What time is it?"

"One in the afternoon." Myron tried to plow through it. "Did you see Suzze yesterday?"

"Is that how you found me? She promised she wouldn't tell."

"Wouldn't tell what?"

"Anything. But especially where I am. I explained it to her."

Just ride it, Myron thought. "Explained what?"

"The danger. But she already understood."

"Kitty, talk to me here. What kind of danger are you in?"

She shook her head. "I can't believe Suzze sold me out."

"She didn't. I found you from her GPS and phone records."

"What? How?"

He wasn't about to head down that road. "How long have you been sleeping?"

"I don't know. I went out last night."

"Where?"

"None of your business."

"Getting high?"

"Get out!"

Myron took a step back, raised his hands as though to show he meant no harm. He had to stop attacking. Why do we always screw up when it comes to family? "Do you know about Suzze?"

"She told me everything."

"What did she tell you?"

"It's confidential. I promised her. And she promised me."

"Kitty, Suzze is dead."

For a moment Myron thought that maybe she hadn't heard him. Kitty just stared, her eyes clear for the first time. Then she started shaking her head.

"A drug overdose," Myron said. "Last night."

More headshake. "No."

"Where do you think she got the drugs, Kitty?"

"She wouldn't. She was pregnant."

"Did you give them to her?"

"Me? My God, what kind of person do you think I am?"

To himself: One who keeps a gun next to her bed. One who had drugs hidden in her purse. One who goes down on strange guys at a club to score. Out loud, he said, "She came by here yesterday, right?"

Kitty didn't reply.

"Why?"

"She called me," Kitty said.

"How did she get your number?"

"She e-mailed my Facebook account. Like you did. She said it was urgent. She said she had things she needed to tell me."

"So you e-mailed her your cell phone number."

Kitty nodded.

"And then Suzze called. You told her to meet you here."

"Not here," Kitty said. "I still wasn't sure. I didn't know if I could trust her. I was scared."

Myron saw it now. "So instead of giving her this address, you just told her the intersection."

"Right. I told her to park by the Staples. That way I could watch her. Make sure she was on her own and that no one was following."

"Who did you think might be following?"

But Kitty shook her head firmly, clearly terrified to answer. This was not a place to go, if he wanted to keep her talking. Myron got back on a more fruitful path. "So you and Suzze talked?"

"Yes."

"What did you talk about?"

"I told you. It's confidential."

Myron moved closer. He tried to pretend that he didn't detest every bone in this woman's body. He put his hand gently on her shoulder and met her eye. "Please listen to me, okay?"

Kitty's eyes were glazed.

"Suzze visited you here yesterday," Myron said as though talking to a slow kindergartener. "After that, she drove up to Kasselton and spoke to Karl Snow. Do you know who that is?"

Kitty closed her eyes and nodded.

"Then she went home and took enough drugs to kill herself."

"She wouldn't do that," Kitty said. "Not to the baby. I know her. She was killed. They killed her."

"Who?"

Another "I won't talk" shake of the head.

"Kitty, you need to help me figure out what happened here. What did you two talk about?"

"We both promised."

"She's dead now. That trumps any promise. You're not breaking any trust here. What did she say to you?"

Kitty reached for her purse and pulled out a pack of Kool cigarettes. For a moment she just held the pack and stared down at it. "She knew it was me who posted that 'Not His' comment."

"Was she angry?"

"Just the opposite. She wanted me to forgive her."

Myron thought about that. "Because of the rumors she spread about you when you got pregnant?"

"That's what I thought. I thought she wanted to apologize for telling everyone I slept around and that the baby wasn't Brad's." Kitty met Myron's eye. "Suzze told you that, didn't she?"

"Yes."

"Is that why you thought I was some kind of whore? Is that why you told Brad it probably wasn't his?"

"Not that alone, no."

"But it contributed?"

"I guess," he said, biting back the anger. "You're not going to tell me that Brad was the only man you were sleeping with back then, are you?"

Mistake. Myron saw it.

"Would it matter what I said?" she asked. "You're going to believe the worst. You always did."

"I just wanted Brad to check, that's all. I'm his older brother. I was only looking out for him."

Her voice was filled with bitterness. "So noble."

He was losing her again. Getting off track. "So Suzze came here to apologize for spreading rumors?"

"No."

"But you just said—"

"I said that's what I thought. At first. And she did. She admitted that she let her competitive nature get the best of her. I told her, it wasn't your competitive nature. It was your bitch of a mother. First place or nothing. Take no prisoners. The woman was a lunatic. Do you remember her?"

"I do."

"But I had no idea how crazy that bitch was. Do you remember that pretty Olympic figure skater from the nineties, what was her name, the one who got attacked by her rival's ex?"

"Nancy Kerrigan."

"Right. I could see Suzze's mom doing that, hiring someone to whack my leg with a tire iron or whatever. But Suzze said it wasn't her mom. She said that maybe her mom pressured her and so she cracked, but that it was on her, not her mom."

"What was on her?"

Kitty's eyes went up and to the right. A small smile came to her lips. "Do you want to hear something funny, Myron?"

He waited.

"I loved tennis. The game." Her eyes had a far-off look to them, and Myron remembered how she was back then, the way she crossed the court like a panther. "I wasn't that competitive compared with the other girls. Sure, I wanted to win. But really, since I was a little girl, I just loved playing. I don't get people who really want to win. I often thought that they were horrible people, especially in tennis. You know why?"

Myron shook his head.

"There are two people in a tennis match. One ends up winning, one ends up losing. And I think the pleasure comes not from winning. I think the pleasure comes from beating someone." She scrunched up her face like a very puzzled child. "Why is that something we admire? We call them winners, but when you think about it, they really get off on making someone else lose. Why is that something we admire so much?"

"That's a good question."

"I wanted to be a professional tennis player because, I mean, can you imagine anything more wonderful than making a living playing the game you loved?"

He heard Suzze's voice: *Kitty was a great player, wasn't she?*

"I can't, no."

"But if you're really good, really talented, everyone tries to make it stop being fun. Why is that?"

"I don't know."

"Why, as soon as we show promise, do they take away the beauty and make it all about winning? They sent us to these ridiculously competitive schools. They pitted us against our friends. It wasn't enough for you to succeed—your friends had to fail. Suzze explained this to me, like I didn't already get it. Me, who lost my entire career. She knew better than anyone what tennis meant to me."

Myron stayed very still, afraid to break the spell. He waited for Kitty to say more, but she didn't. "So Suzze came here to apologize?"

"Yes."

"And what did she tell you?"

"She told me"—Kitty's gaze moved past him, toward the window shade—"that she was sorry for ruining my career."

Myron tried to keep his expression blank. "How did she ruin your career?"

"You didn't believe me, Myron."

He did not reply.

"You thought that I got pregnant on purpose. To trap your brother." Her smile was eerie now. "So dumb when you stop and think about it. Why would I do that? I was seventeen years old. I wanted to be a professional tennis player, not a mother. Why would I intentionally get pregnant?"

Hadn't Myron thought something similar recently? "I'm sorry about that," he said. "I should have known better. The pill isn't a hundred percent. I mean, we learned that first week of health class in seventh grade, right?"

251

"But you didn't believe that, did you?"

"At the time, no. And I'm sorry about that."

"Another apology," she said with a shake of her head. "Also too late. But of course you're wrong."

"Wrong about what?"

"About the pill not working. See, that's what Suzze came to tell me. She said she did it almost as a prank at first. But think about it. Suzze knew that I was religious—that I'd never have an abortion. So what would be the best way to eliminate me, her toughest competitor?"

Suzze's voice from two nights ago. *"My parents explained to me that everything is fair in competition. You do whatever you have to to win. . . ."*

"My God."

Kitty nodded as if to confirm. "That's what Suzze came here to tell me. She switched out my birth control pills. That's how I ended up pregnant."

It made sense. Stunning sense maybe, but it all fit. Myron took a second, let it all sink in. Suzze had been troubled two nights ago when the two of them sat on the balcony. Now he understood why—the talk about guilt, the dangers of being overly competitive, the regrets of the past—it was all a little clearer now.

"I had no idea," Myron said.

"I know. But that doesn't really change anything, does it?"

"I guess not. Did you forgive her?"

"I let her have her say," Kitty went on. "I let her talk and explain everything in full detail. I didn't interrupt her. I didn't ask her any questions. And when she finished, I stood up, walked across this very room, and I hugged her. I hugged her hard. I hugged her for a very long time. And then I said, 'Thank you.'"

252

"For what?"

"That's what she asked. And if you're on the outside, I understand the question. Look at what I've become. What, you have to wonder, would my life be like now if she didn't change the pills? Maybe I would have gone on and been the tennis champion everyone predicted, winning majors and traveling the world in luxury, all that. Maybe Brad and I would have stayed together and had children after I retired, right about now maybe, and lived happily ever after. Maybe. But what I know for sure—the only thing I know for sure—is that if Suzze hadn't switched my pills there would be no Mickey."

Her eyes filled with tears.

"Whatever else happened—what other tragedies followed—Mickey makes up for it ten times over. The fact is, whatever Suzze's motive, Mickey is here because of her. The greatest gift God ever gave me—because of what she did. So not only did I forgive her, but I thanked her because every day, no matter how messed up I get, I get on my knees and thank God for that beautiful, perfect boy."

Myron stood there stunned. Kitty moved past him, back into the main room, and then across to the kitchen area. She opened the fridge. There wasn't much but it was laid out neatly. "Mickey went food shopping," she said. "Would you like something to drink?"

"No." Then: "So what did you confess to Suzze?"

"Nothing."

Kitty was lying. She started glancing around again.

"So why did she go from here to Karl Snow's ice cream parlor?"

"I don't know," Kitty said. The sound of a car startled her upright. "Oh my God." She slammed the refrigerator door closed and peered under a pulled shade. The car passed, but Kitty didn't relax. Her eyes were wide with paranoia again. She backed herself into a corner, glancing about as though the furniture might leap up and attack her. "We need to pack."

"And go where?"

She opened up a closet. Mickey's clothes—all on hangers, shirts folded up top. Man, this kid was neat. "I want my gun back."

"Kitty, what's going on?"

"If you found us . . . It's not safe."

"What's not safe? Where's Brad?"

Kitty shook her head, pulling a suitcase out from under the couch. She started dumping Mickey's clothes into it. Watching this strung-out heroin addict—there was no nicer way to put that—a strange yet obvious realization came to Myron.

"Brad wouldn't do this to his family," Myron said.

That made her slow down.

"Whatever else may be going on—and I don't know if you're really in danger, Kitty, or if you've fried your brain into a state of irrational paranoia—but I know my brother. He wouldn't leave you and his son alone like this—you strung out and afraid for your life, real or imagined."

Kitty's face crumbled a piece at a time. Her voice was a childlike whine. "It isn't his fault."

Whoa. Myron knew to proceed slowly here. He took a half step closer to her and spoke as gently as he could. "I know that."

"I'm so scared."

Myron nodded.

"But Brad can't help us."

"Where is he?"

She shook her head, her body stiffening. "I can't say. Please. I can't say."

"Okay." He put up his hands. Easy, Myron. Don't push too hard. "But maybe you could let me help you."

She looked at him warily. "How?"

Finally—an opening, albeit a small one. He wanted to suggest rehab for her. He knew a nice place not far from the house in Livingston. That was where he wanted to bring her, try to get her cleaned up. She would go into rehab while Mickey stayed with him, just until they contacted Brad and got him up here.

But his own words haunted him: Brad wouldn't leave them like this. So that meant one of two things. One, Brad didn't know how bad his wife was. Or two, for some reason, he couldn't help them.

"Kitty," he said slowly, "is Brad in danger? Is he the reason you're so afraid right now?"

"He'll be back soon." She started scratching her arms hard, as though there were bugs under the skin. Her eyes started darting around again. Uh-oh, Myron thought.

"You okay?" he asked.

"I just need to use the bathroom. Where's my purse?"

Yeah, right.

She dashed into the bedroom, grabbed her purse, and closed the bathroom door. Myron patted his back pocket. Her stash was still there. He could hear the sounds of a frantic search coming from the bathroom.

Myron called, "Kitty?"

Footsteps on the front stoop leading to the door jarred him. Myron whipped his head toward the sound. Through the bathroom door, Kitty shouted, "Who's that?" Working off her panic,

Myron pulled his gun, pointing at the door. The knob turned and Mickey entered. Myron quickly lowered the gun.

Mickey looked at his uncle. "What the hell . . . ?"

"Hey, Mickey." Myron pointed at his name tag. "Or should I say Bob?"

"How did you find us?"

Mickey was scared too. He could hear it in his voice. Anger, yes, but mostly there was fear.

"Where's my mother?" he demanded.

"She's in the bathroom."

He ran over to the door, put his hand on it. "Mom?"

"I'm okay, Mickey."

Mickey leaned his head on the door and closed his eyes. His voice was unbearably tender. "Mom, please come out."

"She'll be okay," Myron said.

Mickey turned to him, his hands curled into fists. Fifteen years old and ready to take on the world. Or at least, his uncle. Mickey was dark, broad, and had that brooding, dangerous quality that made girls weak at the knees. Myron wondered where the brooding came from and then, looking at the bathroom door, figured that he already knew the answer.

"How did you find us?" Mickey asked again.

"Don't worry about it. I had to ask your mom some questions."

"What about?"

"Where's your father?"

Kitty screamed out, "Don't tell him!"

He turned back to the door. "Mom? Come out, okay?"

More sounds of the frantic—and as Myron knew, fruitless—search. Kitty started cursing. Mickey turned back to Myron. "Get out."

"No."

"What?"

"You're the fifteen-year-old kid. I'm the adult. The answer is no."

Kitty was crying now. They could both hear her. "Mickey?"

"Yes, Mom."

"How did I get home last night?"

Mickey gave a quick glare back at Myron. "I got you."

"Did you put me to bed?"

Mickey clearly did not like having this conversation in front of Myron. He tried to whisper through the door, as though Myron wouldn't be able to hear. "Yes."

Myron just shook his head.

Kitty asked, her tone nearly a fevered pitch now, "Did you go through my purse?"

Myron took that one. "No, Kitty, I did."

Mickey turned and faced his uncle full-on. Myron reached into his back pocket and pulled out the heroin. The bathroom door opened. Kitty stomped out and said, "Give that to me."

"Not a chance."

"I don't know who the hell you think you are—"

"I've had enough," Myron said. "You're a junkie. He's a kid. You're both coming with me."

"You don't tell us what to do," Mickey said.

"Yeah, Mickey, I do. I'm your uncle. You may not like it, but I'm not leaving you here with a junkie mom who's willing to shoot up in front of her son."

Mickey stayed between his mother and Myron. "We're fine."

"You're not fine. You're working illegally, I'm sure, under an alias. You get her from bars or she stumbles home and you put her to bed. You keep this place human. You put food in the fridge while she lies around and shoots up."

"You can't prove any of that."

"Sure I can, but it doesn't matter. Here's what's going to happen and if you don't like it, too bad. Kitty, I'm putting you in a rehab center. It's a nice place. I don't know whether they can help you— whether anyone can—but it's worth a try. Mickey, you're going to come with me."

"Like hell I am."

"You are. You can live in Livingston with your grandparents, if you don't want to be with me. Your mom will get cleaned up. We will get in touch with your father and let him know what's going on here."

Mickey kept his body shield in front of his wilting mother. "You can't make us go with you."

"Yeah, I can."

"You think I'm afraid of you? If Grandpa hadn't stepped in—"

"This time," Myron said, "you won't be jumping me in the dark."

Mickey tried to grin. "I can still take you."

"No, Mickey, you can't. You're strong, you're brave, but you wouldn't have a chance. It doesn't matter anyway—you can do what I'm suggesting or I'll call the cops. At the very least your mother is endangering the welfare of a child. She could end up in jail."

Kitty shouted, "No!"

"I'm not giving you guys a choice anymore. Where's Brad?"

Kitty moved out from behind her son. She tried to stand straight and for a moment, Myron saw the old athlete. Mickey said, "Mom?"

"He's right," Kitty said.

"No . . ."

"We need help. We need protection."

"We can take care of ourselves," Mickey said.

She cupped her son's face in her hands. "It's going to be okay," she told him. "He's right. I can get the help I need. You'll be safe."

"Safe from what?" Myron asked yet again. "And really, enough is enough. I want to know where my brother is."

"So do we," Kitty said.

Mickey again said, "Mom?"

Myron took a step closer. "What are you talking about?"

"Brad disappeared three months ago," Kitty said. "That's why we've been on the run. None of us are safe."

25

As they packed their few belongings, Myron called Esperanza and asked her to arrange a stay for Kitty at the Coddington Rehabilitation Institute. Then Myron called Dad.

"Is it okay if Mickey stays at the house with you for a while?"

"Of course," Dad said. "What's going on?"

"A lot."

Dad listened without interrupting. Myron told him about Kitty's drug problems, about her being on her own with Mickey, about Brad being missing. When he finished, Dad said, "Your brother wouldn't just abandon his family like this."

Just what Myron had thought. "I know."

"It means he's in trouble," Dad said. "I know you two have had issues, but . . ."

He didn't finish his thought. This was his way. When Myron was young, Dad somehow pushed Myron to succeed without ever push-ing him too hard. He made it clear that he was proud of his son's accomplishments while never making it seem like it was any kind of precondition to being proud of him. So yet again Dad didn't ask—but he didn't have to.

"I'll find him," Myron said.

During the car ride Myron asked for details.

Kitty sat up front next to him. In the back, Mickey ignored them. He stared out the window, white iPod earbuds in place—playing the part of a petulant teenager, which, Myron surmised, he was.

By the time they reached the Coddington Rehabilitation In-stitute, this was what he had learned: Eight months ago, per the stamp in the passport, Brad, Kitty, and Mickey Bolitar had moved to Los Angeles. Three months ago, Brad had left for an "emergency secret mission" (Kitty's words) to Peru and told them not to say anything to anyone.

"What did Brad mean by that—not to say anything."

Kitty claimed ignorance. "He just said not to worry about him and not to tell anyone. He also said be careful."

"Of what?"

Kitty just shrugged.

"Any clue, Mickey?" The kid did not budge. Myron repeated the question, yelling so he could be heard. Mickey either couldn't hear him or chose to ignore him. Turning back to Kitty, he said, "I thought you guys worked for a charity group."

"We did."

"So?"

Another shrug. Myron asked a few more questions, but there was little more to learn. Weeks passed, but there was no word from Brad. At some point, Kitty felt as though they were being watched. Someone would call and hang up on them. One night, someone jumped her in a mall parking lot, but she managed to run off. She decided then to move with Mickey and stay off the grid.

Myron asked, "Why didn't you tell me any of this sooner?"

Kitty glared at him as though he'd just casually suggested bestiality. "You? You're joking, right?"

Myron didn't want to unearth their old grudge right now. "Or anyone," he said. "Brad's been missing three months. How long did you plan to wait?"

"I told you already. Brad said not to tell anyone. He said it'd be dangerous for all of us."

Myron still wasn't buying it all—something just didn't make sense here—but when he tried to push it, Kitty just shut down and started to cry. Then, when she was sure Mickey wasn't listening (Myron was sure he was), Kitty begged him for her stash back, "just one last hit, please," using the logic that she was heading into rehab anyway—what harm could it do?

The rehab's sign was small and read, THE CODDINGTON REHABILITATION INSTITUTE. Myron took the private road up past the security gate. From the outside the place looked like one of those vinyl-sided, faux-Victorian bed-and-breakfasts. Inside, at least in the reception area, it was an interesting mix of luxury hotel and prison. Soft classical music played on the overhead speaker. A chandelier hung from the ceiling. There were bars on the ornate arched windows.

The receptionist's nameplate read, CHRISTINE SHIPPEE, though Myron knew that she was much more than a receptionist. Christine was, in fact, the hands-on founder of the Coddington Institute. She greeted them from behind what might have been bulletproof glass, though "greeted" might be too strong a term. Christine had a face like a yield sign. Her reading glasses hung from a chain. She looked them over, clearly finding them wanting, and sighed. She slid the forms to them through the kind of chute you see at a bank.

"Fill out the paperwork, then come back," Christine said by way of introduction.

Myron moved over to the corner. He started writing her name, but Kitty stopped him. "Use the name Lisa Gallagher. It's my alias. I don't want them finding me."

Again Myron asked who "them" referred to and again she claimed to have no idea. No reason to argue right now. He filled out the forms and brought them back to the receptionist. She took the forms, put on the reading glasses, and started checking for errors. Kitty's body quake picked up steam. Mickey put his arms around his mother, trying to calm her. It wasn't working. Kitty looked smaller now, frailer.

"Do you have a suitcase?" Christine asked her.

Mickey held it up for her.

"Leave it there. We'll go through the contents before we deliver it to your room." Christine turned her attention to Kitty. "Say good-bye now. Then stand by that door and I'll buzz you in."

"Wait," Mickey said.

Christine Shippee turned her gaze toward him.

"Can I go in with her?" he asked.

"Nope."

"But I want to see her room," Mickey said.

"And I want to mud wrestle with Hugh Jackman. Neither is happening. Say good-bye and then move on."

Mickey did not back down. "When can I visit?"

"We'll see. Your mother needs to detox."

"How long will that take?" Mickey asked.

Christine looked at Myron. "Why am I talking to a kid?"

Kitty still had a bad case of the shakes. "I don't know about this."

Mickey said, "If you don't want to go inside—"

"Mickey," Myron said, cutting him off. "You're not helping."

He said in an angry sotto voce: "Can't you see she's scared?"

"I know she's scared," Myron said. "But you're not helping. Let the people here do their job."

Kitty clung to her son and said, "Mickey?"

Part of Myron felt great sympathy for Kitty. A far bigger part of Myron wanted to rip her away from her son and kick her selfish ass through the door.

Mickey moved toward Myron. "There has to be another way."

"There isn't."

"I'm not leaving her here."

"Yeah, Mickey, you are. It's that or I call the cops or social services or whoever else."

But now Myron could see that it wasn't just Kitty who was scared. It was Mickey. He was, Myron reminded himself, still a kid. Myron flashed back to those happy family photographs—Dad, Mom, Only Son. Mickey's father had since vanished someplace in South America. His mother was about to go through a heavy security door and enter the harsh solo world of detoxification and drug rehabilitation.

"Don't worry," Myron said as gently as he could. "We'll take care of you."

Mickey made a face. "Are you for real? You think I want your help?"

"Mickey?"

It was Kitty. He turned to her, and suddenly the roles were back to where they should have been: Kitty was the mother and Mickey was her child again. "I'll be fine," she said in as firm a voice as she could muster. "You go and stay with your grandparents. You come back and see me as soon as you can."

"But—"

She put her hands on his face again. "It's okay. I promise. You'll visit soon."

Mickey lowered his face into her shoulder. Kitty held him for a moment, looking past him at Myron. Myron nodded that he'd be fine. The nod gave her no solace. Kitty finally pulled away and headed to the door without another word. She waited for the receptionist's buzz and then disappeared inside.

"She'll be fine," Christine Shippee said to Mickey, finally a little tenderness in her voice.

Mickey turned and stomped out the door. Myron followed him. He clicked the remote, unlocking the car door. Mickey reached to open the back door. Myron clicked the remote again, locking it on him.

"What the hell?"

"Get in the front," Myron said. "I'm not a chauffeur."

Mickey slid into the front passenger seat. Myron started up the car. He turned to Mickey, but the kid had the iPod jammed back into his ears. Myron tapped the kid's shoulder.

"Take them off."

"Really, Myron? Is that how you think we're playing this?"

But a few minutes later, Mickey did as he was asked. The boy gazed out the window, giving Myron the back of his head. They were only about ten minutes from the house in Livingston. Myron wanted to ask him more, wanted to push him to open up, but maybe it had been enough for one day.

Still gazing out the window, Mickey said, "Don't you dare judge her."

Myron kept his hands on the steering wheel. "I just want to help."

"She wasn't always like this."

Myron had a thousand follow-up questions but he gave the kid space. When Mickey spoke again, the defensive tone was back. "She's a great mom."

"I'm sure she is."

"Don't patronize me, Myron."

He had a point. "So what happened?"

"What do you mean?"

"You said she wasn't always like this. Do you mean a junkie?"

"Stop calling her that."

"You pick the term then."

Nothing.

"So tell me what you meant by 'she wasn't always like this,'" Myron said. "What happened?"

"What do you mean, what happened?" He swerved his gaze to the front windshield, staring at the road a little too intensely. "Dad happened. You can't blame her."

"I'm not blaming anyone."

"She was so happy before. You have no idea. She was always laughing. Then Dad left and . . ." He caught himself, blinked, swallowed. "And then she fell apart. You don't know what they meant to each other. You think Grandma and Grandpa are a pretty great couple, but they had friends and a community and other relatives. My mom and dad only had each other."

"And you."

He frowned. "There you go with the patronizing again."

"Sorry."

"You don't get it, but if you ever saw them together, you would. When you're that much in love—" Mickey stopped, wondered how to continue. "Some couples aren't built to be apart. They're like one person. You take one away . . ." He didn't finish the thought.

"So when did she start using?"

"A few months ago."

"After your father vanished?"

"Yes. Before that, she'd been clean since I was born—so before you say it, yes, I know she used to do drugs."

"How do you know?"

"I know a lot," Mickey said, and a sly, sad smile came to his face. "I know what you did. I know how you tried to break them up. I know you told my father that my mother got knocked up by another guy. That she slept around. That he shouldn't quit school to be with her."

"How do you know all that?"

"From Mom."

"Your mother told you all that?"

Mickey nodded. "She doesn't lie to me."

Wow. "So what else did she tell you?"

He crossed his arms. "I'm not going through the last fifteen years for you."

"Did she tell you I hit on her?"

"What? No. Gross. Did you?"

"No. But that's what she told your father to drive a wedge between us."

"Oh man, that is so gross."

"How about your father? What did he tell you?"

"He said that you pushed them away."

"I didn't mean to."

"Who cares what you meant? You pushed them away." Mickey let loose a deep breath. "You pushed them away, and now we're here."

"Meaning?"

"What do you think I mean?"

He meant that his father was missing. He meant that his mother was a junkie. He meant that he blamed Myron, that he wondered what their lives would have been like if Myron had been more accepting way back when.

"She's a good mother," Mickey said again. "The best."

Yep, the heroin junkie was Mother of the Year material. Like Myron's own father had said just a few days ago, kids have a way of blocking out the bad. But in this case, it seemed almost delusional. Then again, how should you judge the job a parent does? If you judged Kitty by the outcome—the end result, if you will—then, well, look at this kid. He was magnificent. He was brave, strong, smart, willing to fight for his family.

So maybe, crazy, lying junkie and all, Kitty had indeed done something right.

After another minute of silence had passed, Myron decided to rev up the conversation with a casual starter: "So I hear you play a mean game of hoops."

Mean game of hoops? Oy.

"Myron?"

"Yes?"

"We're not bonding here."

Mickey put the headphones back in his ears, cranked the volume to an undoubtedly unhealthy level, and stared back out the passenger window. They made the rest of the way in silence. When they pulled up to the old house in Livingston, Mickey turned off his iPod and stared out.

"See that window up there?" Myron said. "The one with the decal on it?"

Mickey looked out, said nothing.

"When we were kids, that's where your dad and I shared a bedroom. We used to play Nerf basketball and trade baseball cards and we invented this hockey game with a tennis ball and the closet door."

Mickey waited a beat. Then he turned toward his uncle and said, "You guys must have been the balls."

Everyone's a wiseass.

Despite all the horrors of the past twenty-four hours—or maybe because of them—Myron couldn't help but chuckle. Mickey got out and headed up the same path where last night he'd jumped Myron. Myron followed and for a moment he was tempted to fun-tackle his nephew. Funny what flies through the brain at the strangest times.

Mom was at the door. She hugged Mickey first, the way only

Mom could. When Mom hugged, she gave it her all—holding nothing back. Mickey closed his eyes and soaked it in. Myron waited for the kid to cry, but Mickey wasn't one for waterworks. Mom finally released him and threw the hug at her son. Then she stepped back, blocked their entrance, and fixed them both with a killer glare.

"What's going on with you two?" Mom asked.

Myron said, "What do you mean?"

"Don't hand me 'what do you mean.' Your father just tells me Mickey is staying here for a while. Nothing else. Don't get me wrong. Mickey, I'm thrilled you're staying with us. Too long in coming, you ask me, all this overseas nonsense. You belong here. With us. With your family."

Mickey said nothing.

Myron asked, "Where's Dad?"

"He's in the basement getting your old bedroom ready for Mickey. So what's going on?"

"Why don't we get Dad and we can talk about it?"

"Fine with me," Mom said, wagging her finger at him like, uh, a mother, "but no funny stuff."

Funny stuff?

"Al? The kids are here."

They entered the house. Mom closed the door behind them.

"Al?"

No reply.

They all shared a look, no one moving. Then Myron headed for the basement. The door down to Myron's old bedroom—soon to be Mickey's—was wide open. He called down to his father. "Dad?"

Still no answer.

Myron looked back at his mother. She looked more puzzled than anything else. Panic snaked its way into Myron's chest. He fought it off and half jumped, half ran down the basement stairs. Mickey followed close behind.

Myron pulled up short when he got to the bottom of the stairs. Mickey crashed into him, knocking him a little forward. But Myron didn't feel a thing. He stared in front of him and felt his entire world begin to crumble.

26

When Myron was ten years old and Brad was five, Dad took them to Yankee Stadium for a game against the Red Sox. Most boys have a memory like this—that major-league baseball game with your dad, the perfect July weather, that jaw-dropping moment you come out of whatever tunnel and see the ballpark for the very first time, the almost-painted green of the grass, the sun shining as though it were the first day, your heroes in uniform warming up with the ease of the gifted.

But this particular game would be different.

Dad had secured tickets in the nosebleed upper deck, but at the last minute, a business associate gave him two tickets three rows behind the Red Sox bench. For some odd reason—and to the horror of the rest of his family—Brad was a Red Sox fan. Actually, the reason wasn't all that odd. Carl "Yaz" Yastrzemski was Brad's first baseball card. That might not seem like a big deal, but Brad was one of those little kids who became fiercely loyal to his firsts.

Once they sat, Dad produced the great seats with a magician's flourish and showed them to Brad. "Surprise!"

He handed the tickets to Myron. Dad would stay in the upper deck, sending his two sons down to the box seats. Myron held an excited Brad's hand and made his way down. When they arrived, Myron couldn't believe how close to the field they were. The box seats were, in a word, awesome.

When Brad spotted Yaz scant yards away, his face broke into a smile that even now, if Myron closed his eyes, he could still see and feel. Brad started cheering like mad. When Yaz got into the batter's box, Brad truly lost it. "Yaz! Yaz! Yaz!"

The guy sitting in front of them whirled around, frowning. He was maybe twenty-five and had a scruffy beard. That was another thing Myron would never forget. That beard.

"That's enough," the bearded guy said to Brad. "Quiet down."

The bearded guy turned back to the field. Brad looked as though someone had slapped him in the face.

"Don't listen to him," Myron said. "You're allowed to yell."

That was when everything went wrong. The bearded man spun back around and grabbed Myron—Myron who was ten years old at the time, a tall ten-year-old, but ten nonetheless—by the shirt. The man bunched the Yankee emblem tee in his adult fist and pulled Myron close enough for him to smell the stale beer on the man's breath.

"He's giving my girlfriend a headache," the bearded man said. "He shuts up now."

Myron was stunned. Tears pushed their way into his eyes, but he

273

wouldn't let them out. He felt his chest hitch in fear and, strangely, shame. The man held on to Myron's shirt for another moment or two, then he pushed him back into his seat. The man turned back to the game and put his arm around his girlfriend. Afraid that he'd cry, Myron grabbed Brad's hand and hurried back to the upper deck. He didn't say anything, not at first, but Dad was perceptive and ten-year-old boys are not the world's best actors.

"What's wrong?" Dad asked.

His chest hitching with that combination of fear and shame, Myron managed to tell his father about the bearded man. Al Bolitar tried to stay calm as he listened. He put his hand on his son's shoulder and nodded along with him, but Dad's body was actually shaking. His face reddened. When Myron got to the point in the story where the man grabbed his shirt, Al Bolitar's eyes seemed to explode and go black.

In a too-controlled monotone, Dad said, "I'll be right back."

Myron watched the rest through the binoculars.

Five minutes later, Dad hurried down the lower-deck steps and moved into the third row, behind the bearded man. He cupped his hand around his mouth and began to shout as loud as he could. His face, already red, turned scarlet. Dad kept screaming. The bearded man didn't turn around. Dad leaned in so that his megaphoned mouth was an inch, maybe two at most, from the bearded man's.

He screamed some more.

Finally the bearded man spun around and that was when Dad did something that made Myron gasp out loud: He pushed the bearded man. The bearded man spread his hands as if to say, What gives? Dad pushed him twice more and then gestured with his thumb toward the exit, inviting the man to step outside with him. When the Beard refused, Dad pushed him again.

By now, the crowd had noticed. People started standing. Two security guards dressed in yellow windbreakers hurried down the steps. The players were watching now, even Yaz. The guards broke it up. Dad was escorted up the stairs. The fans cheered him. Dad actually waved to the crowd as he exited.

Ten minutes later, Dad came back to the upper deck. "Go back down again," Dad said. "He won't bother you anymore."

But Myron and Brad shook their heads. They liked the seats up here better anyway, next to their real hero.

Now, more than thirty years later, their hero lay on the basement floor, dying.

Hours passed.

In the Saint Barnabas Hospital waiting room, Mom rocked back and forth. Myron sat next to her, trying to keep it together. Mickey paced.

Mom started talking about how Dad had been out of breath all day—"since last night, really"—and how she had made a joke about it—"Al, why do you keep panting like some kind of perv?"—and how he had said it was nothing and how she should have made him call the doctor but you know how stubborn your father is, nothing is ever wrong, and why oh why hadn't she just made him call.

When Mom said the part about Dad being out of breath since last night, Mickey looked as though he'd been punched hard in the gut. Myron tried to give him a reassuring look, but the kid turned away fast and ran down the corridor.

Myron rose to go after him, but the doctor finally appeared. His name badge read, MARK Q. ELLIS, and he wore blue scrubs with a pink waist tie. The surgical mask was pulled down and bunched up under his chin. Ellis's eyes were red-tinged and bleary, his face two days unshaven. Exhaustion emanated from his very being. He also looked to be about Myron's age, which made him too young to be a top-notch cardiologist. Myron had called Win to find him the best and drag the guy here under gun threat if necessary.

Dr. Ellis said, "Your father suffered a serious myocardial infarction."

Heart attack. Myron felt his knees buckle. Mom let out a small groan. Mickey came back and joined them.

"We have him breathing again, but we aren't out of the woods. There is serious blockage. I'll know more in a little bit."

When he turned to leave, Myron said, "Doctor?"

"Yes?"

"I think I know how my father may have overexerted himself." *I think I know*—not *I think* or *I know*—in short, nervous child speak. "Last night"—Myron had no idea exactly how to put it—"my nephew and I got into a tussle." He explained how Dad had run outside and broken it up. As he spoke, Myron felt his eyes well up. Guilt and—yep, like when he was ten—shame washed over him. He spotted Mom out of the corner of his eye. She stared at him in a way he had never seen before. Ellis listened, nodded, and said, "Thank you for the information" before disappearing down the corridor.

Mom was still staring. She turned her laserlike eyes to Mickey then back to her son. "You two got into a fight?"

Myron almost pointed at Mickey and shouted, "He started it!" but instead he lowered his head in a nod. Mickey kept his eyes up—the kid redefined stoic—but his face had lost all color. Mom kept her gaze on Myron.

"I don't understand. You let your father get involved in your fight?"

Mickey said, "It was my fault."

Mom turned and looked up at her grandson. Myron wanted to say something to defend the kid, but at the same time he didn't want to lie. "He was reacting to something I did," Myron said. "It's on me too."

They both waited for Mom to say something. She didn't, which was a hell of a lot worse. She turned away and sat back in her chair. Mom put her shaking hand—Parkinson's or worry?—up to her face and tried very hard not to cry. Myron started toward her but pulled up. Now wasn't the time. He flashed again to that scene he always imagined, the one where Mom and Dad pull up to the house in Livingston for the first time, baby in tow, starting off on the El-Al family journey. He couldn't help but wonder if this was the final chapter.

Mickey moved to the other side of the waiting room and sat in front of a mounted TV. Myron paced some more. He felt so damn cold. He closed his eyes and started making deals with whatever higher power—what he would do and give and trade and sacrifice if only his father would be spared. Twenty minutes later, Win, Esperanza, and Big Cyndi appeared. Win informed Myron that Dr. Mark Ellis was supposedly great, but Win's friend, the legendary cardiologist Dennis Callahan from New York–Presbyterian, was on the way. They all moved into a private waiting room, except

Mickey, who wanted no part of any of them. Big Cyndi held Mom's hand and cried theatrically. It seemed to help Mom.

The hour passed in torturous slow motion. You consider every possibility. You accept and reject and rail and cry. The emotional wringer never lets up. A nurse came in several times to tell them that there was no new news.

Everyone fell into an exhausted silence. Myron was wandering the hallways when Mickey came rushing up to him.

"What's wrong?"

"Suzze T is dead?" Mickey asked.

"You didn't know?"

"No," Mickey said. "I just saw it on the news."

"That's why I came to see your mom," Myron said.

"Wait, what does my mom have to do with it?"

"Suzze visited your trailer a few hours before she died."

That made Mickey take a step back. "You think Mom gave her the drugs?"

"No. I mean, I don't know. She said she didn't. She said she and Suzze had a big heart-to-heart."

"What kind of heart-to-heart?"

Myron remembered something else Kitty had said about Suzze's OD: *"She wouldn't do that. Not to the baby. I know her. She was killed. They killed her."* Something clicked in the back of Myron's brain.

"Your mom seemed sure someone killed Suzze."

Mickey said nothing.

"And she seemed even more scared after I told her about the OD."

"So?"

"So is this all connected, Mickey? You guys on the run. Suzze dying. Your father missing."

He shrugged a tad too elaborately. "I don't see how."

"Boys?"

They both turned. Myron's mother was there. Tears were on her cheeks. A tissue was balled up in her hand. She dabbed at her eyes. "I want to know what's going on."

"With what?"

"Don't start that with me," she said in a voice only a mother can use on her son. "You and Mickey get into a fight—then suddenly he's going to live with us. Where are his parents? I want to know what's going on. All of it. Right now."

So Myron told her. She listened, shaking, crying. He spared her nothing. He told her about Kitty in rehab and even about Brad vanishing. When he finished, Mom moved closer to them both. She turned first to Mickey, who met her eye. She took his hand.

"It's not your fault," she said to him. "Do you hear me?"

Mickey nodded, his eyes closing.

"Your grandfather would never blame you. I don't blame you. With the amount of blockage he had, you may have inadvertently saved his life. And you"—she turned toward Myron—"stop moping and get out of here. I'll call you if something changes."

"I can't leave here."

"Of course you can."

"Suppose Dad wakes up."

She moved closer to him, craning her neck to look up at him. "Your father told you to find your brother. I don't care how sick he is. You do what he says."

27

So now what?

Myron pulled Mickey aside. "I noticed a laptop in your trailer. How long have you owned it?"

"Two years maybe. Why?"

"Is it the only computer you guys had?"

"Yes. And again I'm asking, why?"

"If your father used it, maybe there's something on it."

"Dad wasn't much with technology."

"I know he had an e-mail address. He used to write your grandparents, right?"

Mickey shrugged. "I guess so."

"Do you know his password?"

"No."

"Okay, what else of his do you still have?"

The kid blinked. He bit down on his lower lip. Again Myron reminded himself of where Mickey's life was right now: father missing, mother in rehab, grandfather suffering a heart attack, and maybe you're to blame. And you're all of fifteen years old. Myron started to reach out, but Mickey stiffened.

"We don't have anything."

"Okay."

"We don't believe in having a lot of possessions," Mickey said defensively. "We travel a lot. We pack light. What would we have?"

Myron put his hands up. "Okay, I'm just asking."

"Dad said not to look for him."

"That was a long time ago, Mickey."

He shook his head. "You should leave it alone."

No need or time to explain himself to a fifteen-year-old. "Will you do me a favor?"

"What?"

"I need you to take care of your grandmother for a few hours, okay?"

Mickey didn't bother with a reply. He headed into the waiting room and sat in the chair across from her. Myron signaled for Win, Esperanza, and Big Cyndi to come out in the hall with him. They needed to reach out to the American embassy in Peru and see whether there were any rumors about his brother. They needed to call any sources at the State Department and get them on the case of Brad Bolitar. They needed to get some computer weenie to break into Brad's e-mail or figure out his password. Esperanza headed back into New York City. Big Cyndi would stay behind to help with Mom and maybe see whether she could coax some more information from Mickey.

"I can be quite the charmer," Big Cyndi noted.

When Myron was alone with Win, he called Lex's phone yet again. Still no answer.

"It's all connected somehow," Myron said. "First my brother goes missing. Then Kitty gets scared and goes on the run. She ends up here. She posts that 'Not His' with a tattoo that both Suzze and Gabriel Wire shared. She sees Lex. Suzze visits her and then Alista Snow's father. It has to all relate."

"I wouldn't say 'has to,'" Win added, "but things do seem to circle back to Gabriel Wire, don't they? He was there when Alista Snow died. He clearly had an affair with Suzze T. He still works with Lex Ryder."

"We need to get to him," Myron said.

Win steepled his fingers. "You are suggesting then that we go after a reclusive, well-guarded, well-financed rock star on a small island."

"Seems that's where the answers are."

"Bitchin'," Win said.

"So how do we do it?"

"It will take a wee bit of planning," Win said. "Give me a few hours."

Myron checked his watch. "That works. I want to head back to the trailer and check their laptop. Maybe there's something there."

Win offered to provide Myron with a car and driver, but Myron hoped the ride would clear his head. He hadn't slept much in the past few nights, so he drove with the sound system on high. He plugged his iPod into the car jack and started blasting mellow music. The Weepies sang that "the world spins madly on." Keane wanted to disappear with that special someone to "somewhere only we know." Snow Patrol, in their search for their lost love, "set the fire to the third bar."

Just right.

When Myron was young, his father played only AM stations when he drove. He would steer with his wrists and whistle. In the morning, Dad would listen to an all-news station as he shaved.

Myron kept waiting for the phone to ring. Before leaving the hospital, he almost had a change of heart. Suppose, Myron had asked his mother, Dad woke up only one more time. Suppose Myron missed his last chance to talk to his father.

Mom had replied matter-of-factly: "What would you say that he doesn't already know?"

Good point. In the end, it was a question of his father's wishes. What would Dad rather Myron do—sit in a waiting room and cry or go out and try to find his brother? The answer was pretty simple when you posed it like that.

Myron arrived at the trailer park. He snapped off the engine. Fatigue weighed down his bones. He half stumbled out of the car, rubbing his eyes. Man, he needed a cup of coffee. Something. The adrenaline had begun to ebb. He reached the door. Locked. Had he really forgotten to get the key from Mickey? He shook his head, reached into his wallet, and pulled out the same credit card.

The door unlocked just as it had several hours ago. The laptop was still in the main room, near Mickey's pullout couch. He flipped it on and while it booted up, he searched the place. Mickey was right. There were very few possessions. The clothes had been packed already. The TV had probably come with the rental. Myron found a drawer of old papers and photographs. He had just dumped them on the couch when the computer dinged that it was all booted up.

Myron sat next to the pile of assorted papers, pulled the laptop toward him, and brought up the Internet history. Facebook was there. Google searches showed that someone had looked up the Three Downing nightclub in Manhattan and the Garden State Plaza Mall. Another Web site had been used to figure out public transportation routes to both. Nothing here. Brad had gone back to Peru three months ago anyway. The history only went back a few days.

His phone rang. It was Win.

"I have set it up. We leave for Adiona Island in two hours out of Teterboro."

Teterboro was a private airport in northern New Jersey. "Okay, I'll be there."

Myron hung up and looked back at the computer. The Internet history hadn't given up anything clue worthy. So now what?

Try some other applications, he thought. He started bringing them up one at a time. No one used the Calendar or the Address Book programs—both were empty. PowerPoint had a few school presentations by Mickey, most recently one on the history of the Mayans. The slideshow was in Spanish. Impressive but not relevant. He brought up the Word file. Again there were a bunch of what had to be school projects. Myron was about to give up when he spotted an eight-month-old file called "Resignation Letter." Myron clicked the icon and read:

To: *The Abeona Shelter*

Dear Juan:

It is with a heavy heart, my old friend, that I resign my position with our wonderful organization. Kitty and I will always be loyal supporters. We believe in this cause so much and have given so much to it. In truth, though, we have been more enriched than the young people we've helped. You understand this. We will always be grateful.

It is time, however, for the wandering Bolitars to settle down. I've secured a position back in Los Angeles. Kitty and I like being nomads, but it has been a long time since we stopped long enough to grow roots. Our son, Mickey, needs that, I think. He never asked for this life. He has spent his life traveling, making and then losing friends, and never calling one place home. He needs normalcy now and a chance to pursue his passions, especially basketball. So after much debate, Kitty and I have decided to get him settled into one place for his last three years of high school, and then he can apply to college.

After that, who knows? I never imagined this life for myself. My father used to quote a Yiddish proverb. Man plans, God laughs. Kitty and I hope to return one day. I know that no one really ever leaves the Abeona Shelter. I know I am asking a big thing here. But I hope you'll understand. In the meantime, we will do all we can to make this transition a smooth one.

Yours in Brotherhood,
Brad

Abeona Shelter. Kitty had posted "Not His" using the profile name "Abeona S." Myron quickly Googled "Abeona Shelter." Nothing. Hmm. He again Googled Abeona and found that it was the name of a somewhat obscure Roman goddess who protected children the first time they left their parents' care. Myron was not sure what that all meant, if anything. Supposedly, Brad had always worked for nonprofits. Was the Abeona Shelter one of them?

He called Esperanza next. He gave her Juan's address and the name of the Abeona Shelter. "Reach out to him. See if he knows anything."

"Okay. Myron?"

"Yes."

"I really love your dad."

He smiled. "Yeah, I know."

Silence.

Esperanza said, "You know the expression that there's never a good time to give bad news."

Uh-oh. "What is it?"

"I'm of two minds on something," she said. "I could wait until things are good before I tell you this. Or I can just throw it on the pile and with everything else going on, you'll barely notice."

"Throw it on the pile."

"Thomas and I are getting a divorce."

"Oh, damn." He thought about the pictures in her office, the happy family shots of Esperanza, Thomas, and little Hector. His heart sank anew. "I'm so sorry."

"I'm hoping it will be peaceful," Esperanza said. "But I don't think it's going to be. Thomas is claiming I'm an unfit mother because of my sordid past and the hours I work. He's going for sole custody of Hector."

"He'll never get it," Myron said.

"Like you have control over that." She made a noise, might have been a half laugh. "But I love when you make definitive pronouncements like that."

Myron flashed back to a recent one with Suzze:

"I just got a bad feeling. I think I'm going to mess up."

"You won't."

"It's what I do, Myron."

"Not this time. Your agent won't let you."

Won't let her mess up. And now she was dead.

Myron Bolitar: Big man with the big, definitive pronouncements.

Before he could take it back, Esperanza said, "I'll get on this," and hung up.

He just stared at the phone for a moment. The lack of sleep was starting to get to him. His head pounded to the point where he wondered if Kitty had any Tylenol in the medicine cabinet. He was about to get up and check when something snagged his attention.

It was in the pile of papers and photographs on the end of the couch. On the bottom on the right. Just a corner stuck out. A royal blue corner. Myron's eyes narrowed. He reached for it and pulled it into view.

It was a passport.

Yesterday he found Kitty's and Mickey's passports in Kitty's purse. Brad had last been seen traveling to Peru, so that's where his passport would be, according to Kitty. That begged the obvious question: Whose passport was this?

Myron flipped it open to the identification page. There, staring him in the face, was a photograph of his brother. He felt lost again, his pounding head spinning now.

Myron was just wondering about his next move when he heard the whispers.

There were times it paid to have frayed nerves. This was one of them. Instead of waiting or trying to figure out where the whispers were coming from or who was doing the whispering, Myron merely reacted. He leapt up, knocking the papers and photographs from the couch. Behind him he could hear the trailer door being smashed open. Myron dropped and rolled behind the couch.

Two men burst into the room holding guns.

They were both young, both pale, both skinny, both on something—what they used to call "heroin chic." The one on the right had a huge, complicated tattoo coming up out of the collar of his T-shirt, rising up his neck like a flame. The other had the practiced tough-guy goatee.

The one with the goatee said, "What the . . . we saw him come in."

"He's gotta be in the other room. I'll cover you."

Still on the floor behind the couch, Myron silently thanked Win for making sure that he was armed. There wasn't much time. The trailer was tiny. It would only take a few seconds to find Myron. He debated jumping out and yelling, "Freeze!" But both were armed and there was no way to know how they'd react. Neither looked particularly reliable, and thus there was an excellent chance they'd panic and start firing.

No, better to keep them confused. Better to make them scatter.

Myron made a decision. He hoped that it was the correct one, the rational one, and not just the emotional one, the one that yearned to lash out and inflict harm because his father was maybe dying and his brother was . . . He flashed back to Brad's passport and realized that he had no idea where his brother was, what he was doing, how much danger he was in.

Clear the mind. Act rationally.

Goatee took two steps toward the bedroom door. Staying low,

Myron shifted to the end of the couch. He waited another second, took aim low at Goatee's knee, and without calling out a warning, Myron pulled the trigger.

The knee exploded.

Goatee let out a shout and collapsed to the ground. His gun skittered across the room. But Myron wasn't paying attention to that. He ducked low, kept out of sight, and watched for Neck Tattoo's reaction. If he started firing, Myron had a bead on him. But Neck Tattoo didn't. He too screamed and, as Myron hoped, he scattered.

Neck Tattoo turned tail and dived back outside. Myron moved fast now. He jumped up and came out from behind the couch. On the floor in front of him, Goatee rolled in agony. Myron bent down, grabbed the man's face, made him look at him. Then Myron jammed the gun into Goatee's face.

"Stop screaming or I'll kill you."

Goatee quieted the scream to animal-like whimpers.

Myron quickly retrieved the man's gun and then ran toward the window. He looked out. Neck Tattoo was hopping into a car. Myron checked the plates. New York. He quickly put the letter-number combination into his BlackBerry and sent it to Esperanza. Not much time now. He went back to Goatee.

"Who are you working for?"

Still whimpering he said in a childlike voice: "You shot me!"

"Yes, I know. Who are you working for?"

"Go to hell."

Myron got down on his haunches. He pressed the barrel of the gun against the man's other knee. "I really don't have much time."

"Please," he said, his voice going up too many octaves. "I don't know."

"What's your name?"

"What?"

"Your name. Never mind. I'll call you Goatee. Here's what's going to happen, Goatee. I'm going to shoot your other knee now. Then I'll move to the elbows."

Goatee was crying. "Please."

"Eventually you'll tell me."

"I don't know! I swear."

Someone in the park had probably heard the gunshot. Neck Tattoo might come back with reinforcements. Either way, Myron had very little time here. He had to show he meant business. With a small sigh, Myron began to pull the trigger—he was that far gone—when a moment of common sense pushed through. Even if he could do it—even if he could shoot an unarmed, helpless man—the result of the shot would probably backfire on him. The pain would more likely make Goatee pass out or go into shock than get him to open up.

Still Myron wasn't sure what he would do when he said, "Last chance . . ."

Goatee came to the rescue. "His name is Bert! That's all I know. Bert!"

"Last name?"

"I don't know! Kevin set it up."

"Who's Kevin?"

"The guy who just left me here, man."

"And what did Bert want you to do?"

"We followed you, man. From the hospital. He said you'd lead us to Kitty Bolitar."

Man, now Myron really knew that he was slipping. These two numb nuts had been behind him this whole time and Myron never spotted the tail? Pathetic. "And when you found Kitty, what were you supposed to do?"

Goatee started crying again. "Please."

Myron put the gun against the man's head. "Look at my eyes."

"Please."

"Stop crying and look at my eyes."

He finally did. He was sniffling, trying to hold it together. His knee was a mess. Myron knew that he would probably never walk again without a limp. One day, that might bother Myron, but he doubted it.

"Tell me the truth and this is all over. You probably won't even have to go to jail. Lie to me and I shoot you in the head, so there's no witness. Do you understand?"

He kept his eyes surprisingly steady. "You're going to kill me anyway."

"No, I'm not. You know why? Because I'm still the good guy here. I want to stay that way. So just tell me the truth and save us: What were you supposed to do when you found Kitty?"

And then, with sirens signaling the approach of police cars, Goatee gave Myron the answer he expected: "We were supposed to kill you both."

Myron opened the trailer door. The sirens were louder now.

There was no time for Myron to get to his car. He ran left, away from the Glendale Estates entrance, as two police cars came into the trailer park. A powerful beacon of light from one of the cop cars hit him.

"Stop! Police!"

Myron didn't listen. The cops gave chase—or at least Myron assumed they did. He never turned around, just kept running. People came out of their trailers to see what the commotion was about, but no one got in his way. Myron had tucked his gun back into his waistband. There was no way he'd take it out and give the cops an excuse to open fire. As long as he wasn't a physical threat, they wouldn't shoot.

Right?

The squad car's loudspeaker came out with a crackle: "This is the police. Stop and put your hands in the air."

For a moment he almost did it. He could explain. But it would take hours, maybe days, and he simply didn't have that kind of time. Win had found a way to get them to Adiona Island. Somehow Myron knew that it was going to come back to that place, back to the reclusive Gabriel Wire, and he wasn't about to give him the chance to slip away.

The trailer park dead-ended into a wooded brush. Myron found a path and started on it. The police called for him to stop again. He darted to the left and kept going. Behind him he could hear movement in the bush. The cops were giving chase into the woods. He picked up his speed, trying to gain some distance. He debated hiding against a boulder or tree while they ran by, but what good would that do him? He needed to get out and free and up to Teterboro Airport.

He heard more shouts, but they were farther back now. He risked a glance behind him. Someone had a flashlight, but they were pretty far away. Fine. Still moving, Myron managed to dig his Bluetooth out of his pocket and jam it into his ear.

He hit the speed dial for Win.

"Articulate."

"I need a ride," Myron said.

He quickly explained. Win listened without interrupting. Myron didn't need to give his location. The GPS in his BlackBerry would help Win track him down. He just needed to stay out of sight until that happened. When he finished, Win said, "You're about a hundred yards west of Highway One. Start north on the highway and you'll run into a fair amount of retail. Find a place to hide or blend. I'll hire a limousine service to pick you up and get you to the airport."

28

Myron found an open Panera Bread. The rich smell of pastry reminded him that he hadn't eaten in forever. He ordered a coffee and bear claw. He sat near a window by a side door in case he needed to make a quick exit. From this vantage point he could see any and all cars pulling into the lot. If one ended up being a squad car, he could get out and be off for the woods in no time flat. He sipped the coffee and inhaled the bear claw. He started thinking about his dad. His dad always ate too fast. On Saturday mornings way back when, Dad would take him and Brad to Seymour's Luncheonette on Livingston Avenue for a milk shake, French fries, and maybe a pack of baseball cards. Myron and Brad would sit on stools and twirl them. Dad would stand next to them, always, as if that was what a man did. When the fries came, he'd lean against the counter and wolf them down.

Dad was never fat, but he was always on the wrong side of the "healthy weight" line.

Was that part of this? What if Dad had eaten better? What if Dad had worked out more or had a less stressful job or had a son who didn't get into jams that kept him up at night? What if his father hadn't come flying out of the house to defend that same son?

Enough.

Myron put the Bluetooth back into his ear and called Chief County Investigator Loren Muse. When she answered, Myron said, "I got a problem."

"What's that?"

"Do you have any sources in Edison, New Jersey?"

"It's Middlesex County. I cover Essex and Hudson. But yes."

"There was a shooting there tonight."

"Is that a fact?"

"And theoretically I might have done the shooting in self-defense."

"Theoretically?"

"I don't want any of this used against me."

"You lawyer types. Go on."

As Myron filled her in, a black limousine slowly cruised by. The window placard read: DOM DELUISE. Win. Myron hurried out, still talking through the Bluetooth, and ducked into the back. The driver offered up a hello. Myron mouthed a hello and then pointed to the earpiece, indicating that he was both on the phone and a pretentious ass.

Loren Muse was not happy. "What exactly do you want me to do with this information?"

"Tell your source."

"Tell my source what exactly? That the shooter called me and said he doesn't want to turn himself in yet?"

"Something like that."

"And when do you expect that you'll have time to grace us with your presence?" Muse asked.

"Soon."

"Well, that should satisfy him."

"I'm just trying to save them some headache, Muse."

"You can do that by coming in now."

"I can't."

Silence. Then Muse asked: "Does this have something to do with Suzze's overdose?"

"I think it does, yes."

"Do you think these guys at the trailer were her drug dealers?"

"They could have been, maybe."

"Do you still think Suzze's death was murder?"

"It's possible, yes."

"And finally, do you think you could just jerk my chain a little harder with all these specifics?"

Myron debated tossing Muse a bone, telling her about Suzze visiting Kitty, that the disposable cell phone Suzze called not long before her death had belonged to his sister-in-law. But then he realized where that would lead—more questions and maybe a visit to the Coddington Rehabilitation Institute—and decided against it.

Instead he tried answering a question with a question. "Do you have any new evidence to suggest it was anything other than an overdose?"

"Ah, I see," Muse said. "If I give you something, you'll continue to give me nothing. Quid pro nada."

"I really don't know anything yet."

"You're so full of crap, Myron. But at this point, what do I care? To answer your question, there is not a shred of evidence that points to foul play in the death of Suzze T. That help?"

Not really.

"So where are you right now?" Muse asked.

Myron frowned. "You serious?"

"Not going to tell me, eh?"

"Not going to tell you."

"So you only trust me so far?"

"You have an obligation as an officer of the law to report anything I say," Myron said. "But you can't say what you don't know."

"How about telling me who lived in that trailer? I'm going to find out anyway."

"No, but . . ." There was a bone he wanted to toss her, even though he had given his word he wouldn't.

"But?"

"Get a warrant on a middle school teacher in Ridgewood named Joel Fishman. He's a drug dealer." Myron had promised ol' Crush that he would not report him, but when you pull a gun on someone in a middle school, well, Joel never called "no crossies."

When he finished giving her enough details to nail Fishman, Myron hit the end button. Cell phones were not allowed in the hospital so he called the administrative desk. They transferred him around until he found a nurse who was willing to go on the record and tell him there was nothing new to report on his father's condition. Terrific.

The limousine pulled right out onto the tarmac next to the aircraft. No luggage check-in, no boarding pass, no security line in which the man in front of you forgets to take the spare change out of his pocket despite forty-seven requests to do so and sets off the metal detector. When you fly private, you pull up right onto the tarmac, you walk up the stairs, and bingo, you're off.

As Win often pointed out, it was good to be rich.

Win was on board already with a couple he introduced as "Sassy and Sinclair Finthorpe" and their twin teenage sons, "Billings and Blakely."

Myron frowned. And rich people made fun of African American names?

Sassy and Sinclair both wore tweed jackets. Sassy was also decked out in riding pants and leather gloves. She had blond hair tied back in a severe ponytail. She was probably in her midfifties with plenty of hard wrinkles from too much sun. Sinclair was bald, paunchy, and wore a real-live ascot. He laughed heartily at everything and said, "Quite, quite," in reply to nearly anything said to him.

"This is so exciting," Sassy said through the clenched teeth. "Isn't it, Sinclair?"

"Quite, quite."

"Like we're helping out James Bond on a secret mission."

"Quite, quite."

"Boys? Isn't this exciting?"

Billings and Blakely looked at her with classic teenage loathing. Sassy said, "This calls for cocktails!"

They offered Myron a drink. He passed. Billings and Blakely continued to look on with haughty scorn, or maybe that was their default genetic facial expressions. The twins both had wavy, Kennedyesque hair and wore tennis whites with sweaters tied around their necks. Win's world.

They all took their seats, and within five minutes of boarding the plane, the wheels were up. Win sat next to Myron.

"Sinclair is a cousin," Win said. "They have a place on Adiona Island and were going to head up there tomorrow. I just asked them to move it up."

"Because Crisp won't know we're on this flight?"

"Exactly. If I had taken my plane or a boat, we would have tipped him off. He may have a man watching the airport though. We'll let my cousins get off first and then sneak out."

"Do you have a plan to get us onto Wire's property?"

"I do. It will require some local help though."

"From?"

"I'm handling it," Win said with a small smile. "There is no cell phone service on the island, but I have a satellite phone, in case the hospital needs to reach us."

Myron nodded. He leaned back and closed his eyes.

"One more rather important thing," Win said.

"I'm listening."

"Esperanza ran a trace on that license plate from the trailer park. The car is currently leased to a company called Regent Rental Associates. She then traced back the company's history. Guess who owns Regent Rental?"

Myron still had his eyes closed. "Herman Ache."

"Should I be impressed?"

"I'm right?"

"You are. How did you know?"

"An educated guess. It's all connected."

"And you have a theory?"

"A partial one."

"Do tell."

"I think it's what we said before. Frank Ache told you that Wire had big gambling debts, right?"

"Correct."

"So we start there—Gabriel Wire and maybe Lex owing money to Herman Ache. But I think Herman really got his hooks into Wire during the Alista Snow incident."

"By protecting him from criminal charges?"

"By making the charges—criminal and otherwise—disappear. Whatever is going on here, it all started the night Alista Snow died."

Win nodded, mulling it over. "And that would explain why Suzze visited Karl Snow yesterday."

"Right, another connection," Myron said. "Suzze is somehow linked into that night too. Maybe via Lex. Maybe via her secret lover Gabriel Wire. I'm not sure. But for whatever reason, she needed to come forward and tell the truth now. She went to Kitty and admitted some wrongdoing by switching out her birth control pills. Then she went to Karl Snow. Maybe she told him what really happened to his daughter, I don't know."

Myron stopped. Yet again something wasn't adding up. Win voiced it.

"And then, after clearing her conscience, a pregnant Suzze T purchased heroin, went back to her penthouse abode, and committed suicide?"

Myron shook his head. "I don't care what the evidence shows. That doesn't make sense."

"You have an alternate theory?"

"I do," Myron said. "Herman Ache had her killed. It was a professional job all the way, so my guess is, Crisp did the deed. He's good at making murder appear to be natural causes."

"Motive?"

Myron still wasn't sure. "Suzze knew something—probably something that could damage Wire, maybe bring back the criminal charges from Alista Snow. So Ache has her killed. Then he sends two men to find Kitty and kill her."

"Why Kitty?"

"I don't know. Again he was cleaning house. Herman figured that she knew something or maybe he was afraid Suzze had talked to her. Whatever, Herman decided to take no chances. Scorch the earth. Kill Suzze and Kitty."

"And you," Win finished for him.

"Yep."

"And what about your brother? How does he fit in?"

"I don't know."

"A lot we don't know."

"Almost everything," Myron agreed. "But here's another thing: If Brad went back to Peru, why was his passport in the trailer?"

"Most likely answer? He didn't go. And if that's the case, what might we safely conclude?"

"That Kitty lied," Myron said.

"Kitty lied," Win repeated. "Wasn't that a song by Steely Dan?"

"*Katy Lied*. And it was the name of an album, not a song."

"Oh, right. I loved that album."

Myron tried to turn his brain off for just a little while so as to rest up before they stormed the castle. He'd just closed his eyes and put his head back when the plane began its descent. Five minutes later they were on the ground. Myron checked his watch. He had arrived at Teterboro Airport forty-five minutes ago.

Yep. It was good to be rich.

29

The shades on the plane were pulled so no one could see inside. The Finthorpe family disembarked. The pilots parked the plane, turned off the lights, got off themselves. Myron and Win stayed in place. Night had fallen.

Myron tried the hospital from the satellite phone. This time Dr. Ellis got on the phone with him. "Your father is out of surgery, but this has been a tough one. His heart stopped twice on the table."

The tears started coming again. Myron forced them back. "Can I speak to my mother?"

"We gave her a sedative and she's sleeping in a room down the hall. Your nephew is asleep in a chair too. It's been a long night."

"Thank you."

Win came out of the bathroom, dressed head to toe in black. "There's a change of clothes for you in there," he said. "There's also a shower. It might help refresh you. Our help will be here in ten minutes."

The plane's showerhead was not designed for the tall, but the water pressure was surprisingly strong. Myron hunched over and used nine of his allotted ten minutes under the nozzle and one minute drying off and slipping into the black garb. Win was right—it did refresh.

"Our ride awaits," Win said. "But first . . ."

He handed Myron two guns. The larger one had a shoulder holster. The smaller was to wrap around the ankle. Myron fastened them into place. Win led the way. The plane steps were slippery. Rain pelted down on them. Win ducked back under the plane for protection. He took night-vision goggles out of their case and strapped them onto his face like a scuba mask. He slowly turned around in a circle.

"All clear," Win said.

He put the goggles back into their pouch. Then he held up his mobile phone and pressed a button. The screen lit up. In the distance Myron saw someone flash car headlights at them. Win started toward the vehicle. Myron followed. The airport, if you will, was basically a landing strip with a concrete building. There was nothing else. A road crossed the front of the landing strip. There were no traffic lights or even a gate to stop cars from going by—one had to guess, Myron assumed, when an incoming plane was on the way. Or maybe it was more of the Adiona Island mystique. You simply *knew* when someone was coming.

The rain kept pouring. A thunderbolt shattered the air. Win reached the car first and opened the back door. Myron slid in and across to behind the passenger side. He looked in the front seats and was surprised to find Billings and Blakely.

"Our local help?"

Win grinned. "Who better?"

The car smelled like an old bong.

"Cousin Win told us you want to get into Wire's place," the twin driving said.

"Which one are you?" Myron asked.

He looked insulted. "I'm Billings."

"And I'm Blakely."

"Right, sorry."

"Blakely and I have spent every summer on this island for as long as we can remember. It can indeed get boring."

"Not enough girls," Blakely added.

"Too right," Billings said. He started driving. There were no other cars on the road. "Last year we made up cruel stories about some of the uglier au pairs."

"So they'd be fired," Blakely said.

"Exactly so."

"And none of these mommies want to take care of their little brats."

"Heavens no."

"So they have to replace the au pairs."

"Often with more attractive ones."

"See the brilliance?"

Myron looked at Win. Win just grinned.

"Pretend I do," Myron said.

"Anyway, this island can get boring," Blakely said.

"Dullsville," Billings added.

"Tedious."

"Tiresome."

"You could die from such boredom, really. And in truth, no one is even sure that Gabriel Wire lives in that estate."

"We've never seen him."

"But we've gotten close to the house."

"We've touched it."

Blakely turned around and flashed the teeth at Myron. "See, we bring the babes there. We tell them that the house belongs to Gabriel Wire and that it's well guarded."

"Because danger is an aphrodisiac."

"If you mention danger to a girl, her panties practically melt off, do you hear what I'm saying?"

Myron looked at Win again. Win still grinned.

"Pretend I do," Myron said again.

Billings continued: "It took us a while—trial and error, don't you know—but we found a safe path to the beach by Wire's house."

"We never get caught anymore."

"Not in the last two summers anyway."

"We go to the beach. Sometimes we bring girls."

"In your day," Billings said, looking at Myron, "you probably called it Lover's Lane or something like that."

"Like in an old movie."

"Exactly. Like, you took them to the malt shop and then you went to Lover's Lane, right?"

"Yes," Myron said. "After the horse-and-buggy ride."

"Right. See, the beach by Wire's house? That's our version of that."

"Billings is very good with the ladies," Blakely said.

"Ol' Blakely here is being too modest."

They both chuckled with their jaws set. Blakely pulled out a hand-rolled cigarette and lit it up. He took a hit and passed it to his brother.

"We also smoke reefer there," Billings said.

"Doobies."

"Weed."

"Hemp."

"Grass."

"Joints."

"A little ganja."

"Marijuana," Myron said, cutting them off. "I get it."

The boys started snickering. This was not their first cigarette of the night.

Win said, "Blakely and Billings are going to lead us down their secret path."

"Where we bring the girls."

"Our honeys."

"Babes-a-licious."

"Glorious hotties."

"Tasties."

"Gnaw-worthy morsels."

Myron looked at Win. "They, uh, seem young to get involved in this."

"Nah, it's cool," Billings said. "They won't hurt us."

"Plus we're brave."

"Especially after we do a little herb."

"Some hay butt."

"A little Doña Juanita."

"A touch of Mary Jane."

"Panama Gal."

They were laughing hysterically now. As hysterically as you can with your jaw clenched. Again Myron looked at Win, wondering about relying on a couple of well-bred stoners. At the same time, breaking into places—finding a way into even the best guarded of edifices—was one of Win's strong points. He had a plan. Myron would just follow it.

They drove past two security stations in the middle of the road with nary a wave. The twins and their reefer-reeking vehicle were clearly well-known on the island. No one bothered them. Billings or Blakely—Myron had already forgotten—drove erratically. Myron fastened his seat belt. During the daytime, this island seemed remote. At night, especially in the rain, it felt totally and completely abandoned.

Billings—Myron remembered now—took the car off the pavement and down a dirt road. The road tested the shocks and found them wanting. Myron bounced around the back as the car traveled through thick woods until they hit a clearing. The car came to a stop near the beach.

Blakely turned around again. He offered Myron a hit. Myron waved him off with a no-thanks.

"You sure? It's premium."

"Primo," Billings added.

"Boss."

"I get it," Myron said. "It's really good."

The twins sat back and for a moment all was silent. "Whenever I'm on the beach," Billings said, "I pick up one grain of sand."

"Oh no," Blakely said. "Here we go again."

"No, I'm serious here. Think about it. One grain of sand. I pick up one tiny grain of sand and I think of how many grains of sand are on this beach. Then I think about how many of them are on this entire island. Then I start thinking about how many grains of sand there are in this entire world. And I'm, like, whoa."

Myron looked at Win some more.

"And the kicker—the real kicker—is that our entire planet is smaller than that grain of sand next to all those other grains. Can you even comprehend that? Our solar system is smaller than that grain of sand when you compare it to the rest of the universe."

Myron said, "How much of this stuff have you smoked today?"

Billings chuckled. "Come on. Let's get you on your way to Mr. Famous Rock Star."

"I hate his music," Blakely added.

"Total crap."

"Self-indulgent dung."

"Pretentious caterwauling."

They stepped out of the car. Myron was about to open the door, but Win put his hand on his knee. "Wait. Let them take the lead. We need to stay hidden."

"Do you really trust these kids?"

"They serve a purpose. Don't worry."

A minute later, Win nodded that it was okay. The rain continued to pound down on them. The twins had gone down a path off the beach. Myron and Win followed, staying a solid fifty yards back. The rain made the visibility tough. They trekked on a serpentine route through a rather hilly wooded area. The path was gone now so that they had to duck under tree branches and step over rocks. Every once in a while, Myron could see the beach to his left through openings in the trees. Finally, Win put his arm in front of Myron, gatelike. They both stopped.

The twins were gone.

"They've reached Wire's property," Win said. "We need to be more cautious now."

Myron let Win take the lead. They slowed their step. The opening looked like a black hole. Myron wiped the rain from his face. Win bent low. He took out the night-vision goggles and pulled them over his face. He signaled for Myron to wait and then he vanished into the dark. A few moments later, Win came back into the woods and signaled for Myron to come forward.

Myron stepped into the clearing and saw via moonlight that they were on a beach. About fifty yards in front of them on the left, Billings and Blakely lay on big boulders. They were on their backs, passing a joint back and forth, the rain not a factor. Waves pounded the boulders. Win's gaze was turned to the right. Myron followed it up the hill and saw what had snagged his friend's attention.

Whoa, Nelly.

Gabriel Wire's palace sat perched alone overlooking the Atlantic. Victorian neo-Gothic with red brick, stone, terra-cotta roof, and cathedral spires à la the House of Parliament, the estate was perfect for the rock-star ego, sprawling and sensual and absolutely nothing like the more understated WASP homes that dotted the rest of the island. The front had a fortress feel with a gated archway that looked like an oversized duplicate of the one on Lex and Suzze's rooftop.

Billings and Blakely sidled over to them. For a few moments they all just stared up at it. "Didn't we tell you?" Billings said.

"Personally," Blakely said, "I think it's gauche."

310

"Spectacularly ostentatious."

"Over-the-top on steroids."

"Showy."

"Pretentious."

"Overcompensating."

Both boys giggled at that one. Then growing more somber, Blakely said, "But man oh man, what a total Babe Lair."

"Love Nest."

"Herpes Haven."

"Penile Palace."

"Beaver Trap."

Myron tried not to sigh. It was like hanging out with a really annoying thesaurus. He turned to Win and asked what the plan was.

"Follow me," Win said.

As they moved back toward the tree line and angled up toward the house, Win explained that Billings and Blakely would approach the house from the front. "The twins have made it to the house several times before," Win said, "but they've never made it inside. They've rung the bell. They've tried the windows. Eventually a security guard chases them. The boys claim that there is only one guard at the house at night, while a second guard covers the gate on the road."

"But they can't know that for sure."

"No, so neither do we."

Myron thought about it. "But they make it all the way to the house before the guard sees them. That means there are probably no motion detectors."

"Motion detectors rarely work on large open estates," Win said.

"Too many animals set off false alarms. There will probably be alarms or some kind of chime on the doors and windows, but that shouldn't concern us."

Burglar alarms, Myron knew, kept out the amateur or run-of-the-mill robber. They did not keep out Win and his satchel of tools.

"So the only big risk," Myron said, "is how many guards are in the actual house."

Win smiled. His eyes had that funny glaze. "What's life without a few risks?"

Still in the trees, Win and Myron reached a spot about twenty yards from the house. Win signaled for Myron to duck down. He pointed to the side door and whispered, "Servants' entrance. That's how we will make our approach."

He took out his cell phone and again flashed it. In the distance, Billings and Blakely started climbing up the hill toward the estate's archway gate. The wind picked up speed, whipping the boys on their ascent. They kept their heads lowered and came closer.

Win nodded at Myron. Both men got on their bellies and commando-crawled toward the servant's entrance. Myron could see that the door led to a kitchen or pantry or something like that, but the lights were off inside. The ground was sopping wet from the rain, making their crawl feel snail-like. The mud oozed beneath them, friction free.

When Win and Myron reached the side door, they remained on their bellies and waited. Myron turned his head to the side and rested his chin on the wet ground. He could see the ocean. Lightning ripped the sky in two. Thunder crackled. They stayed there for one minute, then two. Myron started getting antsy.

A few moments later, through the wind and rain, he heard a shout: "Your music sucks!"

It was Billings or Blakely. The other—the one who hadn't yelled first—came back with, "It's horrendous!"

"Dreadful!"

"Ghastly!"

"Appalling!"

"An offensive audible assault!"

"A ghastly ear crime!"

Win was up and working the door with a thin screwdriver. The lock wouldn't be a problem, but Win had spotted a magnetic sensor. He took a sliver of special foil and jammed it between the two sensors so it would work as a conduit.

Through the rain, Myron could make out the twins' silhouettes running back toward the water. Behind them came another man, the security guard, who stopped once the twins hit the beach. He put something to his mouth—a walkie-talkie of some sort, Myron figured—and said, "It's just those stoned twins again."

Win opened the door. Myron jumped inside. Win followed, closing the door behind them. They were now in an ultramodern kitchen. In the center of the room, there was a giant double oven with eight burners and a silver flume on the ceiling. Various pots and pans hung from the ceiling in decorative chaos. Myron remembered reading that Gabriel Wire was something of a gourmet cook, so Myron guessed that this all made sense. The pots and pans looked pristine—new or lightly used or simply well kept.

Myron and Win stayed still for a full minute. No footsteps, no walkie-talkie shrieking, nothing. In the distance, probably way upstairs, they could hear the faint hint of music.

Win nodded for Myron to go. They had already planned the post-entrance strategy. Myron would search for Gabriel Wire. Win would handle anyone who came to his defense. Myron switched his BlackBerry to a radio frequency and put the Bluetooth into his ear. Win did the same. Win would now be able to warn Myron of any incoming trouble—and vice versa.

Staying low, Myron pushed open the door to the kitchen and into what might have been a ballroom. No lights—the only illumination coming from the screensavers on the two computers. Myron had expected something more ornate, but the room looked as though it'd been converted into a dentist's waiting room. The walls were painted white. The couch and love seat set looked more practical than stylish, like something you'd buy in any highway store. There was a file cabinet in the corner, a printer, a fax machine.

The expansive staircase was wooden with ornate railings and a bloodred runner. Myron started up the stairs. The music, still faint, grew louder. He reached the top of the staircase and started down the long corridor. The wall on the right was loaded up with Horse-Power's framed platinum albums and records. On the left were photographs of India and Tibet—places frequented by Gabriel Wire. Supposedly Wire had a luxury home in posh south Mumbai and often stayed, undercover, in monasteries in eastern Tibet's Kham district. Myron wondered about that. This house was so damn depressing. Yes, it was dark out and the weather could have been better, but had Gabriel Wire really spent most of the last fifteen years cooped up here alone? Maybe. Or maybe that was what Wire wanted people to believe. Maybe he was indeed a crazy, world-class reclusive in the vein of Howard Hughes. Or maybe he had just had enough of being the famous, constantly-in-the-spotlight front man

Gabriel Wire. Maybe the other rumors were true and Wire went out all the time, wearing simple disguises so he could visit the Met in Manhattan or sit in the bleachers at Fenway Park. Maybe he had taken a look at when and how his life had slipped off the rails—the drugs, the gambling debts, the too-young girls—and remembered why he started, what originally drove him, what had made him happy:

Making music.

Maybe Wire's behavior of shunning the spotlight wasn't so crazy. Maybe this was the only way he could survive and thrive. Maybe, like anyone else who makes a life change, he had to hit bottom and how much lower can you get than feeling responsible for the death of a sixteen-year-old girl?

Myron passed the final platinum album on the wall—a record called *Aspects of Juno*, HorsePower's very first. Like any other casual music fan, Myron had heard about the legendary first meeting between Gabriel Wire and Lex Ryder. Lex had been performing at a sketchy pub called the Espy in the St. Kilda area near Melbourne on a busy Saturday night, playing something slow and lyrical and getting booed by the rowdy, drunken crowd. One of those in the crowd was a handsome young singer named Gabriel Wire. Wire would later say that despite the din around him, he was both mesmerized and inspired by the melodies and the lyrics. Finally, with the boos reaching an earth-shattering decibel, Gabriel Wire took to the stage and more to save the poor bastard than anything else, he started jamming with Lex Ryder, changing his lyrics on the fly, speeding up the tempo, getting someone else to pick up a bass and the drums. Ryder started nodding. He came back with more riffs, moved from keyboard to guitar and then back again. The two men fed off each other. The crowd fell into a respectful hush, as though realizing what they were witnessing.

HorsePower was born.

How had Lex poetically put it at Three Downing just a few nights ago? "Things ripple." It had all started there, in that seedy bar on the other side of the world more than a quarter century ago.

Without warning, Myron flashed to his father now. He had tried to keep it out, tried to focus solely on the task at hand, but suddenly he saw his father not as a strong, healthy man but sprawled out on the basement floor. He wanted to run out of here. He wanted to get back on a damn plane and go back to that hospital, where he belonged, but then he thought how much sweeter it would be, how much more it would mean to his father, if he could somehow come back with his baby brother in tow.

How had his brother gotten caught up with Gabriel Wire and the death of Alista Snow?

The answer was obvious and sobering: Kitty.

The familiar anger—Kitty's husband is missing and she's exchanging drugs for sex favors?—rose to the surface as he crept down the corridor. He could hear the music better now. An acoustic guitar and a soft singing voice:

Gabriel Wire's.

The sound was heartbreaking. Myron stopped and listened to the lyrics for a moment:

"My only love, we'll never have yesterday again,
And now I sit through an endless night . . ."

It was coming from the end of the corridor. Toward the stairs up to the third floor.

"My vision blurred by tears,
Hardly feel the bitter cold,
Hardly notice the pounding rain . . ."

He passed an open door and risked a quick peek. Again the room was decorated with frighteningly functional furniture and gray wall-to-wall carpeting. No frills, no flair, no clever accent. Bizarre. Where the huge façade was jaw-droppingly majestic, the interior could double as middle-management office space. This was, Myron surmised, either a guest bedroom or maybe one of the security guards stayed here. But still.

He kept moving. There was a narrow stairway at the end of the corridor. He was nearing it now, getting closer to the plaintive sound:

"Remember our last time together,
Spoke of a love lasting forever,
Our eyes met in some kind of trance,
Everyone vanished as we just held hands,
But now you're gone too. . . ."

There was one more open door before the stairway. Myron took a quick look and froze.

A nursery.

The baby mobile with its potpourri of animals—ducks, horses, giraffes in bright, loud colors—hung over a Victorian bassinet. A butterfly night-light provided enough illumination for Myron to see the Winnie the Pooh wallpaper—the old Winnie drawings, not the more modern ones—and, in a corner, a woman in full nurse garb dozed in a chair. Myron tiptoed into the room and looked into the bassinet. A newborn. Myron assumed that it was his godson. So this was where Lex had run to—or at least, this was where Suzze's son was. Why?

Myron wanted to tell Win, but he didn't dare whisper. With the keyboard on silent, he typed in a text: BABY ON SECOND FLOOR.

Nothing more to do in here. He carefully stepped back into the hallway. The limited light cast long shadows. The narrow staircase ahead of him looked like something that might lead to servants' quarters in the attic. The steps had no runner, just wood, so he padded up them as quietly as he could. The singing was getting closer now:

"In that moment my sun was gone,
And now the rain won't stop falling,
In an endless spell of time,
In the middle of a moment,
And the moment can't move on . . ."

Myron reached the landing. In lesser homes, this level might be considered an attic. Here the entire floor had been cleared out to make one expansive room that ran the length of the entire house. Again the lights were low, but the three big-screen televisions on the far end gave the room an eerie glow. All three sets were on sports—a major-league baseball game, ESPN *SportsCenter*, an overseas basketball game. The volume had been muted. This was the ultimate adult playroom. In the dim light, Myron saw a HorsePower pinball machine. There was a well-stocked mahogany bar with six bar stools and a smoky mirror. The floor was dotted with what looked like upscale beanbag chairs, huge ones, big enough to house an orgy.

One of the beanbag chairs sat center of the three televisions. Myron could see the silhouette of a head. There were bottles of what Myron assumed was booze on the floor next to him.

"Now you're gone too,
And out in the rain, time stands still,
Without you, time stands—"

The music stopped as though someone had switched it off. Myron could see the man in the beanbag stiffen—or maybe that was his imagination. Myron wasn't sure what to do here—call out, approach slowly, just wait?—but the decision was soon made for him.

The man in the beanbag chair stumbled to a stand. He turned toward Myron, the glow from the televisions keeping him a dark silhouette. More as a reaction than anything else, Myron moved his hand toward the weapon in his pocket.

The man said, "Hey, Myron."

It wasn't Gabriel Wire.

"Lex?"

He was teetering, probably from drink. If Lex was surprised to see Myron here, he wasn't showing it. His reactions had probably been dulled by the bottle. Lex spread his arms and moved toward Myron. Myron came toward him, nearly catching Lex as he collapsed into Myron's arms. Lex dug his face into Myron's shoulder. Myron held him up.

Through the tears, Lex kept repeating, "My fault. It's all my fault."

Myron tried to comfort and hush him. It took some time. Lex reeked of whiskey. Myron let him cry it out. He moved Lex toward a bar stool and perched him on it. In his Bluetoothed ear, Myron could hear Win say, "I had to put the security guard down. Safely, don't worry. But you might want to pick up the pace here."

Myron nodded as though Win could see him. Lex was pretty wasted. Myron decided to skip the preliminaries and get right to it. "Why did you call Suzze?"

"Huh?"

"Lex, I don't have time for this, so please listen up. Suzze received a call from you yesterday morning. After that, she ran off to see Kitty and Alista Snow's father. Then she came back home and overdosed. What did you say?"

He started sobbing again. "It was my fault."

"What did you say, Lex?"

"I took my own advice."

"What advice?"

"I told you. At Three Downing. Remember?"

Myron did. "No secrets from the one you love."

"Exactly." He swayed from the booze. "So I told my true love the truth. After all these years. I should have told her years ago but I figured that somehow, Suzze always knew. You know what I mean?"

Myron didn't have a clue.

"Like deep down I thought she always knew the truth. Like it wasn't all a coincidence."

Oh man, it was tough to talk to a drunk. "What wasn't a coincidence, Lex?"

"Us falling in love. Like it was preordained. Like she always knew the truth. You know, deep down inside. And maybe—who knows?—maybe she did. Subconsciously. Or maybe she fell for the music, not the man. Like the two are interwoven anyway. How do you separate the man from the music? Like that."

"What did you tell her?"

"The truth." Lex started to cry again. "And now she's dead. I was wrong, Myron. The truth didn't set us free. The truth was too much to handle. That's the part I forgot. The truth can bring you closer together, but it can also be too much to bear."

"What truth, Lex?"

He started sobbing.

"What did you tell Suzze?"

"It doesn't matter. She's dead. What's the difference now?"

Myron decided to shift gears. "Do you remember my brother, Brad?"

Lex stopped crying. He looked confused now.

"I think my brother might be in trouble because of all this."

"Because of what I said to Suzze?"

"Yes. Maybe. That's why I'm here."

"Because of your brother?" He thought about it. "I can't see how. Oh, wait." He stopped and said something that made Myron's blood chill. "Yes. I guess, even after all these years, it could have led back to your brother."

"How?"

Lex shook his head. "My Suzze . . ."

"Please, Lex, tell me what you told her."

More sobbing. More shaking of his head. Myron had to move him along.

"Suzze was in love with Gabriel Wire, wasn't she?"

Lex sniffled some more, wiped his nose with his shirt sleeve. "How did you know?"

"The tattoo."

He nodded. "Suzze drew that, you know."

"I know."

"It was Hebrew and Gallic letters combined into a love sonnet. Suzze was so artistic."

"So they were lovers?"

He frowned now. "She thought that I didn't know. That was her secret. She loved him." Lex's voice turned bitter. "Everyone loves Gabriel Wire. Do you know how old Suzze was when she started up with him?"

"Sixteen," Myron said.

Lex nodded. "Wire always liked to seduce the young ones. Not prepubescent. He wasn't into that. Just young. So he let Suzze and Kitty and some of the other tennis girls party with us. The famous with the famous. Rock star with tennis starlet. A match made in celebrity heaven. Me, I never paid much attention to them. Enough girls around so that you didn't need someone illegal, you know what I mean?"

"I do," Myron said. "I found a photograph from the Live Wire shoot. Gabriel had the same tattoo as Suzze."

"That?" Lex snickered. "It was temporary. He just wanted a famous notch on his belt. Suzze was so smitten with him she stuck by him even after he killed Alista Snow."

Whoa.

"Hold up," Myron said. "Did you just say Gabriel killed Alista Snow?"

"You didn't know? Of course. Got her doped up on roofies. But he didn't give her enough, dumb bastard. He raped her and then she totally freaked out. Said she was going to tell. In Wire's defense—and no, it's not a defense—he was stoned out of his mind too. He pushed her off the balcony. It's all on videotape."

"How?"

"The room had a security camera."

"Who has the videotape now?"

He shook his head. "I can't tell you that."

But Myron already knew, so he just said it: "Herman Ache."

Lex didn't respond. He didn't have to. It added up, of course. It was pretty much just what Myron had thought.

"We both owed Ache big," Lex said. "Mostly Gabriel—but he used HorsePower as collateral. He had one of his men with us all the time. To protect his investment."

"And that's why Evan Crisp is still here?"

Lex actually shuddered at the mention of his name.

"He scares me," he said in a whisper. "I even thought maybe he killed Suzze. Once she knew the truth, I mean, Crisp had warned us. There was too much money at stake. He would kill anyone who got in the way."

"What makes you so sure he didn't kill her?"

"He swore to me he didn't do it." Lex leaned back. "And how could he? She shot up. That woman investigator, what's her name?"

"Loren Muse."

"Right. She said there was no evidence she was murdered. She said all signs point to an overdose."

"Have you ever seen the videotape of Wire killing Alista Snow?"

"Years ago. Ache and Crisp sat us both down and showed it to us. Wire kept crying that it was an accident, he didn't mean to push her over the rail, but really, what's the difference? He killed that poor girl. Two nights later—I'm not making this up—he actually called Suzze to come over. And she did. Suzze thought he was the victim of the press. So blind—but then again she was only sixteen years old. What's the rest of the world's excuse? Then he dumped her. Do you know how we hooked up—Suzze and me?"

Myron shook his head.

"It was ten years later at a gala for the Museum of Natural History. Suzze asked me to dance and I swear the only reason she came on to me that night was because she hoped that I could lead her back to Wire. She still pined for him."

"But she fell for you."

He managed a smile on that one. "Yes. She did. Really and truly. We were soul mates. I know Suzze loved me. And I loved her. I thought that would be enough. But really, when you stop and think about it, Suzze had already fallen for me. That's what I meant before. About falling for the music. She fell for his beautiful façade, yes, but she also fell for the music, the lyrics, the meaning. Like with *Cyrano de Bergerac*. Do you remember that play?"

"I do."

"They all fell for the gorgeous façade. The whole world, really—we fall for the beauty of the outside. Not a news flash, is it, Myron? We are all shallow. You ever see someone, some guy maybe, and you just *know* from his face he's a nasty SOB? Gabriel Wire was the opposite. He looked so soulful, so poetic, so beautiful and sensitive. The façade. And underneath was nothing but decay."

"Lex?"

"Yes."

"What did you tell Suzze on the phone?"

"The truth."

"You told her that Gabriel Wire killed Alista Snow?"

"That was part of it, yes."

"What was the rest of it?"

He shook his head. "I told Suzze the truth, and it killed her. I have a son to protect now."

"What was the rest of it, Lex?"

"I told her where Gabriel Wire was."

Myron swallowed. "Where is he, Lex?"

And then the strangest thing happened. Lex stopped crying. He smiled now and looked toward a beanbag by the television. Myron felt his blood go cold.

Lex didn't speak. He just stared at the beanbag chair. Myron remembered what he had heard as he came up the stairs. Singing.

Gabriel Wire singing.

Myron slid off the stool. He moved toward the beanbag chair. He saw a strange shape in front of it, low down, on the floor maybe. He came closer, turned his gaze to the floor, and now he could see what it was.

A guitar.

Myron spun back toward Lex Ryder. Lex was still smiling.

"I heard him," Myron said.

"Heard who?"

"Wire. I heard him singing when I was on the stairs."

"No," Lex said. "That was me you heard. It's always been me. That's what I told Suzze. Gabriel Wire died fifteen years ago."

30

Downstairs, Win woke up the security guard.

The guard opened his eyes wide. He was tied up with a gag in his mouth. Win smiled at him. "Good evening," Win said. "I'm going to remove your gag. You will answer my questions and not call for help. If you refuse, I will kill you. Any questions?"

The security guard shook his head.

"Let's start with an easy one," Win said. "Where is Evan Crisp?"

"We did meet at the Espy in Melbourne. But that's the only part of our story that's true."

They were back on the bar stools. Suddenly even Myron needed a belt. He poured them both two fingers of Macallan Scotch. Lex stared down into his glass as if it held a secret.

"At the time I'd already released my solo album. It went nowhere. So I started thinking about putting together a band. So I'm in the Espy when Gabriel sauntered in. He was eighteen years old at the time. I was twenty. Gabriel had dropped out of school and been arrested twice for drug possession and another time for assault. But when he walked in the bar, the way every head turned . . . you know what I mean?"

Myron just nodded, not wanting to interrupt.

"He couldn't sing a lick. He couldn't play an instrument. But if a rock group is a movie, I knew that I needed to cast him as front man. We made up the whole story about my playing in the bar and him coming to my rescue. Actually I half stole the story from a scene in a movie. *Eddie and the Cruisers*. Have you seen it?"

Again Myron nodded.

"I still meet people who swear they were at the Espy that night. I don't know if they're lying to feel important or if they're just self-delusional. Probably both."

Myron remembered his own childhood. Every friend of his had claimed to see a "surprise" Springsteen show at the Stone Pony in Asbury Park. Myron had his doubts. He'd gone three times in high school when he heard the rumors, but Bruce never showed.

"Anyway, we became HorsePower, but I wrote every song— every melody, every lyric. We used backing tapes onstage. I taught Gabriel how to carry a tune but for the most part I dubbed over him or studiofied it."

He stopped now, took a deep sip, seemed lost. To bring him back, Myron asked, "Why?"

"Why what?"

"Why did you need him as a prop?"

"Don't be daft," Lex said. "He had the looks. It's like I told you—Gabriel was the beautiful, poetic, soulful façade. I viewed him as my greatest instrument. And it worked. He loved being the big star, nailing every piece of young ass who crossed his path, making money hand over fist. And I was happy too. Everyone was listening to my music. The entire world."

"But you never got the credit."

"So? That's never mattered much to me. I was about the music. That was all. The fact that the world considers me a second banana . . . well, the joke is on them, isn't it?"

Myron guessed that maybe it was.

"I knew," Lex went on. "That was enough for me. And in a sense, we were indeed a real rock group. I needed Gabriel. Isn't beauty in a sense its own talent? Successful designers put their dresses on beautiful models. Don't the models play a role? Big companies have attractive spokespeople. Aren't they relevant to the process? That's what Gabriel Wire was to HorsePower. And the proof was in the eating. Listen to my solo stuff from before I met Wire. The music is just as good. No one cared. Do you remember Milli Vanilli?"

Myron did. They were two male models named Rob and Fab who lip-synched someone else's music and rose to the top of the charts. They even won a Best New Artist Grammy.

"Remember how the world hated those two guys when the truth came out?"

Myron nodded. "They were vilified."

"Exactly. People actually went out and burned their records. How come? Wasn't the music the same?"

"It was."

He leaned in conspiratorially. "Do you know why the fans turned on those two guys so horribly?"

Just to keep him talking, Myron shook his head.

"Because those pretty boys pointed out the truth: We are all shallow. Milli Vanilli music was pure crap—and they won a Grammy! People listened to it simply because Rob and Fab were handsome and hip. That scandal did more than rip away the façade. It held a mirror up to the fan's face and let him see a total fool. There are many things we can forgive. But we can't forgive those who point out our true foolishness. We don't like to think of ourselves as shallow. But we are. Gabriel Wire looked brooding and deep but he was anything but. People thought that Gabriel didn't do interviews because he felt he was too important—but he didn't give them because he was too dumb. I know I was mocked over the years. Part of me was hurt—who wouldn't be?—but most of me understood that this was the only way. Once I started, once I created Gabriel Wire, I couldn't destroy him without destroying me."

Myron tried to let this information settle. "That's what you meant with all that talk earlier about Suzze falling for you or falling for the music. About being Cyrano."

"Yes."

"But I don't understand. When you say Gabriel Wire is dead—"

"I mean that literally. Someone killed him. Probably Crisp."

"Why would he do that?"

"I'm not sure, but I have my suspicions. When Gabriel killed Alista Snow, Herman Ache saw an opportunity. If they could pull him out of this jam, not only would they get their substantial gambling debt paid, but Wire would owe them for life."

"Yeah, okay, I got that."

"So they saved him from the fire. They intimidated witnesses. They paid off Alista Snow's father. I don't really know what happened next. I think Wire went a little crazy. He started acting erratically. Or maybe they realized that we really didn't need him. I could make the music on my own. Maybe they hatched this plan and decided we were better off with Wire dead."

Myron thought about that. "Seems awfully risky. Plus you guys used to make a mint on the rare concert appearance."

"But touring was a big risk too. Gabriel wanted to do it more, but using backing tracks got more difficult as time went on, what with all the lip-synching scandals. It wasn't worth it."

"So I still don't get it. Why kill Wire? And for that matter, when?"

"A few weeks after Alista Snow was killed," Lex said. "First he left the country. That part was true. If they couldn't clear him, I think Gabriel would have just stayed overseas and become another Roman Polanski or something. He came back when the case against him started falling apart. Witnesses started clamming up. There was no security tape. The last step was for Gabriel to meet with Karl Snow and slip him a bagful of money. Once all that was done, the media and the cops faded away."

"And then, after all that, Crisp kills Gabriel Wire?"

Lex shrugged. It didn't make sense.

"You told Suzze all this on the phone?"

"Not all of it, no. I wanted to. See, I knew it would all come out now, what with Kitty back in our lives. I figured that I should tell her first. I wanted to for years anyway and now we were going to have a baby. . . . We needed to get rid of all the lies, all the secrets. You know what I mean?"

"I do. But when you saw that post that said 'Not His,' I mean, you knew it wasn't true."

"Yep."

"So why did you run?"

"I told you at Three Downing. I just needed time. Suzze didn't tell me about the post. How come? She saw it, and man, I knew right away something was wrong. And think about it. When she came to you, she didn't just want you to find me. She wanted to know who posted the message on the board." He cocked his head to the side. "Why do you think that was?"

"You think," Myron said, "that she still held a candle for Gabriel."

"I don't think. I know. Suzze didn't even tell you because, well, would you have gone looking to help her somehow reunite with another man? No."

"You're wrong. She loved you."

"Of course she did." Lex was smiling now. "Because I was Wire. Don't you see? So when I saw that post, I mean, the shock of it. I just needed time to figure out what to do. So I came up here and made a little music. And then, like I said before, I called Suzze to tell her the truth. I started by telling her that Wire was dead—that he'd been dead for more than fifteen years. But she didn't believe me. She wanted proof."

"Did you see the body?"

"No."

Myron spread his hands. "So then for all you know, he is alive. Maybe he's overseas. Maybe he's disguising himself or living in a commune in Tibet."

Lex almost laughed at that one. "You believed that nonsense?

Oh, come on. We were the ones who spread those rumors. Twice we asked starlets to say that they'd been with him and they agreed just to up their profile. No, Gabriel is dead."

"How do you know?"

He shook his head. "Funny."

"What?"

"That's what Suzze kept asking: How did I know for sure?"

"So what did you tell her?"

"I told her there was a witness. Someone who saw Gabriel's murder."

"Who?"

But even before Lex answered, Myron knew. Whom did Suzze call right after she talked to Lex? Who had posted something that made Lex fear the truth would come out? And who, if he took it to the next level, connected all this to his brother?

"Kitty," Lex said. "Kitty saw Gabriel Wire get killed."

With the security guard still tied up—and the voices of Myron and Lex Ryder in his ear—Win approached the computers in the downstairs room. The austere décor made sense now. Lex might visit to use the recording studio. Crisp or well-trusted security guards might spend nights. But nobody truly lived here. You could feel that hollowness. The security guard was muscle, an old Ache worker. He knew to keep his mouth shut. But even he didn't quite know the circumstances. Guards were changed every few months. All understood that the upstairs was off-limits. This particular guard had never seen Gabriel Wire, of course, but he didn't really question that. He figured that Wire just traveled a lot. Wire was a paranoid recluse, he was told. He was never to approach him. So he never did.

Win had wondered about the lack of security, but now it made perfect sense. "Wire" lived on an island with very few inhabitants, most of whom shunned publicity or craved privacy. Even if there was a breach, even if someone did manage to break into the house, so what? They would find no Gabriel Wire, but what would that mean? Ache, Crisp, and Ryder had concocted enough stories about secret travels and disguises to explain away any absence.

Fairly ingenious.

Win was not much of a computer expert, but he knew enough. With a bit of persuasion the guard had helped him with the rest. Win brought up the passenger manifests. He looked through other files that Crisp had worked on. Crisp was no fool. He would never leave anything incriminating, anything that could be used in court, but Win didn't worry about court.

When he was done, Win placed three phone calls. The first was to his pilot.

"You're ready?"

The pilot said, "Yes."

"Depart now. I'll signal when it's okay to land."

Win's second call was Esperanza. "Any new developments on Mr. Bolitar?"

Al Bolitar has always insisted that Win call him Al. But Win just couldn't.

"They just rushed him back into surgery," Esperanza said. "It doesn't look good."

Win hung up again. The third call was to a federal penitentiary in Lewisburg, Pennsylvania.

When Win finished, he sat back and listened to Myron and Lex Ryder. He considered his options, but in truth there was only one. They had gone too far this time. They had brought themselves to the brink, and there was only one way to back away from it.

The security guard's radio sounded. Through the radio static a voice said, "Billy?"

The voice belonged to Crisp.

Win smiled. That meant Crisp was near. Their big showdown was only minutes away now. Frank Ache had predicted that it would come down to this during the prison visit. Win had joked that he would videotape it, but no, Frank would have to settle for an oral recounting.

Win brought the radio over to the guard. As Win came closer, the security guard began to whimper. Win understood. He took out his gun and put it against the man's forehead. Overkill, really. The man had already tried to be tough. It hadn't lasted.

"You probably have a code word that tells Crisp you're in trouble," Win said. "If you use it, you will beg me to pull this trigger. Do you understand?"

The security guard nodded, eager to please.

Win put the radio to Billy's ear and pressed the talk button. He said, "Billy here."

"Status?"

"All clear."

"The earlier problem was taken care of?"

"Yes. Like I said, it was the twins. They ran when I came out."

"I have separate confirmation that they drove off," Crisp said. "How is our guest behaving?"

"Still upstairs working on that new song."

"Very good," Crisp said. "I'm on my way up to the house. Billy?"

"Yes."

"There's no reason to tell him I'm coming."

The conversation ended. Crisp was on his way.

It was time for Win to prepare.

Myron said, "Kitty?"

Lex Ryder nodded.

"How did she know Wire was dead?"

"She saw it."

"She saw them kill Wire?"

Lex Ryder nodded. "I didn't know about it until a few days ago. She calls me on the phone and tries to shake me down. 'I know what you did to Gabriel,' she says. I figure she's putting me on. I say, 'You don't know squat' and hang up. I don't tell anyone. I figure she'll go away. The next day she posts that tattoo and 'Not His' message. Like a warning. So I call her. I tell her to meet me at Three Downing. When I see her, I mean, wow, she's bad, really wasted. I could have paid her off, I guess, but she's a full-fledged addict now. Totally unreliable. Buzz ends up calling Crisp and tells him what she's babbling about. Then you come barreling into the nightclub. During the commotion, I warn Kitty to get the hell out of there and not come back. She said she's been doing that for sixteen years— since she saw Wire get shot."

So, Myron thought, Kitty hadn't been paranoid. She knew a secret that could cost Herman Ache and Evan Crisp millions of dollars. That explained Goatee and Neck Tattoo following him to

Kitty's trailer. Ache had realized that Myron might be able to lead him to Kitty. He had put a tail on him, and once the men located them, their orders were clear: Kill them both.

So why not use Crisp? Obvious answer: Crisp was busy doing something else. Tailing Myron was still something of a long shot. Hire cheaper muscle.

Win was back in his ear. "Are you done up there?"

"Pretty much."

"Crisp is on his way."

"You have a plan?"

"I do."

"Do you need my help?"

"I need you to stay where you are."

"Win?"

"Yes?"

"Crisp may know what happened to my brother."

"Yes, I know."

"Don't kill him."

"Well," Win said. "Not right away."

31

Two hours later, they were back at the small Adiona Island airport, boarding Win's Boeing Business Jet. Mee greeted them in an aggressively tailored red stewardess uniform topped with a Jackie-O pillbox hat.

"Welcome aboard," Mee said. "Watch your step, welcome aboard, watch your step."

Lex trudged up the stairs first. He was finally sobering up and it wasn't looking good on him. The baby nurse, carrying Lex's son, followed. That left Myron, Win, and a still-wobbly Evan Crisp. Crisp's hands were tied behind his back with several plastic cuffs. Win knew that some people could escape plastic cuffs. Few people, if any, could escape several, especially when the larger ones were wrapped around the forearms and the chest. Win backed these up with a gun too. Crisp had taken chances. Win would not.

Myron looked back at Win. "A moment," Win said.

Mee came back to the door and nodded at Win. Win said, "Okay, now."

Myron took the lead, half dragging Crisp behind. Win took the rear, pushing Crisp up. Myron had carried him before, fireman-style, but now Crisp was starting to regain consciousness.

Win had bought the luxury aircraft from a once-popular rapper who, like many before him, dominated the charts before becoming a trivia question and being forced to liquidate the fruits of his overspending. The main cabin had oversized leather recliners, plush carpeting, a wide-screen 3-D television, serious wood trim. The plane had a separate dining room, plus a bedroom in the back. Lex, the nurse, and the baby were closed off in the dining room. Win and Myron didn't want them in the same room with Crisp.

They pushed Crisp into a seat. Win wrapped him in restraints. Crisp was still blinking through the tranquilizer. Win had used a diluted form of Etorphine, a sedative normally used for elephants and potentially fatal to humans. In the movies, sedatives work instantaneously. In reality, it's hardly a guarantee.

In the end, Crisp had not been indestructible. No one was. As Herman Ache had so poetically put it, no one—not even Myron or Win—was bulletproof. The truth was, when the best were taken, they were normally taken easily. A bomb drops on your house, it doesn't matter how good your hand-to-hand combat skills are— you're dead.

From Billy the security guard, Win had learned the path that Crisp took to the Wire estate. Win had found the ideal spot. He came out with two guns—one with real bullets, one with the Etorphine. He didn't wait. While holding the real gun on him, he shot

Crisp with the Etorphine and kept his distance while the man passed out.

Win and Myron moved two rows back and sat next to each other. Mee, ever the professional flight attendant, ran through a full safety talk, demonstrating how to use the seat belt, how to secure your oxygen mask before helping others, how to inflate the life jacket. Win watched her with his patented rakish grin.

"Demonstrate the blowing in the tube part again," he said to Mee.

Win.

The takeoff was smooth enough to be choreographed by Motown. Myron called Esperanza. When he heard about his father being back in surgery, he closed his eyes and just tried to breathe. Concentrate on the possible. Dad had the best medical care. If Myron wanted to help, there was only one way: Find Brad.

"Did you learn anything about the Abeona Shelter?" he asked Esperanza.

"Not a thing. It's like it doesn't exist."

Myron hung up. He and Win discussed what they already knew and what it meant. "Lex gave me the answer right from the start," Myron said. "All couples have secrets."

"Hardly an earth-shattering revelation," Win said.

"Do we have secrets, Win?"

"No. But we don't have sex either."

"You think sex leads to secrets?" Myron asked.

"You don't?"

"I always thought sex leads to greater intimacy."

"Bah," Win said.

"Bah?"

"You're so naïve."

"How so?"

"Didn't we prove it's just the opposite? Couples—those having sex like Lex and Suzze—those are the ones who keep secrets."

He had a point. "So where are we off to?"

"You'll see."

"I thought we had no secrets."

Crisp started to stir. He opened one eye, then the other. He didn't react. He let it settle, trying to put together where exactly he was and what he should do next. He looked over at Myron and Win.

"You know what Herman Ache will do to you?" Crisp asked. Then: "You can't be this stupid."

Win arched an eyebrow. "Can't we?"

"You guys aren't that tough."

"We keep hearing that."

"Herman will kill you. He'll kill your whole family. He'll make sure the last thing your loved one ever does is curse your name and beg to die."

"Well, well," Win said, "doesn't Herman have a flair for the dramatic? Fortunately I do have something of a plan. A win-win for all involved, including you."

Crisp said nothing.

"We are going to pay dearest Herman a visit," Win said to him. "The four of us will sit down, perhaps over a nice latte. We will all cooperate. We will reveal all. And then we will work out a mutually beneficial understanding so that no one gets harmed."

"Meaning?"

"Détente. Have you heard of it?"

"I have," Crisp said. "I'm not sure Herman has."

Myron's thought exactly. But Win seemed untroubled.

"Herman is a sweetheart, you will see," Win said. "In the meantime, what happened to Myron's brother?"

Crisp frowned. "The guy married to Kitty?"

"Yes."

"How the hell would I know?"

Win sighed. "Cooperate. Reveal all. Remember?"

"I'm serious. We didn't even know Kitty was around until she contacted Lex. I don't have a clue where her husband is."

Myron thought about that. He knew that Crisp could be lying—probably was—but what he said fit with what Lex had told them.

Win unfastened his seat belt and walked over to Evan Crisp. He handed him the satellite phone. "I need you to call Herman Ache. Tell him we will meet him at his Livingston residence within the hour."

Crisp offered up skeptical. "You're kidding, right?"

"I am indeed a mirthful fellow. But no."

"He won't let you in armed."

"That's fine. We don't need weapons. If anyone touches a hair on our heads, the world finds out the truth about Gabriel Wire. Bye-bye, big money. We are also moving Lex Ryder—your cash cow, if you will—to a secure location. Do you see?"

"Cooperation," Crisp said. "Reveal all."

"I love it when we have an understanding."

Crisp made the call. Win stood over him the whole time. On the other end of the phone, Herman Ache didn't like what he was hearing, not at first, but Crisp explained what Win wanted to do. In the end Herman agreed to the meet.

"Wonderful," Win said.

Myron looked at Crisp's smile, then up at Win. "I'm not sure I like being kept in the dark," Myron said.

"You don't trust me?" Win asked.

"You know better."

"I do. And I have it under control."

"You're not infallible, Win."

"Correct," Win said. Then he added, "But I'm also not always your faithful sidekick."

"You may be putting us in a dangerous situation."

"No, Myron, you did that. When you agreed to help Suzze and all those who came before her, you put us where we are now. I'm just trying to find us a way out."

Myron said, "Wow."

"The truth hurts, old friend."

And in truth, it did.

"If there's nothing more . . ." Win checked his watch and smiled at his favorite stewardess. "We still have thirty minutes before we land. You stay and watch our prisoner. I'm going into the bedroom for a little Mee time."

32

Big Cyndi met them at the Essex County Airport in Caldwell, New Jersey. She put Lex, the nurse, and the baby in an SUV. Big Cyndi was going to bring them to Zorra, the cross-dressing former Mossad agent, and then Zorra would find a safe house and would tell no one—not even Myron or Win—where it was. This way, Win had explained, if his plan somehow backfired and Herman Ache grabbed and tortured them, they wouldn't be able to tell them where Lex was.

"How comforting," Myron had said.

Win had a car waiting. Normally he'd use a driver, but why put anyone else in danger? Crisp was fully awake now. They pushed him in the backseat and redid his restraints, adding some to his legs. Myron sat in the passenger seat. Win drove.

Herman Ache lived in a legendary mansion in Livingston, scant miles from where Myron grew up. When Myron was a kid, the estate had belonged to a famed crime boss. Rumors swirled around the playground about the place. One kid said that if you crossed their property line, real-live gangsters shot at you. Another kid said that there was a crematorium behind the house where the mafia boss burned his victims.

This second rumor was actually true.

The gateposts were topped with bronze lion heads. Win took the long drive to the first landing. That was as far as they'd be able to go. They parked. Myron watched three big guys in ill-fitted suits approach. The one in the middle, the leader, was extra beefy.

Win took out both his guns and placed them in the glove compartment.

"Get rid of your weapons," Win said. "We're going to be searched."

Myron looked at him. "Do you have a plan here?"

"I do."

"Do you want to share it with me?"

"I already did. The four of us are going to chat. We will all act rationally. We will learn what we need to about your brother. We will agree not to harm their business interest if they don't harm us. What part of this bothers you?"

"The part where you trust a psychopath like Herman Ache to act rationally."

"He is, first and foremost, interested in business and the air of legitimacy. Killing us would harm that."

The biggest of the beefy bruisers—he had to be six-seven, three hundred pounds—knocked on Win's window with his ring. Win rolled down the window. "May I help you?"

"Get a load of this." Beefy looked at Win like he was something that had just dropped out of a dog's behind. "So you're the famous Win."

Win smiled brightly.

"You don't look like much," Beefy said.

"I could offer up several clichés—don't judge a book by its cover, big things come in small packages—but really, wouldn't that just go over your head?"

"You being funny?"

"Evidently not."

Beefy lowered his brow in a Neanderthal frown. "You armed?"

"No," Win said, pounding his chest. "Me Win. You armed?"

"Huh?"

Sigh. "No, we are not armed."

"We're gonna search you. Thoroughly."

Win winked at Beefy. "I was counting on that, big boy."

Beefy took a step back. "Get the hell out of the car before I put a hole in your head. Now."

Homophobia. Still gets to them every time.

Usually Myron joined Win in these fearless taunts, but this situation seemed too out of control. Win left the keys in the ignition. He and Myron stepped out of the car. Beefy told them where to stand. They did as he asked. The other two men opened the back door and used straight razors to free Evan Crisp from the plastic restraints. Crisp rubbed the circulation back into his wrists. He walked over to Win and stood directly in front of him. The two men stared each other down.

"Can't sneak up on me this time," Crisp said.

Win gave him the smile. "Would you like to go, Crisp?"

"Very much. But right now time is short, so I'll just have my boys here hold a gun on your friend while I pop you one. Just a little payback."

"Mr. Ache gave specific instructions," Beefy said. "No damaging the goods until he talks to them. Follow me."

Beefy led the way. Myron and Win were first. Crisp and the two goons took the back. Up ahead Myron could see the dark baronial mansion that one old mobster described as "Transylvania Classic." It fit. Man, Myron thought, it had been a big night for huge, creepy homes. As they walked, Myron swore he could hear the long-dead call out a warning.

Beefy took them through the back entrance into a mudroom. He had them walk through a metal detector, then he double-checked them with a security wand. Myron tried to remain calm, wondering where Win had hidden the weapon. There was no way he would go into this situation without one.

When he was done with the wand, Beefy did a rough hand-search on Myron. Then he moved on to Win, taking longer.

Win said, "Thorough as promised. Is there a tip jar?"

"Funny guy," Beefy said. When he was done, Beefy took a step back and opened a closet door. He took out two gray sweat suits. "Strip down to nothing. Then you can put these on."

"Are those one-hundred-percent cotton?" Win asked. "I have very sensitive skin, not to mention a reputation for haute couture."

"Funny guy," Beefy said again.

"And gray totally doesn't work with my complexion. It completely washes me out." But now, even Win sounded a little strained by where this was going. His tone had a whistling-in-the-dark quality to it. The other two goons snickered and took out their guns.

Myron looked over to Win. Win shrugged. Not much choice now. They both stripped down to their underwear. Beefy made them take that off too. The, uh, probe was thankfully brief. Win's homophobic jokes had worried them into not being overly meticulous.

When they finished, Beefy handed one of the sweat suits to Myron, the other to Win. "Put them on."

They did so in silence.

"Mr. Ache is waiting in the library," Beefy said.

Crisp led the way with a hint of a smile on his face. Beefy and the Boys stayed behind. No surprise. The Gabriel Wire situation had to be top secret. Myron guessed that no one knew about it but Ache, Crisp, and maybe an attorney on retainer. Even the security guards who worked the property didn't know. "Maybe I should do the talking," Myron said.

"Okay."

"You're right. Herman Ache will want to do what's in his best interest. We have his golden goose."

"Agreed."

When they entered the library, Herman Ache was waiting with a snifter of brandy. He stood by one of those antique-globe wet bars. Win had one too. In fact, the entire room looked as though Win had done the decorating. Bookshelves lined the walls, three stories high, with a sliding ladder so that you could reach the higher volumes. The leather club chairs were burgundy. There was an oriental carpet and deep wainscoting on the ceilings.

Herman Ache's gray toupee was a little too shiny tonight. He wore a polo shirt with a V-neck sweater underneath it. There was a logo for a golf club on the chest.

Herman pointed at Win. "I told you to leave this alone."

Win nodded. "You did indeed." Then Win reached into the waistband of the sweatpants, pulled out a gun, and shot Herman Ache right between the eyes. Herman Ache crumbled in a ragged heap. Myron actually gasped out loud. He turned to Win, who already had the weapon pointed at Evan Crisp.

"Don't," Win said to Crisp. "If I wanted you dead, you'd be dead too. Don't force my hand."

Crisp froze.

Myron just stared. Herman Ache was dead. No question about it. Myron said, "Win?"

Win kept his eye trained on Crisp. "Search him, Myron."

In something of a daze, Myron did as Win asked. There was no weapon. Win told Crisp to get on his knees and lace his hands behind his head. Crisp did so. Win kept the gun pointed at Crisp's head.

"Win?"

"We had no choice, Myron. Mr. Crisp here was correct. Herman would have killed everyone dear to us."

"What about all that talk about his business interest? What about détente?"

"Herman may have agreed for a little while, but not in the long run. You know that. The moment we discovered Wire was dead it became us or him. He would never let us live, holding that over his head."

"But killing Herman Ache"—Myron shook his head, trying to clear it—"even you don't just walk away from that."

"Don't worry about that right now."

Crisp stayed statue-still on his knees, hands on his head.

"So what now?" Myron asked.

"Perhaps," Win said, "I'll kill our friend Mr. Crisp here. In for a penny, in for a pound."

Crisp closed his eyes. Myron said, "Win?"

"Ah, don't worry," Win said, keeping the gun trained on Crisp's head. "Mr. Crisp is merely a hired hand. You have no loyalty to Herman Ache, do you?"

Crisp finally broke his silence. "I don't, no."

"There then." Win looked at Myron. "Go ahead. Ask him."

Myron moved in front of Evan Crisp. Crisp looked up and met his eye.

"How did you do it?" Myron asked.

"Do what?"

"How did you kill Suzze?"

"I didn't."

"Well," Win said. "Now we're both lying."

Crisp said, "What?"

"You're lying about not killing Suzze," Win said. "And I was lying about not killing you."

Somewhere in the distance a grandfather clock started chiming. Herman Ache continued to bleed out on the floor, an almost perfect circular puddle of blood surrounding his head.

"My theory," Win said, "is that you were not merely a hired hand on this but more likely a full partner. It doesn't matter, really. You're a very dangerous man. You don't like that I got the better of you. If our roles were reversed, I wouldn't like it either. So you know already. I can't let you survive to fight another day."

Crisp turned his head to look up at Win. He tried to meet Win's eyes, as though that would help. It wouldn't. But Myron could smell the fear on Crisp now. You could be tough. You could be the hardest guy around. But when you stare death in the face, only one thought comes to mind: I don't want to die. The world becomes very simple. Survive. We don't pray in foxholes because we are ready to meet our Maker. We pray because we don't want to.

Crisp searched for a way out. Win waited, seeming to enjoy the moment. Win had cornered his prey and now it was as though he were playing with it.

"Help!" Crisp yelled. "They shot Herman!"

"Please." Win looked bored. "That won't do any good."

Crisp's eyes widened in confusion, but Myron saw it. There was only one way Win could have gotten that weapon: He had inside help.

Beefy.

Beefy had put the gun in Win's sweat suit.

Win raised the barrel so that it pointed at Crisp's forehead. "Any final words?" Crisp's eyes darted like scattered birds. He spun his head around, hoping to find a reprieve in Myron. And then, looking up at Myron, Crisp made one last desperate move: "I saved your godson's life."

Even Win seemed to catch his breath. Myron moved closer to Crisp, bent down so that they were face-to-face. "What are you talking about?"

"We had a good thing going," Crisp said. "We were all making a lot of money and, really, who were we hurting? And then Lex gets religion and ruins it. After all the years, why the hell did he open his mouth to Suzze? How did he think Herman would react to that?"

"So you were sent to silence her," Myron said.

Crisp nodded. "So I flew into Jersey City. I waited in the garage and grabbed her when she parked. I put my gun against her belly and made her take the stairs. There are no security cameras there. It took a while. When we got up to the penthouse, I told her to overdose on the heroin or, pow, I'd shoot her in the head. I wanted to make it look like an accident or suicide. I could do it with the gun, but it would be easier with the drugs. With her past, the cops would buy an OD easy."

"But Suzze wouldn't shoot up," Myron said.

"That's right. Suzze wanted to make a deal instead."

Myron could almost see it now. Suzze with the gun on her, not blinking. He'd been right. She wouldn't just kill herself. She wouldn't obey an order like that, even at gunpoint. "What kind of deal?"

Crisp risked a glance back at Win. He knew that Win wasn't bluffing, that Win had concluded that it would be too dangerous to let Crisp live. Still, no matter what the odds, man scrambles to survive. This revelation was Crisp's version of the last-second Hail Mary pass, his attempt to show enough humanity so that Myron would persuade Win not to pull the trigger.

Myron remembered the 9-1-1 call from the accented maintenance man. "Suzze agreed to overdose on the heroin," Myron said, "if you called nine-one-one."

Crisp nodded.

How had he not seen it before? You couldn't force Suzze to take the heroin. She too would scramble to save her life. Except under one condition.

"Suzze would do what you asked," Myron went on, "under the condition that you gave her child a chance to live."

"Yes," Crisp said. "We made a deal. I promised to make the call the moment she shot up."

Myron's heart broke anew. He could almost see Suzze coming

to the realization that if she were shot in the head, her unborn son would die with her. So yes, she had scrambled, not to save herself, but to save her child. Somehow she had found a way. It was risky. If she died from the overdose right away, so might the baby. But at least it gave him a chance. Suzze probably knew how heroin overdoses work, how they slowly shut down the system, that there would be time.

"And you kept your promise?"

"Yes."

Myron asked the obvious question: "Why?"

Crisp shrugged and countered with: "Why not? There was no reason to kill an innocent baby if I didn't have to."

The morals of a killer. So now Myron knew. They had come here for answers. There was only one more he needed now. "Tell me about my brother."

"I told you already. I don't know anything about that."

"You went after Kitty."

"Sure. Once she came back and started making noise, we tried to find her. But I don't know a thing about your brother. I swear."

With those last words, Win pulled the trigger and shot Evan Crisp in the head. Myron jumped back, startled by the sound. Blood oozed out onto the oriental carpet as the body slumped to the ground. Win did a quick check, but there was no need for a second shot. Herman Ache and Evan Crisp were both dead.

"Us or them," Win said.

Myron just stared. "So now what?"

"Now," Win said, "you go to your father."

"What are you going to do?"

"Don't worry about it. You may not see me for a while. But I'll be fine."

"What do you mean, not see you for a while? You're not taking the heat for this alone."

"Yes, I am."

"But I'm here too."

"No, you're not. I've taken care of it. Take my car. I'll find a way to communicate but you won't see me for a while."

Myron wanted to argue, but he knew it would only delay and possibly endanger the inevitable.

"How long?"

"I don't know. We had no choice here. There was no way these two would have let us live. You have to see that."

Myron did. He also saw now why Win hadn't told him. Myron would have looked for another way when, in truth, there wasn't one. When Win visited Frank Ache in prison, they promised to exchange favors. Win had made good on it and saved them in the process.

"Go," Win said. "It's over now."

Myron shook his head. "It's not over," he said. "Not until I find Brad."

"Crisp was telling the truth," Win said. "Whatever danger your brother was in, it had nothing to do with this."

"I know," Myron said.

They had come here for answers and now Myron thought that maybe he really did know them all.

"Go," Win said.

Myron hugged Win. Win hugged back. The hug was fierce and

tight and lasted a long time. No words were exchanged—they would have just been superfluous. But Myron remembered what Win had said after Suzze first came to his office looking for help, about our tendency to think good things will last forever. They don't. We think that we will always be young, that the moments and people we cherish are everlasting. But they're not. As Myron held his friend in his arms, he knew that nothing would ever be the same between them. Something in their relationship had changed. Something was gone forever.

When the hug finally ended, Myron headed back down the corridor and changed back into his clothes. Beefy was there. The other two goons were gone. Myron didn't know about their fate. He didn't much care. Beefy nodded at Myron. Myron walked over to Beefy and said, "I need one more favor." He told Beefy what he wanted. Beefy looked surprised but he said, "Give me a minute." He disappeared into the other room, came back, handed Myron what he had asked for. Myron thanked him. He headed outside, slipped into Win's car, and started it up.

It was almost over.

He was a mile down the road when Esperanza called him. "Your father's awake," she said. "He wants to see you."

"Tell him I love him."

"You're on your way?"

"No," he said. "I can't come yet. Not until I do what he asked."

Then Myron hung up the phone and started to cry.

33

Christine Shippee met Myron in the lobby of the Coddington Rehabilitation Institute.

"You look like death warmed over," Christine said. "And when you think about what I see in here every day, that's saying something."

"I need to talk to Kitty."

"I told you on the phone. You can't. You trusted me to take care of her."

"I need information."

"Tough."

"At the risk of sounding melodramatic, it may be a matter of life and death."

"Correct me if I'm wrong," Christine said, "but you called me for help, right?"

"Yes."

"And you knew the rules when you put her in here, right?"

"I did. And I want her to get help. We both know she needs it. But right now my father may be dying, and he's looking for me to get some final answers."

"And you think Kitty has them?"

"Yes."

"She's a mess right now. You know how my protocol works. The first forty-eight hours are pure hell. She won't be able to concentrate. All she'll want is a fix."

"I know that."

Christine shook her head. "You got ten minutes." She buzzed him in and started leading him down a corridor. There wasn't a sound. As though reading his mind, Christine Shippee said, "All the rooms are totally soundproof."

When they reached Kitty's door, Myron said, "One more thing."

Christine waited.

"I need to talk to her alone," Myron said.

"No."

"The conversation has to be confidential."

"I won't tell a soul."

"For legal reasons," Myron said. "If you hear something and one day you're called to testify, I don't want you lying under oath."

"My God. What are you going to ask her?"

Myron said nothing.

"She may freak out on you," Christine said. "She may grow violent."

"I'm a big boy."

She thought about it another minute. Then she sighed, unlocked the door, and said, "You're on your own."

Myron entered. Kitty lay on the bed, half asleep maybe, whimpering. He closed the door behind her and moved toward the bed. He flicked on a lamp. Kitty had the sweats in a big, bad way. She blinked into the light.

"Myron?"

"It's time for the lies to end," he said.

"I need a fix, Myron. You have no idea what this is like."

"You saw them kill Gabriel Wire."

"Them?" She looked puzzled, but then, as though thinking better of it, she caved and said, "Yes. I saw. I went to deliver a message for Suzze. She still loved him. She still had his key. I sneaked in a side entrance. I heard the gun go off and I hid."

"That was why you needed to run off with my brother. You needed to escape because you were afraid for your life. Brad was on the fence. So you added that lie about me—to drive the final wedge between us. You told him that I made a pass at you."

"Please," she said, grabbing at him desperately. "Myron, I need a fix so bad. Just one more and then I'll let them help me. I promise."

Myron tried to keep her focused. He knew that he didn't have much time. "I don't really care what you told Suzze either, but I imagine you just confirmed what Lex told her—that Wire had been killed all those years ago. You posted that 'Not His' message to get revenge and to send Lex a message that he better help you out."

"I just needed a few dollars. I was desperate."

"Yeah, terrific. And it cost Suzze her life."

She started crying.

"But none of that matters anymore," Myron said. "Right now I only care about one thing."

Kitty squeezed her eyes shut. "I won't talk."

357

"Open your eyes, Kitty."

"No."

"Open your eyes."

She peeked out like a child through one eye—then both flew open wide. Myron dangled the heroin in the clear plastic bag in front of her—the bag he'd gotten not long ago from Beefy. Kitty tried to snatch it from his hand, but he pulled away just in time. She started clawing at him, screaming for it, but he pushed her back.

"You tell me the truth," Myron said. "And I will give you the bag."

"Do you promise?"

"I promise."

She started crying. "I miss Brad so much."

"I know you do. That's why you started using again, right? You couldn't face life without him. Like Mickey said, some couples aren't built to be apart." And then, with tears running down his cheeks, still thinking about that five-year-old cheering his lungs out at Yankee Stadium, Myron said, "Brad is dead, isn't he?"

She couldn't move. She collapsed back on the bed, her eyes staring up, unseeing.

"How did he die, Kitty?"

Kitty stayed on her back, her gaze on the ceiling trancelike. When she finally spoke, her voice was a faraway monotone. "He and Mickey were on Interstate Five heading down to an AAU game in San Diego. An SUV lost control and crossed the divider. Brad died on impact—right in front of his son. Mickey spent three weeks in the hospital."

So there it was. Myron had braced himself—had known that

something like this was coming—but the confirmation still sent him reeling. He collapsed into a chair on the other side of the room. His baby brother was dead. In the end, it had nothing to do with Herman Ache or Gabriel Wire or even Kitty. It had just been a car accident.

It was almost too much to bear.

Myron looked across the room. Kitty was motionless now, the quakes momentarily gone. "Why didn't you tell us?"

"You know why."

He did. He knew because that was how he put it together. Kitty had gotten the idea from Gabriel Wire. She had seen him killed—but more important, she saw how Lex and the others had pretended that he was alive. She learned from that.

Pretending Wire was alive gave her the idea to pretend Brad was too.

"You would have tried to take Mickey away from me," Kitty said.

Myron shook his head.

"When your brother died"—she stopped, swallowed hard—"I was like a marionette and suddenly someone cut all my strings. I fell apart."

"You could have come to me."

"Wrong. I knew exactly what would happen if I told you about Brad. You'd have come out to Los Angeles. You'd have seen me strung out—just like you did yesterday. Don't lie, Myron. Not now. You'd want to do what you thought was right again. You'd have petitioned the court for custody. You'd say—just like you did yesterday—that I'm an irresponsible junkie, unfit to raise Mickey. You'd have taken my boy away from me. Don't deny it."

He wouldn't. "So your answer was to pretend that Brad was still alive?"

"It worked, didn't it?"

"And to hell with Mickey and what he needed?"

"He needed his mother. How do you not get that?"

But he did. He remembered how Mickey kept telling him what a great mother she was. "And what about us? What about Brad's family?"

"What family? Mickey and I are his family. None of you had been a part of his life in fifteen years."

"And whose fault was that?"

"Exactly, Myron. Whose?"

He said nothing. He thought it was hers. She thought it was his. And his father . . . how had he put it? We come out a certain way. Brad, Dad had said, wasn't meant to stay home and settle down.

But Dad had based that belief on Myron's lie.

"I know you don't believe this. I know you think I lied and tricked him into running away with me. Maybe I did. But it was the right choice. Brad was happy. We were both happy."

Myron remembered the photographs, the face-splitting smiles. He had thought that they were a lie, that the happiness he'd seen in those pictures was an illusion. They weren't. On that part, Kitty was right.

"So yeah, that was my plan. Just to delay notification until I straightened myself out."

Myron just shook his head.

"You want me to apologize," Kitty said, "but I won't. Sometimes you do the right things and you get the wrong results. And sometimes, well, look at Suzze. She tried to sabotage my career by switching those birth control pills—and because of that I have Mickey. Don't you get that? It's all chaos. It's not about right or wrong. You hold on to the things you love most. I lost the love of my life to a freak accident. Was that fair? Was that right? And maybe if you'd been kinder, Myron. Maybe if you had accepted us I would have come to you for help."

But Kitty hadn't come to him for help—not then, not now. The ripples again. Maybe he could have helped them fifteen years ago. Or maybe they would have run away anyway. Maybe if Kitty had trusted him, if he hadn't snapped when she got pregnant, she would have come to him instead of Lex a few days ago. Maybe then Suzze would still be alive. Maybe Brad would be too.

Lots of maybes.

"I have one more question," he said. "Did you ever tell Brad the truth?"

"About you hitting on me? Yes. I told him it was a lie. He understood."

Myron swallowed. His nerves felt raw, exposed. He heard the catch in his voice as he asked, "Did he forgive me?"

"Yes, Myron. He forgave you."

"But he never got in touch."

"You don't understand our lives," Kitty said, her eyes on the bag in his hand. "We were nomads. We were happy that way. It was his life's work. It was what he loved, what he was meant to do. And now that we were back, I think he would have called you. But . . ."

She stopped, shook her head, closed her eyes.

It was time to go see his father now. He had the plastic bag of heroin. He looked at it, unsure what to do.

"You don't believe me," Kitty said. "About Brad forgiving you."

Myron said nothing.

"Didn't you find Mickey's passport?" Kitty asked.

Myron was confused by the question. "I did. In the trailer."

"Take a closer look at it," she said.

"At the passport?"

"Yes."

"Why?"

She kept her eyes closed and didn't reply. Myron took one more look at the heroin. He had made her a promise that he didn't want to keep. But now, as he held it back up, Kitty saved him from this one last moral dilemma.

She shook her head and told him to leave.

When Myron got back to Saint Barnabas Hospital, he slowly pushed open the door to Dad's room.

It was dark, but he could see that Dad was sleeping. Mom sat next to his bed. She turned and saw Myron's face. And she knew. She let out a small cry, smothering it with her hand. Myron nodded at her. She rose, headed into the corridor.

"Tell me," she said.

And he did. Mom took the blow. She staggered, cried, put herself together. She hurried back into the room. Myron followed.

Dad's eyes remained closed, his breathing raspy and uneven. Tubes seemed to snake out from everywhere. Mom sat back next to the bed. Her hand, shaking with Parkinson's, took his.

"So," Mom said to Myron in a low voice. "We agree?"

Myron did not reply.

A few minutes later, his father's eyes fluttered open. Myron felt the tears push back into his eyes as he looked down at the man he treasured like no other. Dad looked up with pleading, almost child-like confusion.

Dad managed to utter one word: "Brad . . ."

Myron bit back the tears and prepared to tell the lie, but Mom put a hand on her son's arm to stop him. Their eyes met.

"Brad," Dad said again, a little more agitated.

Still looking at Myron, Mom shook her head. He understood. In the end, she didn't want Myron to lie to his father. That would be too much of a betrayal. She turned to her husband of forty-three years and held on to his hand firmly.

Dad started to cry.

"It's okay, Al," Mom said softly. "It's okay."

Epilogue

SIX WEEKS LATER

Los Angeles, California

Dad leaned on his cane and led the way.

He had lost twenty pounds since the open-heart surgery. Myron had wanted him to use a wheelchair to get up this hill, but Al Bolitar would have none of that. He would walk to his son's final resting place.

Mom was with them, of course. And Mickey too. Mickey had borrowed a suit from Myron. The fit was far from perfect. Myron was last in line, making sure, he guessed, that no one fell too far behind.

The sun beat down at them with a fury. Myron looked up and

squinted into it. His eyes watered. So much had changed since Suzze had first come to his office for help.

Help. What a joke when you thought about it.

Esperanza's husband had not only sued for divorce, but he was indeed going for sole custody of Hector. Part of his claim was that Esperanza kept long hours at her job, neglecting her maternal duties. Esperanza had been so freaked out by the threat that she asked Myron to buy her out, but the thought of working at MB Reps without Esperanza or Win was too disheartening. In the end, after much discussion, they agreed to sell MB Reps. The mega-agency that bought it decided to merge companies and get rid of the MB name.

Big Cyndi was using her severance package to take some time off and write a tell-all memoir. The world awaits.

Win was still in hiding. Myron had only gotten one message from him in the past six weeks—an e-mail with a short, simple message:

You are in my heart.

But Yu and Mee are in my pants.

Win.

Terese, his fiancée, was still not able to leave Angola, and now, with all the sudden changes in his life, Myron couldn't go back there. Not yet. Maybe not for a very long time.

As they neared the burial plot, Myron caught up to Mickey. "You okay?"

"Fine," Mickey said, quickening his pace and putting some distance between himself and his uncle. He did that a lot. A minute later, they all came to a stop.

No headstone marked Brad's gravesite yet. Just a placard.

For a long time, no one spoke. The four of them just stood there and stared off. Cars from the adjacent highway zoomed by without a care, without the slightest concern that just yards away a devastated family grieved. Without warning Dad started reciting the Kaddish, the Hebrew prayer for the dead, from memory. They were not religious people, far from it, but some things we do out of tradition, out of ritual, out of need.

"Yit'gadal v'yit'kadash sh'mei raba . . ."

Myron risked a glance at Mickey. He had been in on the lie about his father's death, trying to find a way to keep some semblance of his family together. Now, standing where his father's body lay, the boy remained stoic. His head was up. His eyes were dry. Maybe that was the only way to survive when the blows kept raining down on you. When Kitty had finally come home from rehab, she'd bolted from her son in search of a fix. They found her passed out in a seedy motel and dragged her back to the Coddington Institute. She was getting help again, but the truth was, Brad's death had broken her, and Myron really didn't know whether she could ever be fixed.

When Myron first suggested that he take custody of Mickey, his nephew had unsurprisingly rebelled. He would never let anyone other than his mother be his guardian, he said, and if Myron tried, he would sue for emancipation or even run away. With Myron's parents heading back to Florida and the school year starting up on Monday, Myron and Mickey had finally come to something of an understanding. Mickey would agree to live in the house in Livingston with Myron as an unofficial guardian. He would attend Livingston High School, his uncle and father's alma mater, and in turn, Myron would agree to stay out of his way and make sure that Kitty, despite everything, maintained sole custody of her son.

It was an evolving and uneasy truce.

With his hands clasped and his head lowered, Myron's father finished the long prayer with the words, "Aleinu v'al kol Yis'ra'eil v'im'ru Amein."

Myron and Mom joined in for that final amein. Mickey stayed silent. For several moments, no one moved. Myron looked down at that churned ground and tried to picture his little brother beneath it. He couldn't.

He flashed instead to the very last time he had seen his brother, on that snowy night sixteen years ago, when Myron, the big brother who had always tried to protect him, broke Brad's nose.

Kitty was right. Brad had been on the fence about quitting school and running off to parts unknown. When Dad found out, he sent Myron to talk to his little brother. "You go," Dad told him. "You apologize for what you said about her." Myron argued, pointing out that Kitty was lying about the birth control pills and had a reputation and all the crap Myron now knew was not true. His father had seen through it, even then. "Do you want to push him away forever?" his father asked. "You go and apologize and you bring them both home."

But when Myron arrived, Kitty, in her desperation to escape, made up the story about Myron hitting on her. Brad went crazy. Listening to his brother scream and rant, Myron realized that he'd been right about Kitty all along. His brother was an idiot for getting involved with her in the first place. Myron started arguing back, accusing Kitty of all kinds of treachery and then, he screamed the final words he would ever say to his brother:

"You're going to believe this lying whore over your own brother?"

Brad took a swing. Myron ducked it and, enraged himself, threw a punch back. Even now, standing at Brad's final resting place, Myron could still hear the sick, wet squelching sound as his brother's nose collapsed under his knuckles.

Myron's final image of his brother was Brad on the floor, looking up at him in shock, Kitty trying to stem the blood pouring from his nose.

When Myron got home, he couldn't tell his father what he'd done. Even repeating Kitty's awful lie might give it credence. So instead Myron lied to his father. "I apologized, but Brad wouldn't listen. You should talk to him, Dad. He'll listen to you."

But his father shook his head. "If that was Brad's attitude, maybe this is what's meant to be. Maybe we need to let him go and find his way."

So they did. And now they were all back together for the first time, at a graveyard three thousand miles from home.

After another silent minute had passed, Al Bolitar shook his head and said, "This should never be." He stopped and looked up at the sky. "A father should never have to say the Kaddish for his son."

With that, he started back down the path.

After putting Mom and Dad on a flight from LAX to Miami, Myron and Mickey boarded a plane for Newark Airport. They flew in silence. After landing, they grabbed Myron's car from long-term parking and started up the Garden State Parkway. Neither spoke for the first twenty minutes of the drive. When Mickey saw them pass the Livingston exit, he finally said something.

"Where are we going?"

"You'll see."

Ten minutes later, they pulled into the strip mall lot. Myron put the car in park and smiled at Mickey. Mickey looked out the windshield, then back at Myron.

"You're taking me for ice cream?"

"Come on," Myron said.

"You're kidding me, right?"

When they entered the SnowCap ice cream parlor, Kimberly wheeled over to them with her big smile and said, "Hey, you're back! What can I get you?"

"Set up my nephew here with your SnowCap Melter. I need to talk to your father for a minute."

"Sure thing. He's in the back room."

Karl Snow was going over invoices when Myron entered the room. He looked up at him over his reading glasses. "You promised you wouldn't be back."

"Sorry about that."

"So why are you here?"

"Because you lied to me. You kept trying to peddle how pragmatic you'd been. Your daughter was dead, you said, and nothing could bring her back. There was no way Gabriel Wire would go to jail for it. So you took the hush money to help Kimberly. You explained it beautifully and rationally—and I just couldn't buy a word of it. Not after I saw how you were with Kimberly. And then I thought about the order."

"What order?"

"Lex Ryder calls Suzze and tells her that Gabriel Wire is dead. Suzze is in shock. She's skeptical, so she visits Kitty to confirm that Lex is telling the truth. Okay, I get that." Myron tilted his head. "But why then would Suzze go immediately from Kitty—the only one who witnessed Gabriel's murder—to you?"

Karl Snow said nothing. He didn't have to. Myron knew now. Lex had thought that Ache and Crisp killed Wire, but that made no sense. They had a good thing going with HorsePower.

"Gabriel Wire was rich and connected and going to get away with killing Alista. You saw that. You saw that he would never face justice for what he did to your daughter. So you acted. It's ironic in a way."

"What is?"

"The whole world thinks you sold out your daughter."

"So?" Karl Snow said. "You think that matters to me? What the world thinks?"

"I guess not."

"I told you before. Sometimes you have to love a child privately. Sometimes you have to grieve privately."

And sometimes you have to get justice privately.

"Are you going to say anything?" Snow asked.

"No."

He didn't look relieved. He probably was thinking the same thing as Myron. The ripples. If Snow hadn't gone vigilante—if he hadn't killed Gabriel Wire—Kitty wouldn't have witnessed it and run away. Myron's brother might still be alive. Suzze T too. But you could only take that sort of logic so far. Myron's own father had expressed the outrage of a parent outliving a child. Karl

Snow's daughter had been murdered. Right, wrong, who knew anymore?

Myron rose then and moved to the door. He turned to say good-bye, but Karl Snow kept his head down, studying those invoices with a little too much concentration. Back in the ice cream parlor, Mickey was working on the SnowCap Melter. Kimberly had wheeled her chair over to cheer him on. She lowered her voice and whispered something that made Mickey explode with laughter.

Myron again flashed to his fist heading toward his brother. Only one thing helped now. The passport. Per Kitty's instructions, he had looked at it closely. First he checked the stamps, the many countries they visited. But that wasn't what Kitty wanted him to see. It was the first page, the identification page. He studied it again and looked closely at Mickey's name. His real name. Myron had assumed that Mickey was a nickname for Michael. But it wasn't.

Mickey's real first name was Myron.

Kimberly said something else, something so funny that Mickey put down the spoon, sat back, and laughed—really just let go and laughed—for the first time since Myron had known him. The sound twisted in Myron's chest. The laugh was so familiar, so much like Brad's, as though the laugh had started in some distant memory, some wonderful moment two brothers shared long ago, and had just echoed through the years until it found its way into this ice cream parlor, into the heart of Brad's son.

Myron stood and listened, and while he knew the echo would quiet again, he hoped that maybe it would never go silent.

ACKNOWLEDGMENTS

This is the part where I get to thank the band—and what an eclectic band it is. In alphabetical order: Christine Ball, Eliane Benisti, David Berkeley (the parachute line), Anne Armstrong-Coben, Yvonne Craig, Diane Discepolo, Missy Higgins, Ben Sevier, Brian Tart, Lisa Erbach Vance, and Jon Wood.

This is a work of a fiction. That means I make stuff up. So if you're wondering whether I based the character on so-and-so, or if there really is someone like this in your town or kid's school, the answer is no.

For those who enjoyed meeting Myron's nephew, the story of Mickey Bolitar—and by extension, Myron—will continue in my new young adult novel *Shelter*, coming in fall 2011. For details, and to read a sample chapter, go to www.HarlanCoben.com. Warning:

The sample may contain a *Live Wire* spoiler. Do not read it until you have finished this book.

As always, I thank you.

ABOUT THE AUTHOR

Harlan Coben is the author of nineteen previous novels, including the #1 *New York Times* bestsellers *Caught*, *Long Lost*, and *Hold Tight*, as well as *Play Dead* and the popular Myron Bolitar series. Winner of the Edgar, Shamus, and Anthony Awards, Coben lives in New Jersey.